DONNA TERESA

JC RYAN

BOOKS

By JC Ryan

Rex Dalton K9 Thrillers

Dedicated to my good friend Mitch Pender, a military dog trainer, for giving me the idea for this series and guiding me through the intricate and amazing capabilities and psychology of those majestic four-legged soldiers.

Mitch has a lifetime of experience and exceptional depth of knowledge as a military dog handler and trainer.

Vinci Books

vinci-books.com

Published by Vinci Books Ltd in 2025

1

Copyright © JC Ryan 2019

A CIP catalogue record for this book is available from the British Library.

Paperback ISBN: 9781036704735

About Donna Teresa

Rex Dalton and his best friend Digger, the former military dog, are back in Rome. They are at the famous *Piazza del Popolo*. Seven weeks ago, Rex had to abandon his plans to contact Catia Romano, the woman he's in love with, to help rescue his former CEO, John Brandt.

Now he was back. Catia's apartment was less than a mile away.

But Rex's reverie is interrupted when he notices two women coming through the *Porta del Popolo* in a hurry. One of them looks familiar.

As he keeps watching them, he realizes they are fleeing. Then Rex sees the men — three of them. One behind the women, the other two trying to outflank them, probably to head them off and prevent them from reaching the other side of the *piazza*.

Instinctively, Rex puts his hand out to Digger and pulls him close. "Listen buddy, we've got a situation here. Pay attention."

Thus, a chain of events is triggered that take Rex and

Digger on a harrowing journey to the brink of World War III.

DONNA TERESA is a full-length novel, a nail-biting thriller by best-selling author JC Ryan. It is the ninth book in the electrifying Rex Dalton series.

Part I

NO COINCIDENCE

Chapter One

FASCINATION WITH HEMINGWAY

Port of Civitavecchia, Rome, Italy

Sunday, August 30, 2015

Rex Dalton was a man who could behold a thing of beauty and enjoy it. She was magnificent. He had seen a picture of her, but that was a long time ago. Seeing her in real life took his breath away.

"Digger, would you look at her? Is she not the most beautiful thing you've ever laid your eyes on?"

Digger responded only with a big dog-grin on his face and a wagging tail, which Rex was sure meant, "It's only a boat. We've seen many of them. What's got you so stirred up, buddy?"

The *TOMATS* was exactly what she looked like—a luxury superyacht. Two-hundred and seventy feet of it, three-quarters the length of a football field, and thirty-seven feet wide. A masterpiece, custom designed and built by some of the world's leading exterior and interior designers.

It had only one previous owner, the late prince Mutaib bin Faisal bin Saud, an international black-market arms dealer and human trafficker. A scumbag whom Rex had killed more than a year ago. It was only a few months later that he had learned about the existence of the yacht and appropriated it, along with much of Mutaib's other hidden wealth. He had distributed the money, either directly to Mutaib's victims or to be held in trust for their future needs.

Other matters had then captured his attention, until he and John Brandt, the Old Man, CEO of CRC, his former employer, had landed in a hospital together after Rex was instrumental in rescuing The Old Man from kidnappers. One of the loose ends Rex had found the time to handle while he was laid up was the disposition of this yacht at which he was now staring. He'd signed the yacht over to CRC and agreed that the Old Man would instruct his lawyers to erase the yacht's history, rename it, and hide its new owner's name through an untraceable maze of dummy corporations. In return, Rex would have a permanent home on the yacht for the token amount of one dollar per year for life. Otherwise, CRC could use it as they wished.

The Old Man had kept his word; that he accomplished it in four weeks, was remarkable.

Now, Rex and Digger were on the pier at Roma Marina Yachting, the first marina to be built in Rome's historic, 2,000-year-old port of Civitavecchia, also known as the Port of Rome, about fifty-five miles from the city center.

His reverie was broken when he noticed a sinewy man about six feet tall, with silver-gray hair and sun-tanned skin, dressed in black jeans, dark-blue shirt and matching color windbreaker, with a black baseball cap, descending the gangplank making his way to him and Digger.

This must be the guy the Old Man told me about two days ago. Declan Spencer, the Old Man's best friend and captain of the yacht.

He was right.

When the man was a few yards away, he smiled and said, "Hi there, I'm Declan Spencer, the captain of the *TOMATS*. And you must be Rex Dalton?"

Rex hesitated for a split second before extending his hand to shake Spencer's. He had been living under assumed names for so long, he still found it somewhat unsettling to hear his real name, especially from strangers.

"Yes, I am, and this is my friend, Digger."

Digger, always up to a bit of grandstanding when humans paid attention to him, sat down and raised his right paw.

Spencer laughed and shook Digger's paw. "I've heard all about you, Digger. Apparently, you're one clever boy."

Ah, the Old Man must have changed his mind about the 'damn dog' then.

Brandt and Digger met in the hospital a few weeks before, and there was no love lost between the two of them then. Brandt kept referring to Digger as the 'damn dog', which of course, neither Rex nor Digger appreciated. Brandt kept admonishing Rex about how stupid it was for an agent of his to go around with a 'damn dog'.

But now, Digger was basking in the praise, and Rex immediately relaxed.

Rex was trained to pay close attention to people's micro-expressions and detect when they were deceitful, but since he and Digger had teamed up, he had come to realize that Digger was much better at it. The dog was a living, breathing, four-legged lie detector that outstripped any man-made device or human observation.

Spencer and Digger were off to a good start. And therefore, so were Rex and Spencer.

He invited them to come on board and meet the crew and get a tour of what was going to be Rex and Digger's abode for... well, as long as they wanted it to be.

Rex picked up his grip bag and followed. "*TOMATS*. Peculiar name," Rex said as they approached the gangplank.

Spencer smiled. "I have no idea what went through John Brandt's head when he chose that name. He refused to tell me. I've given up, don't even have a clue what it means. However, he said you would ask, and I should tell you to try and figure it out."

Rex stopped and stared at the yacht and the name painted on the side in gold cursive letters, mumbling softly, "*TOMATS*... hmm *TOMATS*..." Then he started grinning. "The old geezer had to get the last word in, didn't he?"

"What is it?"

"Ernest Hemingway, the first letters of his short novel, 'The Old Man and the Sea'—*TOMATS*. John Brandt is obsessed with Hemingway. He has read everything the man ever wrote and devoured every scrap of information about him. And let me tell you, just between us, I am convinced some of Hemingway's rudeness and abruptness has rubbed off on Brandt."

By now, Spencer was doubling over with laughter. He had known John Brandt all his life. They were bosom friends, born in the same year, in the same hospital, lived in the same neighborhood, grew up together, went to the same school, same university, and joined the Navy SEALS at the same time. John was recruited into the CIA, and Spencer retired as a colonel in the SEALS at the age of sixty-five. Both lost their wives. John's wife, a fellow CIA field agent, had been killed in an operation gone bad. A heart attack took Spencer's wife five years ago. He knew all about his best friend's fascination with Hemingway.

"That's John Brandt for you," Spencer said when he recovered from the bout of laughter. "He always gets the last word."

If Rex knew Declan Spencer as well as John Brandt did, he would also have known that Spencer always had one dream for his retirement—to be the captain of his own yacht and sail the world. This was not Spencer's yacht, he couldn't afford her, neither to buy nor to maintain. But in terms of the deal between John and Rex, he didn't have to worry about any of that, CRC would take care of it. To keep overheads low, he would not get paid for captaining the boat. And that didn't bother him at all; his military pension and savings, as well as the rental income from a mortgage-free house in DC, provided much more than he would ever need. Besides, he had no board and lodging to pay while on the yacht.

What Rex also didn't know was when Brandt had contacted Spencer to offer him the captaincy, he had also asked for his advice and assistance to get the yacht transferred to CRC's untraceable dummy corporation. Brandt wasn't sure at the time how CRC could put the yacht to good use. Spencer came up with the idea that the yacht could be used for R&R by CRC agents and Special Forces operators—free of charge—in exchange for fulfilling crew duties.

Brandt shook his head. "I don't know if that'll work, but you're the captain. Enjoy yourself. Oh, and keep in mind, from time to time, we might want to use it as a base for a quick reaction team, if the need arises."

Spencer had a big smile. "This deal is getting better all the time. Not only will I be out on the sea, I'll be part of some action as well. Music to the ears of a retired SEAL."

"Yeah, I am glad you're excited about it," John said. "But, unfortunately, I have to rain on your parade; you're not a spring chicken anymore. So, don't you start planning on kicking down doors and shooting bad guys. Our use-by dates are gone."

"Yeah, well, we'll have to see about that."

A few days later, Spencer was back in touch with Brandt and told him the registration had been completed; the yacht had its first crew and would be ready to sail in another week or so.

"Who did you have to bribe or lie to, to get it done so quickly?" Brandt wanted to know.

Spencer laughed, ignored the question, and explained that to get the crew all he had to do was let a few of the US Special Forces commanding officers, former colleagues, know about the exceptional holiday deal for Special Forces operators where they could spend some of their R&R on a luxury yacht, free of charge, food and accommodation included, but not alcoholic drinks.

Brandt was shaking his head when Spencer told him, since putting the word out, he had become inundated with applications. Apparently, Spencer's biggest problem now was to manage the waiting list of very keen operatives who wanted to spend time on a luxury yacht, even if it meant they had to attend to menial chores. Obviously, the fact that they could bring a wife or girlfriend with them as long as she performed crew duties, made it even more appealing. Even the chefs were military personnel.

"Okay, Declan, that's great news. Just keep in mind that whatever waiting list you have; my CRC agents always get highest priority."

"Yep, that goes without saying."

The *TOMATS* had three decks, was equipped for ocean travel with ultra-modern stabilization technology, advanced communications equipment, a helipad, and every nod to comfort that one could think of. It had a range of six-thousand nautical miles, a top speed of seventeen knots, and a cruise speed of fifteen. It was powered by two Caterpillar diesel engines producing close to five-thousand horsepower.

Rex was astounded by what he saw as Spencer took him on a tour of the yacht after meeting the crew. He had never seen so much luxury and comfort and elegance in such a small space. Apart from the very comfortable lodgings for the seventeen crew members, including the captain, there were accommodations for fourteen guests in seven luxurious staterooms. There was a hot tub, sauna, Turkish bath, infinity pool, gym, dining room, and several lounges. One of the lounges had been repurposed to house the sophisticated electronics gear and computer equipment that could be concealed when necessary. Another was turned into a secured communications room. Inside the latter was, among others, an impenetrable encrypted satellite video system, the latest technology in communications.

Declan Spencer was the only person on the yacht who knew Rex's background, and that's how it would stay. Spencer assured him it was not going to be a problem, even if the crew would find it strange that Rex was the only non-military person onboard. Being military, the crew understood the need-to-know principle. Besides, they would be on holiday, cruising around on a luxury super-yacht, seeing new places. What more could they wish for?

That night, Rex was treated to an exquisite sea-food dinner with Captain Spencer and his first officer. Digger was a hit with all of the crew from the moment they met him. He, of course, had quickly figured out who was responsible for the food in this new place and became fast friends with the two chefs. When Rex saw what was going on, he had a quick word with Digger's new best friends to let them know that he had no problem if they spoiled him a bit as long as they didn't overdo it and didn't feed him anything that was not good for him such as chocolate, dairy products, nuts, grapes, raisins, and such. It was the first time since Rex and Digger had teamed up that Digger fell asleep during a meal and didn't bother sitting around waiting for someone to give him leftovers.

That night, Rex slept in one of the most comfortable beds he had ever had the privilege of sleeping in. He wasn't sure if Digger had ever slept on a better bed but suspected he would have been happy to sleep anywhere as long as it was close to Rex.

With an adult life that so far consisted of university, military training, special operations training, black ops missions, violence and killing, traveling and hiding, it felt strange to think that it was all over. This was the beginning of a new life, and this yacht would be his and Digger's new place of residence for as long as he wanted it to be. He even allowed himself to fantasize that if everything worked out between him and Catia as he had hoped and dreamed for the past four years, maybe she would soon live with him on the *TOMATS*.

If Rex had any idea of the conversation happening at that very moment about 1,300 miles to the north of Rome, in a restaurant in Narva, Estonia, on the border with Russia, he would have had a very restless night.

Chapter Two

BRAINS IN A TANGLE

Rome, Italy

Monday, August 31, 2015

He'd seen her about seven weeks before, but it had been only for a few fleeting moments, and she wasn't even aware he was there. The last time they'd talked to each other was when he kissed her goodbye, more than four years ago. Since then, there was no contact, but Rex thought of her every day. For the first two years or so after saying goodbye, he was still working for CRC, and they were prohibited from contacting each other or knowing anything about the other, let alone fraternizing. For the remainder of the time, Rex was on the run under a fake identity and couldn't contact her because that would've blown his cover.

Seven weeks ago, when he was in Rome, he had disguised himself in order to check on her first, then he would try to figure out how he was going to contact her. But just as he caught a glimpse of her, he got a call from his IT specialist, Rehka Gyan, telling him John Brandt had been abducted and CRC needed his help in finding him— urgently.

Now, seven weeks later, he and Digger had arrived in Rome in a rental car from Lyon, France, the day before.

This morning, finally, he was ready to pursue his love interest, Catia Romano. He didn't know if that was her real name; in the black ops world people seldom went by their real names. She knew him as Marco, he never gave her a surname, it would have been fake, just like the first name he gave her.

Over the past seven weeks, Rex was able to take care of a lot of unfinished business that had burdened him since that fateful night of the ambush in Afghanistan. But now, he no longer had to live in hiding and didn't work for CRC anymore. For the first time in four years, he had no encumberment, he was free to approach Catia openly. What he didn't know was what her situation was, and there was only one way to find out.

That morning he had woken up with excitement, this was the day he had been thinking and dreaming of for the past four years. He and Digger slept late and had a nice breakfast, served by the chefs on the yacht, before they got into his rental car which he had to return to the agency in Rome not far from the *Piazza del Popolo*, the 'people's square'. It was a little more than half a mile from Catia's apartment located above a little trattoria in *Via delle Carrozze*, close to the famous *Piazza di Spagna*, Spanish Square.

After returning the car to the agency, shortly after 10:00 A.M., he and Digger had to cross the *Piazza del Popolo* to get to Catia's apartment. Rex, with a double major in history and linguistics, always had a keen interest in history and couldn't help but slow down and look around when they entered the historical oval-shaped 'square' bordered by three churches.

The most noticeable feature, right in the center of the piazza, was the obelisk of Ramesses from Heliopolis, Egypt, known as the *Flaminio* or *Popolo Obelisk*, brought to Rome by Augustus, the first emperor of the Roman empire, in 10 BC.

On the north side of the piazza was the *Porta del Popolo*, a large gate, through which Rex and Digger had just entered. Constructed by order of Pope Pius IV in 1562, the sole purpose of the gate was to impress the pilgrims who entered the city from the *Via Flaminia*, one of the first roads built in Rome around 220 BC by emperor Flaminius.

And as with so many historical sites in Rome, and all over Italy for that matter, the *Piazza del Popolo* also boasted its fair share of fountains. After taking a short detour, walking slowly along the perimeters of the square, taking note of all the inscriptions and information boards, Rex ended up on the south side.

From there, all he had to do was continue along the narrow cobblestoned road in front of him, and in less than ten minutes he would have been outside Catia's AirBnB. But then he'd been struck by a spell of doubt. All of a sudden, his brain was swarmed with questions. Should he just walk up to the trattoria and send the coded message to her through one of the waiters? That was if that method of contacting her was still used and if that waiter was still there.

Too many ifs.

Maybe it would be best to do it like he did on a previous occasion—wait for her to come down from her apartment above the trattoria, sidle up to her, and slip a note into her hand or handbag or something like that?

That is all well and good, but she is probably still working for whatever security agency she worked for four years ago, and she might not be allowed to have contact with you without authorization.

Is she still single?

Does she feel the same about me as I about her?

Did she even think of me the past four years?

Worse, would she even remember me?

"Just one way to find out," he mumbled to himself.

There is no danger in it. Just do it.

But why do I feel like there is?

And then it hit him—it was fear of failure.

He had been thinking and dreaming about Catia for so long and was so convinced it was going to be easy. Just take up where they left off and live happily ever after.

A fairytale?

And now, when push came to shove, his courage had all but deserted him.

He had stopped walking and became aware that Digger was staring at him—with a big smile on his face, tongue lolling out. Rex could swear if Digger could talk, he would have said, "Come on, buddy. It can't be *that* bad. You and I have been through much worse. Damn, man, we have been in battle, many times, and we survived. Pull yourself together, let's go see this woman that's got your brains in such a tangle."

"Yeah right. That's easy for you to say," Rex mumbled. "What would you know about the affection between a man and a woman?"

Digger woofed once, sat down, and looked at Rex.

"Exactly my point."

Chapter Three

BE NICE TO HER. OKAY?

Piazza del Popolo, Rome, Italy

Monday, August 31, 2015

Seated on one of the bottom steps of the Egyptian obelisk with his back to the column, facing the *Porta del Popolo*, Rex was slowly lapping on a huge vanilla gelato in a cone while trying to accost his unreasonable fears about seeing Catia.

He and Digger also had a quiet battle going on.

Gelato was the Italian version of ice cream, made from a mixture of custard, cream, and milk—without eggs. It was denser and richer in flavor than other kinds of ice cream. None of it good for Digger, but the dog didn't know that, or if he did, he didn't care. He was staring intently and accusatorily at Rex as he obviously saw how much Rex was enjoying the delicacy, and he was not happy that he wasn't getting any of it. He kept licking his lips to get Rex's attention and trying his level best to make Rex feel guilty for not sharing.

Of course, Digger made no mention of the stack of chicken wings Rex had fed him just a few minutes ago. He wanted gelato, and it was not on offer. The chicken wings were already forgotten.

Rex, fully aware of Digger's act but not letting him know about it, was wondering if he'd put chicken wings and gelato in front of him, which one Digger would've chosen. Needless to say, he'd have both; it was just a matter of which one would be gulped down first.

Rex deliberately made no eye-contact with Digger—he knew if he did, he would not be able to resist the beseeching eyes, he would just give in and hand over the gelato.

In the next moment, this silent battle of wills was interrupted as Rex's attention was drawn to two women coming through the *Porta del Popolo*—they were in a hurry. He immediately noticed the one on the left kept looking over her shoulder—it looked as if she were frightened by something behind them. But Rex couldn't see what.

Something stirred in his subconscious as he looked more intently at the woman on the right. She was a good six inches taller than her companion, and something about her was familiar. She had a large sunhat and large sunglasses on, but was still too far away to identify. There was however enough recognition to arrest his attention.

He looked back at the woman on the left again.

What is scaring her?

All of that got him distracted, causing him to let his guard down with Digger. Involuntarily, his hand with the gelato had lowered.

Digger must have thought he had won the battle,

because he snatched the delicacy out of Rex's hand and gulped it down in one go.

Rex didn't even realize what had happened, all his senses were now directed at the two women heading in his direction. A few seconds later, he concluded they were unaware of him. Something or someone behind them was occupying their minds.

Then, in quick succession, he spotted the men. Three of them.

They could've been Italian, definitely Mediterranean. One was tall, Rex estimated about five ten or eleven or so, the other two were stocky. None of them looked friendly; in fact, they looked like thugs the world over, tattoos, piercings, greasy hair, big rings on all fingers, gold chains around their necks, unzipped jackets, and dark glasses. And, of course, low riding pants and the typical swaggering, ambling gait with a pronounced bounce and faux half-limp known as the 'pimp roll' or the 'gangster glide'. They were trouble, and they were about fifteen yards apart from each other. One of them was following the women directly, the other two looked like they were trying to outflank the women, probably to head them off and prevent them from reaching the other side of the *piazza*.

The middle one looked as if he had his cellphone glued to his ear.

To Rex it was clear, those women were scared, and those three men were the reason for it. The women seemed to need help, and he was there. Besides, he thought he knew one of them, although he didn't know who she was, yet. He couldn't let it go, he had to act. If he were wrong about it, he would apologize and move on. If he were right, well, then he'd helped someone in need. Something he seemed predestined to do as he went through life and lately had come to accept.

He put his hand out to Digger and pulled him closer. "Listen buddy, we've got a situation here. Pay attention."

Rex had to take his attention off the women and their followers while he fitted Digger's harness. It was equipped with a video camera the size of a pencil eraser, which was located on the top of Digger's head, and practically invisible unless an observer were brave enough to get very close to Digger and knew where and what to look for. The mini earphones were fitted in his ears, completely invisible unless one would want to take the chance to look into Digger's ears. A mini microphone, not much bigger than a pinhead was fitted on the harness between his front legs. All of it was wirelessly connected to an iPad mini, which Rex carried in a small backpack and could strap to his forearm if he wanted.

By the time the women arrived at the obelisk, Rex had the harness fitted and every device tested, and he could pay attention to the women and their followers again. The women had joined the largest group of people milling around the obelisk. Two of the followers had moved, one to the west side and one to the east side of the obelisk, the third was on the north side.

The women were now less than fifteen paces away from him, but they were among a throng of people and had their backs turned to him. He stood, took Digger's leash in his hand, and made his way to the north side. When he passed close behind the bearded man, he looked down at Digger, touched his own nose, and motioned slightly with his head toward the man. It was the sign for Digger to acquire that man's scent.

Digger did that quickly, and with raising hair on his back and a soft low growl that Rex could hear in his earphone, Digger had let him know that he didn't like this guy. They moved on, making a wide circle around the obelisk so that Digger could get the scent of the remaining men. And Digger made sure Rex knew about his immediate dislike for both of them as well.

From what Rex could see, the women remained nervous and restless. It was as if they were caged in. The tall one with the sunhat and sunglasses repeatedly glanced to the south end of the piazza as if she were expecting help from that direction or thinking of heading in that direction. They were mostly obscured by the people around them, and the tall one was still nagging his memory.

I know her. But from when and where?

And then, as if she wanted to give Rex a chance to have a good look at her, she moved a few steps to her right, away from the people, and slowly turned in a full circle holding her phone up while she apparently recorded a video.

She moved slowly enough for Rex to get his first good look at her before she moved back among the people again. It was more than enough time to set his pulse racing before his brain registered who she was.

Catia!

Gone were all his worries and hesitancy of earlier about contacting her—it didn't even cross his mind.

Catia is here, and she's in some kind of trouble.

Rex was a lethal and very successful operator because of a number of traits, among them his ability to rapidly assess a situation, form a plan based on the realities, not caprices, and execute it.

Therefore, he and Digger walked over to Catia. He was fully aware that because of the stress she was under, as well as his baseball cap pulled low over his face and his wrap-around sunglasses, she would probably not recognize him immediately. He edged up right next to her on her left side. He bent his knees just enough to scratch Digger's ears, and that made Catia look at him.

He whispered, "Lady, don't say anything, just listen. I'm here to help."

Catia started to take a step back but he told her, "Don't do that. Stay close. Please, I swear to you I mean you no harm. I might be able to help you and your friend get away from those men following you. I know who you are."

The next moment, Catia's jaw dropped and her hand flew to her mouth to stifle an exclamation which, fortunately, she was able to do in time.

"Marco!?" She whispered. "What... how..."

By now, Rex was standing up straight but not looking at her. He had the iPad mini in his hand, holding it above the people, as if he was taking a video, his focus on the screen while he continued talking to her softly.

"Yes, I'm Marco. I know you're being followed by three men. Are you in trouble?"

She nodded slightly as she also held her phone up. "Serious trouble, I think."

"I thought so. Who is the woman with you?"

Catia hesitated for a split second but remembered Marco was the one who saved her from the Camorra. "That's Sophia. The woman who you helped to escape from Naples a few years ago."

It was Rex's turn to be surprised. "But... she doesn't look..."

"No, she doesn't. I'll explain later. What you need to know is that her name is Simona Bellucci now, and those people following us are probably working for the Camorra. And strange as it might sound after all this time, they've caught up with her. They're here for her... and by the looks of it, me as well… and now… I don't know how they…"

Rex shook his head. "Okay, it sounds complicated. Let's get rid of those hoodlums, go to a safe place, and you can tell me all about it."

"But, why are you here? I mean now, at this specific time, just when these men turned up? How did you know?"

"I'll have to explain that to you later. When I do, remind me not to use the word coincidence—I don't believe in it, and I suspect neither do you."

Catia was grateful that Simona stood with her back to them, about three paces away, scanning the people, still trying to make out who was following them. She was totally unaware of the conversation going on behind her. Just as well, if she would have been closer and had a look at Marco, she would have recognized him, and there was no telling how she would react.

Rex knelt down next to Digger and motioned for Catia to do the same. He stroked Digger's back a few times, then leaned in close to his ear and whispered, "Hey boy, this is Catia, the one I told you so much about. Be nice to her, okay?"

Catia heard that and smiled. She slowly extended her hand for Digger to sniff, and when he was happy, she started scratching his back, very gently.

Digger had gone on high alert the moment Rex had placed the harness on him. It was something that only happened when they were either training or going into danger, and then he never allowed someone other than Rex to touch him or give him orders.

This was the first time ever Rex saw him not being grumpy about someone else touching and talking to him when he was in mission mode.

But, before they could continue, Simona had turned around and appeared to panic when she at first couldn't immediately find Catia where she expected her to be. However, before it could turn into full-fledged panic, she saw Catia on her knees stroking the back of a big, black dog who seemed to be very happy about it.

Catia caught her eye and gestured for her to kneel down next to her.

Knowing she wouldn't recognize Marco, Catia told her in a low whisper who he was. Fortunately, Catia had preempted Simona's reaction and had placed her index finger on Simona's lips when she started talking to her—it worked—her mouth remained shut—only her eyes had shot wide.

Chapter Four

IF ONLY

Rome and Naples, Italy

August, 2015

For four years Simona had practiced restraint and made no contact with her mother or sister. It was tough, she couldn't even ask someone to find out how her mother was doing, neither could she send her an anonymous letter. She didn't even know if her mother was alive. She couldn't make just one phone call to say, *Hi mom, it's Sophia, your daughter, I'm alive, I am well, I miss you terribly. I can't contact you again, but don't worry about me. I hope you're okay, mom. I love you.*

And then, one day, after more than four years and many days of agonizing, in the last week of August 2015, it had become too much. She went out and bought a throw-away mobile phone, in cash. She got on her scooter and found an empty park bench, miles away from where she lived and worked, and she called her mother.

She spoke to her for only ten minutes. After she disconnected the call, she took the SIM card out and crushed it under her feet, got on her scooter, and left. On her way back to her apartment, she stopped on a bridge crossing the Tiber River and dropped the phone into the water.

She tried to convince herself that everything would be okay, that no one would know about the call and no one would be able to track her down. But instead of feeling relieved that she had at last spoken to her mother, she could not shake an ominous feeling that she had done something terrible.

By the time Simona had reached her apartment, Rinaldo Fara, a corrupt policeman who was heavily involved with the Camorra, was listening to the audio file of the recorded conversation between mother and daughter.

It was exactly as Catia had warned Simona. The Camorra had been watching her mother and sister. For four years they had been waiting for that call.

Now the Camorra knew two things; one, Sophia was alive. Two, at the time of the call, she was in Rome because it was made from the *Parco del Colle Oppio*, a park located on the Oppian Hill, the southern part of the Esquiline Hill, one of the famous Seven Hills of Rome.

That same night, the elderly and ailing Mrs. Rosa Maiorani had what seemed to the nursing staff as a minor stroke, so they called an ambulance to take her to the emergency ward of a nearby hospital.

The staff didn't make enquiries to the hospital about Mrs. Maiorani's condition until late the next morning when they were told that no one by that name had been admitted.

They then proceeded to call all hospitals in the area only to get the same answer.

It was shortly after mid-day when two homicide detectives turned up at the nursing home to tell them that Mrs. Maiorani's body was found on a bench in a nearby park. It was not necessary for an autopsy to know the cause of death — she had multiple broken fingers, and bruises all over her head and body caused by a blunt instrument. The detectives wanted to know how Mrs. Maiorani got to the park. All the staff could tell them was that she was taken away by an ambulance the night before.

It was only two days later when Simona overheard a conversation between some of her colleagues at work about the hideous assault and killing of an old lady in Caserta. She immediately left the room, went to the bathroom, locked herself in one of the cubicles, and Googled it on her smartphone.

"Oh my God! What have I done?" were the only words she got out before she started throwing up. Half an hour later, one of her colleagues found her sitting on the bathroom floor, pallid and shaking uncontrollably. How she did it she would never know, but she managed to keep the presence of mind to answer her colleague's question with, "Food poisoning, I think."

Her manager told her to go see a doctor and then go home and not to worry about anything as they would cover for her until she was better.

Simona was inconsolable and alone. There was no one who she could tell. At some stage, she had her phone in her hand to send the SOS message to Catia but then realized she would have to tell her that she had broken the no-contact rule.

It was in this state of emotional turmoil that she made the second mistake. If only she did phone Catia. Instead, she phoned her manager the next morning and lied to her that the doctor had booked her off for four days.

And then she got on a train to Caserta to attend her mother's funeral.

It was a small funeral, attended by about twenty people including her sister, without a husband if she still had one, staff from the nursing home, and a few long-time friends of her mother's.

Simona sat at the back and recognized most of the mourners. What she didn't know was among those she didn't recognize were two Beneduce-Longobardi henchmen who attended the funeral for one purpose only—to spot her if she turned up. She also didn't know that the entire event was recorded on video by hidden cameras that were streaming live to a TV screen in Teresa Lombardi's study where she, Valter Li Voti, and Rinaldo Fara were carefully studying the faces of everyone. They had photos as well as the names and addresses of every one of the funeral goers, and it didn't take them long to match all but one of the faces on the TV screen with their list.

The exception was the woman with bob-styled wavy auburn hair and slightly slanting brown eyes.

At the grave-side, Simona also kept a distance, didn't approach her sister, and left immediately after the interment ritual. Back on the train to Rome she had cried a lot, but her large sunglasses kept most of it hidden from onlookers.

However, she was unaware that the two young lovebirds a few seats behind her, were not in love at all. They were there for one purpose only—to follow her and find out everything about her.

Within two days after her arrival back in Rome, while she was at work, the couple had entered her apartment, searched it from corner to corner, learned that she went by the name of Simona Bellucci, and planted a number of very small listening devices in obscured places.

And four days later, a day before they were going to pack up and go back to Naples because they couldn't find any more information of interest about Simona, they were listening to a heated exchange between Simona and a woman who she called Catia.

During this conversation, Simona was highly emotional, she cried a lot, and they heard when she said, "I missed my mother so much, Catia. I couldn't stand it anymore. I thought it was safe. It's been more than four years. I was wrong, and my stupidity got my mother killed."

The two watchers didn't have the background information to know what a momentous breakthrough this was, but they made sure that every word of it was recorded.

When Catia left Simona's apartment a few hours later, they emailed the audio file as an attachment to a police officer in Naples, Rinaldo Fara.

If only Simona had not made that call to her mother.

Chapter Five

TO THE PIAZZA DEL POPOLO

Rome, Italy

Monday, August 31, 2015

Catia understood that Simona was devastated by her mother's death and that she needed emotional support, not reproach. She did her best to provide the solace Simona needed. But it didn't make her any less furious about Simona's imprudent behavior. Simona knew it was her irresponsible action that led to her mother's death. That was bad enough, but what she didn't know was that she had also put herself and by extension, Catia, at risk as well.

Nevertheless, Catia was ultimately responsible for Simona's safety. She couldn't simply break off all contact, and that was why she arranged to meet with Simona again this morning despite going to her apartment the night before, when she had received the emergency text message.

They met at a street café where they had coffee and

pastries. Simona was still in a bad way, although a little better than the night before. Regardless of Simona's sadness, Catia thought it was the right time to make her aware of the potential danger she was in now. She did, however, stop short of telling her that she had endangered both of them. The woman had enough guilt to deal with as it was. Catia spent most of the time doing her best to console Simona, telling her that it was impossible to know if it was the Camorra who killed her mother and, although she didn't entirely believe it, she said that it was possible that nothing else would come of it. She did, however, make it very clear that it was imperative that Simona never make such a mistake again, ever.

When Catia was ready to leave, Simona said she had to pop into a small convenience store to get some groceries before going home. The two of them walked together for about a hundred yards to the entrance of the convenience store, said goodbye, and Catia continued.

When Simona had entered the store, Catia, having been on high alert ever since she'd found out what Simona did, performed an SDR, Surveillance Detection Route, also known as a surveillance detection run. It was a street craft tactic used by field agents to flush out any unwelcome followers. And that's when she noticed the first one. She saw a Mediterranean-looking male for the third time that morning and realized she'd not only seen his face three times, but he had changed, or tried to change, his appearance all three times, as well. The first time he was wearing a blue jacket, the second time it was beige, a reversible jacket, and now he had gotten rid of the jacket but was wearing a baseball cap and sunglasses which he hadn't worn before. But she'd seen his face, and she was trained not to forget faces.

Catia stopped at a shop window, and he walked past her. She turned back the way she had come, and less than a block later she made out another one whose face she'd seen twice that morning, a man with a beard, also stupid enough to try to change his appearance but not face. Not long after that, she spotted the third man, following the same amateurish countersurveillance routine to hide himself from her.

It was quite a team to follow one person. Clearly, they'd had some training to do this type of thing but obviously not to the same level as she had gotten from the Mossad.

She didn't need anyone to tell her that what she told Simona before about nothing coming of her irresponsible actions was wishful thinking. Simona had been compromised. She had little doubt that these men worked for the Camorra.

And now, they had seen her, Catia's face, and were following her, not Simona. The only reason for that was they already knew where to find Simona.

Catia had to make decisions, quickly. She couldn't just leave Simona to fend for herself. Those thugs, or their associates, had already shown their coldblooded cruelty when they killed Simona's mother, a defenseless, innocent, seventy-six-year-old, ailing woman. If she shook these men off, which she was confident she could, they would go straight for Simona and torture her for information; when they realized she had none, they would kill her, like they had her mother.

The challenge was to get herself *and* Simona away from these men immediately.

Her training kicked in; remain calm and act normal, don't run, don't hurry, take your time, browse the shops, blend in. Keep wandering around like a sightseer with no definite destination or haste. Do boring things, bore them stiff, let them drop their guard, and then shake them off.

With her level of street craft that would've been relatively easy. She was trained by the best, and she was good at it. But to do it while having to take care of Simona, an untrained civilian, at the same time, was going to be near impossible.

While these thoughts were going through her mind, she couldn't help but remember Marco. As far as she knew, he was the only person she ever met who could follow her without her knowledge. And she couldn't help but wonder where he was and what he was doing. But there was no time to ponder on that.

She had no gun, but as she was trained in Krav Maga, she could give good account of herself if necessary. However, it was highly unlikely that a physical encounter with three big men at the same time would go her way. If she had only herself to take care of, she could have tried to keep them separated and take them down one at a time.

Catia could kick herself for choosing to walk from her apartment that morning instead of using one of her motorbikes as she did the night before when she visited Simona.

She was a motorbike enthusiast. In a little garage, just around the corner from her apartment, she kept two of them. A Ducati Multistrada 1200 S Touring which she had loaned to Marco when he was on the Naples mission in 2011, and the second one, her beloved Ducati Streetfighter S, which she used for amateur racing and road trips whenever she had the opportunity. The bikes were both in immaculate condition, the tanks were full, and she had the keys in her handbag—either of them would have been an ideal getaway vehicle.

As she strolled back to the convenience store in an

ostensibly very relaxed manner, she tried to order her thoughts. The first thing, even before reaching Simona, was to get hold of David Sternberg and tell him what was going on.

After she reached Sternberg, the next task was to get hold of Simona and explain to her what was going on and what had to be done. The latter was probably going to be the most difficult part of the plan as she anticipated that Simona was going to panic. If she did, the followers might pick up on it and know they'd been made.

Her call to David Sternberg went to voicemail without ringing. His phone could have been switched off, out of order, or he could be in a bad reception area. It didn't matter which, she had to reach him. She phoned the embassy reception and was told that she could leave a message for David but shouldn't expect an answer very soon.

Whatever that means, she thought.

With no immediate help from Sternberg, and without her own transport, she had limited options. Trying to shake off the tail with Simona in tow was not one of them. Getting into a taxi was an option, but the followers could do the same, and all they would be doing is driving around Rome without being able to get away from the men. Unless she could get to the Israeli embassy and ask for protection; that was, if they would allow her in.

But she and Simona were Italian citizens, not Israeli. Harboring them at the Israeli embassy could cause a major diplomatic upheaval which she was sure the ambassador would want to avoid at all cost. She no longer had access to the Mossad safehouses; she didn't even know if the ones she knew about were still operational, and even if she did and they were, she would have to get herself and Simona to one of them unnoticed.

There was no benefit in bemoaning the fact that the Mossad could not be of assistance immediately—she knew she was on her own. She would fetch Simona and try to make her way to the garage where she kept her motorcycles. Astride one of those would be the best chance to get away from her followers. She still had no idea where she should go, but she would worry about that once she had escaped them.

While she made her way back to the convenience store, she stopped often to 'take photos' of the buildings and statues and people, making sure she got the faces of her followers in the process. She hoped the extensive Mossad database would be able to identify their faces easily—that was if she could get hold of Sternberg.

All the way back to the convenience store she was quietly hoping and praying that Simona was still there. She was.

Catia got herself a shopping basket and went straight to Simona among the shelves. One of her followers was loitering outside the shop, smoking. Fortunately, he couldn't see Catia or Simona from where he was standing.

Pretending to take stuff off the shelves and studying the labels carefully, then putting the items back, she spoke to Simona in a whisper and explained what was going on and what had to be done.

Simona's eyes were wide with shock and, as expected, she started to panic. Exactly what Catia didn't need now. It took a few harsh words from Catia to get Simona to focus and to pull herself together and cooperate.

"Now, listen to me," Catia said. "If you want to get out of this alive, you'd better do exactly as I say. Understood?"

Simona nodded.

"No, that's not good enough. I want to hear you say it."

"Yes. I understand, and I will do exactly as you say."

As they walked out onto the street and turned to the right, Catia did her best to keep up what she intended to sound like a normal conversation, interspersing it with whispered instructions to Simona to follow her example.

"Relax, walk slowly, don't look back, don't give them the idea you're nervous. Its critically important that they don't know that we know about them."

But willing as she was to do as told, it soon became apparent that Simona was unable to control her anxiety. Several times she frantically peeked around trying to identify the followers. Then she quickened the pace, and Catia had to call her back.

Within a few minutes, Catia couldn't help but think they might as well have had big red targets painted on their backs and a trumpeter following them just to make sure their followers didn't lose them.

After a few hundred yards, Catia stopped, and pretending to look around, shot some more photos. To her horror, she realized that their followers had recognized that they'd been discovered. All three of them had their cellphones against their ears, and they were now just a few paces apart from each other. They'd narrowed the gap between themselves and Simona and her. Catia speculated that the men were possibly making arrangements to close in and apprehend their charges. It was only a matter of time before this was going to turn into a pursuit.

Catia knew they had to get out of the narrow street as quickly as possible and onto the open square at *Piazza del Popolo*, hoping the followers would back off if they were among the crowds. Maybe there would even be police around.

She started walking faster. They were just about running when they stormed through the *Porta del Popolo* onto the *Piazza del Popolo*.

Catia sighed in relief when she saw the crowds. But there were no police in sight. Usually there would be at least one police vehicle with at least two police officers somewhere on the perimeter of the square. Sometimes there were two, even three police vehicles, but not today.

Catia steered straight for the Egyptian obelisk in the middle of the *piazza* where there were plenty of people sitting on the steps and standing around taking photos or hanging around in small groups, talking.

Her mind was too occupied to take more than momentary notice of the man with a big black dog who'd been sitting on the bottom step of the obelisk.

Chapter Six

LET'S GO

Rome, Italy

Monday, August 31, 2015

Now that he had gained Catia's trust, Rex's plan was to go back the way he and Digger had come earlier after he'd dropped off his rental car at the agency. On the way there were a few narrow alleys, a few people, and many nooks and crannies, doors, and little shops. It would be ideal if Catia and Simona could lead the thugs on that route. He and Digger would follow and take them out, one by one. Hopefully he could do it before the thugs could get backup.

He told Catia what he had in mind, and she said, "That could work, but before we settle on that idea, I'd like you to know I have two motorbikes in a garage about seven hundred meters from here. I have the keys with me. That's where we were heading, but then they discovered we've made them."

"Which direction?"

"You remember where I live?"

Rex nodded. There was no time to tell her he had been there seven weeks ago, that he was actually heading that way today before he got cold feet, and that he was there at the obelisk trying to build up the courage to go and see her.

"The garage with the motorcycles is just around the corner from my apartment. It's less than twenty meters from the front door."

"Okay, that might work better than what I had in mind. Let's just hope those goons won't make a move to snatch you off the street in broad daylight. If they do, we're in for a street fight."

Catia nodded. "Okay. If we can make it to the bikes, I'll take Simona on the back of one of them with me. But will your dog be all right to get on a bike?"

"Never tried it, but I'm sure he'd be good."

Catia nodded again. "Okay, let's start moving."

Rex held his hand up. "Let's exchange phone numbers. I'll call you, and we'll stay in touch until we reach the garage."

"Good idea."

When she took her phone out, Rex looked at it and asked, "Secured?"

"Yep. And untraceable."

"Great."

Less than a minute later they were connected and ready to go. Catia had retrieved a mini Bluetooth earpiece from her handbag, fitted it to her ear, and switched it on. It was well hidden from view behind her hair. Now she could stay in touch with Rex without having to hold her phone to her ear, which could make the followers unnecessarily nervous.

Rex and Digger remained among the people and

watched Catia and Simona making their way to the south side of the crowd very slowly and unobtrusively. When they got to the edge of the crowd, they started walking away at a brisk pace and had a good thirty-yard lead when the three men realized what was happening and started moving.

Rex gave the goons a head start of about thirty yards and then followed with Digger right next to him. To a casual observer it would have looked as if Digger was on leash, but he was not. The end of the leash was shoved under one of the straps of his harness but not clipped onto it to allow him to move wherever Rex wanted him to without having to wait to be unleashed.

The followers were oblivious to the fact that they were now being followed.

Rex kept Catia abreast of where the three men were and what they were doing.

The biggest worry was that more thugs could show up, and that would complicate matters. If more were on the way, they were probably in a vehicle in which they could stow the women once they had overpowered them.

However, Rex thought if that was the thugs' plan, they would close the gap between them and the women as soon as they approached such a vehicle.

After covering about half the distance to the garage, the trio walked together, no longer trying to hide their presence but keeping a distance of about twenty yards behind the women. There was no indication they were about to make a move yet.

A few minutes later, Catia and Simona arrived in front of the rollup door of the garage; Catia unlocked it and started rolling up the door.

The three men had quickened their pace when they saw the women at the door and must have thought their charges were about to escape out of sight. From about twenty yards away, just when Catia started opening the door, they broke into a full run.

They were too occupied with their charges getting away to notice Rex and Digger were now about five yards behind them.

Catia had kept the approaching men in the corner of her eye, and when she had the door fully opened, the men were less than three yards away. She pushed Simona into the garage and turned to face the men.

Fortunately, there were no people on the street to see the short and almost noiseless mayhem that ensued inside the garage.

The first man that came through the door fell flat on his face with Digger on his back.

The second had barely put his foot inside when he collapsed in a bundle from a brutal karate chop to the side of the neck from Rex.

The third man was too slow to realize what was going on around him. He entered the garage and walked right into a vicious kick in the groin from Catia. He jackknifed into her left knee which broke his nose and laid him out flat on his back.

The only attacker who was still conscious and making a sound, was Digger's charge. Rex took one step, kicked him in the side of the head, and he went quiet.

The whole event lasted less than four seconds.

Catia moved back to the entrance, rolled the door down, and switched on the lights.

Simona had backed up into the far corner and slumped to the floor. Her hands were covering her eyes and mouth, she didn't see any of it, but she was shaking like a leaf in the wind. Thankfully, she made no noise.

Rex said, "We have to gag and tie them up, search them, take their cellphones, wallets, and anything else we can find to tell us who they are and who they work for."

Catia nodded and went to work on the guy she'd kicked in the groin. With no rope or cloth in the garage, she and Rex used the thugs' own boot laces and stinking socks to tie and gag them.

When Catia had finished her guy, Rex nodded toward Simona, and Catia went over, sat next to her, and put an arm around Simona's shoulder. She spoke softly. "It's over, Simona. We're going to be okay now. Try to take a few deep breaths, it will help to calm you down."

Simona nodded slowly and started sobbing silently.

In the meantime, Rex had collected the cellphones, switched them off, and removed the batteries and SIM Cards. He was looking through their wallets. "You idiots never thought you'd end up like this, did you? Thanks guys, you were a great help. Now we won't have to guess who you are." He stuffed everything into his backpack.

Catia said it was time to get out of there.

Rex had no problem with that, the only question was to where.

"Let's just get out of Rome first and make sure we haven't been followed. Then we can decide what to do," Catia said.

The garage had only the one door and no windows. They had no idea what was going on in the street outside.

Catia suggested they should turn the bikes to face the door. Simona should get on the one bike in the passenger position, Rex and Digger on the other. Then she would open the door so they could leave, quickly.

"Wait," Rex said, "I'd like to see if the coast is clear

before we charge out of here. I'd prefer if we could get away unnoticed."

"How?"

"You'll see in a moment," Rex said and retrieved the iPad mini from his cargo pants' pocket, switched it on, and checked that the devices on Digger's harness were all still working. Then he stood to the side, rolled the door up about twelve inches, and said to Digger, "Scout."

Digger crawled through the opening; Rex closed the door and followed him on the screen of the iPad mini. "Digger, go right."

Catia grinned. "Military dog?"

Rex nodded while keeping his eyes on the screen. "And a very clever one."

Catia stood next to him watching the screen.

Digger walked slowly along the narrow street for a hundred or so yards, crossing the street and approaching a few parked vehicles a few times on Rex's commands until Rex called him back.

By now, Simona had calmed down and was also standing next to Rex, following the feed coming from Digger's camera with great interest.

Just as Digger returned to the garage door, and Rex told him to go to the left, a white van with tinted windows driving slowly toward their position appeared on the screen.

"Digger, stop," Rex said.

Digger did exactly as he was ordered, and the three of them watched the van approaching. When it was only a few yards away, the face of the driver came into clear view through the driver-side window.

Simona drew a sharp breath. "I know that man. I've seen him."

"Where?" Catia asked.

"Outside my apartment, every morning the last few days. He was with a woman, every time. I thought they were waiting for someone to give a lift to work."

"Don't think so," Catia said.

"Oh my God! They were… they were… watching me."

Catia placed her hand on Simona's shoulder and said, "It will be all right. He doesn't know where we are."

She was wrong.

There was no one else in the van besides the driver, a young man. The van stopped right in front of the garage door, and the driver got out and approached the door. He paid no attention to the dog sitting a few yards away to his right facing him.

With his hand, Rex motioned for Catia to wait for his signal to raise the door. Just as Rex saw the young man bending down to grab the handle to raise the door, Rex whispered softly to Digger, "Take him down, now!" at the same time he signaled for Catia to raise the door.

In a flash, the garage door had been half opened and shut again and there was now one more guest inside. This one lay on the floor in a growing puddle of his own urine, his eyes as big as saucers, stock-still from the shock, and unable to make a sound because of Rex's hand over his mouth.

It didn't take much persuasion, just a few growls from Digger, to find out that the young man was there on police business. Although he was not a policeman himself, he explained that he was helping a policeman in Naples, Rinaldo Fara, who was investigating the 2011 murder of Matthew Benedict, and this woman who called herself Simona Bellucci is actually Sophia Maiorani, and she was a suspect.

For a moment, Rex contemplated knocking the young

man out or putting him in a sleeper hold but decided against it and instead tied and gagged him, like the others, with his own shoelaces and socks. He too was relieved of his mobile phone and wallet.

Now, for the first time, Rex paid attention to the motorbikes and immediately recognized the one Catia had provided for him on the Naples mission in 2011. "These yours?"

"Yep, both of them." She smiled as she handed one of the black helmets to Simona and one to Rex and fitted the third one over her own head.

"Well, I'll be damned. I would've never…"

"To be explained later," Catia said.

Rex nodded and said, "I've got a place we can go."

Catia didn't hesitate to respond, "Okay, let's go. You lead the way."

"Before we go," Rex said before donning his helmet, "we have to stay in touch through our mobile phones as we did previously."

Catia nodded. "The helmets have got built in earphones and microphones which can be connected wirelessly through Bluetooth with your phone." She showed Rex what to do, and within a few minutes, they were talking to each other through their helmets.

"Okay," Rex said. "Final thing, make sure Simona's phone is switched off, SIM card out, and the battery out."

Catia quickly took care of that while Rex straddled the Multistrada, looked around for Digger, and found him standing next to him. To his surprise, Digger looked excited. "Hey buddy, want to go for a ride with the two lovely ladies here?"

The next moment, Digger leapt onto the front of the bike, shifted his rear into Rex's lap, placed his front feet on the handlebars, lowered his belly onto the petrol tank, and looked back to Rex as if to say, "Let's go."

"Ah, I see you've done this before. That's great. No need to tell you to sit still then?"

Digger woofed as if he was getting impatient.

Catia made sure Simona was ready, started the Street-fighter, quickly opened the door all the way, jumped onto the bike, and told Simona to put her arms around her and hold on.

Chapter Seven

TO BE EXPLAINED LATER?

Cerveteri, about 27 miles out of Rome, Italy

Monday, August 31, 2015

Riding out of the city they performed surveillance detection runs. They didn't stay together, took different routes to predetermined locations, doubled back on routes they had already covered, and when they were on the same road, they kept a distance between them. Once out of the city, they kept off the main roads as Rex led them in the direction of Roma Marina Yachting.

Digger was happy on the bike; he didn't move except for his head every now and then to look around. It reminded Rex of a few weeks previously, when he had to perform a high-risk HALO (high altitude low opening) parachute jump with Digger. Something he had never done before with a dog. Digger was an exemplary tandem partner then just as he was now.

Simona had been on a bike before with Marco, from Naples to Rome in 2011. Back then she was in a bad condition with a broken arm and bruises thanks to two Camorra brutes who assaulted her, and she was in a daze from the painkillers Marco had given her. This ride was much better than that one. Clearly, Catia was an accomplished rider, and it helped her to relax.

She couldn't help but think that this was her second escape from the Camorra. Both times on the back of a speeding motorcycle, and both times Marco was involved in the escape. She was also wondering how it came about that he had turned up at the *Piazza del Popolo* that morning as if he had been sent. Notwithstanding the eerie happenstance of his arrival at just the right moment that morning, she was grateful for it.

Catia was also happy to see Marco. Four years ago, there was definitely a romantic spark between them. She knew if they were in a different situation then it could have turned into a serious relationship. She had thought of him often but alas, it was as Lord Bryon so eloquently stated when he rebutted the adage of 'absence makes the heart grow fonder' and said, "Absence—the common cure of love."

Eventually, over the years, she had given up on seeing Marco again.

Besides, up until a year ago she was also in the spy business, and when it came to relationships in the spy business, there were a few givens. Short term, also known as one-night stands, was okay as long as you were sure you were not sleeping with the enemy. Long term relationships were not okay; they almost never worked out in the long run. Apart from the fact that real field operators never had a prospect of longevity, the spy business was also the business of deception. It was all but impossible to live a dual life, one of a hundred percent honesty with a partner when at home and one of a hundred percent deception when doing your job. It would have been near impossible to have a working relationship even if the partners were both spies and both worked for the same outfit, forget about it if both of those conditions were not met.

He'd come to her through MI6 when she trained him in 2010. He spoke Italian with a Northern Italian accent, as if he was born and bred in Italy. At the time, she thought he was from Milan or Venice or Turin. But then, when she worked with him on the Naples mission, she was surprised to learn that he worked for an American private military contractor, CRC, under the auspices of the CIA. How it came about that he worked for the CIA when he was clearly an Italian, she had no idea.

Nonetheless, Catia often played the if-then game—there was no harm in it. If she were not a spy and she could choose a man she'd like to settle down with, and had the option to pick out of the many men she'd met and who were interested in her over the years, and there were quite a few, Marco would've been one of those at the top of her list. He could very well have been the number one on her list, it depended if he lived up to what she observed and learned about him and thought he would be, in the little time they had spent together. But that was only the if-then game.

Now, as they were on the road to a yet unknown destination, she had time to think about Marco's uncanny appearance at the *Piazza del Popolo* just when she was at wits' end. If it was not coincidence, which she had learned during her training with the Mossad not to believe in, then what was it? Did someone send him? Did he perhaps know more than he had said so far? But then again, she remembered his strange reply when she asked him how it came about that he turned up there earlier, and he said he would explain it later but that she should remind him not to use the word coincidence. Did that mean it was exactly what he was trying to say—coincidence? She knew that sometimes those happened, it was just not good spycraft to not have a healthy sense of paranoia. Whatever it was that happened that morning, as far as she was concerned, God had sent him.

She found herself wondering if she could even trust him. But that was just a passing thought. Since joining her and Simona there on the piazza, every action testified to his commitment to help them get to safety. It bothered her a little that he didn't tell her where they were going yet. And she was about to ask him when his voice came through on her headset saying, "Let's take the turnoff to Cerveteri. I need to make a few phone calls and tell you where we're going."

She shook her head slightly, *now he even knows what I'm thinking.*

They had covered about thirty miles to their destination when Rex saw the turnoff for the small town of Cerveteri, known by the ancient Romans as Caere. It dated back to

600 BC, and just outside the modern-day town were more than a thousand tombs from ancient times. It was the largest ancient necropolis in the Mediterranean area.

Rex wanted to get off the roads and find a place where they could be out of the eyes of the police and anyone else who might be looking for them by now. He wanted to let Catia know what he had in mind, and if she agreed, he wanted to make the necessary arrangements.

He told Catia to drop back and drive around the outskirts of the town while he found a place for them to be out of sight and able to plan what they wanted to do next.

Three quarters of an hour later, he called Catia again and gave her directions to an address about two miles out of town. It was a guesthouse on an estate with a vineyard and winery. He had used one of his many passports, this one in the name Rowan Donnelly, and credit cards to book and pay for one night. The hostess had no problems with Digger; she loved animals, especially dogs, had a few of her own, and thought Digger was a fine specimen. Rex didn't have any intentions of staying the night, but he wasn't going to tell her that.

The place had two bedrooms, a kitchen, a small sitting room, and bathroom. To Rex, most appealing of all was the lockup garage with an internal door opening in the kitchen.

There was a basket of fruit; apples, oranges, pears, and dates, on the kitchen table, an espresso machine with a dozen pods as well as milk and tea, and two bottles of cold white wine in the fridge.

About fifteen minutes after giving Catia the address of the guesthouse, the bikes were in the garage, each of them had an espresso in hand and were seated at the kitchen table, nibbling on the dates.

Digger was placed on guard outside after being properly introduced to Simona and Catia, both of whom he took an immediate liking, and vice versa. Rex struggled to hide his delight when he saw how taken Digger was with Catia. Much more so than with Simona. He wasn't sure if it was because he so desperately hoped Digger would like her that his judgment could have been clouded, but he was sure he had never seen Digger take so much of a liking so quickly in a strange person. It could also have been that Digger could sense that Rex was so enamored of Catia, and he wanted to please his alpha.

Rex looked at Catia and Simona and smiled. "I'm sure there are many questions, and I'm happy to answer them. However, I suggest we first talk about the men who were following you. Who were they? And why were they following you?"

Catia replied, "My best guess is Camorra, and the why is a bit of a long story. Can we shelve that for now, plan next steps, and the reasons to be explained later?"

Rex nodded. "Fair enough. I'll accept your assessment that they're working for the Camorra, and until we have evidence to the contrary, let's assume that's who they are. The fact is, irrespective of who they are, they have clearly demonstrated their intentions, and they saw our faces. It seems they know where Simona lives, and they have seen the garage where Catia parks her motorcycles. It wouldn't take much for them to find out where she lives, put a trace on those bikes, and find out who she is. I'd guess before long they'd have the police and every man and his dog looking for us."

"Yes, that'd be about right," Catia said.

"I have a place where we could go, but before I tell you about it, I'd like to hear what you had in mind," Rex said.

Catia shrugged. "I don't really have a specific place. I have a good friend up north and thought I would ask her to put us up for a few days while we decided where we could go." She considered whether she should tell him about her former handler, David Sternberg, and that she was hoping to be able to get in touch with him to help them, but in the end, decided not to tell him, yet.

Simona sighed and said, "I only know people in Naples and Rome." She started crying. "This is all my fault. I'm so sorry."

"Simona, there's nothing to be gained from beating yourself up." Rex said, "We are in this together now, and we'll work it out."

"So, what's *your* idea?" Catia asked.

Rex told them about the *TOMATS* without going into all the detail and was happy when he saw the relief washing the strain off their faces.

Catia and Simona were smiling when he finished, and Catia said, "Well, as far as I'm concerned, that would be an ideal hiding place, provided of course, we can get onto the yacht unnoticed."

Rex grinned slightly. "Okay, I'm glad we're in agreement. Now, if you'd excuse me for a few minutes, I need to call the captain to make arrangements."

Rex left the guesthouse, called Digger, walked to a large umbrella pine tree about thirty yards away, sat down on the bench in the shadow, and called Declan Spencer on his secured satellite phone.

Half an hour later, he returned to the guesthouse to share with them the plan. "And just to put your mind at ease," he said, "the captain is very excited to meet you ladies. You'll be his first guests since he became the captain."

"You're not a guest?" Catia asked.

Rex laughed. "No, not really in that sense," and when he saw the probing look on Catia's face, he said, "to be explained later."

He would have a lot of explaining to do once 'later' came.

Part II

THE PREDECESSOR

Chapter Eight

THE DON

Naples, Italy

Ricardo Lombardi was the leader of the Beneduce-Longobardi clan, the Campania region's most powerful Camorra crime boss. He'd become an exceedingly rich and powerful man from running the biggest drug and counterfeit-goods empire in Europe.

He imported cocaine from Colombia, heroin from Afghanistan, and hashish from Morocco. In Naples, the cocaine and heroin were diluted and provided to the piazzas, as well as the extensive wholesale networks in Italy, Germany, France, and further afield.

He manufactured counterfeit brand-name goods such as Louis Vuitton, Dolce & Gabbana, Versace, Gucci, Prada, and others that lined the shelves of outlets in Western Europe, Brazil, and the United States. Some of the counterfeits were made by the same factories that produced the originals and were identical down to the stitching.

Unlike many other crime bosses across the globe, Lombardi had not arbitrarily killed his way to power from the back-street slums. Nevertheless, no crime boss could attain and stay in power without, from time to time, having to rely on the persuasive powers of violent measures such as beatings, killing, kidnapping, torture, and robbery—those were a given in the power struggles of the underworld of organized crime.

However, when Lombardi resorted to such measures, it was because it was necessary—for strategic reasons, never indiscriminately—so he believed.

Regardless of his power and money, he went to great lengths to stay out of the limelight and off the radar of law enforcement. He lived a reclusive life in the same house where he grew up as a child, secured behind steel shutters, bolted gates, and a contingent of guards. He almost never had contact with anyone outside of his family, his chief of staff, also known as a consigliere, and very occasionally, a few trusted deputies.

Yet, he wielded immense political clout and influence in high places. He was a perpetual benefactor to good causes such as schools, hospitals, and nursing homes. He funded scholarships, took care of widows and orphans, and donated to political parties, not just one party, all of them, even those who advocated to voters that they would crush the Camorra.

His donations always had two conditions: One, it was anonymous, and the benefactor insisted that it remained that way. Two, please remember the Beneduce-Longobardi clan in your prayers.

He contributed generously to the unofficial pension funds of those high-ranking government officials who assisted him and included, among others, police officers, prosecutors, judges, and others who might be of use to him someday.

And above all, he passionately supported the Catholic Church, anonymously. The clergymen in his area never fell on hard times, neither would he allow any church building to fall into disrepair.

He provided jobs to his clan members, and he extended low or no interest business and personal loans.

Under his reign, there was a period of rarely known peace among the people who lived on his turf and beyond. On many occasions, he had also stepped in to settle feuds between belligerent clans not under his control.

The message was simple: you can do whatever you like, on one condition—you don't do it in our territory.

Those who were hard of hearing or slow of understanding about this matter soon found themselves in a basement of an abandoned building where they were beaten with rubber hoses until they collapsed.

Of course, there was no ill-will, it was just a matter of getting the wrongdoers to concentrate on what they were told they could or couldn't do on Beneduce-Longobardi turf.

The police and anti-Mafia law enforcement agencies 'knew' he was a crime boss and a major player in organized crime in Italy and beyond, but they were unable to link him directly to any crime that they could charge him for—in Campania, silence was what kept you alive. Truth known, law enforcement was not really that motivated to bring him up on charges. The Don's methods of law enforcement worked much better than their own in many cases. So, why would they interfere with someone who was doing their job for them? The end justifies the means, they argued.

Throughout Campania, Don Ricardo Lombardi, or simply, the Don, was a well-respected man even among his adversaries.

Chapter Nine

THERE ARE NO DOUBTS

How had Italy managed to escape the jihadi terrorist attacks that had afflicted Western European countries such as France, Belgium, Germany, Spain, and the United Kingdom, since the invasion of Iraq in 2003?

Western Europe was besieged by hundreds of thousands of refugees from war-torn Middle Eastern countries. Among them, security analysts say, were tens of thousands of Islamic extremists. Refugee shelters were the breeding ground for jihadists. The security agencies of Western European countries were inundated as radical Islamic jihad bloomed, and they were forced to keep thousands of persons of interest under constant surveillance.

Their counterterrorism efforts foiled hundreds of plots but not all of them. Since the 2004 Madrid train bombings in which Rex Dalton's parents and siblings had been killed, Islamic terrorists regularly slipped through the security dragnets killing hundreds and injuring thousands more with bombs, guns, trucks, and knives in the cities of France, Belgium, Germany, Spain, and the United Kingdom.

But not in Italy.

Some security analysts called it a mystery. Some called it the Italian paradox.

It wasn't because Italy had strict immigration policies – they didn't – refugees from Africa and Middle Eastern countries arrived in droves on Italy's shores.

However, for some reason or another, these Italian refugees seemed to be of a different brand – they never made any trouble, they didn't send suicide bombers to blow up the Vatican, the epitome of the infidel, or any other historic place in Italy, they didn't plant bombs in Italy, and they never drove trucks into crowds of Italian people. In fact, most of the refugees reaching the shores of Italy didn't even settle there—they moved on to other Western European countries.

Plenty of theories existed to explain the phenomenon. Most were poppycock.

The official reason, according to Italian authorities; they had the best security and intelligence service in Europe and therefore prevented these things from happening by nipping the plans in the bud, before they could come to fruition. They said they had decades of experience with anti-mafia policing, had learned harsh lessons, and were applying those tactics to prevent terrorism.

Even the Italian people laughed at that.

The true reason, the unofficial one, that every self-respecting security agency in the world knew, was that Italy had the organized crime syndicates. Often referred to by non-Italians as the Mafia, as if it was one big nation-wide organization responsible for the racketeering, drug-trafficking, and murders associated with organized crime.

The Italians, however, knew that what outsiders thought of as one big crime organization were in reality five major organizations that established themselves in Italy over a period of more than five-hundred years: The Cosa Nostra, meaning 'Our Thing' or 'This Thing of Ours', were the original 'Mafia' also known as the Sicilian Mafia. The second group was the 'Ndrangheta operating in Calabria, the region in the toe of Italy, wedged between the Camorra of Naples and the Cosa Nostra of Sicily, they were considered to be among the biggest cocaine smugglers in Europe. The third group was the Camorra of the Campania region with Naples as the capital. The fourth and fifth groups were the Stidda of the central-southern part of Sicily and the Sacra Corona Unita of Apulia. The latter two were established during the 20th century

Although no one talked about it, everyone suspected, and some knew, the organized crime syndicates had made a deal with the terrorists.

It was clear as daylight that the organized crime syndicates' role in this demonic partnership was to make available their established infrastructure and trade routes to help the terrorists smuggle weapons through Italy back to their countries to cause more mayhem. The terrorists paid with drugs from their home countries, which the crime syndicates then sold throughout Europe. Naturally, the terrorists didn't want to upset their trading partners, and therefore Italy was exempt from terrorist incidents. This barter system worked very well for both parties, a true win-win situation for them, but not so for those on both receiving ends.

A former agent of Italy's Secret Service hit the nail on the head when he said, *"Our country has a vast territory, difficult to control and full of places that could be considered sensitive targets. So, it would be foolish, not to say ridiculous, to say we are secure despite constant monitoring of public transportation, major shopping* centers, and airports. The real protection is the indirect one exercised by criminal organizations.

"Italy is able to protect itself from terrorist attacks in just two ways: the precise monitoring of 'weak signals' that allows wiretapping and targeted preventive interventions, and with the Mafia."

The Camorra clans, operating out of the Campania region and Naples, its capital, dwarfed the Sicilian Mafia, Cosa Nostra, the 'Ndrangheta and any of Italy's other organized crime gangs, in numbers, in economic power, and in ruthless violence.

Where the Cosa Nostra's families organized themselves in a pyramidal structure, the Camorra was an integral part of the region's culture, consisting of more than a hundred self-directed clans, ten thousand plus immediate associates, and an even larger group of dependents, clients, and friends.

"You can't really cut the head off the Camorra, because it doesn't have one," – said John Dickie, a Professor of Italian Studies at University College London.

For centuries, the Camorra had been a way of life in Campania. It had been in existence longer than the modern-day Italy. It provided justice and created and distributed wealth. It offered work, lent money, suppressed street crime, and protected the clans' people from the government.

People trusted the Camorra for their livelihood more than their government. They have a saying in Campania; The Camorra never sleeps.

They were also the largest drug supplier to the European market. In Scampia, a suburb of the city of Naples, they operated one of the most lucrative retail operations in the world, drug bazaars—known as piazzas—outlets for low-grade heroin and cocaine. Depending on location and demand, the largest of these piazzas operated twenty-four-seven and employed lookouts as an early warning system to cover all approaches. They watched driveways and parking areas from higher floors in surrounding buildings, some on scooters patrolling the streets, and some hanging around in groups at entry points. The piazzas were protected by steel bars in front of windows and steel doors. Drugs and money safely exchanged hands through a small portal cut through a door or wall.

Those setups could not stop the police from entering, but it made their raids futile because they would never find vendors in possession of the drugs. So, the police didn't even bother.

With the rise of Islamic radicalism in Europe, the name of the Camorra more frequently started to pop up in conversations about terrorism in Western Europe.

Franco Roberti, a prominent anti-mafia prosecutor said, "*Naples has been, for many years, a central logistics base for the Middle East. The Camorra is also active in the world of Jihadist terrorism that passes through Naples. Naples lends itself to this type of activity. In the past there have been contacts between Jihadi militants and the Camorra clans.*

"*Campania, especially the province of Caserta and Castel Volturno, is one of the main gateways into Europe for those who want to become a terrorist. It has been demonstrated by numerous investigations. On this now, there are no doubts.*"

Pierluigi Vigna, Italy's national anti-mafia prosecutor, once noted, "*We have evidence that groups of the Camorra are implicated in an exchange of weapons for drugs with terrorist groups.*"

Chapter Ten

THE DEAL

South of Naples, Italy

2009

About thirty miles south of the center of Naples there was a small beachfront enclave, covering an area of about five or so square miles. It was a no-go area for anyone who didn't live there, and even law enforcement toed the line.

In 2009, the enclave had a short but sad history. Over a period of two years since 2007, a few hundred Muslim refugees had settled in the area, and Sharia law became the only law of that piece of land.

The newcomers were not welcomed by the Neapolitans, in fact, they were despised. Most of the Camorra clan leaders were driven by one psychiatric defect: raging paranoia. Their suspicion toward the foreigners was direct and irrepressible. They made sure the intruders got no jobs and subjected them to insulting stares and comments whenever they dared to leave the enclave where they lived in dismal conditions in dilapidated buildings.

The message was clear; *you are locked in, you have no future here, we don't want you here, pack up and leave.*

These people's only source of income was the drugs which they smuggled in from Afghanistan, Pakistan, and North Africa, and tried to peddle on the streets of the towns and cities of Campania.

The issue?

Selling drugs in Camorra territory.

For that they were regularly singled out for brutal beatings by clan members.

But then, in early 2009, things came to a head when one of the Camorra clans, a rival group to the Don's Beneduce-Longobardi clan, took it upon themselves to solve the problem once and for all. Ethnic cleansing of the area to get rid of these obnoxious, unwelcome, infidel-hating, illegal aliens who were threatening their livelihoods.

Eight clan members entered the streets of the enclave in two dark SUVs with tinted windows, guns blazing, and indiscriminately killed fifteen men, women, and children and wounded forty more.

And thus, this irresponsible, short-sighted bunch of vigilantes brought Italy and their beloved Naples to the brink of an Islamic holy war, jihad.

However, Don Ricardo Lombardi had not survived and thrived in one of the most malevolent surroundings on earth without a sixth sense of recognizing danger when he saw it. Throughout his life, it was the Don's logic and paranoia that kept him alive and made him rich.

His minions expected him to explode in rage about the news of the senseless killings, but it didn't happen. It was a lesson he had learned at a young age—when faced with tribulations, decorum and gentlemanly calm will win the day.

For more than an hour, the Don was quiet and then, speaking in a tranquil voice, he ordered his consigliere to identify, interrogate, and kill the thugs who did it, and do so quickly.

Within twelve hours of the shootings, the offending clan numbered eight less men.

It was a rare show of force from the Don.

The police were still mobilizing and trying to gather evidence when it was all over, and although they didn't close their dossiers, they didn't investigate any further. They knew better than to try to unravel the entire chain of events and bring anyone else to justice when it had already been served.

However, Don Lombardi knew there was still much to do. He ordered his consigliere to get the name of the imam of the afflicted Muslim community and set up a meeting, immediately.

Another rare event took place a day later, when the Don left the sanctuary of his home shortly after midnight to travel under heavy guard to the home of Imam Kazim Al-Sadiq in the enclave.

Prior to the Don's arrival, as per agreement, the street and surroundings where the imam lived had been cleared and secured. The Don's men took up positions on the street corners and outside the house while the two men had a private meeting inside.

At the outset, it was obvious that Imam Al-Sadiq was not in the mood for small talk. He avoided shaking the Don's hand by keeping his hands behind his back. He greeted with a curt nod and pointed to the small living room. The drapes on the windows were black plastic rubbish bags, a cardboard box turned upside down served as a table, and two derelict double seats, ripped out of old cars, were the sofas. Wordlessly, he pointed the Don to one of the 'sofas' and sat down on the one opposite.

The Don started to explain why he was there, but the imam interrupted and said, "No need for that. All I want to know is, who killed my people and why?"

Although nobody had spoken to Don Lombardi in that manner for a very long time, he remained impervious to the imam's rudeness. He kept his composure, continued where he was interrupted, and explained that he was there to offer his condolences, express his anger at what had happened, and offer his help. Without admitting or even alluding to the fact that he knew who the killers were or that he had already dealt with them, he gave Al-Sadiq his personal assurance that he would do everything in his power to make sure such a thing would never happen again.

Not only was Al-Sadiq inconsolable about the loss of innocent lives, he also made sure to express his outrage about the inhumane treatment of his people by the locals, the Don's people.

Al-Sadiq's ranting didn't surprise Don Lombardi, he had expected it.

Notwithstanding the fact that the conversation became less strained after the Don had managed to convince Al-Sadiq of his bona fides, it required another two and half hours of painstaking negotiations before they had forged an alliance between them.

The Don would divert a considerable amount of money from his vast income to the reconstruction and upliftment of the enclave and its people. In return, Al-Sadiq would use his influence to pacify his fellow Muslims in the enclave and the Campania region.

That part was relatively easy, and it would have been an excellent outcome if that constituted the entire agreement, but it didn't.

Al-Sadiq was an astute negotiator; Don Lombardi had quickly come to realize that. What the Don didn't know then and would only discover much later, was that the imam was also a highly placed terrorist mastermind. In fact, there were less than a handful of people on the planet who knew that Al-Sadiq was not who he purported to be.

Kazim Al-Sadiq, whose real name was Hassan Walid, was a member of the external wing of Hezbollah's secret service, known as Amn al-Muddad. This secret service had been described by some as 'one of the best in the world', rumored to have infiltrated the Israeli army. Hezbollah, a political party in Lebanon and sworn enemy of the state of Israel, was declared a terrorist organization by the United States, Israel, Canada, the Arab League, the Gulf Cooperation Council, the United Kingdom, Australia, and the European Union.

Mossad, the Israelis' branch of their Intelligence Community responsible for intelligence collection, covert operations, and counterterrorism had Hassan Walid on a watchlist for years. But they'd lost track of him a few years ago. There were rumors that he was killed in one of Israel's air raids on a target in Lebanon.

As top-secret agent of Amn al-Muddad, Al-Sadiq had received specialized intelligence training in Iran and North Korea.

When he was sent on the mission to Italy to establish a mission support base for the jihadis operating against targets in Western European countries, the brief from his handlers was to blend in, play the role of a true refugee, maintain a very low profile, don't radicalize anyone, and keep his sermons peaceful and reconciliatory.

The result of the second stage of the negotiations between them was, to put it mildly, portentous.

Very shrewdly, Al-Sadiq had assured that the Don understood about the untold pressure put on him by his congregation to declare jihad against the people of Naples, even Italy. He explained in spine-chilling detail to the Don about the far-reaching implications jihad would have. Not only for Naples, but for all of Italy, and Al-Sadiq didn't neglect to mention that included the Vatican.

Of course, he also told the Don that he was a man of peace, a follower of a religion of peace, and surreptitiously hinted that, in fact, it was only peace-loving people like the Don and himself that stood between Italy and the dire consequences of jihad.

That was when the Don got the first inklings that the imam was not just the spiritual leader of the few hundred Muslims in the enclave, but a man with a much wider sphere of influence. Possibly a man with terrorist connections. The Don soon came to the realization that in order to keep his clan, the region, his country, and his church safe, he *had* to make a deal.

Although he knew it was the case, he couldn't bring himself so far as to admit what Al-Sadiq was so eloquently extracting from him was an agreement to a protection scheme. That which the organized crime syndicates were so good at in the good old days when they still ruled supreme.

Now the shoe was on the other foot, and it didn't fit well.

Imam Kazim Al-Sadiq promised that he would keep his end of the deal by assuring that drugs smuggled into the country by his people were delivered to Don Lombardi's warehouses. The Don's part of the deal was to pay them for it—some in cash and some in weapons. Al-Sadiq also mentioned that over time, this agreement could expand to much larger quantities of both commodities and become extremely lucrative.

A true win-win situation for both parties.

The Don was not entirely happy to agree to such a deal, but once he had extracted a solemn promise from Al-Sadiq that the weapons would never be used on Italian soil, including the Vatican, the deal was clinched.

By the time they shook hands, for the first time, they were both smiling and thanking each other for the candid discussions and letting sensibility prevail over emotions.

Within a few months, the enclave had literally risen from the ashes like the fabled Phoenix. Some of the houses and buildings were demolished and new ones constructed, others only required renovation, electricity, water, and sanitation services restored, and cash started to flow into the pockets of the impoverished residents.

In this manner, the foresight, cool-headedness, and quick action of Don Lombardi had spared Italy and the Catholic Church the horrors of jihad which was besetting the rest of Western Europe.

Part of the deal was also that the enclave would remain a no-go zone for any outsiders who were not specifically invited, including the police.

It had become what it was intended to be from the start; an exclusive safe haven for refugees of the Muslim persuasion.

Chapter Eleven

THE CONNECTION

CRC Headquarters, Arizona, USA

2011

Crisis Response Consultancy, CRC, nominally commanded by the CIA, was a private military contractor under the command of John Brandt, the Old Man as his underlings liked to call him. The name, Crisis Response Consultancy, was one of those nondescript names that simultaneously said nothing and everything about the activities of the organization. One had to be one of them to know what crises they were consulted about and how they responded to them. CRC was a private contractor business specializing in black operations on behalf of their clients such as the CIA and other US security and law enforcement agencies.

One of CRC's agents, Matthew Benedict, had been sent on the mission to Naples to infiltrate the Camorra and collect information about a weapons-for-drugs deal. He'd been successful in doing so, but his rise in clan business, however, had attracted unwanted attention and gotten him killed.

His body was found by Italian authorities floating in the harbor, a knife wound in his back that an autopsy showed had penetrated his heart.

John Brandt wanted the murderer punished as well as the mission completed.

Naples, Italy

2011

Rex Dalton was up for the next mission, and he was perfect for it. He was fluent in Italian and spoke it with a perfect accent of someone who was born and raised in the northern part of the country. His dark hair, eyes, and skin would stand him in good stead, as well.

In Rome, he met with Catia Romano, a mission support specialist who had provided part of his European tradecraft training the year before. He thought she worked for MI6 and would have been surprised to learn that she was associated instead with the Mossad. The Mossad had trained her as a support specialist, a *sayan* in Hebrew.

The Mossad was a small intelligence agency and cash strapped, therefore they had devised a brilliant plan to overcome their limitations with the use of helpers, *sayanim*, Jewish volunteers across the world. They were bankers, restauranteurs, homeowners, hoteliers, owners of guest houses, AirBnBs, rental car companies, travel agents, lawyers, doctors, nurses, journalists, and many others. They numbered more than ten thousand and whenever needed, provided mission support to Mossad's covert operations, free of charge.

Catia was not an ordinary *sayan* who only owned an AirBnB in Rome that the Mossad could use for a safehouse; she was one of their trainers. Therefore, she was trained in hand-to-hand combat and the use of weapons to take care of herself if required; she was highly skilled in street-craft, surveillance and counter-surveillance, how to set up weapons caches, and providing false identity documents when required by operatives; and she was trained to lead surveillance teams to check out targets. Sometimes, she was even tasked to monitor some of the agents she supported to make sure they were not double agents.

Rex knew Catia could help when he found his informant, Sophia Maiorani, beaten by Camorra thugs after giving him information that would turn out to help him break a major drugs-for-weapons deal.

Rex had tried to talk to Sophia at the restaurant where she worked, but when he asked her about Matthew Benedict, she was scared out of her wits and ordered him to leave and never come back. Rex left when he noticed that Sophia was under the watch of two mean-looking Italian goons, no doubt Camorra henchmen. He didn't want to get her into any trouble with them. He returned the next day, hoping that her 'bodyguards' would not be there. They weren't. Neither was Sophia. She was in the hospital.

On arrival in her room at the hospital, with the first look at her, Rex noticed her lumpy and misshapen face, bruises, one eye swollen shut, and her left arm in a cast. She had been badly beaten.

The two thugs who did it to her turned up and made

the mistake of attacking Rex. Both ended up unconscious, tied up and gagged, in the shower, sporting their own bruises and broken bones.

Sophia was almost out of her mind with fear, telling Rex that he had now signed not only his own death warrant but also hers. He'd spirited her away on the back of a motorcycle.

———————

Sophia had provided Rex with enough information to expand his investigation. He called in assistance from CRC to help him with surveillance, and soon he had all the information he needed.

By the time Rex had the full picture, though, there was not enough time to plan and launch a sophisticated clandestine operation before the transaction would take place. Definitely not on Italian soil. After thorough reconnaissance of the location where the drugs and weapons would change hands, Rex had put a plan forward. It was simple and brilliant and accepted by CRC's John Brandt, the CIA's DDO, and the Director of the Mossad. The latter two, of course, also liked the fact that if the plan failed, no fingers could be pointed to Israel or the USA, and the good relations with Italy would remain unscathed.

Rex and his team had rigged the warehouse where the deal would go down with explosives, including a large tanker parked inside and filled with liquefied petroleum gas, LPG. The resultant explosion that night, when all the offending parties were gathered around their trucks loaded with more than sixty tons of opium on the one side and trucks packed to the brim with AK-47 rifles, rocket-propelled grenades, RPG 7 rocket launchers, landmines, and hundreds of thousands of rounds of ammunition on the other side, killed every single person inside that warehouse and obliterated the merchandise. The building was reduced to dust and rubble, and a few more warehouses in the vicinity also suffered some damage.

Thirty were dead, including a local Camorra Don, Ricardo Lombardi, and two of his sons. What the Don was doing in the warehouse with twenty-nine other men, half of whom were of Middle Eastern heritage, no one could or would explain.

Most of the media was quick to blame the explosion on a gas leak, which wasn't so far from the truth. After all, sixty-five tons of LPG when ignited like that causes a big explosion.

Some of the media speculated, though only vaguely and briefly, about terrorist activity, but they were soon reminded that Italy had the best security services in Europe; therefore, they had no terrorist problems.

Chapter Twelve

HOW AWFUL WOULD THAT HAVE BEEN?

Mossad safehouse, Rome, Italy

2011

It was ten days before wiping out the Camorra warehouse with all the drugs, weapons, and thirty people inside it, when Rex had delivered Sophia to Catia Romano late at night to a safehouse very close to the Jewish Quarters in Rome.

Rex didn't know that his mission was a joint Mossad-CIA operation. It didn't matter, he didn't need to know that to execute his brief.

Catia was shocked when she saw Sophia's bruised face and left arm in a cast. She was surprised that Rex had managed to transport her in that condition all the way from Naples on the back of a motorcycle without incident and asked him how he did it.

"I strapped her to my back."

Although Sophia was able to walk, it was clear that the stress of the trip and the painkillers that Rex gave her before they left Naples had weakened her. She was unsteady on her feet. Rex and Catia supported her as they led her to her bedroom.

Half an hour later Sophia was asleep, and Rex and Catia had a bit of time to talk before he had to turn back for Naples.

Over an espresso and two arancini balls (rice stuffed with ragù, meat or mince, coated with bread crumbs and then deep fried) which Catia had heated up for him, without giving away too many details, Rex told her how it came about that he had to get Sophia out of harm's way and about the valuable information she had given him.

She got her instructions for Marco's (the name she knew Rex by) mission from her *katsa*, Hebrew for handler, David Sternberg, stationed at the Israeli Embassy in Rome. She knew it was a joint Mossad-CIA operation but didn't tell Marco. He either knew or didn't, if it was the latter there was a reason for it—need-to-know.

She had been listening to him without interrupting, and when he finished, she said, "Okay, Marco, I understand. I'll see to it that she's kept safe here and taken care of. I'll get instructions from my people about what must happen once she has recovered. I guess she will not be returning to Naples, at least not soon?"

"Not for the foreseeable future. In Campania it seems as if people are born into the Camorra, they're part of it whether they like it or not, and by the same token they can't just leave them when they feel like it. I think it's important that you let her know that she should not make any attempt whatsoever to contact any of her acquaintances, including her family."

"I'll take care of it."

Rex looked at his watch and realized, with regret, their time was up. He would have loved to stay with Catia for a little longer, but he had to leave within the next few minutes to reach Naples before sunrise. He downed another espresso to keep him alert, gave Catia a hug and a kiss which set his heart racing, and left with a big smile on his face.

True to her promise, Catia had seen to it that Sophia was taken good care of. The middle-aged lady who owned the apartment was Jewish, also a *sayan* working for the Mossad, but not trained for mission support like Catia. She had made her apartment available as a safehouse for Mossad missions when they needed it, for which they paid her a monthly retainer. Part of her duties were to tend to the guests who arrived from time to time and ask no questions.

Catia left the safehouse after checking on Sophia and giving the landlady instructions. She returned that afternoon to check on Sophia again and took time to explain to her, her responsibilities about her own security. Part of which was that she should not leave the apartment for any reason whatsoever and not to contact anyone. Sophia, with the memory of the brutal assault still fresh in her memory, promised to abide by every rule laid down by Catia.

The landlady and Sophia got along very well. By the second day, after getting the nod from Catia to incur the expenses, she took Sophia's measurements and went out clothes-shopping for her.

In the meantime, Catia had been in contact with her *katsa*, David Sternberg. He had more information about Marco's mission than she had but no need to share it with her, yet. His instructions were that Sophia had to be kept at the safehouse until the end of Marco's mission.

Depending on the outcome, decisions about Sophia's lot would be made at that stage. He had no idea how long the operation would last; it could be over in a few days, maybe a week or two, it could even be a few months. For the time being the Mossad were happy for Sophia to remain at the safehouse.

Trattoria near Trevi Fountain, Rome, Italy

2011

In her apartment above the *trattoria* in Via delle Carrozze, about fifty yards away from the *Piazza di Spagna*, Spanish Square, Catia was awake and busy with research for a master's dissertation about the history of the Jewish Community in Rome when the news of the explosion in Naples broke. She couldn't help but immediately think of Marco. She saved and closed the document she was working on, turned up the volume on the TV, got up, and made herself a cup of tea while she watched the news unfolding.

Within a few hours the stations were continually repeating the same story. The so-called expert analysts were clueless. The official story was that a gas leak caused it. Any suggestions that it could have been terrorism were quickly rejected.

When Catia finally went to bed, shortly before midnight, her last thoughts were of Marco. She had no reason to make a connection between the explosion and Marco, yet she could not shake the feeling that there was one.

Shortly after 6:00 A.M. she got an encoded message on her encrypted mobile phone.

$$7 @ L4 - S.$$

She had a meeting at 10:00 A.M. (the first number plus three) at L4, Location Four, a trattoria close to Trevi Fountain, about five minutes' walk from her apartment with S, David Sternberg.

Both of them made sure they were not followed before entering the *trattoria*. The owner, another *sayan*, always kept a table at the back of the restaurant reserved for special guests such as Catia and Sternberg.

After serving them with espresso and a plate of delectable pastries, the *sayan* left the two of them to attend to his other patrons.

Sternberg took a bite of the cannoli followed by a sip of espresso and started. "Marco's mission is over."

Catia instantly knew Marco was somehow involved in that explosion. "Is he okay?"

Sternberg must have noticed her disquiet. He grinned. "Yep, he's all good. No casualties on our side. Mission was a big success."

Catia couldn't help but let out a sigh of relief.

David smiled. "Catia, looks like you got the hots for this guy."

Catia blushed a little. "He's a nice guy. But I know the rules."

"Yeah, well, the rules can't stop one's emotions, can they?"

Catia smiled and changed the subject. "David, I know if I was supposed to know more about the operation, I would've been told, but I suspect he had something to do with that explosion in Naples last night."

Sternberg nodded. "Well, that's part of the reason for the meeting. Your suspicions are correct. That explosion prevented a major drugs-for-arms deal. It was one of the biggest illicit arms shipments in the history of Israel's existence. The explosion killed thirty coldblooded criminals, and it saved the lives of thousands of innocent people.

"Sophia's information helped us uncover that evil conspiracy and thwart it."

For the next twenty or so minutes, he told Catia all about the operation starting with the information they got from their informant in Hezbollah, Matthew Benedict's failed mission and Marco's mission, including the role Sophia played in all of it.

"However, that information she gave to Marco came at a price—to her," Sternberg said. "I'm afraid she can never go back to Naples. Before long the Camorra will know that was no gas leak. They'll make the connection, and they'll leave no stone unturned to find her."

Catia nodded. She didn't have to be told that the Camorra, whose tentacles reached far beyond Campania, would get hold of Sophia sooner or later. "I take it you want me to make arrangements for her to set up a new life?"

Sternberg nodded. "Yes. We always look after our assets, especially those who didn't do it for money. New ID, new looks, new country if necessary. Just let me know what you need."

Catia nodded. She had helped people disappear before and understood what had to be done. "Okay, leave it with me, I'll talk to her and get back to you. Say tomorrow nine o'clock at L5?"

Sternberg agreed. He remained at the table after Catia

had left, finished the pastries, and had another espresso and a short chat with the owner before he left.

Mossad safehouse, Rome, Italy

2011

When Catia turned up at the safehouse that afternoon, Sophia was in a state of shock and anguish in the family room, staring at the TV.

By now, the names of the deceased had been released, and Sophia knew almost all the Italian men. Those were the names she'd given to the blonde man she knew as Marco. The man who had saved her from those Camorra thugs who had beaten her.

She had recovered well. There were no more bruises on her face. The only physical reminder of the nightmare was the cast on her left arm. Over the past ten days since her arrival at the safehouse, she'd had time to think about her situation. She knew the Camorra, and she knew she could not go back to Naples, at least not soon. Other than her mother and sister, she had no family, friends, not even acquaintances in Rome or anywhere else in Italy, or anywhere else in the world for that matter. She had spent her whole life in Naples. Thoughts of what would become of her when she had to leave the sanctuary of the safehouse worried her. But whenever she had asked Catia about it, the answer was always the same. "Don't worry about it, Sophia. When you are ready to leave here, I'll make sure that you're kept safe."

She would have liked it if Catia told her what the plan was, but Catia always evaded the question. It was as if Catia was waiting for something to happen.

Now Sophia knew what Catia had been waiting for, and it was driving her to the edge of hysteria.

———

Catia had one look at Sophia and realized she had to act quickly. She had a quick word with the landlady, who told her that Sophia had been sitting in front of the TV the whole day, crying most of the time. It was a difficult situation as she could not ask Sophia why she was upset, although she knew it must have had something to do with the news out of Naples.

After the landlady had left the house with the excuse of visiting a friend, Catia took a seat on the sofa next to Sophia, who took yet another tissue out of the box wiped her tears away and blew her nose. She pointed at the TV screen and said, "I think I'm responsible for that, Catia. I killed those people… didn't I?"

Catia was surprised that Sophia had made the connection. In a way, Sophia was right. It was the information she'd given Marco that set the chain of events in motion, eventually leading to the explosion.

"Why are you saying that?"

Sophia sniffed and said, "Those people, the Italians, I knew them. I gave their names, almost all of them, to Marco. I am sure Marco is behind this."

Catia knew it would serve no purpose to try and sugar-coat the facts. It was best to help her get over the remorse and understand the bigger picture. But how much should she tell Sophia?

"Sophia, I want you to listen carefully to what I say. Will you?"

Sophia nodded and sighed again.

"I can't tell you everything, but I'm going to tell you things you can never repeat to anyone. I want your word about that."

"You have it," Sophia said.

"Those people who were killed in that explosion deserved it. I know it might sound harsh, but if they'd been allowed to carry out their plans, thousands of innocent people were going to die. It was your information that helped us track them down and stop their evil plans."

"What plans?"

"Just think about it, Sophia. Fifteen of those names were Italian and fifteen were from the Middle East. Why would fifteen Italians, Camorristi, no less, want to meet in a big warehouse in the Port of Naples with fifteen Middle Eastern men?"

Sophia had turned and was staring at Catia blankly for a long while, and then it must have dawned on her. "Drugs and weapons?"

Catia nodded. "One of the biggest black-market weapons shipments destined for the Middle East ever. Have you any idea how many people would have been killed with those weapons? Have you any idea how many people would have been killed, here in our own country and across Europe, by those drugs?"

"But… but… I've never killed anyone… I… I am not a murderer," she started crying again.

"You didn't kill those people. They were responsible for what happened to them. You didn't make criminals, drug dealers, or terrorists out of them. They chose their own destiny. They didn't care about you or me or anyone. Need I remind you how they treated you?"

Sophia shook her head. "I understand, but it doesn't make it less awful."

"No, it doesn't. But there is nothing to be gained by blaming yourself for what those people brought on themselves. Thousands of innocent people would have died, Sophia. How awful would that have been?"

It took another two hours and a few more cups of tea to calm Sophia and get her to face the reality of the situation. Only then was it time for her to face another reality—her life as Sophia Maiorani had come to an end.

Part III

THE SUCCESSOR

Chapter Thirteen

WHO WILL BE THE SUCCESSOR?

Naples, Italy

2011

With the news of the death of Don Ricardo Lombardi and two of his three sons and many of the senior leaders, the Beneduce-Longobardi clan were flung into a state of mourning. And they were also given to conjecture and anxiety about the Don's successor.

The Don's wife was terminal with late-stage bowel cancer.

Mattia Lombardi, thirty-four years of age, the youngest of the Don's sons, and the Don's only daughter, thirty-two-year-old Teresa, were his only children who were not at the fateful business meeting that night.

No one spared a moment of serious thought that Teresa Lombardi would ever take over the leadership of the Beneduce-Longobardi clan. She was an enigma, in all regards. With her skinny and petite physique, blond hair, fair skin, and blue eyes, she was very beautiful; it was obvious she had inherited her mother's genes. But, not only did she bear no semblance of the Lombardi men's stocky, dark haired, dark complexion familial features, she never acted as if she was a Camorrista or even remotely interested in their business. At least not as far as they could see.

Other than her immediate family and the Don's consigliere, who took an oath under penalty of death to never divulge the secret, no one actually knew what became of her after she had finished school.

There were rumors among the Camorra, there always were, that Teresa got married to an Australian or a New Zealander, and she was living somewhere Down Under. Other rumors had it that she was living with a partner somewhere in Sweden or it could have been Norway. Whatever, she was not even living in Italy. Clearly, she had no interest in the clan's business.

The truth was, from a very early age, Teresa had proven to be a gifted painter. After school, she had left Naples to study art at the Florence School of Fine Arts where she attained a Master of Arts with high distinction.

Part of the reason the people didn't know what had become of her was because when she left Naples, she assumed a new name. It might have been because she wanted to sever or obscure ties with the Beneduce-Longobardi clan, or it might have been for more devious reasons. In any case, Liana Verdi was what it stated on her driver's license, credit cards, bank accounts, passport, and graduation certificates.

Upon completion of her studies, she and her father had

entered into a joint business venture. They purchased a historic, run-down building in Rome, which they renovated and converted into the Liana Verdi Art Studio. With her father's business acumen and her artistic talents, they soon had a thriving business.

There was never a shortage of students nor of rich clients who wanted to buy the art, her own, her students', and those of others. She sold some of the art through her own studio, but the most lucrative part of the business was the sales that went through a network of outlets located in Rome, other Italian cities, and major cities across Europe.

Contrary to what outsiders thought, despite her apparent decision to choose a different path in life than the rest of her family, Teresa actually loved her family dearly, all of them, even her youngest brother, Mattia.

Her father was her business partner, mentor, and hero, and her mother was her role model of gracious comportment.

And just like her father, Teresa understood how important it was to keep a low profile. Other than turning heads with her exquisite beauty and elegance, she went to great lengths to stay out of the limelight by running the business at arm's-length.

The times when she visited her family in Naples, she arrived under the cover of darkness, stayed inside the family home, and left again under the cover of darkness.

Therefore, in the minds of those who knew and those who speculated, the reality was; this tragedy had left them with only one choice for a leader, Mattia Lombardi.

Although it was never said openly, clan-members knew why Don Lombardi never involved his youngest son in the family business. Mattia was a brutal psychopath. He wore his hair in dreadlocks and always dressed in gothic style. Even his finger- and toenails were painted black. Heavy-set gold chains decorated his neck and hairy chest, hundred-thousand-dollar Swiss watches, a different one for each day of the week, decorated his left wrist, another heavy gold chain on his right wrist, and a twenty-carat diamond ring, set in platinum on his right pinky. And he always carried a concealed gun.

He was almost never without the company of a throng of similarly-clad gothic-looking contemptuous young gunmen. Lower-class girls were thrilled by his style and aggressive demeanor. In short, he was a pompous windbag constantly in pursuit of nothing but his own pleasure.

He regularly got into trouble, and it was only his father's sway over the authorities that kept the young man out of jail.

There were many whispers about Mattia's involvement in a number of killings, armed robberies, kidnappings, and rape. None of his alleged crimes were ever solved by the police because in Campania silence was a birthright.

The clan's people knew that to keep their mouths shut assured longevity.

Up until the untimely death of the Don and his two oldest sons, everyone who knew Mattia quietly thanked God that his youngest son would never be his successor to the reins of the powerful Beneduce-Longobardi clan.

But now, Don Lombardi wasn't there to prevent it, and they were worried.

Likewise, when the authorities learned about the Don's demise, they knew they had a lot of trouble heading their way soon. They could only hope that the clan's surviving leaders would prevent Mattia from ascending the 'throne' of his late father. If not, maybe the other clans might prevent it in short order. But the latter meant the streets of Naples and the other cities of Campania would become a war zone, and they already anticipated that they might soon miss the days when the Don was in charge.

Chapter Fourteen

INEXCUSABLE NEGLIGENCE

South of Naples, Italy

2011

In the Muslim enclave thirty miles south of Naples's central
business district, the news of the explosion and bloodbath in
the harbor soon also reached Imam Kazim Al-Sadiq. He
hadn't attended the ill-fated meeting because he had to
maintain his cover, and of course he counted himself as
fortunate for not having done so.

Within the hour, Al-Sadiq had enough information to
report the disaster to his handlers in Lebanon via an
encrypted website. He was told to collect every scrap of
information about the event he could get and pass it on.
Although it was too early to tell with any degree of certainty
if there were any survivors, the images on TV told him not
to hold out any hope.

Within another few hours Al-Sadiq knew it was no accident—definitely not a gas leak, and no one had survived. He also grieved for his fallen comrades but contrary to the Camorra, he didn't think about successors. The question uppermost in his mind was who was responsible? He didn't know, but the principle of *cui bono*—to whom was it a benefit? —immediately came to mind, and he started creating a list.

It could have been one or more of Don Lombardi's rival Camorra clans who saw their chance to wipe out the Don and his top leaders and step in to fill the gap. It was even possible that a mutinous group within the Don's clan staged a palace revolution. But, Al-Sadiq had his doubts about either of those. Don Lombardi had not been challenged by anyone in many years, he was just too well-informed and too powerful and too well protected. He would have known if there was a challenger waiting in the wings for the right moment to take him out.

Notwithstanding, killing the Don and his men could be beneficial to a contending clan or rebels on the inside. So, that idea, unlikely as it was, could not be discarded outright.

The next potential beneficiary that came to mind was the 'Ndrangheta of Calabria. Their name meant the Honorable Society. Historically they were a mixed breed of Greek and Phoenician and spoke a dialect of Italian derived from Greek, almost unintelligible to the rest of their countrymen. They were, according to law enforcement agencies, impossible to infiltrate because membership was based on family and blood—no stranger was ever allowed to join them. The 'Ndrangheta prided themselves that they were the only one of the organized crime syndicates in which the oath of utter silence, the *omertà*, had never been broken.

They were the biggest cocaine smugglers in Europe, and a ruthless bunch. They almost never collaborated with the other crime syndicates; in fact, they loathed them and had no compunction to visit brutal violence on their adversaries, especially if they encroached on their business.

Al-Sadiq had the 'Ndrangheta high on his list of suspects because they might have felt the pinch from Don Lombardi's ever-expanding empire infringing on their business and decided it was time to send a clear message to the Camorra.

They certainly stood to gain a lot by removing the Don's clan from the playing field.

Last, but not least, he also considered Western Europe's security agencies such as the French DGSE or Britain's MI6 and, of course, the CIA and Mossad. It could even have been a joint operation between two or more of them. The benefit to them was obvious—neither weapons nor drugs on the streets of their cities.

But the chilling aspect of that scenario was the realization that, at the very least, either Al-Sadiq's side or the Don's had at least one mole in its midst.

After a few more hours of watching the news and passing on information to his handlers in Lebanon while trying to figure out who could have done it, the stations were all repeating the same information. The commentators were speculating widely, and quite clearly none of them were prepared to call it what it was—a deliberate and well-planned attack by some yet unknown group.

By now another idea had also started to take shape in Al-Sadiq's mind. The deal and the exchange of merchandise was made on Don Lombardi's territory. Surely, the Don was responsible for the safety of everyone involved. The more he thought about it the more he became convinced that there was no way around it, this whole tragedy could only be blamed on the gross negligence on the part of the late Don Lombardi and his henchmen. The facts spoke for themselves—that warehouse was not inspected and secured before the meeting. The Don's people were obviously so confident that no one would even dare to enter their territory and their building, let alone kill them, that they neglected to sweep and secure the place before the meeting.

Inexcusable negligence that cost the lives of fifteen of my fellow Muslim brothers.

Al-Sadiq had passed his opinion about this on to his handlers together with his recommendation that the deal he and the Don had reached two years before be called off. He also suggested that the Camorra, all of them, and all other organized crime syndicates should be put on notice; Italy was now fair game, and that included the Vatican and every symbol of Christianity.

Al-Sadiq wasn't privy to the discussions in Beirut, between the Al-Qaeda and Hezbollah masterminds. If he were, he would have learned that his proposal came to within a hair-width of being accepted.

The al-Qaeda contingent demanded immediate retaliation in the form of suicide attacks in various Italian cities and the Vatican to announce the jihad on Italian soil.

However, the Hezbollah leader managed to stall their plans with a compromise suggestion. "Let's give them a week or so to appoint a new don who we can negotiate with. Let's first get all the information before we rush in. The deal we had worked well until now. We made a lot of money from the drugs we sold to them, *and* we also got a lot of weapons from them. Unless we could get proof positive that they deliberately betrayed us, it would be better for our cause in the long term if we could continue the deal. Let's not make a rash decision without all the facts."

Chapter Fifteen

BREAKING THE NEWS

Lombardi family residence, Naples, Italy

2011

Her name was Estella Lombardi, and she was seventy-nine, the wife of Ricardo Lombardi, and matriarch of the Bene-duce-Longobardi clan. She was a petite but once-strong woman. In her young days she had shoulder-length blonde hair and deep blue eyes. She was beautiful. But what was left of her now was only an apparition of her former image. Lifeless, painfilled-eyes, an emaciated body, literally a living bag of bones, with no hair—the result of the chemo treatments, which the oncologist had stopped.

"It's of no use to her," he told the Don. "It's only intensifying her discomfort. She has maybe another week, two at the most, to live. I suggest we put her on a morphine drip to ease the pain and make her as comfortable as possible until the end."

The Don had tears in his eyes when the oncologist spoke to him. Over the past eighteen months it had been almost unbearable to see his beloved Estella wither away before his eyes.

It was shortly after 9:00 P.M., and Estella was asleep. Her fulltime nurse and the Don's consigliere, Valter Li Voti, were at the kitchen table having a late dinner when they both heard it. They looked at each other. The sound was distant but unmistakable, an explosion, a huge one. It was not something they often heard in Naples. Gunfire, police, and ambulance sirens, yes, but not explosions.

"Explosion?" The nurse asked.

Li Voti nodded. "From the harbor I'd say." A frown creased his forehead.

The nurse took the remote and switched on the TV.

Within minutes, TV and radio stations reported that there was a massive explosion in the harbor; camera crews and journalists were on their way to investigate.

Later, more details and video footage started to come through.

As the Don's consigliere, Li Voti was the Don's right-hand man, advisor and confidant. At barely five foot ten, very skinny, and almost seventy, he was not a bodyguard—he was hired by the Don for his intellect. He was a former banker who had an intimate understanding of financial matters, national and international, which included among others off-shore banking, money laundering, counterfeiting, and fraud such as pension fund fraud, investment fraud, revenue and taxation fraud, financial market fraud, card fraud, and identity fraud.

After the Don and his wife, he was the most senior person of the Beneduce-Longobardi clan.

He knew all about the deal with Imam Al-Sadiq made

two years before and every transaction concluded between them since then. He also knew all the details, including the time, place, commodities, and the name of every person involved in the exchange in the harbor of Naples that night. He was the one responsible for the forgery of all the shipping documents.

And now, when he saw the video footage broadcast by the TV crews onsite, he also knew that everyone who was inside that warehouse had been killed.

Unmoving, he stared at the screen in silence.

The nurse could see something was wrong with him, but strangely, it seemed as if he was devoid of emotion. He didn't respond to her questions. It was as if she was not there. She had never seen him like this. After a few minutes, she gave up and went to check on her patient.

Li Voti's encrypted cellphone rang for close to fifteen seconds before he realized it, picked it up, and pressed the answer button but didn't say a word.

The caller, the chief of the Fire-Rescue Department of Naples, was onsite with his team. They had arrived within minutes after the police. They had gone through the warehouse, as far as the raging fire allowed them. There were no humans to rescue; they had only found parts of humans, and not many of those. All they were doing now was putting out the fire.

Without saying a word Li Voti disconnected the call.

His phone started ringing again. It was a senior officer in the Naples Police Department. Li Voti ignored the call, dropped his head into his hands, and started crying.

Another half an hour of crying inaction followed.

The nurse had popped into the kitchen a few times to check on him but still didn't get any responses from him. She knew something very bad had happened, and it must have been related to the explosion, which was now being reported about on the TV. But she was not on the Don's need-to-know list.

Finally, Li Voti managed to compose himself, got up from the table, and went out to get hold of the commander of the guards.

After giving his orders to the commander, he went back into the house, called Teresa, and told her it was imperative for her to come to Naples immediately. But he refused to give her more information over the phone.

After ending the call, he went to Estella's room, where he ordered the nurse to wake her up and then to leave the two of them alone.

Chapter Sixteen

I AM THE NEW DON!

Naples, Italy

2011

The explosion happened just a few miles away from the members-only White Lily, a nightclub, strip club, piazza, and brothel all under one roof, Mattia Lombardi's favorite hangout. He owned the place.

A few of the staff and patrons heard and felt the explosion but didn't pay it any attention. Most didn't hear or feel it because either the music was deafening, or their senses were too dulled by alcohol and drugs.

When the commander of the Don's guards arrived at the White Lily, accompanied by two subordinates, they were refused entry. The irate commander explained who they were and why they were there. It didn't work. He then had to resort to threatening with strong-arm tactics which produced the desired outcome, and he was escorted to Mattia's private lounge.

He was not shocked about the company or condition in which he found his employer's youngest son, he had seen it many times. The commander's biggest problem was that he didn't know what the crisis was, yet he had to convince the pig-headed young man that there *was* a crisis, and had orders to take him to his parents' home immediately.

An altercation followed during which Mattia's gun-toting gothic friends threatened to step in and help their friend.

Fortunately, the guards were sober and didn't escalate the threat of violence. In the end, they were able to persuade Mattia to come with them. Of course, it didn't happen without protest. As he was led away, he was all but kicking and screaming like a spoiled brat, which he was.

He kept asking what was so important that his fun had to be interrupted. The guards told him they didn't know what the problem was, but his mother knew and would tell him.

Forty minutes later, Mattia entered his mother's room where her atrophied body lay on the bed, pale as the sheets that covered it. Other than himself, she was the only person on the planet who he really loved. He hated his father and brothers and was ambivalent about his sister. It was gut-wrenching for him to see his mother like that, and he couldn't help but think that if he knew he was going to see her that night, he would have taken more alcohol and drugs to completely desensitize his emotions. Fortunately, he didn't, otherwise he would have been unconscious.

Valter Li Voti sat in a chair next to her bed.

Estella's eyes opened when her son entered. With a soft

and labored voice, she said, "Please come and sit beside me, Mattia."

He nodded and took the chair on the opposite side of the bed from where Li Voti sat.

Although Li Voti had always been polite to him, he knew the man didn't like him, and the feeling was mutual. It was a source of immense irritation to him that Li Voti was closer to his father than he could ever be. He blamed Li Voti for the fact that his father obviously loved his older sons more than him, involved them in the clan's matters, and excluded him.

Mattia was too egotistical to even contemplate for one second that he could have been the sole cause of the deficient relationship.

Estella was weak and fragile before she had received the devastating news. Now, having learned of the death of her husband and sons, she was on the verge of total collapse. The nurse told Li Voti, "She could die any moment, the human body can only handle so much, and then it will stop functioning."

Li Voti watched her closely as she broke the news to Mattia and was stunned by her will to stay alive for just a little longer to complete what she believed was probably going to be her last, but most important task on this earth.

She had to pause often to regain strength before continuing.

Mattia looked as if he was in a stupor, and he was. To Li Voti, it was obvious that very little of what his mother was saying, or the implications thereof registered with him.

At some stage Li Voti took Estella's hand and whispered

to her to get a bit of rest while he continued the conversation with Mattia.

She smiled faintly and nodded.

Fifteen minutes later, Li Voti got the first sensible, but definitely not pleasing, response from Mattia as some of what was said to him must have registered somewhere in his brain.

"I am the new Don!" he shouted.

Estella's eyes flew open.

Li Voti nodded slowly and decided it was not the right time to explain that 'Don' was an honorary title bestowed on his father by the people out of love and respect, and it didn't pass on to him by default.

Mattia had gone quiet again. Li Voti suspected that ever becoming his father's replacement was a thought that almost never crossed Mattia's mind. On the few occasions he'd mentioned it, and that was when he was much younger, he joked about it as something as unlikely as him becoming the Pope.

Yet, there he was, although he still had no chance of becoming the leader of the Catholic Church, he *had* somehow become the leader of the Beneduce-Longobardi clan.

And unless Li Voti was mistaken, he had not the first idea what to do or where to start.

Li Voti remained quiet as he allowed Mattia to assimilate what he had heard. He carefully studied the young man's facial expressions and tried to guess what was going on in his mind. And he couldn't help but think; *It's the law of nature and of gangland; when the king is dead, long live the next king.*

"What now?" Mattia finally asked.

Li Voti almost shrugged and wanted to say, *just go back to your club, do whatever it is you do, and leave it to me; I'll take care of everything.* Instead he said, "First you have to decide if you want me to be your consigliere?"

"Yes, of course. How the hell am I supposed to run the damn show without you?"

"Good. Thank you for the confidence," Li Voti said. "There will be a lot of anxious people out there now. We have to allay their fears and stabilize things quickly. I suggest we let them know that they are not leaderless."

Mattia was staring at him in a daze of witlessness.

"You will have to start leading immediately, show them you have stepped into your father's shoes, let the people see you're in control and you know what you're doing."

"How… would I… what…"

"I will call a meeting, tonight, of a few of the most trusted family heads, and we'll announce it to them. It has to be handled delicately as we have to show respect for the memory of your father, brothers, and others who died tonight."

"But will the Camorristi accept me?"

Li Voti was a little surprised, they were the first intelligent words he heard out of Mattia's mouth all night.

Before he could answer, Estella stirred and said in a barely audible whisper, "Yes, they will." She turned her head to Li Voti and said, "Valter, please bring them all here, I'll talk to them."

Li Voti nodded and left to make the calls.

Estella closed her eyes and fell asleep again.

The nurse came in, made sure that Estella was comfortable, and then led Mattia to the kitchen where she started feeding him near lethal-strength coffee. Though coffee would not sober up a drunk person, it could help to make the person more alert, which, given the situation, was the best Li Voti could hope for.

Leaving Rome just after 10:00 P.M., understandably Teresa was extremely worried and, in her mind, she started going through the possible scenarios that awaited her in Naples. She discarded every one of them except the one about her mother. Soon she had convinced herself that could be the only reason for Li Voti's call and hoped she would be in time to say goodbye to her mother. She was too tense to think about other possibilities or the fact that if it were about her mother, Li Voti would have told her so. Too occupied by the thoughts of her beloved mother, she didn't turn the radio on. If she did, she would have heard the news about the explosion and the people killed, and she would have heard her father and brothers' names mentioned.

It was a little over one hundred and fifteen miles from Rome to Naples, and she did it in less than an hour and a quarter. It was shortly before midnight when Teresa arrived and Valter Li Voti opened the front door for her. She had known him for most of her life and held him in high regard. One look at him brought the first suspicion that she was not called home on account of her mother. When Li Voti led her past the kitchen, she saw Mattia sitting at the table with the nurse next to him, but Li Voti tightened his grip on her arm, and led her to the living room. He didn't allow her to greet her brother or the nurse. Her suspicion had turned into the sure knowledge that she was about to receive horrific news.

Chapter Seventeen

EVERYONE RAISED A HAND

Lombardi family residence, Naples, Italy

2011

An hour later, Mattia, Li Voti, and six of the most senior and trusted members of the Beneduce-Longobardi clan, five men and one woman, stood in pious silence around Estella's bed.

The nurse had collected Teresa from her mother's side and took her to the kitchen where she served her a cup of tea and tried her best to console the grief-stricken young woman.

It was as if the arrival of Teresa and the bit of time she had spent with her mother had invigorated the latter so that she was able to sit up and speak in a more audible voice.

She asked Li Voti to first give them more details about the tragedy. He did so without divulging the details of the transaction that was supposed to be concluded that night and why the Don and his sons and other senior leaders were there.

All of them probably had questions about that on their minds, but they knew not to ask—they would be informed if they needed to know.

Estella took over and explained that traditionally she would have been the one to take over the leadership of the clan. She didn't have to explain to them why she couldn't, but rather told them that as her oldest surviving child, Mattia would be the new leader.

The drawing of a few sharp breaths could be heard in the room, but a stern look from Li Voti nipped any protests in the bud.

"Now, I want you, each and every one of you, to take an oath, in the presence of all of us in this room, and before God, that you will accept Mattia as your leader. That you will be as loyal and respectful to him as you've been to my late husband."

There were tears in her eyes when she finished.

Li Voti nodded to each of them in turn to step forward and make the pledge as he watched them carefully. The look on his face and his demeanor left no doubt, they had no choice but to abide by the wishes of the dying wife of their beloved Don. One by one they stepped forward and said out loud, "Signora Lombardi, I swear before everyone here and before God that I will be loyal to your son, Mattia, as our new leader."

Throughout the whole ritual Mattia had been sitting silently in the chair next to his mother's bed. Impassively, he stared at the floor and never looked anyone in the eye.

When they had all made their promise, Li Voti motioned for them to leave the bedroom and wait for him in the living room.

The nurse came back with Teresa in tow and helped Estella to lie down again and made her comfortable. It was clear that Estella was exhausted to the point of death.

It was a miracle that she was still alive.

———————

Mattia had followed Li Voti to the living room where they would have the first meeting under his leadership. In the hallway, before entering the living room, Li Voti said to Mattia, "Don't worry about it, I'll run it for you. We only have a few urgent matters to bring to their attention for now."

Mattia didn't answer, he just nodded and entered the room.

Li Voti started by explaining that, although it was necessary to prevent panic among the clan members, the announcement of Mattia's ascension to power had to be done in a manner which would show reverence for the deceased. He suggested that a message should go out to let the people know they had nothing to worry about, they were not without leadership, things would continue as usual.

Li Voti was about to continue when Mattia seemed to have found his voice and interrupted him. "Why should it be a secret?"

"It's not a secret, I'm only suggesting…"

"Bullshit! I am the new Don, tell the people. I don't give a shit about what they think."

If Li Voti were surprised at Mattia's sudden outburst, he didn't show it. This was the Mattia he knew, given to irrational behavior more often than not. The reprobate had no idea what it meant to lead people. Bullying and intimidating, yes, that he knew, but not the difference between leadership and tyranny. For as long as Li Voti had known him, Mattia had lived in the delusion that his family and society were to blame for his miserable existence.

Calmly, Li Voti held his hand up and said, "Please Mattia, just listen to me, I know the people. I know how they think. Let's do it my way. Trust me, it's for your own good."

Mattia glowered at the others. "You all agree with him?"

They all nodded.

"Well, I still think it's a load of crap, but let's do it as you said then. Now, what about the other clans?"

Li Voti and the others looked at him with raised eyebrows.

"Why are you staring at me like idiots? Don't you get it? The other clans will see this as an opportunity to take over the Beneduce-Longobardi empire. I want a message sent to them."

The only woman in the room, Dina Martelli, spoke for all of them. "Mattia, there are no problems with any of the other clans. There haven't been for many years. Your father…"

"Where have you been the past few hours? My father is dead! I'm the Don, and I say we need to send a strong message out. Right now. Let them know there will be hell to pay if anyone dares to interfere with our clan in any manner."

The attendees went quiet and stared at each other for a while. Li Voti tried to explain again that it was going to do a lot more harm than good to send out an unwarranted threat like that.

But Mattia interrupted him and said, "I've spoken. Make it happen."

Li Voti didn't reply, he only sighed and nodded slowly.

"Next. Who did this? And don't tell me you don't know. You *must* know who is so stupid to attack the mighty Bene-duce-Longobardi clan. I want their names, right now."

Li Voti said, "Mattia, unbelievable as it might sound to you, we don't know, yet. There was no prior…"

"What! You're the consigliere of this clan, and you," he pointed to the rest of the people in the room, "are the leaders of this clan, and you're telling me you don't have an idea?"

Among the attendees were one of Naples's senior police officers, Rinaldo Fara. Some would have thought of him as corrupt; others would have thought him to be wise. Life in Naples under the Camorra was complex and multifaceted.

He is the one who said, "It's too early Mattia. We don't have all the information yet. There will be an investigation, not only by the police but also at least by the AISI, if not DIS and the AISE as well. We'll do our own investigations, but I'd strongly suggest that we don't rush to judgment until we have all the facts."

The AISI, *Agenzia Informazioni e Sicurezza Interna*, (internal information and security agency) was the Italian equivalent of America's FBI. DIS, *Dipartimento delle Informazioni per la Sicurezza* (security information department) was something similar to America's Department of Homeland Security, and the AISE, *Agenzia Informazioni e Sicurezza Esterna* (external information and security agency) their equivalent of America's CIA.

"You chickenshit!" the red-faced Mattia shouted at Fara. "You know who did it, but you're too much of a coward to say or do anything about it."

Fara shook his head and said, "Honestly, Mattia, I don't know and neither does anyone else in this room. I can only say I'm convinced it was not another Camorra clan. It could be the 'Ndrangheta or Cosa Nostra, but I doubt…"

"Let me tell you what I doubt. I doubt that you." He was pointing at Fara. "And for that matter, all of you are competent to find out. I can't believe that my father was able to put up with you morons for so long. But then again, you were never his first choice—they were all killed tonight, except for that lucky bastard." He was pointing at Li Voti.

For Li Voti, the meeting was a disaster, he had achieved nothing of what he hoped he would. Mattia took every well-meant suggestion as a personal insult. Apart from never learning how to control his temper, it was clear that he had also never learned how to handle differing opinions. Not to mention that he had no clue what concepts such as heeding good advice, negotiation, and consensus meant.

Despite his insufferable impertinence and stupidity, they kept trying to mollify him, but he just became more aggressive, louder, and more brazen.

Finally, the meeting turned from bad to ugly when, in a fit of rage, Mattia pulled out his gun, waved it around while screaming at them to shut up. When he had their attention he said, "I've had enough of your stupid ideas and incessant sulking. Who is with me, and who is against me? Put up your hand if you're going to be loyal to me and to our clan."

Staring at the gun, not at Mattia, everyone raised a hand.

Mattia told them the meeting was over and that he was going to get some sleep and didn't want to be disturbed.

Chapter Eighteen

I LIKE THE SOUND OF THAT

North of Naples, Italy

2011

About twenty miles out of Naples, on the north side, Dina Martelli owned a vineyard which had been in her family for more than three-hundred years.

It was at this estate, Vinicola del Martelli, where at about 3:30 A.M. Dina welcomed her six guests and led them to the magnificent antique-appointed study. It was the same six who had left the meeting with her at the Lombardi residence less than an hour before.

There were no dissidents among the seven of them—Mattia Lombardi could not be allowed to be Don of the Beneduce-Longobardi clan. If he was, the Camorra clans would soon be in a protracted and bloody civil war.

One of them suggested they wait until after the funeral.

The rest, however, said that would be too late. It had to be done quickly. The funeral was at least a week away, by then that lunatic would have caused irreparable damage to their clan. Violence and killing would be rampant on the streets of Naples and throughout Campania.

The question was how to stop him.

They all agreed that it would be wishful thinking to expect Mattia to step down voluntarily to make way for another, better qualified person.

They discussed the option of abducting him and keeping him imprisoned somewhere. It was not a practical and easy-to-execute solution; it would involve too many additional people and would leave too many loose ends.

Fara suggested that there were many unsolved crimes in which, as they all knew, Mattia had been involved. All they had to do was get some witnesses to talk, then he could be arrested, charged, and put in prison for a long time. It was better than the first idea, but the problem was then they had to rely on the government's legal system, which they didn't trust, to take care of their problem. Not to mention how long it would take.

Li Voti had been quietly listening attentively to all arguments before he said, "Julius Caesar."

Everyone looked at him with a huh-expression on their faces.

He explained, "Look, we're descendants of the Romans, we all know about Julius Caesar. A little more than two-thousand years ago, our ancestors had a similar problem with Julius Caesar threatening their way of life when he indicated he was going to abolish the Senate and become the sole ruler, a dictator.

"A handful of senators had the guts to stand up to him.

And they did so on the Ides of March 44 BC, stabbing him twenty-three times with their knives and killing him."

Everyone was staring at Li Voti.

Although they were not in Rome, and it was not the government that was threatened, there were indisputable similarities between the scenario of two-thousand and fifty-five years earlier and the one they were facing now.

After a long silence, Dina Martelli was the first to start nodding her head slowly, then Rinaldo Fara, and one by one the rest of them followed suit.

It was not March, neither were there senators to do it for them, nor would they need knives. It was decided that one man with a syringe filled with undiluted heroin would do it. That man had to be Valter Li Voti, he was the only one of them who had unfettered access to the Lombardi house and could get close to Mattia.

It was Fara who asked the logical question, "Who will take Mattia's place?"

"Teresa, of course," Martelli said in jest.

All but Li Voti laughed.

"She won't, she's got no interest in the clan's business," one of them said.

"Never had, never will, if you ask me," another added.

"She doesn't have the skills or experience we need. We don't want to have another meeting like this in a day or two. That's if she even takes the job," the third one said.

"So, let's forget about her, who's the new leader then?" asked Fara.

"I guess we have to elect one," said Martelli.

But then they realized that Li Voti hadn't participated in their discussions and wanted to know what his thoughts were.

"You might be right that Teresa might not want the job," he said. "Although, I think she could be persuaded. I know her better than anyone of you. In fact, I know all about her since she's left school and what she's been doing all these years. Trust me, with the right guidance, she'd be an excellent leader."

"That's of course if she's not as crazy as her brother and would *accept* guidance when given," Fara said.

"Again, you can trust me on that. She's nothing like her brother; she'll listen to good advice. But the challenge is to get her to accept the role in the first place."

Martelli grinned. "Donna Teresa, hmm... I like the sound of that."

Fifteen minutes later, Li Voti left the Martelli estate and drove back to the Lombardi house where he found Mattia passed out in one of the spare bedrooms.

Teresa and the nurse were with Estella.

No one saw him slipping into Mattia's room.

When the sun rose that morning, it was over Mattia's dead body.

But it wasn't until nearly mid-day when the nurse went to the room to check on him, and she saw the wrapping and an empty syringe on the floor next to the bed.

She immediately felt for a pulse, found nothing, and collapsed to the floor in a bundle, crying.

That was where Li Voti found her, and only with great effort learned from her that Mattia was dead. "Probably from a drug overdose," she said.

The coroner would later confirm it was heroin, and the

JC RYAN

police would find only Mattia's fingerprints on the wrapping and the syringe and conclude there was no foul play.

For the second time in less than twelve hours, the thought, *the king is dead,* crossed Li Voti's mind, but this time there was not a new king to hail a long life to.

Not yet.

Chapter Nineteen

THEN IT'S TIME TO TELL MY MOTHER

Lombardi family residence, Naples, Italy

2011

Li Voti sat on the floor with his arm around the nurse's shoulder in an attempt to comfort her despite the fact that he was relieved that the Mattia problem had been resolved so quickly and easily.

His mind soon became occupied with a new question: How to broach the news of Mattia's death with Estella and Teresa.

When he got the nurse calmed down, he stood, held his hand out, and helped her off the floor. He led her out of the room and closed the door behind them. In the kitchen he made her a cup of tea while he asked her what her advice about the effect of the news of another death would be on Estella.

The nurse told him it could be the straw that would

break the camel's back. "After all she's been through and how much it has set her back already, Estella will surely die if she gets this news."

Li Voti nodded. "That might be so, or it might not. The thing is if we don't tell her now, for how long can we keep it from her? Her mind is functioning properly, we won't be able to deceive her for much longer than a day or so at most."

"In her current condition she'd probably not be alive by the time of the funeral. If by some miracle she is, and we haven't told her…" She started crying again.

Li Voti couldn't help but think about euthanasia. After all, she *was* dying, she had already accepted it, and so did everyone else. The question was, should they make her last few hours on earth more miserable than they already were, or would it be merciful if they helped her out of this life of pain and suffering?

Whatever he decided about Estella, in the end he couldn't get away from the fact that Teresa had to be told about her brother's death without delay.

He went and fetched her from her mother's room, sat down in the living room with her, sighed deeply, and told her about Mattia's death.

Teresa was shocked, it was to be expected. Although she and Mattia drifted apart over the years, they were still blood relatives. Li Voti knew they had a much happier relationship as children than lately.

He was worried that the news was going to send her into a state of utter emotional despair, but to his surprise, it didn't.

She had wiped her tears away and in a calm voice said, "Maybe it's for the better."

"What do you mean?"

"Valter, you know better than anyone that Mattia was going to cause a lot of trouble. He would've destroyed the Beneduce-Longobardi clan that my father had dedicated his life to. My father constructed an empire; Mattia was going to destruct it.

"Not only that, he would have caused strife and war among all of the Camorra clans whom we have been living in peace with for all these years."

Surprised by what he heard, he nodded slowly. "You're right."

"My father would never have handed the reins to him."

He nodded again and hesitated as he considered whether it was the right time to raise the matter of the leadership. He decided it was, because she had opened the door for him to do so with her last comment.

"Teresa, we have two important matters to talk about now. I wish it could've waited but..."

She interrupted. "I think I know what it is. My mother and the new leader. Right?"

Li Voti was stunned by her perceptiveness and calm. It took him a few seconds to compose himself. "Yes. That's correct."

He was about to continue when she started. "As for breaking the news about Mattia to my mother, I think, notwithstanding her condition, she deserves to know the truth. It might hasten her death, I know. Nevertheless, I'd prefer if we're honest with her."

He was relieved, *one less thing to worry about.*

"As for the new leader, I have the distinct impression you have something in mind. Or am I wrong?"

Li Voti shifted uneasily in his chair. He shook his head slightly. "No, you're not, but..."

"You left the house after the catastrophic meeting with

Mattia. You were gone for about one and a half hours. Enough time to have had a second meeting with those who were in the first meeting," she said in a soft but unwavering voice while she looked him straight in the eyes.

An ice-cold chill ran down Li Voti's spine. *Is it possible that she could have seen me going into Mattia's room? Definitely. Be very careful now.* Therefore, he made no reply. He just looked at her, letting her know he was expecting her to continue before he would consider a response.

"So, what did you decide?"

Li Voti was experiencing a side of Teresa that he never knew existed. She was always nice and friendly, delicate, ladylike, impeccably behaved. He had not expected her to be so calm and collected, insightful, straightforward in such dire circumstances. Admittedly, it caught him on the wrong foot. It was unsettling not to be in control of the situation.

If he had known as much about Teresa as her father had known, he would not have been so surprised and unsettled.

That she was an artist and owned a successful art studio in Rome was all true, and Li Voti knew all of that. The thing is, that was only part of the picture. Not even Estella knew the full story.

What was kept from everyone, including Li Voti and Estella all these years, was that Teresa didn't only make money from selling her own and her students' artwork. In fact, her income from that was paltry compared to what she made from the buying and selling of the creations of others. People who had lived centuries, even millennia, before.

Teresa and her father had over the years carved out an extremely lucrative niche in the multi-billion-dollar antiquities marketplace.

They bought and sold ancient artifacts. All of it illegal.

Their suppliers were terrorist groups from the Middle East and Africa who looted ancient sites and sold the artifacts to fund their war efforts.

The two Lombardis were smart, they never dealt in artifacts stolen from extant collections where provenance was properly documented. They only bought stock that was illegally excavated. Those artifacts were never laid eyes on in modern times. When they bought them, the artifacts had not been recorded in any official database yet. Therefore, no official provenance existed. All they had to do was to create falsified documents that stated the artifacts were legally excavated thus establishing the first provenance and enabled them to sell them openly.

As it were, Li Voti knew absolutely nothing about it. He didn't even suspect that she could be involved in illicit activities of any kind.

He knew he had to tell her some of what was decided at that second meeting, but he couldn't tell her everything. He cleared his throat and started lying. "We all agreed that Mattia was not the right person…"

"I very much doubt those were the words used, but I appreciate the effort to spare my feelings. Please continue."

Li Voti grinned and continued. "We decided to ask him to step aside so that you could be the leader."

Teresa smirked. "Interesting… I have two questions though. One, what made you think I'd be interested? Two, do you expect me to believe, after what you experienced with Mattia, that you were really so naïve as to think he would've stepped down of his own volition?"

"Well, you are the next person in the line of succession. And no, we were not *that* naïve, but we had to at least try."

Teresa was smiling, clearly enjoying Li Voti's discomposure as he tried to skirt around the truth. She had no intention to let him off the hook too easily. "Okay, so you anticipated he was going to throw a tantrum and wouldn't accept it. What was your plan B?"

Li Voti realized she had maneuvered him into a tight corner. She obviously knew he had not been entirely forthcoming so far. He couldn't tell her there was no plan B—she wouldn't believe him. He could tell her the truth—that would be the end of him and his co-conspirators. He tried to look her in the eyes as he said, "Teresa, it serves no purpose to discuss that. Neither plan A nor plan B was necessary."

Teresa now had a stern look on her face when she interjected, "No, I don't agree. It serves a purpose for me to know. I insist."

The blood had drained from his face as he tried one more lie. "Plan B was to get rid of him."

"How?"

"Getting the witnesses who didn't want to testify against him before to do so now, which would've landed him in jail."

"A rather cumbersome and long-winded way to take care of a problem that needed immediate action. Wouldn't you say?"

Li Voti just shrugged.

"Valter, I've known you for more than fifteen years. My father always spoke very highly of you. He trusted you unreservedly with almost everything. You've been loyal to him all these years. Yet, without blinking an eye you are sitting there, and you're lying to me."

"I'm not. I just don't want to cause more heartache and pain. I'm sorry…"

"Okay, let's leave it at that for now. Let's talk about the

rest of the plan. The part about what you were going to do when Mattia was out of the way."

Li Voti almost sighed in relief. At least now he could be honest. "It was suggested we approach you to take over the leadership."

"And how did *that* go down?" She was smiling again.

"Well, as you know there are only three people alive now that know the truth about you." He was referring to himself, Estella, and Teresa herself. "So, the others thought you would not be willing to do it. None of them have seen you or know anything about you after you left school."

"And?"

"I told them that I know you, and you'd make a fine leader for our clan."

"Right. So, what's plan B for me? If I *don't* want to do it."

"We'd have to elect someone."

"What do you, Valter Li Voti, want?"

"I want *you* to be our leader."

"Even if I turn out to be like Mattia?"

"I know you won't."

"And can I rely on you to be my consigliere?"

"Absolutely."

"And that those lies you told me before were the last ones you will ever tell me?"

"Yes."

She smiled and said, "Then it's time to tell my mother about Mattia and about our new leader."

Chapter Twenty

IT WAS A TERRIBLE LOSS

Lombardi family residence, Naples, Italy

2011

Teresa and Li Voti sat down in the chairs on either side of Estella's bed. Teresa took her mother's hand and Li Voti let her do the talking. The last hour or so he had become acutely aware just how much he had underestimated her and how little he really knew about her. She had not only demonstrated extraordinary intellect and perceptiveness but also a cool-headedness and steel will which assured him she would match, if not outdo, her late father. She had inherited her mother's looks, but she definitely got her brains and acumen from her father.

Estella had no more tears to shed. She was completely broken. She had just about enough life left in her to hear that Teresa would be the new leader. It had put a little smile on her face as she passed away.

It was time to call the police and to start making the funeral arrangements.

The Beneduce-Longobardi clan were in a state of mourning. Thirteen families lost loved ones. Twelve of them lost one person. The thirteenth, the Lombardi family, lost three as a direct result of the explosion, and two more as an indirect result.

The men died the way they lived—violently.

The only women among them died heartbroken but peacefully.

It was a terrible loss. Without doubt the darkest moment in the history of the Beneduce-Longobardi clan of Naples.

However, if only by sheer numbers, the clan's tragedy paled in comparison to the ten to twelve thousand annual drug related deaths in the European Union. To which had to be added the deaths caused by terrorism in European Union countries plus the tens of thousands killed every year in war-torn Middle Eastern and African countries with weapons obtained from the merchants of death— international illicit arms dealers.

All of which the Beneduce-Longobardi clan of Naples contributed to, either directly or indirectly.

The Muslim funeral

Although the Shiite and Sunni Muslims held different views on a number of religious issues, they didn't differ much when it came to funerals. Sharia law stated that the body had to be washed and shrouded followed by the Janazah Salah (funeral prayer) and buried as soon as possible. Usually within twenty-four hours of death. They didn't bury their dead in coffins; the body was wrapped in cloth. Cremation was strictly forbidden.

As it were, Imam Al-Sadiq was unable to follow the rituals of a traditional Muslim funeral. He had no bodies to wash or shroud. He couldn't claim the bodies, or rather, parts of bodies, retrieved from the warehouse; that would have blown his cover.

Shortly after mid-day, the media reported that police forensics experts advised that so far, they had established the death of at least thirty people in the explosion. That was when Imam Al-Sadiq held a short and quiet ceremony, attended only by himself, where he said the Janazah Salah.

Muslims believed that by doing good deeds in life, entry into Paradise would be gained on the Day of Judgment, also called the Last Day, when the world will be destroyed. The exception was those who were killed on the battlefields of jihad. They didn't have to wait for the Day of Judgment for they had Allah's promise of immediate entry into Paradise, Jannah. The place where, some believed, seventy-two virgins awaited them.

Al-Sadiq had no doubt that the fifteen men who perished in the explosion were now all in Jannah.

Chapter Twenty-One

A BRILLIANT STRATEGY

Lombardi family residence, Naples, Italy

2011

Li Voti suggested to Teresa that it was important to meet with the rest of the leadership group as soon as possible. She agreed but insisted on getting a full brief from him about all of the clan business first.

The need-to-know principle was at work as Li Voti told her everything about her father's business dealings, past, present, and future, but she told him nothing about her antiquities business.

Three hours later, at around 4:00 P.M., she had enough details to determine priorities, and her first priority was for Li Voti to arrange an urgent meeting with Imam Al-Sadiq. After that she would meet with the leaders.

Li Voti had dealt with Al-Sadiq on many occasions since the deal made in 2009. He knew Al-Sadiq was shrewd and at times short-tempered. The imam had lost fifteen people and so far, no one from the Beneduce-Longobardi clan had been in contact with him. What with all Li Voti had to deal with in the aftermath of the explosion he thought he had good reason not to have contacted the imam as yet.

Nevertheless, he didn't exactly expect to hear the voice of a very jovial man on the other end of the phone.

He was right, Al-Sadiq's voice was arctic.

Li Voti started to sympathize, but Al-Sadiq cut him short and said, "We need to meet. Save your excuses for then."

"That's the reason for my call. 11:00 P.M. tonight?"

"Yes. My house."

The phone went dead.

Li Voti stared at it in alarm wondering if he should call again to explain that Teresa would accompany him. He fully expected Al-Sadiq to throw a tantrum when he turned up at the man's door with Teresa by his side. He shrugged and decided to leave it at that and rather prepare *her* for what to expect, and how to behave. That was if she would even be allowed to enter the man's house. And of course, there was also the chance that Teresa might have a similar reaction if she heard how she'd have to comport herself in the presence of a devoted Muslim man.

While Li Voti made the call to Al-Sadiq, Teresa had gone to her father's study and made a call to her business manager in Rome to let him know about her tragic loss and not to expect her back in Rome for the next two to three weeks.

She didn't tell him that she was now the leader of the Beneduce-Longobardi clan and that she would in all likelihood have to settle in Naples. He was her right-hand man and confidant, whom she trusted implicitly with all her business, legal and illegal.

He sympathized with her loss and assured her that she wouldn't have to worry about anything—he would take care of it.

When she ended the call, Li Voti came in and told her of the meeting at 11:00 P.M. that night. He started to explain what he thought they could expect, but she stopped him and said, "We can discuss that later. I want to meet with the other leaders now."

He looked at his watch and said, "I called them after I spoke to Al-Sadiq and arranged for them to be here at 7:00 P.M. I hope that will be enough time for the police to do their work and remove the bodies.

"I already told them about the passing of Mattia and your mother. And of course, about your decision."

She nodded.

Li Voti was bone-tired, and he could see that Teresa was in no better shape, but he was amazed at how well she still kept up. He didn't tell her that he had also told the six that they should be prepared to be surprised by their new leader —pleasantly so.

By 6:30 P.M. the police had left, the bodies had been moved to the morgue, and the nurse had gone home.

By 7:00 P.M. the six had arrived, and the meeting could start. Mindful of the meeting with Al-Sadiq later that night Teresa asked that they keep this only about the most critical matters. None of the six knew about the meeting with Al-Sadiq. In fact, none of them knew about the arms-for-drugs transaction that was supposed to have been concluded in the harbor the night before. As the new leadership group, they would have to be informed—in if necessary.

Dina Martelli said she was speaking on behalf of the six, confirmed by their nods, when she first conveyed their condolences to Teresa. Then she thanked her for taking up the reins under such difficult circumstances and assured her of their loyalty and support.

Teresa nodded, thanked them, and continued with the business at hand. Setting the agenda for the meeting, she told them what she thought were the most important matters: Anonymity. A message to the other clans. The funeral. An investigation. She gave them an opportunity to add any matter that she and Li Voti might have overlooked.

There were none.

Li Voti had known the six for many years, could discern their facial expressions and body language, and was pleased to notice that within just a few minutes Teresa had demonstrated that she was going to be nothing like Mattia.

"Anonymity. For strategic reasons, I'd like to keep a very low profile, just like my late father. It worked well for him, and I believe it's in our best interest to continue doing so."

Everyone agreed.

"A message to the other clans. I have been told that Mattia wanted to send a warning message to the other clans and that you disagreed with him."

Everyone was staring at her probably wondering if they were going to have a repeat of what happened with her brother. But were instantly relieved when she said, "I agree with your view, not Mattia's. There is no need to threaten anyone. My father lived in peace with everyone, I intend to continue doing so. Therefore, I'd like a message to go out to our own people first. Let them know that they've not been forsaken. The Beneduce-Longobardi clan will continue to provide and care for them as always.

"A second message should go to the other clans. Tell them that my late father's policies will remain. Nothing is going to change, and no one has anything to fear from us."

Again, everyone agreed. This time with big smiles on their faces.

"The funeral. It is my wish that there would be a mass funeral out of the *Viscuvato 'e Napule* in five days' time."

The cathedral that the Neapolitans called the *Viscuvato 'e Napule* had been commissioned by King Charles I of Anjou and was completed in the early 14th century. It was the main church of Naples and the seat of the Archbishop of Naples.

"I'll leave the specific arrangements to Valter and yourselves. Let me know if you need me for anything."

"We'll take care of it," Li Voti said.

"Finally, the investigation." She paused and nodded for Li Voti to give them the background.

For the next twenty minutes or so, Li Voti explained to the six what had happened and why Don Lombardi, his two older sons, and twelve other clan members were in the warehouse at the time of the explosion.

By now, forensic experts had been fine-combing the site for more than eighteen hours and had formed their first opinions about the chain of events. Fara, the police officer, took over and gave them the information, which was not public knowledge, and probably would never be. According to the experts, the devastation was caused by a combination of gas and military explosives. They found an LPG tanker, or rather enough remnants to identify it as such, among the debris. They also found numerous bits and pieces of AK-47 rifles, rocket-propelled grenades, RPG 7 rocket launchers, landmines, and an inestimable quantity of exploded ammu-nition. Reconstructing the possible chain of events, they opined that the gas tanker was filled with LPG and was set off with Semtex explosives, the evidence of which they found on some parts of the tanker. The gas explosion would have triggered the subsequent explosions of the ordnance.

The expressions of devastation and disquiet on the faces of the six were unmistakable. It was not because of the illegal deal that ended in disaster, the clan was deeply involved in all manner of illicit business, including black market arms deals, but the realization that it was no acci-dent. It was crystal clear to them that this had been a delib-erate and pre-meditated attack.

"There is only one question. Who did it?" Teresa said in a soft but measured tone, "we are going to find out and punish them."

In silence, everyone nodded their accord.

"We are not going to run amok. We will not be running around intimidating people, shaking trees and rattling cages. On the contrary, we are going to create the impression that we've accepted the media's claptrap about a gas leak. But surreptitiously we will conduct our own investigation.

"We have a sprawling network of informers out there—thousands of them. People will be talking, gossiping, specu-lating… we want to know about it. All of it. We will gather and analyze what we hear, and somewhere in there will be a lead, which will provide the next lead and the next, until we know who did it."

Rinaldo Fara was smiling. In less than an hour, Teresa Lombardi had managed to impress him profoundly. And it didn't escape him that it seemed she had the same effect on the others. "I think yours is a brilliant strategy, Teresa. I support it one hundred percent. That's how we will get to the bottom of it."

Chapter Twenty-Two

South of Naples, Italy

2011

It was exactly 10:55 p.m. when a very nervous Valter Li Voti, driving a black Alpha Romeo SUV with tinted windows and Teresa Lombardi in the passenger seat, pulled up to the sidewalk in front of Imam Al-Sadiq's house in the Muslim enclave on the south side of Naples.

His anxiety had a number of causes. Their telephone conversation earlier informed him that Al-Sadiq was deeply troubled and he, Li Voti, was about to add to the man's distress by turning up with Teresa unannounced. The next troubling matter was that Teresa had refused to be accompanied by bodyguards. The third was, when he tried to educate her about the appropriate behavior in the presence of the imam, she waved him off and said, "Don't worry, I know what to do."

But when they got into the car earlier, and he saw her dressed in a dark pantsuit, he just sighed. She obviously didn't know how women were supposed to dress in the presence of a religiously observant Muslim man. *This is not going to go well.*

He did however notice the black tote bag she had put on the back seat but didn't ask what was in it.

When Li Voti had killed the engine and switched off the lights, Teresa said, "Just one moment," opened the tote bag, and took out two pieces of what, in the dim streetlights, looked like cloth to him. Then she stepped out of the car, and to Li Voti's bewilderment, donned a black full-length abaya, a robe-like dress, which covered her from shoulders to feet. This she followed with a half niqab, a type of hijab which covered her head and shoulders leaving only the bridge of her nose, eyes, and part of her forehead visible.

When she was done, she said, "I'm ready," closed the door, and walked around the car to meet Li Voti who was staring at her wordlessly.

Little did he know he was in for a few more surprises.

Teresa made sure that she stood at a respectful distance behind Li Voti when he knocked on the front door.

Within the first few seconds after opening the door the imam's eyes shot wide in shock, quickly replaced by anger, when he noticed Li Voti was not alone and then realized his companion was a woman.

"Who is this?" he snapped.

"My apologies, I wanted to…"

"You didn't ask my permission to bring someone with you. Neither did I invite you to do so…"

By now, Teresa had stepped forward and with downcast eyes she said, "*Ya Mu'aleem* (oh learned man), I am Teresa Lombardi, *As-Salamu Alaykum* (peace be upon you)."

Li Voti had gone slack-jawed as he heard Al-Sadiq responding in a whisper to Teresa's traditional Muslim greeting with, "*Wa alaikum assalaam*" (and upon you be peace).

Li Voti barely had a chance to draw breath when Teresa continued with, "*Ya Mu'aleem*, please accept our deepest and heart-felt condolences for your loss."

Although Li Voti couldn't begin to fathom what was going through Al-Sadiq's mind, he could see that the imam was as stunned or more than he was. It could have been that the man had realized he was talking to the late Don's daughter or, for a western woman, she was so subservient and observant of Muslim tradition, or maybe it was because she addressed him as *Mu'aleem*, learned man, or it could have been a combination of it all.

Al-Sadiq shrugged a little and said, "To Allah we belong, and to Him is our return."

Teresa had one more reply. "The Prophet, peace be upon him, said, '*no fatigue, no disease, nor sorrow, nor sadness, nor hurt, nor distress befalls a Muslim, even if it were the prick he receives from a thorn, but that Allah expiates some of his sins for that*'."

Al-Sadiq nodded impassively, looked at Li Voti, and said, "Come in… Both of you."

Li Voti was still half dazed, but somewhat relieved as he and Teresa followed the imam to the living room. Getting the two of them into the house was only a minor victory in what he expected was going to be a tough meeting. Li Voti knew, and briefed Teresa, that Al-Sadiq was not really an imam in the true sense of the word, that, according to her father, he worked for an undisclosed terrorist organization somewhere in the Middle East, and that he was a shrewd negotiator.

Neither of them knew what the living room looked like

two years before when Don Lombardi set foot in it for the first time. Had they been there they would have noticed that since then the house had been renovated and extended. Instead of a cardboard box serving as a coffee table, car seats as sofas, and black plastic bags as window drapes, the living room was now tastefully appointed with Persian carpets on the floor, four comfortable chairs, a three-seat sofa, and an oak coffee table in the middle of the room. The windows were covered with beige-colored drapes, and the walls decorated with various pieces of framed calligraphy in Arabic script, quotes from the Quran.

Al-Sadiq took one of the chairs and motioned for them to do the same. He didn't offer them anything except for his half-hearted condolences after which he got right to the point.

Addressing Li Voti, he said, "I'm waiting for your explanation."

"It was an accident... a gas..."

Al-Sadiq's face was contorted with rage when he interrupted. "Bullshit! Absolute-unadulterated one-hundred percent bullshit. Do you think I'm an idiot?"

Li Voti was not a man who handled confrontations very well, definitely not when it was as aggressive as this one. "Ah... why... I mean... why would you say that?"

"Gas leak? Really. That building is probably not even on the gas grid. There is no need for it. It's a warehouse."

"Sorry, I... well... but there were also a terrible lot of explosives and ammunition onsite... that could've..."

"Li Voti, you believe whatever you want, I'm telling you it was deliberate, and I hold you, the Beneduce-Longobardi clan, responsible for it."

"Why? How could we..."

"Negligence, Li Voti. Inexcusable, gross negligence."

Li Voti stared at him in shock. He expected a tough stance from Al-Sadiq but not to be accused of negligence.

"How... I mean... what... in what manner could we've been negligent?"

"If I invite you into my house, am I not responsible for your safety?"

Li Voti nodded hesitantly.

"You invited us to your warehouse to conclude a business transaction. You were responsible for our safety. You should have inspected the place and made sure it was safe. You obviously didn't."

Teresa had been quietly listening and waiting for the right moment. This was it. "*Ya Mu'aleem*, my apology for interrupting..."

Al-Sadiq looked at Li Voti as if to ask, who gave this woman permission to speak?

But Li Voti was staring at Teresa.

Teresa continued, "It is my humble opinion that it is too early to reach any conclusions. Therefore, again in my humble opinion, also too early to blame anyone for it. Negligent or not. We just don't have enough information."

Al-Sadiq stared at her for a long while without saying a word. "That doesn't exonerate you from responsibility to safeguard your guests."

"*Ya Mu'aleem*, that may be so, but how do we know if anyone *was* in fact negligent?"

Li Voti saw that Teresa had backed the imam into a corner, if he agreed with her, he had lost the argument. If he didn't, he had to answer her question. Li Voti was worried that Al-Sadiq was not going to take kindly to the embarrassment, especially since it was caused by a woman.

Al-Sadiq turned to Li Voti again. "Why is this woman talking when she has not been spoken to?"

Li Voti clenched his jaw, leaned forward in his chair, looked Al-Sadiq straight in the eyes, and was about to reply when Teresa beat him to it.

She spoke in a soft, calm, and measured voice. "*This* woman is the daughter of Don Ricardo Lombardi. She has not only lost her father and three brothers, she has, just a few hours ago, also lost her youngest brother and her mother. Yet, despite her own pain and sorrow, *this* woman thought it was important to meet with you as soon as possible. To sympathize with you and to assure you that you and your people will receive the same respect and support you got from her father. *This* woman intends to honor those agreements, every one of them. Finally, if it hasn't occurred to you by now, *this* woman is the new leader of the Beneduce-Longobardi clan."

Al-Sadiq was pallid and speechless.

Li Voti was biting the inside of his cheek nervously.

By now, Teresa had risen to her feet and continued. "*Sayyid,* (sir), I came here tonight with nothing but good intentions. I was told you are a friend of our clan. An honorable and trustworthy man. I came to your house and respected you, your culture and traditions, and throughout I've addressed you with respect. However, and I'm sorry to say so, *Sayyid,* you have treated us with nothing but *disrespect.*"

In one smooth movement she removed the hijab and shook her head slightly to let her blonde hair drop to her shoulders.

Al-Sadiq and Li Voti were gawking at her.

Unfazed, she continued, "Therefore, *Sayyid,* there remains only one thing to be said before we go; *you* need to decide if you want to continue enjoying the protection and goodwill of the Beneduce-Longobardi clan or not. I'll give you time to think about it."

She turned and started toward the door.

Al-Sadiq was shaking his head and held his hand up in a gesture to stop her. He spoke in an almost inaudible whisper. "I'm so sorry. My own sorrow has clouded my judgment to the exclusion of everyone else's. Please accept my sincerest apology for my rudeness. I'm ashamed of myself.

"I thank you for your gesture of kindness to me and my people; I'm grateful for it. And you can be assured of my loyalty to you… Donna Teresa."

Teresa simply nodded and left the house with Li Voti right on her heels.

Chapter Twenty-Three

WHO DID IT?

Lombardi family residence, Naples, Italy

2011

In the lead-up to the funeral, Dina Martelli and some of the other leaders took responsibility for the arrangements, which freed Teresa and Li Voti to work on the business plans for the future and what they considered to be the most critical issue facing the clan—who was responsible for the attack?

The two of them agreed that as long as the perpetrators were on the loose, their business, all of it, was vulnerable to another attack. And just like Al-Sadiq, they considered all possibilities, which included rival Camorra clans and rival crime syndicates from other parts of the country. All of those were possibilities, but as far as they were concerned, highly unlikely.

As for rival Camorra clans, they argued it would have

been near impossible for such a group to plan and execute an operation like that in total secrecy—not with the hundreds of informants the Beneduce-Longobardi group had planted throughout the Campania region and beyond.

As for rival crime syndicates such as the Cosa Nostra of Sicily, the 'Ndrangheta of Calabria, or one of the others, there was an unwritten rule among the syndicates that they each had their areas where they operated and stayed off the turf of others. Not that every one of them always followed the rules, but if they didn't, they knew what the consequences would be.

Teresa didn't take long to conclude that what they were looking at was in all probability the work of a government counterterrorism team. The question was: from which country? They were sure it was not the Italian government, but there were quite a few other possibilities. Ranking top of the list were, Israel, the USA, the UK, France, and Germany. It was even possible that it could have been a joint operation between two or more of those.

Teresa laid out her theory, seated behind the desk in the study, as Li Voti sat on the opposite side listening intently to her reasoning. And he couldn't fault it.

She continued, "Spine-chilling as that thought is, even more disturbing is the realization that not only had the Beneduce-Longobardi clan managed to land themselves on the radar of the best security agencies in the world, we've also in some way been infiltrated by those agencies."

Li Voti had his elbows on the desk and his hands were covering his face as he let out a long and troubled sigh. "You're right." He looked up at Teresa absentmindedly.

"What?"

"I just remembered something. I don't have all the details, but there was this American guy who arrived here in

Naples about four or so months ago... mhh what was his name? Ahh... Luke... no wait, ahh... Matt, ah got it, Matthew Benedict. I never met him, neither did your father, but we were informed about him. You see, he said he wanted to settle here in Naples. Claimed to be a third generation Beneduce and wanted to get back to his roots. Apparently, his grandfather moved to America about fifty-odd years ago where they had Americanized their name to Benedict. He quickly made it known that he wanted to be a member of our clan and was seeking permission to set up a business under the auspices of the clan. Your father gave Rinaldo Fara the job to check out this guy's claims. At the time, everything checked out. He was who he said he was."

"What type of business?"

"He claimed to have had a small but very discreet, extremely affluent, niche market for high quality heroin and cocaine back in the States. He said he had enough money to start up the business.

"Your father was willing to give him the nod but not immediately. He wanted the guy to prove himself to be trustworthy. So, the message to him was, 'Your request is being considered, you will be informed in due course'."

"And how did that turn out?"

"By all accounts, he was quite a likeable guy. His Italian was perfect, although accented, and he was keen to learn about the clan and assimilate. All in all, he made a favorable impression on those who knew him. He even insisted on changing his last name back to Beneduce."

Teresa nodded.

Li Voti continued and explained that he couldn't remember all the details, but the gist of it was that Benedict raised suspicions when he started asking too many intrusive questions about their suppliers and delivery methods. Then one of the clansmen, a restaurateur, Vinicio Scaletta, reported to his capo that Benedict had also been asking questions about obtaining weapons from the black market, apparently to export to America, and from there over the border to the drug cartels into Mexico and further south.

"That's when alarm bells started ringing. It makes no sense to smuggle weapons into America and then to South America instead of directly to the end users.

"We also have a very clear understanding with our South American suppliers—we stay out of each other's territories. We buy their product, process them, and distribute them. We don't get involved in their conflicts, definitely never pick sides, and absolutely never provide weapons to any side.

"Getting involved in the South American drug cartel wars and illicit weapons dealing was stupid."

Teresa took a sip of her tea and nodded for him to continue.

Li Voti told her that Benedict's behavior was enough to get their hackles up, and they decided it was better to be safe rather than sorry.

He didn't have to explain what that meant, she knew.

"So, why do you think this Benedict's story is relevant to our issue?"

"I'm not sure that it is, but a few weeks ago, your father and I received a report about a man who was here in Naples asking questions about this Matthew Benedict."

"I see. So, what happened with that?"

"I don't know. We didn't get further reports about it. And at the time, your father and I were very busy with all the arrangements for the exchange with Al-Sadiq's group."

"Okay. So, you think it could be worth looking into it?"

"Yes, I'd like to know more about this man who asked those questions."

Teresa nodded. "Agreed. Let's put Rinaldo onto it."

"I'll brief him," Li Voti said.

The Catholic funeral

Catholic funerals usually took place between two days and one week after death. Apart from burial, cremation and embalming were also permissible.

Five days after the explosion, a mass funeral was held for the members of the Beneduce-Longobardi clan. It was a closed casket ceremony. Although there were seventeen caskets, only two of them contained bodies. The rest held only small bags with parts of bodies. A large picture of each of the deceased were displayed on their designated caskets which were surrounded by flowers.

It was one of the biggest and most emotional funerals in Naples's modern history, conducted at the Naples Cathedral.

Catholics, like all Christians, believed that the soul lives on after death, either in Heaven or Hell, depending on how righteous a life the deceased had lived. However, Catholics also believed in an intermediate state of the soul: Purgatory. The doctrine of purgatory held that, "all who die in God's grace and friendship but still imperfectly purified" undergo a process of expiatory purification (the act of atoning for sin or wrongdoing), "so as to achieve the holiness necessary to enter the joy of heaven."

Therefore, the Catholic funeral is an opportunity for the

living to appeal to God for forgiveness of their departed loved ones, to be merciful on their souls.

At Catholic funerals, there is no eulogy. However, friends and family who wished to say something about their loved ones could do so at the wake or at a reception after the funeral, if there was one.

At the Beneduce-Longobardi funeral, there was no wake. There was a reception and a few family members did say a few words about their beloved departed.

Everyone understood that Teresa was in too much emotional pain to be able to say anything. If, however, she would have said anything, she would only have expressed her hatred for those who killed their loved ones and the revenge she intended to visit upon them.

Part IV

IN PURSUIT OF REVENGE

Chapter Twenty-Four

THE CRUCIAL LEAD

Palazzo Scaletta Ristorante, Port of Naples, Italy

2011

It was two days after the funeral when Fara visited the restaurateur, Vinicio Scaletta, at his Palazzo Scaletta Ristorante in the Port of Naples. Despite the fact that Scaletta was part of the Beneduce-Longobardi clan and knew that Rinaldo Fara was a senior police officer, he knew nothing about the latter's role in the clan. In fact, he didn't even know Fara was part of the clan.

Fara was not about to enlighten him. He explained to Scaletta that the police were still investigating the death of one Matthew Benedict, an American who relocated to Naples a few months ago, and he was hoping Scaletta might have information that could be helpful.

With feigned insouciance, Scaletta shrugged and said,

"You're wasting your time. I don't even know who you're talking about."

Unperturbed, Fara grinned and said, "Not what I've heard. My sources say Benedict was a regular patron here. Maybe it will refresh your memory if you have a look at this photo?" He opened his briefcase, took out a large photo, taken postmortem, and slid it over the table.

Scaletta, moved uneasy in his chair but leaned forward and looked at the photo. "Hmm… yeah, I vaguely remember him. Isn't he the poor guy who fell off a boat in the harbor and drowned?"

Fara nodded, still grinning. "Yes, apparently he did, but the strange thing is, before he went overboard, he had stabbed himself with a knife, through the heart, from the back."

"I wouldn't know anything about that."

"I'm sure you don't. But just to put you at ease, you're not a suspect. So, I'll appreciate if you don't withhold any information from me. Okay?"

Scaletta nodded cautiously while his eyes were darting around the room as if he were expecting backing from his staff or maybe clients.

"Tell me about Sophia Maiorani."

Scaletta had gone quiet and bone-white in the face. Slowly he started nodding as he probably realized that Fara knew a lot more than he was letting on, and that his affair with Sophia was known by everyone including his wife.

"So, this Benedict got a bit too cozy with her?"

Scaletta started biting the nail on his index finger. "Wait a minute. I think I need to get hold of my lawyer."

Fara smiled. "I won't stop you if you think you need one. But as I've said before, you're not a suspect. In fact, I know you didn't kill Benedict. I checked it out, you were in

Rome at the time of the murder. You went there two days before and only returned three days after. So, stop worrying about that. Just answer my questions."

Scaletta nodded hesitantly.

"Well, she's your mistress, isn't she?"

"Was, not is." Scaletta tried to smile. "Okay, the thing is, yes, Sophia *was* my mistress, but I broke up with her more than a year ago. Truth be told, it was actually by mutual agreement that we ended the relationship. Part of our agreement was that she would manage this restaurant, and she did a fine job of it... until..."

"Until what?"

"She disappeared."

"Disappeared?"

Scaletta nodded.

"Obviously I need to know all about that," Fara said. "Start from the beginning and leave nothing out."

Over the course of the next half an hour or so, Scaletta told him how he met Sophia and employed her as a waitress at first and how she had worked her way up from there. Other than mentioning that Sophia became too demanding, expecting more from the relationship than he was prepared to commit to, he didn't give much information about their affair.

Fara was not really interested in that.

He told Fara how Matthew Benedict started frequenting the restaurant and showing a lot of interest in Sophia. How he, Scaletta, then had a long chat with her and discovered that Benedict was aksing all these weird questions about the drug trade in Naples and about buying illicit weapons.

"I told Gilberto Trapani about it."

"Who is Gilberto Trapani?" Fara knew very well who Trapani was. He was Scaletta's caporegime also referred to as a capo, captain, skipper, or crew chief. Trapani had been appointed by the Don to exert control over groups of Camorristi. But Fara was not going to let Scaletta know about it.

"My business mentor," Scaletta said.

Fara grinned slightly, it was the first time he heard a capo described as a business mentor. "Okay, continue."

"Well, all I know is not long after that, Benedict's body was found in the harbor."

Fara nodded. "So, when did Sophia disappear?"

Scaletta took a deep breath and started. "About three weeks ago, apparently a man turned up here at the restaurant and started asking her questions about Benedict."

"Apparently?"

"I've never seen this man, can't tell you anything about him. So, what I'm telling you is hearsay. Got it from my security staff. They told me they saw this stranger talking to her and they had questioned her after he left."

Fara had to suppress a smile when he heard Scaletta calling his goons, security staff.

"They told me they got the impression she was lying about the conversation she had with this stranger. Well, it seems they got a bit too zealous with their questioning… and… she landed in the hospital."

"Yes, and then?"

"So, according to them, they took her to the hospital and guarded her to make sure this man didn't talk to her again. Then, according to them, this stranger turned up at the hospital accompanied by three more men. The four of them attacked my men and left both of them in very bad shape, tied up, and unconscious in the shower of Sophia's room.

"By the time my men were discovered, Sophia was gone.

I have no idea where she went, and so far, all my inquiries have come to naught."

He continued to tell Fara that Sophia's only family, that he knew of, was her sister who lived in Naples, and her mother who lived in a nursing home in Caserta, half an hour away from Naples. He had been in contact with them, but they had no idea what had happened to her, and they were worried about her. She didn't have many friends, but the few she had, that he was aware of, also had no clue as to her whereabouts.

Fara asked to talk to the restaurant staff and the 'security staff'.

While Scaletta made the calls to summon his men to the restaurant, Fara spoke to the two staff members who had contact with the stranger.

They remembered the man mainly because he asked them, on two separate days, to talk to Sophia, their manager. They saw the two of them talking and remembered that she was visibly upset after. They didn't have a name for him. The stranger was of athletic build, between five eight and five eleven, weighing around hundred and fifty pounds or so, blond hair, and blue eyes. None of them had a long conversation with him, but from the little they had, both of them were sure he spoke with a north Italian accent.

Although Scaletta had mentioned that his men got quite a beating from the stranger and his cohorts, Fara was still surprised to see their abject condition even though it was almost three weeks since the attack on them.

Adelfo Naro, a tall, overheavy man with straight, dark hair, which he kept in a ponytail, clearly had esotropia; a condition where one or both eyes were turned inward, more commonly known as cross-eyed. Fara didn't know whether

Naro suffered from the condition before or as a result of the assault. Apart from that Naro also sported a cast on his left arm and metal braces on three fingers of his right hand. He explained that on top of the broken wrist and fingers he also sustained a few broken ribs and broken nose.

Lamberto Gugliotti was pushed in on a wheelchair. It was obvious that he took the worst beating of the two. He had dark, curly hair. In fact, he was quite hairy all over. Apparently, his jaw was broken and was wired shut. He was also missing some of his front teeth, which Fara thought could have been missing from before or as a result of the assault. His right elbow was in a cast and so was his left knee.

Fara couldn't help but think, *the two of them got mauled by a troop of gorillas, not four humans.* He was about to be even more surprised.

He interviewed them separately. Gugliotti's interview, due to the wired jaw, was more cumbersome than Naro's. Nevertheless, it was not too difficult for a policeman of thirty-five years to quickly find numerous inconsistencies, especially in the narrative of the assault on them. Fara thought it was important and pushed them on that until he finally got the truth—it was the work of one man, not four.

And it took Fara a while to convince himself to rather believe that than the four-man assault team. These guys were big and rough and clearly no strangers to a brawl.

What kind of man would be able take on these guys and kick their asses so badly? A highly trained martial arts expert? A special forces operator maybe?

Fara's mind was working overtime, and he soon reached the juncture where he seriously considered the possibility that there was a nexus between this stranger and the explosion. It intrigued him that this stranger knew he had to contact Sophia to find out about Benedict. Clearly, she was the crucial lead they were looking for, if they could find her.

In parting, Fara made it very clear to Scaletta and his goons that he was less than happy about their neglect to report the assault and Sophia's disappearance to authorities.

They simply nodded in silence, and Fara left it at that.

Within a few days, Fara had collected photos of Sophia from the restaurant staff, as well as her mother and sister. Identikits of the stranger were drawn.

The princely sum of two million Euros was placed on Sophia's head and four million on the head of the stranger.

Of course, none of that was made public. Nonetheless, a select group of private investigators were made aware of it, as well as a select group of law enforcement and government officials. Among the latter group, people with access to some of the best facial recognition systems in Europe.

At some stage, one or both of the suspects were going to land in their dragnets.

Chapter Twenty-Five

A DISH THAT TASTES BEST WHEN IT'S COLD

Naples, Italy

Teresa Lombardi, or Donna Teresa as they liked to call her, turned out to be the best leader the Beneduce-Longobardi clan could have hoped for. Even better than her late father, Ricardo Lombardi, the Don, and that was no small feat.

During his lifetime, the Don had built the biggest drug and counterfeit empire in all of Europe. Within three years, Donna Teresa had more than doubled it. She had an open hand, spreading the wealth more than her father ever did. There were more jobs, more loans, more small business startups, more charitable donations to schools, nursing homes, clinics, churches, and such.

Her father was known to insert himself, without invitation, between feuding clans from time to time to settle disputes. Donna Teresa was known as the mediator; the clans were bringing their disputes to her instead of killing each other.

Frequently, her father had to resort to heavy-handed

tactics to keep his underlings in check. Donna Teresa almost never had to sanction such actions.

Don Ricardo Lombardi was revered. Donna Teresa was sacrosanct.

A year after the deaths of her family, not wanting to keep living in the house that constantly reminded her of her loved ones, Teresa sold the Lombardi family home. She was now living in a luxurious six million Euro, three-bedroom villa on one acre of land, in the sought-after residential area of Posillipo, an area on the Gulf of Naples with panoramic views that had been a favorite holiday spot for the Roman elite since the first century BC. The immaculately restored two-century-old home was located right on the cliff, giving her uninterrupted sea views all the way to Mount Vesuvius from the living room, kitchen, main bedroom, and of course from the large beautiful terraced Mediterranean garden where she spent many hours enjoying the views, reading, painting, and cogitating.

Despite her ostensibly tranquil and laidback lifestyle, Donna Teresa carried within her, which very few people knew about, a deep-seated hatred and a consuming obsession for revenge against those who killed her family.

To her it was frustrating to know that the explosion was no accident, but, despite the vast resources available to her, unable to find out who did it. Undoubtedly it was a black operation authorized by one or more government agencies. A few Western European countries ranked high on her list but the top three were the usual suspects; America, Israel, and Britain.

Even more upsetting was the realization that an informant was at work among them.

She had a discussion with Imam Al-Sadiq about it. At the time, she told the imam that they now knew it was not a gas leak but a well-planned covert military operation. Fortunately, the imam had the wisdom not to try and play the blame game with her and Li Voti again. Understandably, he was a bit reluctant to accept that a leak could have come from his side; after all, Hezbollah's secret service was the best in the world.

However, she told him what Rinaldo Fara had to say after talking to Vinicio Scaletta, the owner of Palazzo Scaletta Ristorante. It was clear that whoever did it must have heard something about the deal in the making but didn't have all the details. Hence, they sent first Matthew Benedict who had asked questions about drugs and weapons, and a few months later another man who had asked questions about Benedict and abducted Sophia Maiorani. The explosion took place shortly after Sophia disappeared. Admittedly, Sophia must have given this man some information, but she had no way of knowing the details of the deal. The evidence, as far as she was concerned, pointed to an initial piece of information that must have originated from either the imam's side or the clan's side.

"Therefore, I'd say it is incumbent upon both sides to clean house in an attempt to find the traitor."

Al-Sadiq nodded slowly, deep in thought. "You have a point. It also means we can't even think of making another deal until we find the traitor."

Hezbollah went on a mole hunt and found him. It took almost twelve months, but they found him. The man was tortured for weeks before he gave it up and told them that he worked for the Mossad. He was the one who alerted the Mossad about the drugs-for-arms deal in the making.

They hung his body in a market square in Beirut with a board around his neck with an inscription that read:

THIS TRAITOR WORKED FOR THE JEWISH DOGS

The Beneduce-Longobardis found no mole on their side, but they knew Sophia Maiorani could lead them to the one who was responsible for the explosion.

However, after more than three years they were no closer to finding her than the day they learned about her role in it. She might as well have been dead and buried in an unmarked grave in an unknown location.

They had tabs on her mother's and sister's phones, emails, social media accounts, even the neighbors were cooperating, but so far, they had zilch. Not even a hint, only speculation and conjecture.

Vexing as it was, Donna Teresa knew eventually they would find her, dead or alive. Therefore, she kept working on her plan of revenge, often remembering the words of Don Corleone, a character in the 1969 novel *The Godfather* by Mario Puzo, who said, "Revenge is a dish best served cold."

Chapter Twenty-Six

THE RISE OF THE VORY

Russia

Many people think that the Russian mafia came into existence in the wake of the collapse of the Soviet Union and the end of the Cold War. That is not correct. The Russian mafia, the *Bratva*, Russian for brotherhood, could trace its history back to the imperial era of the Tsars.

But it was not until the Soviet era when the *vory v zakone*, thieves-in-law, while interned in prisons and forced labor camps, organized themselves and defined their code of honor. Among the members the term *Vor* (plural: *vory*) literally meaning thief, was an honorary title bestowed only on those who had demonstrated significant leadership skills, personal ability, intellect, and charisma.

In the flourishing lawlessness and black market that sprung up after the fall of the Soviet Union, they rapidly gained prominence and power. At some stage they controlled about two-thirds of the Russian economy. In modern times, it was estimated that there were more than six thousand groups and more than two hundred of them with global reach.

Their members are no longer only former prisoners; their ranks had been bolstered by corrupt officials, ex-KGB officers, former soldiers, and business leaders. And the title *Vory* was conferred only on the most successful crime groups, the super mafia so to speak.

Alain Bauer, a French criminologist, once described the Bratva as "one of the best structured criminal organizations in Europe, with a quasi-military operation."

In 1995, Italian authorities uncovered a joint Camorra-Russian Mafia operation in which the Camorra were bleaching US $1 bills and reprinted them as $100 bills destined for distribution in former Eastern-Bloc countries in return for firearms smuggled into Italy.

President Vladimir Putin, after coming into power in 1999, had quickly abandoned the tough stance on organized crime and offered the elite of the underworld a kind of unwritten 'social contract' that defined the terms under which they were to operate within Russia and beyond.

By 2010, there were more than three hundred thousand Vor, and it was not a big secret, at least not to western security agencies, that the most powerful Bratva bosses had close ties with the Russian president, Vladimir Putin. While the Kremlin vehemently denied any links to organized crime, the truth was that the *vory* drew much of its power and influence from its ties with the Russian government.

Moscow, Russia

June 2014

It was in June 2014 when Donna Teresa, without the knowledge of the Beneduce-Longobardi leadership, made a secret trip to Moscow. She told Li Voti that she had to attend to some business in Rome and would be away for a few days. That was not unusual, she frequently traveled to Rome to confer with her business manager in charge of her Liana Verdi Art Studio. Li Voti was the only one of the leadership group who she had let in on the secret about the studio's existence, ownership, and nature of its business.

She *did* travel to Rome, and she *did* meet with her business manager—for one day—and then she flew to Moscow where she met with Olesya Kharlamova, a *vor* who had done work for her late father.

Olesya was in her mid-sixties, not a beautiful woman anymore, although there was undeniable evidence of beauty that once was. A full body of thirty years ago was now on the verge of obesity. A face that was perfectly lined was now wrinkled. The startling shoulder-length wavy dark brown hair of her youth, now short, thin, and white as snow, barely covered her ears. A lifetime of chain-smoking and long spells of overindulgence in alcohol left her skin blotched and mottled, and her once striking brown eyes hazy, almost lifeless.

She was recruited by the KGB directly out of Moscow University in 1976, and she gave them twenty-five years of undivided loyalty and hard work. And she reaped the benefits, for as long as communism existed. By December 1991, she had reached the rank of major when the Soviet Union collapsed, and communism had ended. But then the KGB was disbanded and replaced by the *Sluzhba vneshney razvedki Rossiyskoy Federatsii*, (Foreign Intelligence Service of the Russian Federation) or just the SVR RF, and she was laid off. She didn't have enough years of service to get a state pension. And she quickly discovered that there were very few to no job opportunities for ex-KGB field agents, especially women, in the new Russia.

It took her a while, and many nights of going to bed on an empty stomach, to realize she actually had marketable skills and experience; her intimate knowledge of what was known in the lexicon of spies as sexpionage.

When she was recruited into the KGB it was not only for her brains and language skills, it was for her beauty and elegance. Six months of training at the Swallows Nest, the KGB's facility where they trained young beautiful women in the art of seduction and information gathering, made her an expert in all methods of manipulating the male ego, and more tangible areas, in order to get access to the secrets the men carried. The graduates were called swallows or sparrows. Of course, the SVR fervidly denies that the Swallows Nest, swallows or sparrows, ever existed. But Olesya Kharlamova knew different, and so did every agent in the world who knew anything about the spy business.

But the Russian underworld was dominated by bigots who didn't believe in gender equality. To them, women members of their syndicates were only of use as seductresses, prostitutes, and drug pushers. It took her many years to build up her own business among the *vory*—a world infested with male chauvinist egomaniacs, who wouldn't allow the sun to shine on her.

Nonetheless, by June 2014, on what Muscovites would call a balmy summer's evening, when Olesya met with

Teresa Lombardi in the Grand Café Dr. Zhivago across the street from the Kremlin, she had made her mark in the Russian crime world. She was not nearly as affluent as the most successful of her fellow *vory*, but she had an enviable bank balance, many well-paying investments, and the men of the *Bratva* had accepted her presence in their industry.

Her organization specialized in the gathering and selling of information. Her all-female crew of beautiful young women, handpicked and trained by herself from all over the world, enabled her to carve out a niche in the harsh world of the male dominated *Bratva*, because no one else had the skills, the resources or the experience she had. They often used her services to get their hands on hard to come by information or to get blackmail material. And they paid handsomely for it.

The food at the baroque-style brasserie with large statues, elaborately decorated ceilings, and bright red chairs was exquisite; the ambience was buoyant, and the business talk lasted only a few minutes, leaving the rest of the evening to enjoy and talk about everything but business. Teresa could only speak Italian and English, Olesya spoke many languages including French, German, Swedish, and English, but not Italian.

Teresa's request was uncomplicated. "I would like to know who was responsible for the explosion in the Port of Naples in 2011. I already know about the Mossad's involvement. Were there any others? And what would be most appreciated," she was rubbing her thumb and index finger together in the international gesture for money, "would be any names, photos, addresses and such, of those involved. The more details I get the more valuable the information becomes."

Olesya had nodded and said, "I'll need a few details

from you about the event. I also need a non-refundable deposit of one hundred thousand US to get me started. All expenses to be covered by you, including any bribes, if required. Any expenses over five thousand I will clear with you first. The name of the countries and their organizations that might have been involved, if there were any other than the Israelis, will be seventy-five thousand US per country including the name of the organization. The names of individuals will be much more difficult to come by. Therefore, those would be one hundred to one hundred and fifty thousand each, depending on how much information I can collect for you."

Teresa had raised her glass of very expensive red wine in a gesture of sealing the agreement. At more than seven hundred US dollars per bottle, it was one of Italy's most expensive red wines, made entirely of Merlot by Tenuta dell'Ornellaia on the Masseto vineyard on the coast of the Tuscany region of Italy.

To stimulate Olesya's enthusiasm, Teresa mentioned the bounties on the heads of Sophia Maiorani and the unknown man who made off with her out of Naples in 2011. "If your information leads to the capture of one or both of them, the bounty is yours."

For the first time that night, Olesya's eyes had gained a sparkle.

Chapter Twenty-Seven

ALL THE DO'S AND DON'TS

Rome, Italy

The past four years

Her driver's license, bank accounts, bills, and all other identification said her name was Simona Bellucci who grew up in Milan. She spoke with a Milanese accent and used their idiom. She had bob-style wavy auburn hair and brown eyes.

About four years ago she underwent extensive cosmetic surgery which included not only a facelift but also rhinoplasty to change the shape of her nose, V-line jaw surgery to contour and slim her lower jaw giving her a more streamlined profile, liposuction, a tummy tuck, and blepharoplasty. The latter was a procedure known as 'ethnic plastic surgery', popular among Asian people who wanted a more 'western' look by taking away the slanting of their eyes. In her case, the surgeons actually did the opposite by giving her slightly slanted eyes, hinting at an Asian ancestor in her lineage. She had spent weeks in a private clinic, it was painful, but it was necessary, and the result left her with a stunning new look that took at least ten years off her real age.

No facial recognition system would have been able to identify her.

The only identification she carried with her that could potentially have betrayed who she really was, was her gait, voice, fingerprints, and DNA. If those would have been captured and analyzed it would have shown that her real name was Sophia Maiorani, former resident of Naples.

However, she had been assured by Catia that the chances of that happening were slim to none. Catia had explained that for the authorities to find a match between her fingerprints or DNA and her real identity, she had to be in the system. In other words, they had to have those on record, usually from a previous encounter with them such as being fingerprinted or DNA'd when arrested for a crime.

And although the erstwhile Sophia Maiorani had been involved in some petty crimes in her youth, she was fortunate enough to never have been arrested. Neither her name nor her fingerprints or DNA had ever landed in the police or any other government records. As for her voice and gait, it was the same, she had to be in the system, and she was sure she was not.

What Catia didn't tell her was that the Mossad had a network of contacts throughout Italy in high places, and they had made sure that the system will show Simona Bellucci who grew up in Milan who now lived in Rome, to be the owner of those identification markers.

Although Simona often wondered who had paid for the surgery and which organization she helped back there in

Naples, she would never have guessed it was the Mossad and CIA. Her only contact with that chapter of her life was Catia, and she knew Catia would never tell her.

Catia had helped her find a steady job as an assistant at the National Etruscan Museum (*Museo Nazionale Etrusco*), housed in the Villa Giulia in Rome about half a mile from the Piazza del Popolo and about one and a half miles from where Catia lived. Although she didn't know where Catia lived—it was part of their security measures.

Thanks to Catia's employer, who remained anonymous, Simona had received a generous gift of fifty-thousand Euros as token of their appreciation for her help with the Naples mission, and they provided her with a small studio apartment, one room serving as a sitting room, bedroom, and kitchenette, plus a bathroom. From her apartment to her work was about two miles, an easy commute with her Vespa scooter.

She enjoyed her work; it was much more satisfying to take people on a tour through the museum than dealing with impertinent customers in a restaurant under the constant watch of Camorra brutes.

In the days after she had left the private clinic, Catia had spent a lot of time with her to make sure she settled in and to coach her about security. It was agreed that contact would always be made by Catia not Simona, unless there was an emergency. In which case Simona had to send a pre-agreed text message to a mobile number Catia gave her. Catia also gave her a little bit of training about countersurveillance so that she could spot when someone was following or surveilling her.

Catia made it very clear to her that she, Simona, was responsible for her own security. Not that Catia and her employer would leave her to her own devices and not protect her if it was necessary, but she was the first line of defense.

"You have to live a normal life, do the things people normally do—blend in and act normal. Be mindful that someone from your past may turn up when you least expect it. Not that anyone would recognize you, but how are you going to react?

"Be cautious, never get blasé about your security, never. Make no mistake, they *are* looking for you, they will be scouring and trolling the internet. They will be monitoring the phone lines of your former friends and family. You cannot ever contact them again."

It was harsh but necessary, and with the beating she had received from Scaletta's bullies still fresh in her memory, Simona understood all too well what the consequences would be if she didn't.

Catia didn't tell her about the two million Euro bounty on her head, which had come to the Mossad's attention, or about the four million on Marco's head.

Within a few months, Simona was getting used to all the do's and don'ts, and she was grateful for the fresh start. The Camorra and crime, and the fear and abuse were gone. She could be herself and soon realized what she made of her life was in her own hands, not in those of a bunch of ruthless criminals.

By nature, Simona had a friendly and outgoing person-ality, but under the Camorra she could never be herself. Now she was able to come out of her shell. She started to make new friends. And, as can be expected with a woman of her beauty, she had no shortage of male admirers. But after Vinicio Scaletta—she still couldn't believe she had fallen for the scumbag—and the beating by his thugs, Adelfo Naro and Lamberto Gugliotti, she was wary of men.

Short of the suitor appearing in shining armor on a white horse, sword in hand, saving her from the jaws of a dragon, she would rather keep her distance.

Maybe someday I will overcome the demons of my past and allow someone to get closer.

But of all her emotional trials and tribulations, the most difficult was not being able to contact her mother and sister. Her mother much more so than her sister who was twelve years younger and in her third marriage. All her former husbands and the current one were Camorra hardliners and drug abusers. Fortunately, there were no children. Simona had always done her best to help and protect her little sister, but it was never easy, and most of the time not even possible. Unless she wanted to cross swords with the Camorra thugs.

Growing up, their mother worked as a seamstress in one of the many counterfeit clothing factories in Naples. Their father, a dockworker in the Port of Naples, an honest, hard-working and good man, was killed in a gang shooting in the first summer after she had finished school. Gunned down right in front of Simona's eyes on the pavement while the two of them were on their way home from the grocery store.

Simona had to give up her dream of higher education and find a job to help her mother make ends meet. And in Campania, no one got a job without the say-so of the Camorra. After countless job applications, Vinicio Scaletta, the restaurant owner, gave her a job as waitress at his restaurant at a sub-minimum wage. She had no choice, after six months of trying, every day, it was the only job offer she had. Since then, for more than twenty years, she worked as waitress, head waitress, and eventually manager in Scaletta's restaurant.

Between her and her mother they had managed to get her sister through school, pay the rent, put food on the table. Many days the food on their table was the leftovers she brought from the restaurant.

Those were hard times, but the good that came out of it was the very special bond that had developed between her and her mother. Her mother was seventy-six, living in a government nursing home in Caserta, half an hour outside of Naples.

Now that bond was broken, and her loneliness was complete.

Chapter Twenty-Eight

A PLAN TO GIVE IT TO THEM

Naples, Italy

February 2015

It was February 2015, eight months and $270,000 USD after meeting with Olesya Kharlamova, when Teresa finally knew the attack that killed her father and brothers had been the result of a joint Mossad-CIA operation. The mission support was provided by a Mossad agent in Rome, a female *sayan*, but her name, address, and photo evaded Olesya's swallows. They learned that the person responsible for the explosion worked for a black ops private contractor, operating out of Arizona, Crisis Response Consultancy, CRC, to whom the CIA had outsourced the mission. However, to Teresa's utter disappointment, Olesya's agents were only able to find out that this man went by the pseudonyms *El Gato*, the cat in Spanish, *Alshaytan*, the Devil in Arabic, and the Ghost.

But at least now she knew at which countries and organizations to direct her hatred.

Ever since the explosion, Donna Teresa had been thinking and searching for a method of retribution. She would not be gratified with an eye for an eye or a tooth for a tooth—killing only thirty-two of those who did it and their associates was not going to be enough. That would only avenge the deaths of those who were killed in that explosion. What she was looking for was a method of revenge to account for the pain and suffering of the loved ones of those who died, and that would send a clear message, not only to the culprits but also to the rest of the world—don't mess with the Camorra.

In her quest for the perfect solution she had come to the realization that she had much in common with Islamic terrorist groups such as ISIS, Al-Qaeda and Hezbollah. Not in their fanatical religious stances—she was Catholic—but their insatiable hatred for Israel and America.

The media and politicians often claimed that terrorism always had its origins in poverty and deprivation, among those who the author Frantz Fanon called, 'the wretched of the earth'. But they were wrong, history told a different story. One only had to look at the history of terror across the globe over the past century or so; the IRA of Ireland, the EOKA of Cyprus, the Baader-Meinhof and Red Army Faction of Germany, the Red Brigades of Italy, ETA in Spain, and many others. They were without exception the brainchild of a theorist from the middle-class who had never gone to bed hungry in their lives. No, it was not wretchedness that stoked the fires of terrorism; the common denominator that besieged them all was hatred. Whether it was motivated by a desire for freedom, anti-capitalist passion, or religious zeal, it was always preceded by hatred.

The same kind of hatred Teresa Lombardi carried within her.

She was not going to start another terrorist organization, for she already had access to them through Imam Kazim Al-Sadiq. What remained to be finalized was the method to exact her revenge. A method so audacious and so destructive it would motivate and excite the terrorists to do her bidding.

And now that she knew who she hated; she could dedicate her thoughts to finding such a method.

She knew the Islamic terrorists would not be satisfied with a few dead Jews and Americans—they killed two thousand seven hundred and fifty-three people on September 11, 2001 and they'd danced in the streets, chanting, "Death to America!" They were not satisfied, they wanted more—hundreds of thousands more.

But the terrorists didn't have the means, or the weapons, to do it. They had experimented in the caves of Afghanistan, in secret facilities, above and below ground, throughout the Middle East, with toxic gases and germs in search of the weapon of mass destruction they so desired, but thus far they were unable to build such a weapon.

Teresa Lombardi was working on a plan to give it to them.

Part V

PS: BADR. ALLAHU AKBAR

Chapter Twenty-Nine

A SIP OF COFFEE

CIA Headquarters, Langley, Virginia, United States

May 2015

The CIA analyst on duty had been assigned to the Middle East desk because of his knowledge of the region acquired through university studies, his fluency in Arabic and Persian or Farsi, and a working knowledge of Punjabi, the most widely spoken language in Pakistan. He knew the Quran and the history of Islam better than most Arabs.

It was late afternoon, he was tired, and he'd been looking forward to going home. He had been staring at the intercepted message he'd translated from Arabic to English, for more than two hours. The original message was in plain text Arabic. An email between two businesspeople, one located in Saudi Arabia, the other in London. On the face of it, the entire email seemed to be a benign conversation to arrange for an upcoming visit by the guy from London to the guy in Riyadh, Saudi Arabia's capital. But what gave him reason for pause that afternoon, after translating it and retranslating and thinking of it in every way possible until it threatened to do his head in, was the three-word postscript at the end of the email—PS: Badr. *Allahu akbar*.

He knew that Badr, full Arabic name Badr Hunayn, was a town in Saudi Arabia, about eighty miles from Medina, where the famous battle of Badr took place in 624 AD, a battle of immense significance in Islamic history.

The Quraysh was a polytheist Arab tribe that inhabited Mecca and surrounding areas at the time of the Prophet Muhammad's birth. Although Muhammad was born into the Banu Hashim clan of the Quraysh tribe, the tribal leaders had resolutely opposed his new religious idea about monotheism. When Muhammad learned of the Quraysh's plans to wipe him and his followers out, he and his followers had migrated to Medina, two hundred miles north of Mecca, in 622 AD, in what became known as the Hijra. It was during this journey to Medina that the battle of Badr took place in the year 624 AD between the Quraysh and Muhammad's forces. Muslims believed that Muhammad's decisive victory in the battle of Badr that day was attributable to divine intervention. It was one of only a few battles noted in the Qur'an where mention was made of thousands of angels that were present on the battlefield that day. Secular sources ascribed the victory to Muhammad's strategic prowess.

Although there were no descriptions of the battle prior to the 9th century, it was said to be Muhammad's first military victory and regarded as a turning point in Islamic history, establishing Mohammed's followers as a noteworthy force in the Arabian Peninsula.

In 630 AD, the Quraysh converted to Islam en masse.

The last two words of the postscript, *Allahu akbar,* also known as the *Takbir,* were usually translated as 'God is greatest' or 'God is greater'. Traditionally it was used by Muslims and Arabic speaking Orthodox Christians alike as an expression of their faith. It meant no matter the situation or emotion, God is always greater than any real or imaginary entity. The phrase appeared on the flags of several Muslim countries, including Afghanistan, Iraq, and Iran.

However, in modern times, especially in western society, the phrase had come to be associated with terrorism. Some called it the battle cry for terrorists. Some went so far as to suggest that it meant Allah and Islam were dominant over every other form of government, religion, law, or ethic. Or a proclamation of Islamic superiority over all religions, comparable to Hitler's idea of a superior Aryan race or a white supremacist shouting, 'heil Hitler'.

Notwithstanding the diverting interpretations, the analyst found it a strange postscript. *Allahu akbar* without the preceding reference to Badr would not have raised his suspicions, but in combination it did. One of the questions he had was; if the body of the email was what it purported to be an innocent conversation between friends, or a hidden message, what did a battle that took place almost fourteen hundred years ago have to do with the contents of the email? Did the word Badr actually hold a different meaning?

Eventually, he gave up. He could not think of a legitimate alternative explanation. Hidden messages, decoding, and decryption were not his bailiwick. Therefore, he kicked it upstairs to his manager with a short note explaining his perplexity about those three words and his subsequent suspicions about the entire email. He suggested that it might be worthwhile to add those words and variations of them to

the computer algorithms used to scan electronic communications from across the globe to see if it showed up again in
other messages.

The next morning, his manager, a very intelligent man
but hopelessly overextended with all his responsibilities, read
the email and report, sighed, and tagged it as NFA—not for
action. But before he archived the message, he took a sip of
his coffee while he stared at the message again. When he
put the mug down, he sighed again and mumbled, "Maybe,
just maybe. No harm in checking." He changed the flag to
FA—for action—and assigned a priority two to it. It was
supposed to be actioned within the next twenty-four to
forty-eight hours.

It was only months later when it would become evident
what a monumental impact a sip of coffee could have on
world affairs.

Chapter Thirty

ANOTHER TURNING POINT?

The US Intelligence Community

In the reverberations of the September 11 attacks in the US, analysts, scholars, commentators, and others wanted to know how such a complex plan of attack could have gone undetected by the US intelligence community. It didn't take them long to label the disaster as an intelligence failure. A board of inquiry found that the information on the attacks was there prior to the attacks. Had the agencies been sharing and collating the bits and pieces they had, it was entirely possible that the attacks could have been prevented.

Since then the US intelligence community had grown in size, budget, and effort. By 2010, there were reported to be 1,271 government organizations and 1,931 private companies in 10,000 locations across the United States working on counterterrorism, homeland security, and intelligence. More than 850,000 people held top-secret clearances.

By 2015, the Intelligence Community of the United States consisted of what some called a veritable alphabet soup of 17 intelligence agencies operating on a federated model to perform intelligence activities, separately and in collaboration to support foreign policy and national security. It was estimated that between them they had eyes and ears on close to, if not more than, 90% of all intelligence gathered on the planet by licit (overt) and illicit (covert) means during any given twenty-four-hour period. Its total budget in 2015 was almost seventy billion dollars.

By 2015, their sharing of information and collaboration were orders of magnitude better and more efficient than at the time of the 9/11 attacks.

The immensity of data collected was mindboggling. The analysis, classification, and prioritization was an operation of industrial magnitude. Then came the collation of relevant pieces of intelligence, putting together the pieces of the jigsaw puzzle that made up the picture, and that was where the entire effort at times still fell flat on its face. Despite the directive from the Director of National Intelligence, "It's no longer about 'need to know'. Our guiding principle is 'responsibility to share,'" the agencies were still not always efficient in their sharing of information. The reality was that the shift to digital intelligence gathering had cataclysmic impacts on the intelligence gathering effort because of the colossal amounts of data collected, pushing them to the development of computer systems capable of artificial intelligence and machine learning. Thus, taking the human touch out of the equation all too often.

Five Eyes

July 2015

The prioritization and request for actioning of the Badr email was received and actioned, keyword search algorithms were duly updated, and confirmation duly sent to the requesting manager within twenty-four hours, by an employee of the National Security Agency (NSA).

The NSA's existence was once so secret they were often referred to as 'No Such Agency'. That was before 2013 when Edward Snowden revealed to the world the existence of PRISM and other mass surveillance programs under the NSA's control. Their focus was on what was known in the intelligence world as SIGINT, signal intelligence—the monitoring, collecting, and processing of communications and other electronic information as well as the cracking of secret codes.

As for the Badr request, up until that point, everyone had done their job, properly. The NSA's powerful computers had gone to work and gotten several hits on the keywords Badr and *Allahu akbar* in existing and new communications including in voice communications. Naturally, hits on the words *Allahu akbar* ran into the millions, on the word Badr not so much. The hits would be duly reported by the computers to one or more of the seventeen agencies if they had registered an interest in communications between certain parties in the first place. In some cases, there were no interested agencies, so the report was not sent to anyone.

This turned out to be the case that exposed the flaw in the logic, identified in a 'lessons learned' review after the event. The recommendation of the review committee was that applications and algorithms had to be updated, immediately, to add a feature that would enable agencies to subscribe to the reports generated by the NSA computers so that they could get all the reports based on all the hits on their keywords irrespective of whether they were interested in the parties using the keywords.

If the recommended software update had existed at the time when the Badr request was submitted to the NSA in May 2015, the manager who requested it would have received a flood of reports. All he would have had to do was filter out all appearances of *Allahu akbar* without an accompanying Badr or look for the appearance of the word Badr on its own. That would have given him a list of ten communications with those words in them in May 2015 already. He would have known that within twelve hours of receiving confirmation from the NSA that his request had been processed and implemented.

As it was, it was the 3rd of July, almost two months after his initial request, when he received the first NSA report, which was triggered because of an email the original sender, from back in May, had sent to another person, someone who lived in Naples, Italy. Up until then, the original requester had not received a report because neither the sender nor receiver of the May email had used those keywords in their communications.

When he saw the report, he had to think long and hard to recall the email that had prompted him to request it. Once he did, he quickly found it and compared the attached emails with the emails in the report. He started thinking. *I wonder if there are more of these.*

He requested a report from the NSA for all communications, going back six months, containing those three words or the word Badr on its own, no matter who the sender or reccivers were. Twenty-four hours later, he was looking at the list—there were twenty-one entries, the oldest dating back to April 2015. He read the report and found there were five different people communicating with each other using those keywords. All of them seemed to know each other, at least by email they did. One in Rome, one in Riyadh, one in Pasadena, California, one in Naples, and one in Beirut.

He read the analyst's May report again and wondered, *Badr, the turning point in Islamic history. Are we at the dawn of another turning point?*

He picked the phone up and made an appointment with his manager, the person in charge of the Directorate of Analysis, Bryan Shafer.

Chapter Thirty-One

ENOUGH REASON TO CONTINUE

The ops room, CIA Headquarters, Langley, Virginia, USA

June 2015

Within a week a senior analyst, Stacie Barrett, assisted by a team of five of her experienced colleagues were assigned and ready to start work on Operation Badr.

At fifty-four, with all her working life after university at the CIA, it was not Stacie's first rodeo. She had a reputation as a meticulous worker, near anal retentive, an uncanny ability to see connections between seemingly unrelated pieces of information to reveal the whole picture, and a remarkable ability to recollect. Her human relations skills sometimes left a bit to be desired, but her colleagues knew her and didn't even notice it anymore. In fact, most of them liked her. She was a straight shooter, not a single bone of political correctness in her body, and she got results. She never claimed the accolades following success for herself neither did she blame failure on her underlings.

Soon the five individuals in those emails would be under the most sophisticated surveillance systems in existence, and a tenacious analyst and her team would be on their trails. The other agencies in the US Intelligence Community would be briefed as well as the heads of the intelligence agencies of the Five Eyes countries and Israel.

Five Eyes or FVEY was formed in 1941 between the US, UK, Australia, Canada, and New Zealand to share signals intelligence with each other.

Although the team had the best computers, software, and technology available to do their job, and Stacie was well versed in computer use, she still liked to also have the good old-fashioned link chart or investigation board, as some called it, on the wall. For the operation, she and her team had been allocated a fully equipped operations room with two big TV screens, secured telephones, computers, water cooler, fridge, microwave oven, and espresso machine.

She started off by sticking five squares with faceless gray silhouettes on the board. Below each of them was a name, a city, and an email address. Then she retrieved a ball of string from her desk drawer and connected the images to each other in a crisscross.

"That's what we know today," she said to her team as she stepped back from the board. "Those five blank faces know each other. They've come to our attention because they have used the words Badr and *Allahu akbar* in their communications with each other. Something which we believe holds some significance, although we don't under-stand why, yet. For what it's worth, I've invited the analyst who noticed the anomaly to give us a historical perspective of those words."

She nodded for him to take over.

This was the analyst's first encounter with Stacie Barrett, also known as M1 or Abrams, a reference to the US M1 Abrams battle tank. Her nickname had nothing to do with her looks—she was tall, in good shape, with curly dark brown hair and sparkling brown eyes—in fact, she was quite attractive.

Fifteen minutes and a few questions later, the analyst was done and left the room with the impression that Stacie Barrett was well deserving of her title as the Battle Tank of the Analysis Directorate.

"Okay, there you have it," Stacie said when the door closed behind him. "Not much to start with. We need full names, pictures of faces, and real addresses in those blank spaces. Followed by aliases, if any, family, friends and associates, phone numbers, date of birth, employment, financial data, travel habits, you name it we want it. Nothing about them is unimportant.

"Each of you pick a name from the board. That person is going to become the 'love of your life'. You are going to find out everything there is to know about him or her.

"If you need anything, let me know. We have the authority of our deputy director behind us. So, if anyone anywhere gives you any grief at any time, you let me know.

"This might be a wild goose chase, but I've got a gut feeling it's not.

"Any questions?"

There were none, the team had done this kind of work before, many times. And more than once with M1 Abrams in the lead. More than ninety percent of the time it turned out to be nothing; the rest of the time they were instrumental in thwarting terrorist plots that could have killed thousands.

Within five days, the blank images on the link chart had been replaced with images of real people. And the impact of what they had learned about their subjects had set off alarm bells that had quickly reached the ears of the Director of the CIA, Howard Lawrence.

Early on the morning of July 16, Stacie and her manager, Bryan Shafer, found themselves in a secured board room facing a plethora of high-ranking CIA mandarins including Director Lawrence.

Stacie nodded and thanked the Director when he asked her to present her findings after Bryan Shafer had given the attendees a brief overview about Operation Badr. She brought up the first picture.

"Aziz Abdul-Salam Awad, a part time professor of Middle Eastern Studies at Università Cattolica del Sacro Cuore, Rome campus. A devoted Muslim of the Sunni persuasion. An Italian citizen by birth from parents origi-nally from Saudi Arabia. No indications of radicalism. No known aliases and not on the radar of any of the US, other Five Eyes, or Israeli intelligence agencies."

There were no questions, and she continued.

"Haroun Najm al Din Hadad, homegrown—got his PHD in chemical engineering and electronics from the Cali-fornia Institute of Technology, Caltech, only last year. A Muslim of the Sunni persuasion. Devoted, but no indica-tions of radicalism. No known aliases and not on the radar of any of the US, other Five Eyes, or Israeli intelligence agencies.

"But we don't know his present whereabouts. His friends —and he didn't really have any, they'd rather qualify as acquaintances than friends—were surreptitiously ques-tioned but had no idea where he is. According to them he is a loner and introvert. Two months ago, he resigned from his temporary teaching position at Caltech and told them he was going on a pilgrimage, first to Mecca and then to the rest of the world's Muslim countries. No one knows where he is now. He has left no electronic footprints; in other words, we have not been able to track down any emails, Internet usage, or social media activities from him since he left the US."

"So, for all we know he could be sitting somewhere quietly building diabolical bombs, and we wouldn't know?"

"Yes, sir. That could be so."

Some eyebrows raised, but there were no further questions.

Stacie continued, "Saiyyad Rahal, businessman in Riyadh, Saudi Arabia. Owner of a big shipping company. Muslim of the Sunni persuasion. No indications of radicalism. No known aliases and not on the radar of any of the US, other Five Eyes, or Israeli intelligence agencies."

Again, there were no questions.

"Esam Abbas Bitar from Beirut, a well-known politician in those parts of the world, member of Hezbollah's political wing, Loyalty to the Resistance Bloc, and member of the Lebanese parliament. He is known to have close ties with Hezbollah's paramilitary wing, the Jihad Council. He is a Muslim of the Shi'a persuasion. The Mossad has an extensive file on this man, and although he is not on their hitlist, they are keeping a close watch on him and his associates."

There were a few nods around the table including the Director who said, "Three Sunni's and one Shiite so far?"

Stacie nodded slightly and brought up the next slide. "And here is the second Shiite. Imam Karim Al-Sadiq, Naples, Italy. This is the guy who raised our hackles. We had no record of him, neither did the other members of Five Eyes. But the Mossad did. And they were, to put it mildly, most unpleasantly surprised. They thought they had killed him in an airstrike in Beirut years ago. His real name is Hassan Walid, a Shiite Muslim, not a Sunni as he had been portraying himself since his arrival in Naples in 2009. He is a member of the external wing of Hezbollah's secret service Amn al-Muddad. One of their top agents, trained in Iran and North Korea."

"And this guy is now posing as a Sunni Imam in Naples, Italy on Camorra turf. Any connection there?" Lawrence asked.

"We're working on that, sir. We have reason, albeit not much, to believe there could be a connection."

"How?"

"In 2011, there was a joint CIA-Mossad operation in Naples to stop an arms-for-drugs deal between Camorra and a Hezbollah-Al-Qaeda group operating out of Lebanon. At the time, and to this day, Hassan Walid lived in a Muslim enclave south of Naples under this pseudonym Imam Karim Al-Sadiq. We think he might have been involved in that deal."

For the next half hour, they discussed and speculated, and eventually agreed that if for no other reason than the presence of the names, Hassan Walid and Esam Abbas Bitar were cause for concern and more than enough reason to continue Operation Badr, with full backing of the Director.

Chapter Thirty-Two

FOLLOWING THE BREADCRUMBS

The ops room, CIA Headquarters, Langley, Virginia, USA

July 2015

There was a lot more information to be collected and analyzed. If what they were looking at was a sinister plot in the making, what was it? Who else was involved? How far had it progressed and when would it happen?

As for timelines, Stacie told them, "We don't know. Therefore, we're on twenty-four seven from here on in. Eight-hour shifts. You keep on working; I'll get us a bigger room and more people."

Less than two hours later she told the team to pack up their stuff and follow her to the new room where seven additional staff members were already waiting for them. Five minutes after that, five of the new members were teamed up with the existing team of five, two to a target. The newcomers were brought up to speed.

No one even bothered to ask her if someone would relieve her. They already knew, from previous experience, that when an operation reached a critical stage like Operation Badr had, she survived on catnaps, in her chair, at her desk.

By the third week of July, they had delved into the lives of their five subjects and knew much of their life-history from the day they were born up until the present. It was time to expand their research to cover friends, family, associates, and how the five got to know each other. Telephone records, emails, financial records, Internet usage, travel records, and such were requested and scrutinized.

It was late July when the Naples team, while unravelling the calls received by the 'Imam' over the past four years, backtracking, identifying, and matching names to numbers of each caller, found the name Valter Li Voti.

When the analyst, Leigh-Anne, a red-haired woman in her mid-thirties, ran the name through the NSA databases like they did with everyone else they found, a flag came up that suggested this individual had a Camorra connection.

The Italian law enforcement databases that the *Direzione Investigativa Antimafia* (Anti-Mafia Investigation Directorate) knew as the DIA, the Italian multi-force agency dedicated to solving and preventing mafia-related crimes, had graciously shared with the FBI, provided more information about the Camorra connection.

Valter Li Voti was on the DIA's watch lists, suspected to be the financial manager of the most powerful Camorra group in the Campania region, the Beneduce-Longobardi clan. He was thought to have been the consigliere of the late Ricardo Lombardi, the don of the Beneduce-Longobardi clan, who was killed in an explosion in the Port of Naples in 2011.

The Naples mission, Stacie thought when she heard that. She was let in on some of the details of that top-secret operation, but not all of it. "How often has this Li Voti been in contact with the 'Imam' since the date of the explosion?"

The analyst looked at her computer screen. "Hmm, quite often, once or twice a month by the looks of it. But short calls, most of them less than a minute. Ah, and one on the day after the explosion."

"To set up appointments," Stacie said.

"What?"

"The short calls were to set up meetings," Stacie said.

Leigh-Anne nodded.

"Calls before the explosion?"

Leigh-Anne looked at her screen again, scrolled down, and replied, "Yep, quite a few, same frequency and durations."

Stacie nodded. "Get me a picture of Li Voti, put it up on the link chart, and link him to the 'Imam'. Then dig up his details. Who is he working for now? Who replaced Lombardi as leader of the Beneduce-Longobardi clan? My understanding is that most of their leadership group were killed in that explosion, so, I'd like to know who'd replaced them."

Less than twenty-four hours later, Leigh-Anne gave Stacie the report. The Beneduce-Longobardi clan now had a leadership group of six, excluding Li Voti. Among the six were a Naples police officer, Rinaldo Fara, and a woman by the name of Dina Martelli, owner of a wine estate, Vinicola del Martelli, outside Naples. Li Voti was, according to DIA sources, still playing a part in the clan's business, but they had no more details. The new leader was Teresa Lombardi,

Ricardo Lombardi's only daughter. She had been keeping a very low profile and had, thus far, not given them reason to arrest her. Two of Ricardo Lombardi's sons had died with him in the explosion, his third son died of a drug overdose the day after the explosion, and Ricardo Lombardi's wife, who was terminal with cancer at the time, also passed away the same day.

Stacie was shaking her head when she read the part of the report detailing the deaths of the Lombardis. The deaths of the father and his two sons involved in the arms-for-drugs deal left her cold, but she couldn't help to feel a small measure of sympathy with Teresa Lombardi for also losing her brother and mother the day after the death of her father and two brothers.

Depending on how close the family bonds were, a tragedy like that could leave irreparable emotional scars on anyone. And I'm sure, with their resources and wide-ranging influence, by now, they'd know that explosion was no accident.

"Okay Leigh-Anne," she said, "you know the drill; pictures, addresses, biographies for all of them. I'm especially interested in this Teresa Lombardi who I guess could also be known among the clan members as Donna Teresa or Donna Lombardi."

Stacie sat there thinking for a while longer before she left the room to talk to her manager. With these kinds of investigations, the team could easily end up entangled in a web of irrelevant information, mesmerized and sidetracked by the discovery of new information with no bearing on the original case. It was part of her job as operational lead to coordinate the team effort and make sure they didn't get caught up in such a mesh.

This was one of those moments where she had to decide to pursue the Camorra connection or drop it. She had only her gut instinct, cultivated over a period of twenty-seven years of CIA analysis work, to motivate her request for full access to the files about the 2011 Naples mission. And of course, there were the suspicions, not entirely unfounded, that Hassan Walid, also known as Imam Karim Al-Sadiq, by not only his mere presence in the area at the time, but also his regular contact with Valter Li Voti, could somehow have been involved in that arms-for-drugs deal in 2011.

Legal principles such as innocent until proven guilty, were not applied in the same manner in the world of counterterrorism as elsewhere. Guilt by association or proximity, more often than not, was a starting point for any counterterrorism analyst. The Imam was in the vicinity at the time of the deal and the explosion—he and his associates had to be investigated. What his ongoing connection with the Camorra might have to do with Operation Badr, she didn't know, but she felt they had to follow the breadcrumbs just a little further.

Chapter Thirty-Three

OLD-STYLE SPYING

The ops room, CIA Headquarters, Langley, Virginia, USA

July 2015

Bryan Shafer had been Stacie's manager for the past five years, and by now he should have known to trust her instincts and not ask, "Apart from your gut feeling, have you got anything more substantial to help me convince the Director to open that file to you?"

If looks could have inflicted a handicap, Shafer would have landed in a wheelchair. Without so much as another squeak, Shafer wisely decided; *rather the wrath of the deputy director than Abram's,* and picked up the phone. He was relieved to see the Battle Tank leaving his office.

The next day, Stacie got her access to the Naples mission file, and Bryan Shafer was still in good health. She studied the file carefully, garnered a lot of new information, but no connection to Al-Sadiq.

Leaning back in her chair, she took stock.

There was obviously something going on between Li Voti and the Imam. But all her team had so far was the record of the telephone calls between the two, and those were always short—less than a minute on average. They had not discovered any connection between Li Voti or anyone of the Beneduce-Longobardi leadership group and the remaining four original Badr subjects. But she knew the fact that there was no evidence of electronic communications didn't mean there weren't any communications. It was quite possible that Al-Sadiq and Li Voti could have been the messengers between the two groups.

She was old enough to remember the Cold War and the methods used for both sides to spy on each other, and the countermeasures used to hide spying activities. In those days before the Internet and mobile phones, things were done in person, and electronic surveillance and countermeasures meant the bugging of rooms and telephones—landlines, not mobile phones. Terms such as dead-letter boxes, invisible ink, poisonous or exploding pens, street surveillance, and such made up the jargon of spies in those days. And she knew that modern-day terrorists were using those, what western intelligence agencies called archaic, methods because western intelligence had all but forgotten about them as they came to rely on technology and computers to do the work for them.

She was back in Bryan Shafer's office. She had given him a sitrep, and he was now looking at her inquisitively—eyebrows raised.

"Feet on the ground, Bryan," she said. "Tracking

devices, bugs in rooms, street teams, etcetera. On all of the original targets and the eight people in the top echelon of that Camorra outfit."

"It's a big operation you're talking about now, Stacie."

"The size of the operation is irrelevant. We've agreed, weeks ago, the presence of Hassan Walid alone was enough impetus for the operation. Terrorists like Walid don't just turn into angels overnight. Not to even mention abandoning the Shiites and joining the Sunnis. That's what both sides call apostacy and deserving of stoning or beheading. Oh, and don't forget the Camorra has become involved as well. So, what's it going to be?"

Shafer grinned and nodded. "I agree. Old-style spying is what we need. Leave it with me, I'll take care of it."

By the second week in August, Stacie's team was receiving reports from the street teams.

The CIA had outsourced their surveillance request to their most efficient private contractor, Crisis Response Consultancy, CRC, to spy on the Beneduce-Longobardi clan's leadership and Imam Al-Sadiq in Naples as well as Professor Aziz Abdul-Salam Awad in Rome. The CRC agents quickly had surveillance on every one of their charges except Teresa Lombardi. It didn't take long to learn that she lived an almost cloistered life behind the walls of her home under the protection of a contingent of no less than three armed guards.

"We'll find a way or make a way to get to her," CRC's CEO, John Brandt told Stacie and Shafer.

Haroun Najm al Din Hadad, the chemical engineer, was still unaccounted for. It irritated Stacie endlessly that they couldn't get a trace on him.

Saiyyad Rahal, in Riyadh, was under the watch of the

General Intelligence Presidency, Saudi Arabia's primary intelligence agency.

Esam Abbas Bitar, the Hezbollah politician from Beirut, was already on the Mossad's watchlist but got a lot more attention now.

Chapter Thirty-Four

A MULTI-MILLION-DOLLAR DEAL

Narva, Estonia

Sunday, August 30, 2015

Narva, a medieval stronghold dating back to the 13th century, is located in the eastern most point of Estonia and is the country's third largest city, separated from Russia by only a partially frozen river. Narva became a border town in 1991 when the Soviet Union collapsed, and Estonia regained its independence. In 2004, to the chagrin of the Russians, Estonia became part of the European Union and NATO.

It was Estonian law; to gain citizenship one has to speak the Estonian language. However, the fifty-six thousand inhabitants of Narva are almost all Russian speaking and ethnically Russian who refuse to learn Estonian. Many of them are either Russian citizens or stateless residents of Estonia, who possess gray 'resident alien' passports.

The 'Narva scenario', as some military strategists called it, was a cause for concern because it reminded them so much of the 2014 incident when Russia invaded the Ukrainian territory of Crimea and annexed it. At the time, Russian president Vladimir Putin justified his action as "my duty to protect Ukraine's Russian-speaking minority."

Over the years, Narva had produced some notable people, such as Professor Emmanuel Steinschneider (1886–1970), one of the top USSR infectious diseases specialists, Nikolai Stepulov (1913–1968), an Olympic boxer, Paul Keres (1916–1975), a chess grandmaster, and Fedot Frolov born in 1945 to Russian parents. Frolov, however, never became as well-known as the others, but he certainly gained notoriety among the few who knew what he had been up to in his life after finishing school.

After school, he studied at Moscow's Military Institute of Foreign Languages and was recruited by the KGB shortly after graduation. In the KGB, he had attained the rank of full colonel by the time the Soviet Union collapsed in 1991. During his time in the KGB he was responsible for elaborate covert operations to supply weapons to anti-Western terrorist groups and governments across the globe. He had been involved in arms supply to war torn countries on four continents and countless islands and had learned all the stratagems of the trade.

As with many of his KGB colleagues, when the KGB ceased to exist, Frolov seized the opportunity to become a capitalist and set up his own business. He used his experience and contacts in the KGB as well as the Russian and former Soviet Bloc military to go into business for himself. In the years of chaos that followed the collapse of the Soviet Union, military commanders were in control of staggering inventories of materiel. With no war to prepare for, no supply chain command, and uncertainty about their own futures, they set themselves up as wholesalers.

Those industrious military commanders were ideal partners in Frolov's fledgling business venture, and soon he had a fleet of cargo planes and secret warehouses in various places across the globe stocked to the brim with military equipment and supplies and no shortage of clientele.

By 2015, he went by the name of Egor Zubarev, one of many pseudonyms he used throughout his life to remain untraceable and become one of the world's foremost merchants of death, a black-market arms trader.

There was only one kind of weapon of mass destruction he was unable to get his hands on—nuclear weapons—but not for a lack of trying. He could however supply his clients with a wide range of other weapons of mass destruction such as biochemical weapons, poison and nerve gases, biological toxins, and infectious agents.

Since 1992, when he had opened his doors for business, he had operated under names suggesting origins from Bulgaria, Slovenia, Hungary, and many others. He was a man with more *noms de guerre* than intelligence agencies were able to keep track of, mainly because every few years he had staged his own death. Frolov was camera shy, therefore, the only two photos of him in existence in the archives of intelligence agencies outside Russia, was one in the Mossad database where his name was Saburo Szabó, from Hungary, and according to their information, dead for more than a decade. The second photo was in the CIA database describing him as a KGB colonel, Fedot Frolov, born in the Estonian border town of Narva. According to the CIA's database he had died in a tragic car accident in 1993. Neither the CIA nor the Mossad ever made the connection between the KGB colonel and the arms dealer, the worst, most ruthless and heartless son of a bitch imaginable.

It was in this potential hotspot of Narva, at the four-star Narva Hotel on Aleksander Puškini drive, where Teresa Lombardi had a secret meeting with Frolov, though she believed his name was Egor Zubarev. Whether Egor Zubarev was his real name or a pseudonym was of no consequence to Teresa. This man, she was told by Olesya Kharlamova, would be able to supply her with what she wanted.

Teresa told Li Voti she was going on a three-day trip to Rome. But she spent only one day with her business manager. From there, with her Liana Verdi passport, she traveled by plane to Tallinn, the capital of Estonia, and by private charter from there to Narva.

She was unaware that her departure from Naples had been captured by one of the CRC-operated surveillance drones, which had been circling at twenty-thousand feet above her home for the past week. Neither was she aware that her arrival in Rome as well as the lunch with her manager of Liana Verdi Art Studio had been noted and meticulously photographed by various sightseers and pedestrians. Likewise, she missed the welcoming committee, a young Estonian couple, at Lennart Meri Tallinn Airport. And that night during the dinner with Egor Zubarev in the restaurant of the Narva Hotel, neither of them paid much attention to the noisy conversation of the two couples at the table diagonally across from them.

Maybe their inattention was caused by the gravity of their own discussion—a multi-million-dollar deal.

Part VI

PRESENT DAY

Chapter Thirty-Five

I PLAN TO FIND THEM QUICKLY

Rome and Naples, Italy

Monday, August 31, 2015

When Rex and Catia with their passengers left the garage on their motorcycles, they had left the door open. They had to get away as far and quickly as possible. Within minutes after they had left, passersby found the four men in the garage, untied them, and tried to assist them.

One of the well-doer's question, "What happened?" was met with a curt, "Mugged by a gang."

The helpers found it very strange that these men, despite their obvious shock and injuries, didn't want an ambulance to be called, neither to get the police involved.

"Just help us get into the van, and we'll be okay," one of them said.

They did as they were asked, the young man with wet

pants, the only uninjured person of the four, thanked the good Samaritans and drove off.

Half an hour later, the van had one more passenger, a young woman. Shortly thereafter, it pulled into a large service station complex off the A1, the main road from Rome to Naples.

The woman got out and went to a pharmacy in search of bandages, plaster, and painkillers while the young man made a call to Naples. He had the speakerphone on so that the three passengers could hear and participate in the conversation.

Rinaldo Fara, the Naples police officer, was livid, swearing like a sailor as he strung together long phrases made up only of swearwords without repeating a single one of them.

When he had calmed down a bit, Fara said, "I just can't believe that you got your asses kicked by two women."

The young man knew very little of what had happened before his arrival at the garage, but he was absolutely sure there was nothing wrong with his brain, and that besides the two women in the garage, there was also a man with a big black dog. He was wondering if he should point that out to Fara. But a quick look at the three men with their damaged egos and in pain, convinced him it was not a good idea to get on their bad side right now.

"Well, boss," the one whom the unknown woman had kicked in the groin said, "they had help."

The young man relaxed.

"What help?"

"A man with a big black dog... I... have no idea where they came from... they... well they just appeared there... right there when I moved in to grab one of the women. I don't remember anything after that."

"Like a ghost, appearing from nowhere? Is that what you monkeys want me to believe? And let me guess, none of you got a look at those apparitions?"

Silence.

"I thought so, Pietro," Fara said to the young man with the wet pants. "Apparently, you're the only one who was not injured. What do you remember? Have you seen these ghosts?"

"No sir, I mean yes, sir. I saw them. They weren't ghosts, they were real. The man and the dog. But I only arrived on the scene after the others were already... ah... neutralized. I have no idea what happened before that."

"I know you came late on the scene, you dimwit. What I want to know is can you describe the man and the dog?"

"No sir, I... well no... I can't."

"Why the hell not? You were conscious, you saw it was a man and a dog, why can't you describe them to me?"

"Ah... I... don't know... I..."

"He was too scared, he pissed himself," one of the men said from the back.

Fara let out another string of profanities, sighed, and said, "Okay, so two women, one of them we know is Sophia, the other we know nothing about. Then there is this man and a dog whom none of you can describe but thank God we know they're not ghosts. I don't suppose any of you had the ingenuity to get the registration numbers of the motorcycles?"

A chorus of noes followed.

"But you have photos of Sophia and the woman who was with her?"

A chorus of yeses followed.

"Any others I should know about?"

Another chorus of noes followed.

"Okay, Stefano," Fara said to the leader of the group, the one whom the unknown male had karate chopped in the neck. "Talk me through everything again, slowly. Step by step from this morning when you guys started following Sophia now known as Simona Bellucci. Make sure you don't miss anything. The rest of you listen carefully and fill in any gaps."

Over the next fifteen minutes, Fara got the entire story out of them, and by the end of it, he felt like he could get into his car, drive out on the A1, and where he met the van and its occupants, commit four justifiable murders.

Naples, Italy

Li Voti was fuming. "I told you days ago we should pick up Sophia. Had you listened to me, at least we would have had her instead of nothing."

Fara chose not to respond.

Donna Teresa, although tired from her travels, having arrived back in Naples only a few hours ago, was pragmatic. "Of course, it's disappointing to have lost Sophia. But it is what it is. Let's move on.

"We know Sophia must have had cosmetic surgery. And now that she's been discovered she might have another round of it. So, we need to find out who would do such surgery and where. Put tabs on them.

"We have photos of this woman who helped Sophia. Let's find out who she is and where we can get hold of her.

"Rinaldo, from the taped conversation between you and your men, I got the impression that this woman might be trained in street craft. I'd like to have a look at the videos they took, and I suggest you also question your men more closely about this woman's behavior while she and Sophia escaped from them. If she is a professional, who does she work for?

"We don't know who the man with the dog was. But let's check every photo and every bit of video footage your men have, and don't forget the footage of the CCTV cameras in Rome. Let's find photos of him and his dog and take it from there."

"I'll get onto it right away. I plan to find them, quickly," Fara said.

Chapter Thirty-Six

TO THE TOMATS

Roma Marina Yachting, Rome, Italy

Monday, August 31, 2015

Spencer was a bit surprised when Rex's call came through on his secured satphone. However, the surprise quickly made way for excitement as he listened to Rex. He had retired about three years ago and since then his life had been boring. The most exciting things he did was play golf twice a week and go on daytrips with friends who had a sail-boat, once a month or so when the weather permitted. Getting the tap to captain the *TOMATS* was one of the most exhilarating moments of his life. And now, by the sounds of it, there could even be a bit of action. Just what a retired Navy SEAL needed to spice up his life.

Rex had given him enough background information to enable him to swing into action and make the necessary arrangements for their arrival that night.

It was about 1:00 P.M. in Italy, 4:00 A.M. in Arizona, when Spencer had called John Brandt, who, although still recovering from injuries sustained during his abduction, was back at CRC headquarters. Brandt had interrupted Spencer on a few occasions with a few choice words for the Camorra who had killed one of his boys, as he called them, Matthew Benedict, in 2011. They were still on the phone when Brandt ordered his orderly to wake up his second in command, Chris McArdle and his IT specialist, Greg Wade, and tell them to report to his office immediately.

Greg Wade's team of computer hackers were among the best in the business. With a few keystrokes, they could create havoc, black out a city, take control of their traffic lights, enter their databases and extract the plans for any building, and much more. They were not going to break a sweat to get control of Roma Marina Yachting's lights and security systems.

It took Wade and his team less than two hours to locate the security cameras at the marina and up to five miles away, hack into them and load a twenty-minute clip of the previous night's recordings. They were ready to play those clips on Brandt's order. They also told him that the security lights could be switched off on his command as well.

Brandt phoned Spencer and told him they were ready. Spencer in turn informed Rex.

At 9:50 P.M. that night, Spencer's phone rang; it was Rex telling him they were about eight miles away. Spencer told him to wait for his call as he needed to let Brandt know. Three minutes later, Spencer was back on the phone with Rex telling him the cameras were taken care of, and they had twenty minutes to get onboard.

It took Rex and Catia six minutes to cover the distance to the entrance of the marina. Just when they entered the marina the security lights flickered a few times and went out.

Three minutes later, the two motorcycles, riders, and passengers had vanished, and the security lights flickered twice before they came on again. The crew had used the onboard crane to hoist the two motorcycles from the pier straight into a storage space below the lower deck where they were properly tied down and covered with canvas.

Ten minutes after the security lights came on, the *TOMATS* lifted its anchor and started making its way out of Port Civitavecchia, also known as the Port of Rome. It would take them a bit more than an hour to get out of the territorial sea of Italy.

Spencer couldn't help but be excited as he steered the yacht westward toward the open sea. Since he got on board a week before he had made sure that she was stocked with food and water, fueled up, and ready to go. All he had been waiting for was the order to set sail. He didn't care where it would take him, as long as he could get out there on the open sea.

When they were out of the harbor, Spencer sent a brief message to John Brandt to let him know that Rex and company were safely on board and then handed it over to his first officer and went down to the second deck to attend to his guests. They were in the smaller of the two lounges with Rex, wading into food and hot drinks that one of the chefs had prepared for them. Digger, who was happy to see Spencer, got up and walked over to say hi and get a quick backrub from his new friend. Spencer smiled when he saw the look of incredulity on the faces of the two ladies as they stared around them at the opulent furnishings and decorations.

Rex introduced them to each other, in English. Other

than to say hello, goodbye, please, and thank you in Italian, Spencer knew just enough of the language to say, *non parlo Italiano*, I do not speak Italian. Catia spoke fluent English, albeit with what Rex thought an endearing Italian accent. Simona's English was passable, although she understood much more than she could speak. After the introductions, Spencer offered to take them on a tour of the yacht like he did with Rex the day before, show them their rooms and introduce them to the crew.

Rex accompanied them and wondered if the two of them were going to be as impressed with the yacht as he had been the day before. He was not disappointed. Their mouths were hanging open almost all the way. When Spencer showed them their rooms, the two of them all but shrieked in excitement.

And that's when Rex realized that Catia and Simona had only the clothes they were wearing, and no toiletries. His mind went into overdrive trying to figure out what could be done about it.

Spencer saw the look on Rex's face and asked about it, and he smiled as Rex told him what worried him. He looked at the two ladies and said, "The toiletries, no problem, we have some basic items stocked up. I'll arrange with one of the female crew members to take care of it. The clothes, well, that's a bit more of a problem. We do have various sized female uniforms. I'm sure some of those might fit you ladies. It would only be for a day or so until we can get you to a shop."

Catia and Simona smiled, thanked them for being so considerate, and assured them they would be okay.

Chapter Thirty-Seven

ANOTHER ARMS DEAL IN THE MAKING

*The Badr Ops Room, CIA Headquarters, Langley,
Virginia, USA*

Monday, August 31, 2015

Stacie Barrett had been studying the photos and video footage that came in from the CRC surveillance teams. She looked at the pictures of Teresa Lombardi first. "Ahh, so you're also Liana Verdi," she mumbled. "Well, at least now we know what you look like. Let's see who you keep company with."

Five minutes later, Bryan Shafer was in the ops room staring at the images on the big TV screen. The first one was of a petite, blond-haired, fair-skinned, blue-eyed, beautiful woman whom he estimated to be in her mid-thirties.

"Teresa Lombardi," Stacie said, "also known as Liana Verdi, owner of Liana Verdi Art Studio in Rome."

"Interesting," Shafer said deep in thought. "We, or

rather the Italian anti-mafia squad, think she's the boss of the Beneduce-Longobardi clan?"

Stacie nodded and said, "Now hold onto your britches," as she flipped to the next slide. "Recognize this guy? When he is not teaching students about the Middle East, he is the business manager of Liana Verdi Art Studio."

Shafer took a step closer to the screen, studied it for a moment, and then turned his head to the link chart on the wall. "Bingo! Professor Aziz Abdul-Salam Awad. There's your link to the Camorra. Excellent work, Stacie."

Stacie waved her finger. "No Bryan, the honor goes to the excellent work of the street teams. Now, exciting as that might have been, we still don't know what they're planning. But I have a gut feeling this next guy might give us an indication of what they're up to."

She advanced to the next slide. Everyone in the room was looking at the images of the man who had been dining with Teresa Lombardi in Narva the night before. He was thin and bony, with hollow cheeks and a big nose that didn't fit his lean face. His dark-brown eyes, deep-sunk into their sockets, were piercing, the eyes of a pitiless soul.

"These photos were taken last night in the restaurant of the Narva Hotel in Narva, Estonia. We've got no idea who this man is," Stacie said, "but the location of the meeting, right there on the border with Russia, and with the presumed leader of the most influential Camorra clan in Italy, could not have been to make Christmas party arrangements."

"You'll get no arguments from me," Shafer said. "I'll get the backing from someone higher up to assign top priority to the facial recognition effort."

The CIA's and FBI's computerized facial recognition systems were the best on the planet. They were programmed to capture facial features that were unique to each individual, like fingerprints. The size and shape of eyes, the distance between the pupils of the eyes, shape and size of ears and noses, jawlines, and hundreds more features were measured and stored. Those powerful computers could sometimes find matches within seconds, never longer than two hours, as long as there was at least one photo in their databases to compare it to.

One of the major tasks of intelligence agencies around the world was to collect pictures and upload them to their facial recognition databases. Pictures of criminals and potential criminals, officials, politicians, diplomats, trade delegates, visitors, tourists, scientists, and many more were collected annually in their hundreds of thousands. Spies from the Cold War era and thereafter had gotten their hands on the files of adversaries and potential adversaries. Between the members of Five Eyes and the Mossad there existed archives of many millions of pictures, all of them scanned and measured by the facial recognition software and just waiting to be called upon to match what it had with a new picture given to it. These databases were never purged, they simply kept growing.

Stacie and Shafer were looking over the shoulder of the facial recognition analyst when the system produced its first report. It was a list of potential names ranked by percentage match. All the scores except one were below fifty percent. The eighty percent match was of an erstwhile KBG colonel, Fedot Frolov.

"That photo in the database is probably a quarter of a century old. Can you age it by twenty-five years and run it again?"

"No, problem," the analyst said.

Ten minutes later, they had no doubt that the man who

had dinner with Teresa Lombardi in Narva the night before was the presumed dead former KBG colonel, Fedot Frolov, in charge of arms distribution to anti-Western terror groups and governments during the Cold War. And he was very much alive and in apparent good health.

"So, now to find out what the resurrected Colonel Frolov has been up to since his death in 1993," Shafer said as they walked back to the ops center.

"Definitely more than only treating beautiful Camorrista ladies to cozy dinners in Narva," Stacie said.

CIA Headquarters, Langley, Virginia

The photos and facial recognition results were sent to the Five Eyes partners and Mossad to compare with their databases and to comment. And it caused quite a stir at the Mossad headquarters in Tel Aviv, Israel. So much so that less than three hours after the information was sent out, Samuel Naor, the second in charge of Mossad's Research Department, tasked with intelligence production, made a secured call to his old friend Bryan Shafer.

After the usual greetings and questions about health and well-being of each other and their families, Shafer said, "Samuel, I appreciate your call, but I'm sure you didn't stay in the office until ten at night your time just to check that I'm still in the office at three on a Friday afternoon or to find out how my family and I are doing?"

Naor laughed. "C'mon Bryan, we're old friends, that's what friends do."

"Yeah, right, of course."

"But now that you've mentioned it, there *is* another reason for my call."

"Uh-oh, here it comes."

"Those photos that your teams have collected the last few days. Man, they have certainly raised more than a few eyebrows over here."

"Samuel, can you just hold the line for one second," Shafer interrupted. "I have the feeling that what you're about to tell me will be of much interest to Stacie Barrett, the team leader of Operation Badr. That okay with you?"

"No problem, I'll hold."

Thirty seconds later, Stacie was in Shafer's office, the phone was on speaker, and Shafer introduced Stacie and Naor to each other.

Naor started with Teresa Lombardi, whom the Mossad knew as Liana Verdi, and told them that the Mossad had been watching her for quite a few years because of their suspicions that she had been dealing illegally in Middle Eastern antiquities. Not only that, that they had unsubstantiated information that some of her illicit deals were with certain anti-Israeli terrorist groups. But they have not been able to catch her in the act as yet.

"It was, to put it mildly, a nasty surprise to learn that she's actually Teresa Lombardi, the daughter and, by the looks of it, the successor of the late Ricardo Lombardi who tried to send an enormous shipment of weapons to Hezbollah and Al-Qaeda in 2011. The deal that ended in disaster for Lombardi and his cronies, as you know," Naor said.

"So, Miss Lombardi's good looks are indeed deceiving," Shafer said.

"Yep, you've got that right, and I'll tell you why. It's her association with that guy with the remarkable ability to raise from the dead, the one who you know as Fedot Frolov, the former KGB colonel. We had him in our database as Saburo Szabó from Hungary, an international illicit arms dealer who died in 2005 from a heart attack."

Stacie said, "Well, Samuel, I'm not entirely surprised that this guy was, and I'm willing to bet, still is, involved in black market arms trading. After all, that's what he was trained to do in the KGB. What *is* surprising though is how he has managed to evade detection by the world's intelligence agencies for so long."

"Well, he seems to be a master at cheating death. He has certainly managed to pull the wool over our and your eyes for many years. And my guess is, just by looking at the backgrounds of our two diners there in Narva, we've got another arms deal in the making."

Chapter Thirty-Eight

I FELL IN LOVE WITH YOU

Off the coast of Italy

Monday, August 31, 2015

When they were a few miles outside Italy's territorial waters, Spencer had sent another brief message to John Brandt to let him know they were out of the Italian jurisdiction en route to Corsica. He then plotted a course to the port of Bastia on the east coast of the French island of Corsica, birthplace of Napoleon Bonaparte, and the fourth-largest island in the Mediterranean. It was about one-hundred and forty nautical miles away. At a cruise speed of fifteen nautical miles per hour it would take less than ten hours to reach.

Rex decided it was time to sit down, bring Spencer up to date, and plan what they were going to do next. No one had to tell him that neither Catia nor Simona, and probably not even himself, could go back to Rome, or Italy for that matter, until they had addressed the threat posed by the Camorra.

Simona had to let her manager know she would not be coming back to work for the foreseeable future. It was decided that she would call her manager in the morning and spin a story about her father who took ill, that she was an only child, her mother had passed away years ago, and there was no one else who could take care of him.

Catia had to plan for someone to mind her AirBnB until further notice. That turned out to be easy. She had hired an assistant the year before when she commenced her PHD studies. The assistant would be more than capable of running the place for an indefinite period, if required. Catia would contact her in the morning and make the necessary arrangements.

Rex told them that he had no such issues to deal with and that, in fact, he was in his home. Seeing the inquisitive looks on their faces he told them about the agreement he had with CRC about the yacht but withheld the part about how it was acquired. Spencer knew the history but was not going to tell anyone without Rex's or Brandt's say-so.

The next topic was how to remain anonymous and off the grid which meant no Internet use and no mobile phones unless it was secured and untraceable. It was a topic Rex knew a lot about. Catia, as a *sayan* for Mossad, had helped people, including Simona, disappear before and knew what it took to remain in hiding. Simona of course, had her personal experience which worked well for four years until she broke the rules and almost got them captured was it not for Marco's and Digger's timely arrival.

Catia told Rex and Simona about the bounties on their heads. Simona was shocked. Rex just laughed and said, "Finally, someone realized how valuable I am. Four million you say. That means between Simona and I we're worth six million Euros. Not too shabby, I'd say. What do you reckon Simona?"

Rex's wittiness soon had Simona laughing.

Finally, they got to the question that had been bothering Catia since that morning. "Marco, I think this is a good time to explain your presence at the *Piazza del Popolo* at such a very appropriate time this morning. Oh, and remember you asked me to remind you not to use the word coincidence in your explanation."

Rex grinned and exhaled. He was on the spot. For four years he wanted to see this woman and tell her that he loved her. In his dreams, awake and asleep, thousands of times, he had envisaged the moment when he would tell her. But not in one single one of them had he envisaged the current situation.

He looked at Digger, but he was half asleep. Digger opened one eye and peaked at Rex, with a look that could only have meant one thing. "Don't look at me. What would I know about the affection between men and women, right?" He sighed and went back to sleep.

"Okay, hmm… where shall I start? Okay, I guess the best place is with my real name." But before he could continue, he was interrupted by a loud yawn from Digger. He looked at him and saw Digger had both his eyes open, and that yawn probably meant, "Mate, get on with it, stop beating around the bush."

Rex decided to ignore Digger and continued to tell them what his real name was. Spencer only knew him by his real name, and neither Catia nor Simona were much surprised.

When Rex stopped, Catia said, "Okay, Rex, thanks for that. You know Simona's real name, and I don't have an alias. But what's that got to do with your mystical appearance this morning?"

Rex cleared his throat and started, "Catia, in 2010 and 2011 when we worked together, I fell in love with you..."

Before he could continue, Spencer cleared his throat, pushed his chair back, grabbed Simona's hand, helped her to her feet, and said to Rex and Catia, "Please excuse us, we've been overwhelmed by a sudden need of something to drink and nibble on. We'll be in the small lounge."

Catia smiled, nodded to them, and then turned back to Rex who looked very uneasy, and in Italian she said, "Please continue."

"Yeah, well... like I said, I fell in love with you... and I'm still... ah... in love with you," Rex replied, in Italian.

Catia's smile had grown bigger.

Rex caught a quick glimpse at Digger and saw the smile on the dog's face. Rex had regained enough of his composure to discern that Catia's smile was not because she found what he said amusing, it was because she liked what she heard. It was encouraging.

It took more than thirty minutes, including questions from Catia, for Rex to explain what he had been doing, some of it in not too much detail, since he saw her the last time in 2011. He told her how he had been at her doorstep seven weeks before, saw her but had to leave, and that he was now back again to see her and tell her that he loved her. By then she had placed her hand on his and her eyes had acquired that knee-buckling aquamarine color.

"So, there you have it," Rex said. "As for how it came about that Digger and I were there this morning, at that specific time, you can pick from the following: providence, prescience, divine intervention, luck, or none of the above."

"Rex Dalton, that is the longest compliment any man

has ever given me and by far the most beautiful and most romantic. Thank you. And although I can't say that I have thought as much about you as you apparently have of me, I can assure you I *did* think a lot about you. And if I have to pick the reason for why you were there this morning, I'd go for providence and divine intervention."

Rex didn't exactly expect that she would have felt the same about him, but what she said surely gave him hope and inspiration. And he was relieved that she apparently had no one else in her life at the moment, otherwise she would have told him so.

She must have read his mind. "I'm glad you're here, not just because you've saved us, but because I'd very much like to continue where we left off in 2011."

In that moment, Rex Dalton would not have believed it if anyone told him there was a happier man on the planet. He looked at Digger, pointed at the door, and said, "Digger, go get Declan and Simona. Go boy, get them."

When Digger went through the door, Catia looked at Rex in wonder. "Digger understands that?"

Rex shrugged. "I think he did. I've never learned to give him proper commands. So, over time he must have figured out what I want. We'll soon know if he understood that one."

A few minutes later, Spencer and Simona walked through the door with Digger behind them as if he was herding them.

Spencer said, "I guess Digger was sent to fetch us?"

Catia started clapping her hands and went to meet Digger. "You are one clever boy, Digger."

And of course, Digger was on cloud nine, with Rex.

Chapter Thirty-Nine

ANOTHER GHOST FROM THE PAST

En route to Corsica

Tuesday, September 1, 2015

On the *TOMATS*, it was past midnight and no prospect of sleep for Rex as yet. The next important matter was to have a video call with John Brandt. Rex decided it was best to let the women get some sleep while he and Spencer had the call with the Old Man. If necessary, they could have another call in the morning with Catia and Simona present.

When John Brandt's face came on the big screen in the communications room on the *TOMATS*, he characteristically, without any greetings, started the conversation with, "Dalton, I thought you were done with me and CRC, and I had the right to ignore your calls after making the yacht available to you."

Spencer, unaccustomed to the way Rex and John sometimes interacted, shifted uneasily in his chair.

Rex shrugged. "Yeah, well you're the one who told me never to say never. I guess you were right. Oh, by the way, thanks for everything you did to get the yacht ready. Though, I suspect you must have had a few glasses too many of Hemingway's Death in the Afternoon when you chose the name."

Hemingway loved Champagne and reportedly once said, "If I have any money, I can't think of any better way of spending money than on Champagne." But Hemingway liked to 'enhance' his Champagne with absinthe, a green, bitter herbal anise-flavored spirit known for its hallucinogenic side effects to create his own unique cocktail that became known as Death in the Afternoon.

Spencer was shaking his head. It would take him a while to realize that the apparent belligerence between the two was all a charade. They respected and held each other in the highest regard.

Just then, Digger came into view, and to Rex's surprise the Old Man's face lit up, and instead of saying, 'there's that damn dog of yours', he greeted him with a very polite, "Hey Digger, good to see you again, boy."

Digger wagged his tail, smiled, woofed once, and sat down on the floor next to Rex.

Someone, probably Josh Farley, must have told the Old Man that Digger was the superstar of his rescue operation a few weeks ago.

"Okay Dalton, I've answered your call, I might as well listen to what you have to say."

The Old Man soon turned serious as he listened in silence to Rex telling him what had happened since he met Catia and Simona at the *Piazza del Popolo* and what the two ladies told him since he had rescued them.

"I questioned that young guy who drove the van, he told me that they worked for a police officer in Naples, Rinaldo

Fara. He told us that they knew Simona Bellucci is actually Sophia Maiorani and that the Naples police want to question her about Matthew Benedict's murder in 2011.

"So, I am pretty sure there is some connection to the Camorra. That same outfit that was involved in the drugs-for-arms deal that we stopped during the 2011 Naples mission."

"Hmm, Rinaldo Fara you said?"

"Yes, that's the name the van driver gave me."

"Hang on for just a second, I want to check something." Brandt turned to his computer screen next to him and typed on the keyboard. A minute or so later, he turned back to face Rex and Spencer again. "You're right about the Bene-duce-Longobardi outfit's involvement in this."

"Are you saying that Fara is connected to the clan?"

"Yes."

"How do you know?"

"I'll get to that in a moment. Let me first give you my opinion why I think the Beneduce-Longobardis are involved. I think they've been hunting those who ruined their deal and killed their leaders back in 2011. Those organized crime groups never take kindly to anyone meddling in their business. So, I reckon they've been looking for Sophia, or Simona as she is now known, for years, couldn't find her until she was so stupid to contact her mother, and attended the funeral. I think that's how they discovered her and followed her."

"Okay, that makes sense," Rex said. "But what doesn't make sense is that Simona told us she saw that van driver and a woman in front of her apartment every morning for the last few days. In other words, they knew where she was. Why didn't they pick her up earlier?"

Brandt shrugged. "Your guess is as good as mine. I'd say

they didn't make a move because they knew where to get hold of her and kept a watch on her to find out who she has contact with. I'll place a bet that they bugged Simona's apartment."

Rex nodded slowly in agreement. "And when they realized that Catia had discovered them, they decided it was better to move in and capture Simona rather than risk losing her again."

"Yep."

"Okay, so what's the story with this policeman, Fara?"

"Now that's a bit more of a prickly problem."

"Why?"

"Well, Declan works for CRC, he's got security clearance. But you're not working for me. So, I can't share top secret information with you."

Rex went quiet for a few moments before he said, "Okay, you've got some mission on the go. And I get the impression it involves this Camorra mob. If that's the case, I'm available for a contract."

Brandt grinned; it was exactly what he hoped Rex would say. "In that case, welcome back, and with that your clearance has been reinstated. Just one question though; what about the woman you told me about? The one that got your head so messed up that you *had* to leave CRC?"

Rex smiled. "You'd just love to know, wouldn't you?"

Brandt grinned and made no reply.

"But, and just to put your mind at ease, I found her, she's right here on the yacht. It's Catia."

Brandt grinned. "Ahh, I see. And I guess you're now going to regale us with a tale about the princess who kissed the frog?"

"None of your business, Old Man. What's the story with this mission?"

Brandt and Spencer laughed at Rex's discomfiture.

"Well, John," Spencer said when he stopped laughing, "I have to come to Rex's rescue here. I've seen the princess, and although I wasn't there for the kissing ceremony, because I left during the prelude, let me tell you, I can only compliment Rex on his exquisite taste."

"Yeah, that might be so," Brandt retorted, "but regardless of not having had the privilege of meeting the princess, I already know I won't be complimenting her on *her* taste."

Rex was shaking his head. "With friends like you, I need no enemies."

When the gibing came to an end, Brandt became serious again and told them about Operation Badr and his agents' work in Italy. He told them about the worrying discoveries made by his team over the past twenty-four hours when they had not only learned about Teresa Lombardi but also about Fedot Frolov aka Saburo Szabó, the illicit arms dealer.

"So, by the sounds of it we're looking at another potential arms deal?" Rex said.

"Yes, that's what we're thinking." Brandt said.

"Okay, and this reference to Badr that the CIA picked up in intercepted communications, what's the take on that?" Spencer asked.

"I'm not a history buff like Rex is, but my understanding is it could be a reference to some important battle in Islamic history. What the significance of it could be for this group, I don't know."

They both looked at Rex.

"Badr or Badr Hunayn is a town in Saudi Arabia, not too far, about eighty miles, from Medina. That's where, circa 624 AD, if my memory serves me, Muhammad's forces battled the forces of the Quraysh tribe from Mecca and kicked their asses. It was not the first of Muhammad's battles, but it was the first one where he emerged victorious. Muslims regard that battle as a turning point in Islamic history. That's when they established themselves as the new force to be reckoned with on the Arabian Peninsula."

Spencer, not familiar with Rex's near eidetic memory, was surprised at his ability to recall and recount the historical facts with so much ease and confidence.

"Okay, so what do you reckon could be the connection between that battle and this Badr outfit we're talking about today?" Spencer asked.

Rex shrugged. "All I can think of is that this group has something in mind that would be another watershed moment in Islamic history."

Brandt and Spencer were staring at Rex. "So, the question is, what would it take for them to cause such a defining moment?" Brandt said.

"Another battle. Not in the conventional sense, they know they'd get annihilated in an open confrontation with any of the western militaries. But if they could get their hands on nukes and obliterate a few cities such as DC, New York, London, and others, it might create such a moment for them," Rex said.

"I agree that would be a major event for them," Spencer said. "But it would also be the end of them, and they know that. The thing is, they've been trying forever to get nukes but, thank God, have never been able to get them."

Brandt nodded. "A former Director of the CIA once told me, that there is a kind of unwritten but very clear understanding between the US and all Muslim countries that if anyone from their countries, whether their government knew about it or not, ever sets off a nuclear bomb anywhere in the West or Israel, they should expect a nuclear retaliation from America. And it won't be just a like for like response; it would be a response of the kind that would send them back to the time before Muhammad walked the earth."

"Okay, let's assume for now it's not nukes they have in mind," Rex said. "There are a lot of other weapons of mass destruction such as biochemical and chemical that they're able to acquire with much less hassle and a lot easier to hide and transport."

Brandt said, "Well, a panel of top analysts at CIA head-quarters had the same discussion since we gave them those photos yesterday, and I'm told they ended with the same conclusion as us—they don't know. And that's why CRC has been briefed by Martin Richardson, deputy director in charge of CIA operations, to get more information—urgently."

"Okay, before we get to my mission briefing," Rex said, "just a few more things, if you don't mind, John?"

"Go for it."

"The thing is, those men that tried to abduct Catia and Simona saw their faces, probably took photos of them. Through all their connections, which we know include the police and, in all likelihood, other government agencies, they'd be looking for them now. We need to think how we can get the two of them to safety."

"I've already been thinking about it," Brandt said. "Maybe we can bring them over to the US and keep them here in a safe place until this is all over. But I guess we need to ask them about it first?"

"Agreed. Next question, you haven't told me about the policeman, Rinaldo Fara and his link to the Camorra yet."

"Ah, yes, of course. Well, while I'm at it, let me give you a quick rundown of the clan's leadership and where he fits in. You see, after you killed most of the clan's leaders in that explosion in 2011, they did a bit of organizational restructuring.

"Teresa Lombardi is now the new boss, known among the clan members as Donna Teresa. As I've told you before, she sometimes uses the alias Liana Verdi. That's the name she used a day or so ago when she met that scumbag Frolov in Estonia. And according to the Mossad, she used the name in the past when she was involved in what they believed was illicit antiquities trading. She is the owner of the Liana Verdi Art Studio in Rome.

"Her consigliere is Valter Li Voti, he did the same job for her late father, Ricardo Lombardi.

"Below them they have six more people in their leadership group, and Rinaldo Fara, the Naples police officer, is one of them."

Rex had a grim look on his face when Brandt finished.

"What's the matter, son?"

"This is like phase two of the Naples mission of 2011, another ghost from the past."

"Yeah, probably is. But remember this, son; you and I didn't ask for or start this war, they pushed it on us. So, I've always felt it's good manners to oblige the bastards and take part in it."

Rex smiled wryly. That was John Brandt, sharp and to the point. "Yep, I'm not going to be rude and disappoint them either."

Brandt looked at the array of clocks on the wall, set to the different time zones in the major cities of the world, and said, "You had a long day over there already. I suggest you get a few hours' sleep, and let's meet again at six your time."

"Good idea," said Spencer. "I can do with a bit of shuteye."

"Oh, Rex, I think for the first part of our meeting later, it's best if you bring in only Catia. There are a few things that we need to talk to her about which Simona doesn't need to know."

"No problem. See you in a few hours."

Chapter Forty

I'M NOT RUNNING AWAY

Onboard the TOMATS and CRC HQ in Arizona, USA

Tuesday, September 1, 2015

By 6:00 a.m. local time, Rex, Catia, and Spencer were seated in the communications room and connected through the secured satellite link with John Brandt. He had Chris McArdle, his second in command with him. Simona had bribed Digger with a few treats to accompany her to spent time with some of the female crew.

When Rex introduced Catia to Brandt and McArdle he noticed the mischievous grin on Brandt's face and expected another round of gibing.

Brandt didn't disappoint. "Declan," he said, "I can see what you told me about the princess earlier was spot on."

Catia had no idea what Brandt was talking about and looked at Rex for help, but he was staring out the window.

She kicked him lightly on the shin, leaned over, and asked in a whisper, "What's he talking about?"

"Not important for now. I'll tell you later."

Rex was still under the impression that Catia worked for Britain's MI6 and was very surprised when Brandt turned his gaze back to Catia and said, "So, Catia, you're the *sayan* who trained Rex in 2010 and supported him during the 2011 Naples mission?"

"Wait, hang on. You two know each other? And did I hear you say *sayan*?" Rex interrupted before Catia could respond. "That means you're Mossad not MI6. Why... how come... I..."

Catia grinned and nodded. "John and I don't know each other, Rex. We know *of* each other. As for being a *sayan*, it was about need-to-know; you didn't need to know at the time. And by the way, you haven't exactly been forthcoming, either."

"Yeah... but I would've liked..."

Brandt laughed and said, "She's right, Rex. You didn't have to know it was a joint CIA-Mossad operation. Would it have made any difference if you knew?"

Rex shrugged. "I guess not."

Brandt continued. "Catia, Rex briefed me about everything that happened yesterday and also told me all about Simona. Our immediate concern is to get the two of you to safety as quickly as possible. I need Rex to take care of a few things for me, so he will have to stay for a while longer.

"So, my suggestion is that I make arrangements for you and Simona to fly over to the US as soon as you arrive in Bastia. When we have you over here, I will make sure you are set up in a safe place and arrange for your protection. Unless, of course, you'd prefer the Mossad to take care of it? If you want to, I'll be happy to give Yaron a call to set it up."

Yaron Aderet was the head of the Mossad's largest department, Collections, tasked with all the many aspects of conducting espionage overseas.

"Huh, you know Yaron?" Catia asked, very surprised.

"Indeed, I do. For a long time. He always pays me a visit when he comes over to the States, and I return the favor when I'm in Israel. We've known each other for... let me see... wow! I can't believe it... almost thirty years. In our young days Yaron and I had a few joint missions and more than just a few glasses of arak."

Arak is a potent drink made by distilling grapes into what is known as neutral alcohol, ninety-five percent pure, to which anise is then added, rendering a clear, licorice-flavored drink served with ice, to which water, lemonade, or grapefruit juice could be added.

Catia smiled. She had never met Yaron Aderet, but she knew all about him. He was a highly respected man among his friends and feared by the enemies of Israel. "I'd appreciate it very much if you could give him a call and clear the way for me to talk to you openly. I tried to get hold of my *katsa* yesterday but was told he would be unreachable for an unknown period. I also have to let you know that I have a kind of unusual relationship with the Mossad at the moment. I asked them to release me from my duties about a year ago to focus on my PHD studies. They agreed to my request but with the proviso that I'd continue to be Simona's *sayan* and keep in touch with my *katsa*."

"Okay, let's take a break. I'll see if I can get hold of Yaron," Brandt said.

Half an hour later, Brandt and McArdle were back on the screen. "Catia, I just had a great conversation with

Yaron. He said he'd never met you, but while we were on the phone, he pulled your file and read me a few very flattering comments about you."

"Thanks," Catia said, a bit embarrassed.

"But, having said that, unfortunately, I have some sad news. Your handler or *katsa* as you call them, David Sternberg, apparently had a stroke three days ago. He's in intensive care, unable to talk at the moment."

Catia's hand had flown to her mouth but couldn't stifle the, "Oh my God. He's only forty something."

"However, Yaron told me," Brandt continued, "according to the doctors, if he doesn't have another stroke, there is a good chance that he'll make a near full recovery over the next few months."

Catia's eyes were swimming in tears when she said, "I can only hope and pray he'll make it through this. He's got a wife and two young children."

"I'm sorry to be the bearer of such bad news," Brandt said.

Catia nodded.

"Okay, the rest of our conversation was much happier than that," Brandt continued. "Yaron said he'd leave it to you to decide if you want the Mossad to step in and help you and Simona get to safety or if you want to take up my offer. He also said he's got no problem if you want to share sensitive information with us and vice versa. He left it to you to make the call about what we need to know or not.

"Finally, he also said I could give you his direct number to confirm what I said is true or if you need his advice on anything. Here's his number if you'd like to write it down."

Catia held her hand up. "Thanks for clearing things up on my behalf, John. I don't need to call him; I know I can trust you and everyone else here."

"Thanks, Catia. I want you to know the trust is mutual. Let's move on then," Brandt said. "I take it you'll need a bit of time to think about who you want to take you and Simona under their wings. Us or the Mossad?"

"I can't speak for Simona. I'll put the options to her. But as far as I'm concerned, Italy is my home. Yes, I am Jewish, but I was born and bred in Italy, my ancestors have been living in Italy for more than four and a half centuries. We were there before the Camorra even existed. If there is any operation, and I suspect there is one, against those Camorra hoodlums, I want to be part of it. So, thanks for your offer, but no thanks, I'm not running away from those criminals."

If they were not in the presence of other people, this would have been the moment when Rex would have taken her into his arms and kissed her. As it were, instead, he smiled like a proud father at the birth of his first child.

Brandt looked at McArdle, got a slight nod from him, then at Spencer, got another nod from him, and then at Rex, saw the smile on his face, and turned his eyes to Catia. "Yaron told me that's exactly what he'd expect you to say. So, let me tell you what's cooking. But before I proceed, please know there is no obligation on you to participate in it. If at any stage you want out, feel free to say so."

Catia nodded and said, "I'm all ears."

Brandt took fifteen minutes to give Catia a rundown of Operation Badr, and when he got to the end, he asked her, "You still in?"

"Absolutely. Wouldn't miss it for the world."

Brandt smiled, thanked her, and asked McArdle to lead the planning session.

Over the course of the next hour they agreed that Rex and Spencer would set up a virtual joint operation center on the *TOMATS*, similar to the one they had a few weeks before when Rex and a few other people he now considered his crew, Rehka Gyan, Josh Farley, and Marissa Bisset, based themselves on the family estate of Rex's friend, Margot Lemaire, in Lyon France. They had established a secured permanent audio and video connection with the ops center at CRC headquarters in Arizona. It had been the proximity of the Lyon ops center to the ship where John Brandt had been kept after his kidnapping that enabled Rex, Josh, and Digger to reach and rescue Brandt in the nick of time.

It didn't take much from Rex to convince Brandt and McArdle to let him have his old team back—Rehka, his IT specialist, and Josh and Marissa, former colleagues who still worked for CRC. It did however take a bit more of Rex's persuasive powers to get Brandt's and McArdle's agreement to let Greg Wade, CRC's head IT specialist, join his team as well. When they finally gave in to Rex's demands, they noted the smile on his face and wondered if it was caused by the fact that he got his way or for some other reason.

Rex didn't tell him that apart from how well the two worked together on the previous mission, he'd also noticed the vibes between Rehka and Greg. And that was the other reason he wanted to give them the opportunity to meet each other in person and work together.

McArdle said he would arrange with Josh, Marissa, and Greg to meet them in Bastia in the next day or two. Rex had to make his own arrangements directly with Rehka. As soon as the team was aboard, they had to sail to Naples and wait outside the Italian territorial waters until further notice.

Catia had to talk to Simona and find out what she wanted to do. Brandt told her to convey his and Yaron's offers and their recommendation that she took one of them up to let them take her to safety.

Chapter Forty-One

I'LL BRIEF THE PRESIDENT

CIA Headquarters, Langley, Virginia, USA

Thursday, September 3, 2015

It was 10:00 A.M. in Virginia, Thursday the 3rd of September, when Bryan Shafer and Abrams were back in the secured meeting room, briefing the Director of the CIA, three deputy directors, and two of the most senior analysts from the Directorate of Operations, on the progress they had made on Operation Badr.

If the discovery of the connection between the original Badr five and the Camorra was not already enough cause for deep concern, the name of Fedot Frolov popping up in the mix really had their hair standing on end.

With Frolov's picture on the screen, Stacie elaborated, "According to information in our archives, last updated twenty-two years ago, shortly after the Cold War, and in the

Mossad's archives, last updated a decade ago, this guy was one nasty son of a bitch. And we believe he still is."

Lawrence and the others grinned slightly at Stacie's choice of words.

"Until yesterday, we, the CIA, believed he died in 1993. The Mossad had him in their archives as Saburo Szabó from Hungary, suspected of being involved in supplying arms to Hezbollah. Apparently, he only came to their attention in 2002 when one of their undercover agents took a photo of him in Beirut where he met with a prominent figure of Hezbollah's Jihad Council. But then he died, yet again, in 2004. Until yesterday, when we showed them this picture and a few others, they didn't know he was Fedot Frolov, the former KGB colonel and of course, neither of us knew he had risen from the dead—twice."

Stacie nodded at Shafer who took over and told them about Frolov's work in the KGB and the little that the Mossad had on record. "So, it must be obvious that we have a serious lack of intelligence about this guy. However, until we get evidence to the contrary, we think it's prudent to assume he is a low-life black-market arms dealer."

Lawrence nodded and said, "Agreed. Bryan can you give us an overview of the parts of the puzzle you've managed to assemble so far?"

"Sir, the picture that has emerged so far has three parts; the original Badr Five, the Camorra, and this Frolov character.

"Of the Badr Five, the two most worrisome characters because of their links to terrorist groups, are Esam Abbas Bitar, the Hezbollah politician with links to the Jihad Council and Hassan Walid aka Imam Karim Al-Sadiq in Naples, member of Amn al-Muddad. We now also know he has regular contact with the consigliere of the boss of the

Beneduce-Longobardis. Aziz Abdul-Salam Awad, the professor of Middle Eastern Studies at Università Cattolica del Sacro Cuore, Rome, we have discovered, is also connected to the same Camorra clan as Walid.

"Of course, the missing scientist, Haroun Najm al Din Hadad, purely because of his technical knowledge and the malicious ends to which he can use it, remains a major concern. We have not found him as yet and that—the fact that it seems he doesn't want to be found—is an indication that he might be up to no good."

The Director nodded and looked at deputy director Martin Richardson. "Martin, double the effort, pull out all the stops if you have to, talk to our allies, get them to double their efforts. We need to know where this guy is and what he's up to."

"Will do, sir."

Shafer continued. "The Camorra part of the picture consists of Teresa Lombardi the leader of the Beneduce-Longobardi clan, her consigliere, one Valter Li Voti, and of course the rest of their leadership group of six which includes a high-ranking Naples police officer, Rinaldo Fara.

"Teresa Lombardi, referred to by her clan members as Donna Teresa, sometimes uses the alias Liana Verdi. She is the owner of Liana Verdi Art Studio in Rome which we discovered is managed on her behalf by Professor Aziz Abdul-Salam Awad, mentioned before. The Mossad knows her by her Liana Verdi alias which she used in the past for, what they believe to be, illicit dealing in Middle Eastern antiquities with terrorist groups.

"The last part of the picture is this Fedot Frolov aka Saburo Szabó, assumed international illegal arms dealer, twice dead but still very much alive."

"Did we ever find out who supplied the arms to that

Camorra clan for their deal with the terrorists in 2011?" Lawrence asked.

"No, sir. Not to my knowledge."

"Nonetheless, Frolov's reputation as an arms dealer precedes him, so I'd say there is a good chance we're looking at another illegal arms deal in progress," Lawrence said.

Shafer nodded. "Yes sir, Stacie and I concur. We called a group of senior analysts together yesterday to evaluate the information and discuss possible scenarios. The takeaway is, as you have concluded, at this stage everything points to an arms deal.

"We've also ventured into the aspects of the target, the what, how, when, and where. However, with the limited amount of intelligence available to us at present, those discussions were obviously quite speculative. Even so, the group is of the opinion that, given the information we have and the involvement of Frolov and the Camorra, this might not be the usual small arms, ammunition, rocket launchers, and explosives type deal…"

"Why?" The deputy director in charge of operations, Martin Richardson, to whom Shafer reported interjected.

"Sir, it's the use of the word Badr by the original five, all of them Muslims. The word has only appeared in communications between those five. So far, there has been no other explanation for the word than the significance it holds in Islamic history. The analysts are of the opinion that one of the possible scenarios is that we might be facing an attempt to create another Badr type event. In other words, another momentous episode in Islamic history."

"And what did the group think would constitute such an event?" Lawrence asked.

"Well, sir, bearing in mind at the moment it's only

conjecture, one possibility is the use of one or more weapons of mass destruction such as a nuclear bomb in one or more strategic locations. As you know, for the Islamic radicals, to get their hands on nukes has proved to be an impossible dream so far. And it might still be the case. However, getting their hands on chemical and biochemical weapons of mass destruction is not nearly as difficult as acquiring nukes."

"All the more reason to track down that chemical engineer," Lawrence said.

A protracted silence descended in the room as everyone processed the information.

Finally, Lawrence broke the quiet and said to Richardson, "Martin, are we in agreement that Operation Badr is of this moment of the highest priority?"

"Absolutely," Richardson replied without hesitation.

"Okay, I'll brief the President. Meeting adjourned."

Chapter Forty-Two

HEAVYWEIGHT WEAPONRY

CIA Headquarters, Langley, Virginia, USA

Thursday, September 3, 2015

Richardson stopped Stacie and Shafer at the door of the meeting room on the way out. He looked at his watch and said, "Grab yourselves a drink and meet me in my office. We've got work to do."

At 11:30 A.M. Shafer and Stacie entered Richardson's office each with a takeaway cup of coffee in hand. Richardson smiled when he noticed that all three of them had a cup displaying a green and white logo of a topless mermaid known as the Siren, the most recognized logo among coffee-lovers in the world. "Good to see that we're in agreement that Starbucks makes good coffee."

The Starbucks at CIA headquarters, known as 'Store Number 1', was the only outlet of their 20,000 outlets across the globe where customers were served by baristas with security clearances, and who would never ask for a client's name. Instead, they paired faces with the favorite drinks of their customers.

For the next hour, Shafer and Stacie stepped Richardson through the minutest detail of every bit of information the Operation Badr team had collected so far.

When their briefing ended, Richardson said, "Okay, no doubt we've got a serious lack of intelligence. Let's talk about how we're going to rectify that at the best possible speed."

Stacie said, "I suggest we up the surveillance and intel gathering on Fedot Frolov, Hassan Walid, the imam, and Teresa Lombardi immediately. Not to say the others should get less attention, but those three seem to be the potential linchpins."

Richardson nodded. "Agreed. And they might lead us to that absconded chemical engineer," Richardson said, "Let's start with Frolov. Bryan?"

Shafer nodded. "The Estonian Internal Security service is keeping a watch on him while he is still in country. Although they're competent, I have to point out that they were reluctant to do more than just street surveillance. I'd like to assign a team to get much closer than that. We need a team that will, if necessary, bend the rules in order to put the closest possible electronic and any other kind of surveillance on him, and keep the tabs on him if he leaves the country. Estonia's Foreign Intelligence Service, I'm afraid, might neither have the skills nor the willingness to do anything outside Estonia."

"Do you have a team in mind?"

"Yes, sir. I'd like to put John Brandt's CRC onto the case."

"Authorized," Richardson said.

"Hassan Walid and Teresa Lombardi," Shafer continued, "as you know, we've already outsourced their surveillance to CRC, they're the best in the business. On our instructions they've kept their surveillance low key so far. They've been waiting for us to give them permission to take their feet off the brakes."

"Authorized," Richardson said.

Shafer and Stacie nodded. They liked Richardson. He was a man who took his job seriously. He had no political ambitions and believed that we were created with two ears and one mouth because we were meant to listen twice as much as we speak. He listened to his underlings, asked intelligent questions, and was not afraid to make decisions and stand by them.

"Now, there's something I've been wondering about," Richardson said. "If we're correct in our assumption that we're looking at an arms deal, the guy in Riyadh with his shipping company could be responsible for the shipping of whatever it is Frolov will be supplying them. And this guy with the PHD in chemical engineering and electronics..."

"Could be building a bomb," Stacie completed for him.

"That's what's bugging me. What is Frolov supplying them with?"

"Well," Shafer said, "to create a Badr-like event, AK47's and rocket launchers won't cut it. They'd need some heavyweight weaponry."

"Such as a chemical or biological weapon that a guy with a PHD in chemical engineering might be able to construct," Richardson said.

"Exactly," Stacie said.

"We need to find that guy, Stacie."

"We will, sir. We will. He *will* have to make an appearance somewhere. As we are expanding our intelligence gathering and surveillance, we're bound to bump into him sooner or later."

Richardson let out a long breath. "Let's hope it's the former."

The three of them would have been horrified to know what Doctor Haroun Najm al Din Hadad was doing at that exact moment about 6,570 miles east of Langley, Virginia in a specially equipped warehouse on the outskirts of a city in eastern Sudan known as Port Sudan. It was Sudan's main port, 210 miles from Mecca.

Chapter Forty-Three

WHEN WE'RE STATESIDE AGAIN

Bastia, Corsica, France

September 1-3, 2015

It was just before mid-day on Tuesday, September 1, when the *TOMATS* moored at the pier in the marina Le Vieux at Port de Bastia, Corsica. Catia, Simona, Rex, and Digger would not disembark; they would stay out of sight while they were at anchor and only come outside when the yacht was back on the open sea again.

Rex had spoken to Rehka a few hours earlier. She had been back in Mumbai for only a little over a week after her visit to Lyon, France where she had helped Rex, Josh, and Marissa in John Brandt's rescue operation. After the operation, by invitation of Margot Le Maire, in whose rescue operation, nine months ago, she also played a significant role, she had stayed on at the Le Maire family estate for a few more weeks to spend time with Margot and her baby, Rowena.

When Rex told her he needed her for another mission, Rehka didn't hesitate.

"On a luxury yacht off the coast of Italy you say?"

"Yep, equipped with the latest and greatest computer and communications technology you can dream of."

"Well, what else can a girl wish for." She chuckled. "I just love working for you Rex—never a dull moment, *and* I get to meet new people *and* see the world."

"Exactly, that's what's called job satisfaction. Oh, and on the topic of meeting new people, just so you know, Greg Wade will be joining us."

There was a brief silence on Rehka's end, and when she asked, "When should I start packing?" Rex was sure there was a very big smile on her face.

"Right about now would be good. I need you here as quickly as humanly possible."

"Okay, I'm already on my way to my room to pack."

"Send me your itinerary when you have it."

"Will do. I'm looking forward to seeing you and Digger soon."

And Greg of course.

"We're looking forward to seeing you too, Rehka. Have a safe trip."

Chris McArdle must have been talking to Josh and Marissa at about the same time as Rex spoke to Rehka, because less than two minutes after ending the call, Rex got a call from Josh.

"Hey buddy, what's up?" Josh started. "I thought you'd sworn off violence, handed in your gun and your badge, and entered the priesthood."

Rex laughed. "Yeah, well I did all of that and applied

for entry at the Catholic seminary in Rome, everything went well, they accepted me and all. The problem came when they had to check my references. The only one I had was the Old Man. Need I say any more?"

Josh was roaring with laughter. "I can just imagine how that conversation would have gone."

"So, Josh, I take it this call from you is to tell me how excited you and Marissa are to see me again?"

"Indeed, we're excited," Josh said, "but don't flatter yourself. It's not because we've missed you, it's about the prospect of a cruise on a luxury yacht. We should be there by mid-day tomorrow your time."

"I knew this was an offer you couldn't refuse."

"Yep, you're right about that. We'll be heading to the airport in the next hour. Greg will meet us there."

"Great. See you tomorrow."

In the meantime, Catia had a long conversation with Simona and recommended that she take John Brandt up on his offer to fly her over to America where he would see to it that she would be safe. Simona seemed to understand it was for her safety and appreciated it, but Catia soon realized she was reluctant and asked her about it.

"I trust Rex and his people, but I don't trust anyone as much as you Catia. I know it's for my own safety, and I appreciate it, but for now I'd feel much better if I could stay here, on the yacht with you and Rex and the rest. Maybe in a few days or so I'd be in a better emotional state to go to America or Israel. It's just the idea of going to a country where I don't know anyone and can't even speak the language properly. It scares me. However, if you and Rex or this John Brandt, order me to go to America I'll do it, I don't want to be a burden for you. I've caused enough trouble already."

"Simona, no one is going to order you to do anything you don't want to do. If you prefer to stay here, it's not a problem. Declan, Rex, and John have already said the choice is yours. I'll let them know about your decision to stay."

Simona nodded and thanked her.

Catia then told Simona, in very broad terms, about the mission, taking great care not to divulge any sensitive information.

Simona was perceptive enough to rapidly get an idea of what was going on and understand not to ask too many questions. When Catia ended her explanations, Simona said, "Well, if I understand you correctly, part of this operation involves the Camorra, if so I might even be of some help. As you know, I've been born and raised among them. I'm pretty sure when it comes to the Beneduce-Longobardi clan there is probably no one else on this yacht who knows them better than I do. And don't forget, they killed my mother, I have good reason to want them destroyed."

Catia nodded. "Good point, Simona. Very good point. Your knowledge might indeed come in very handy."

After arrival in the port of Bastia, Rex had asked two of the female crew, the wife of one of the SEALs and fiancée of another, to go ashore with their partners and do some shopping on behalf of Catia, Simona, and himself. The ladies required clothes and toiletries. Rex provided the money for Catia's and Simona's shopping. He didn't want them to make any financial transactions as he thought it was possible that their bank accounts could have been flagged to report any activity.

There was no need to buy food for Digger, Spencer had stocked up on big bags of kibble in Italy before Rex and Digger had arrived. How much of the kibble Digger was going to eat remained to be seen with all the treats and spoils he got from everyone onboard the yacht. Rex had however told everyone what types of food they were allowed to give him and what not.

Digger was having the time of his life with everyone giving him so much attention and spoiling him with treats. But Rex knew Digger would soon be getting restless as he would miss his daily runs. Digger had already made known his opinion of the artificial turf of Spencer's putting green for his 'business', much to the latter's distress. Fortunately, the yacht was equipped with high-pressure hoses with which to clear the decks.

As for Digger's other daily exercise, and for that matter Rex's own, there was the gym. To test his idea to give Digger some exercise, he had taken him to the gym and introduced him to the treadmill. Within a few minutes, Digger understood what he had to do and enjoyed it so much Rex had a hard time getting him off it.

Josh, Marissa, and Greg had flown from DC to Paris where they met Rehka who had arrived on a direct flight from Mumbai. The Air Corsica flight from Paris to Bastia was a little over one and a half hours. It was late afternoon on Wednesday, September 2nd when the four of them stepped aboard.

Digger was somewhere on the lower deck with Catia and Simona when they arrived and must have heard the familiar voices. Rex had just enough time to shake hands with Josh and Greg, kiss Marissa on the cheek, and as always, give Rehka a hug and a kiss on the cheek when Digger stormed in and went straight for Rehka. He almost knocked her off her feet as he jumped up, placed his front legs on her shoulders, and tried to 'kiss' her in the face with his wet nose.

Catia, Simona, and Spencer arrived shortly after Digger, and Rex made introductions all around. Spencer welcomed his new guests aboard, showed them to their rooms, took them on the royal tour of the yacht, and introduced them to the crew. Rex and Digger had one room, Catia and Simona had a room each, Josh and Marissa had the biggest one, and Rehka and Greg had one each. Now only one of the seven staterooms was unoccupied.

After taking them to the lounge where the chefs had tea, coffee, and cookies for them, Spencer asked to be excused and joined his first officer on the bridge to prepare for departure. Within twenty minutes, the engines started and the *TOMATS* maneuvered out of its berth and set course for Naples, 258 nautical miles away which would take them about seventeen hours to reach.

Shortly before dinner that evening, Josh had taken Rex aside, and in great confidence, told him about a surprise he had in mind for Marissa that night. He was a little nervous and wanted to know what Rex's thoughts were.

Rex listened to his friend, smiled, clapped him on the back, and said, "You'll be okay, buddy. You've made it through much more danger than that in your life."

For dinner, the chefs had prepared a seafood feast to welcome their new guests. When the dessert was served, Josh took Marissa's hand and led her out on the deck to look out over the open ocean in the moonlight. It was out there that he took her in his arms and kissed her long and passionately, and when they came up for breath, he had slipped a tiny black box out of his pocket, opened the lid, turned it so that she could see what was inside, and said, "Marissa Bisset, I love you with all my heart. Will you please marry me?"

Marissa tried to fake hesitation but couldn't keep it up

past the two-second mark before she broke out in an ear-to-ear smile and said, "Yes, I will."

When the two returned to the dining room, Rex first noticed the smiles and then the ring on Marissa's finger. He smiled, nodded, and showed them a thumbs up. By then everyone had gone quiet and was looking at the radiant couple. It took just a few seconds for the women in the room to figure out what had happened. The men only realized what was going on when the women descended on Marissa and grabbed her hand to ooh and ahh over the ring. After that, the men either slapped Josh on the back with a congratulatory word or shook their heads in mock despair that he'd allowed himself to be 'caught'.

Later that night, by the time quite a few Champagne bottles were empty, Rex sidled up to Josh and Marissa and asked when they were going to tell the Old Man.

Marissa waved her hand in dismissal, and said, "Tomorrow... maybe."

Josh with a bit of a slur in his speech said, "Yeah, well, I don't know about tomorrow... maybe when we're Stateside again."

No one knew how the Old Man would take the news. It had never happened before, since he'd previously kept the knowledge that he employed female agents from his larger group, the men. Chances were there'd be momentous repercussions.

When Rex eventually went to bed late that night, after kissing Catia goodnight, he couldn't help but yearn for their relationship to soon progress to the status of Josh's and Marissa's.

Chapter Forty-Four

OUTRANKING THE POPE

*CRC Headquarters, Arizona and CIA Headquarters,
Langley, Virginia, USA*

Friday, September 4, 2015

It was Friday, September 4, when John Brandt and Chris
McArdle were in a secured video conference with Richardson, Shafer, and Stacie from CIA headquarters getting
briefed about the expansion of CRC's mission parameters
on Operation Badr.

After the meeting with Richardson three days before, in
preparation for their meeting with CRC, Stacie had collated
every bit of information she and her team had gathered,
encrypted it, and sent it to John Brandt via a secured link.
He'd now had a chance to review it and consult with his
team on how they'd prefer to proceed.

It took them the best part of two hours to discuss all the
information and agree what was expected of CRC.

Richardson's said, "John, as you can see, we've got a lot of reasons to be nervous about this. As far as I'm concerned, the summary of my brief is simply this; get that information, whatever it takes."

Brandt grinned. "That, I'll do. And, I assume, with the usual caveat, if any of this goes pear-shaped, you don't know me and have never heard of CRC?"

Richardson grinned. "As much as I hate it, yes. Unfortunately, that's still the only way we get the things done that need doing. It keeps the politicians happy and you and me in a job and our country safe."

Brandt nodded. He had no comments; that's why private black ops organizations such as CRC were created, and that's how they had been operating in the new political environment for the past decade or longer.

"Okay, a request for you, Stacie."

"I'm listening," Stacie said.

"My team would like you to use your clout with the NSA and others to get us a report of phone calls, Internet usage, financial records and such, related to Teresa Lombardi and her alias Liana Verdi—everything you can get."

"Will do," Stacie said.

Before the meeting ended, Brandt said he'd like to have a word in private with Richardson.

When Shafer and Stacie had left, Brandt said, "Martin, I'd appreciate it very much if you could use your influence to find out if any of the Italian authorities have a BOLO (be on the lookout) for two women; Sophia Maiorani, also known as Simona Bellucci and Catia Romano. Both are Italian citizens."

Richardson nodded and wrote the names down. "Leave it with me, I'll let you know."

It was part of the arrangement with the private contractors employed by the CIA that the names of their employees would be kept secret. Richardson assumed that the names he just got from Brandt were CRC agents but knew not to ask.

Rex's name was not mentioned.

"One more request, Martin. Can you also check if the yacht, the *TOMATS*, has been flagged by any of the Italian authorities? I suspect there won't be any, but I'd like to have the assurance."

Martin frowned. "A yacht? What... okay, never mind. I'll get it checked."

Aboard the TOMATS

Saturday, September 5, 2015

It was shortly after 4:00 P.M. on September 4 in Arizona and 1:00 A.M. on the 5th aboard the *TOMATS*, off the coast of Italy, when Brandt called Spencer and asked him to wake the team and gather them in the communications room for an urgent briefing.

Within ten minutes, Spencer, Rex, Josh, Marissa, Catia, Greg, and Rehka were staring through sleepy eyes at Brandt and McArdle on the big screen.

Brandt grinned as he looked at the dull faces staring back at him and said, "Well, I'm not apologizing for waking you up, the holiday is over. We've got bad guys to chase."

McArdle took over and gave them a rundown of the instructions from the CIA.

They were about eight hours away from Naples, enough time to plan and be ready to go into action when they arrived there. Just when McArdle reached the end of his briefing, Brandt held his hand up and said, "I've got an important call coming through. Hold the discussions, I'll be back momentarily."

The screen went blank and Spencer said, "I guess we're all in need of a caffeine boost?"

He was answered with a chorus of yeses, except Rehka who asked for tea.

Three minutes later Brandt and McArdle were back. Brandt said, "Perplexing but good news. I just received confirmation that none of the Italian law enforcement agencies, and that includes the Naples police department, has a BOLO on Simona or Catia. Neither has any of them flagged the *TOMATS*. The latter I expected, the former I didn't."

"Strange indeed," Rex said. "Like you, I'm not surprised they have nothing about the *TOMATS*, but having nothing on Simona and Catia, I think, should be treated with great circumspection."

"Agreed," said Brandt. "But at least we know, for now, the yacht can enter Italian ports without problems." He nodded for McArdle to continue.

McArdle told Greg, Rehka, and Marissa that their first task was to get access to as much of the electronic communications and Internet activities of Teresa Lombardi and Imam Karim Al-Sadiq aka Hassan Walid as they could. The next task was to get access to the computer networks of not only the port authorities in the Port of Naples but also to every shipping company. Then they had to do the same for the rest of the Beneduce-Longobardi leadership and everyone that they were in contact with, which already included professor Aziz Abdul-Salam Awad in Rome.

"I'm aware that it might not be easy at first, but the plan is to plant bugs that will get you more information. In the meantime, we have drones watching Teresa Lombardi and Hassan Walid. We can request more drones if necessary."

Greg nodded. "Every bit of help we can get will be welcome."

McArdle nodded and continued to explain that CRC agents have been assigned to put tabs on Fedot Frolov aka Saburo Szabó and that they were expecting to see a stream of information coming in soon. "We don't know who initiated the first contact between him and Teresa Lombardi or who introduced them to each other in the first place. We're working on that from our end."

McArdle paused to take a sip of coffee and continued. "Let's talk about the field teams. Rex, you'll oversee the teams in Italy. The surveillance teams we have now will keep their distance from the targets while they continue unobtrusive observation. Your mission is to get into the targets' homes, offices, cars, phones, up their asses if necessary, to plant bugs. Josh has with him the latest and greatest surveillance gear, fresh out of the CIA's research labs. All of it properly tested."

Rex's mind was already working at warp speed. "Okay, the fact that the *TOMATS* is not on a watchlist will help us to get ashore fairly easily, but then we'll need transport. Using taxis and Uber are options, but I'm not too keen on those because they not only leave trackable financial transactions, they also give other people the chance to see and remember our faces and the locations where we're going. Maybe the surveillance teams could hire a few rental cars and keep them ready for us. What do you think?"

McArdle nodded. "Yep, I'll look into that and let you know."

Spencer was looking at Catia. She noticed and must have realized what he was thinking. She smiled and said, "And... we could use my motorbikes."

Rex bumped his open palm against his forehead and said, "Of course! I completely forgot about the bikes. But... there's just one problem though."

"What?" Catia asked.

"Your use of the word 'we'; you and Simona cannot go ashore."

Catia looked dejected for a few moments, then started laughing.

Before Rex could ask what Catia found so amusing, Catia continued, "I understand it might put the operation in jeopardy if Simona and I go on shore and get recognized. The reason I'm laughing is when I bought the Street-figther S, I took an oath that nobody will ever ride it but me. At the time, in 2011, when I gave Rex the Multistrada to use on the Naples mission, I told myself that the only exception I would make would be for the Pope, but only as a passenger."

By now everyone was laughing.

"But don't worry, my thinking about the matter has evolved. Therefore, although it pains me, I'd allow Rex, but only Rex, to ride my beloved Streetfigther S, and of course Digger may accompany him."

Rex stared at Catia; mouth agape. *There is so much I still have to discover about this amazing woman.*

"There you have it, Rex, you're the chosen one," Brandt winked at Catia.

"Jeez, thanks Catia, I'm honored to know I'm outranking the Pope, or is it actually Digger who outranks the Vicar of Christ?" was as far as Rex got before he started laughing.

When the mirth subsided, McArdle brought them back to task. "We'll probably need a few sets of different number plates. I'll see what I can arrange."

Rex and Josh asked McArdle to give them access to all the photos, reports, and video footage of Teresa Lombardi and the Imam, collected by surveillance teams thus far, so that they could study them.

Chapter Forty-Five

I'LL KEEP YOU POSTED

*CRC Headquarters Arizona and CIA Headquarters,
Langley, Virginia, USA*

Saturday, September 5, 2015

By the time the *TOMATS* had reached the Port of Naples
and headed for its berth in the Marina Molo Luise, Brandt
and McArdle were poring over the NSA report Stacie had
sent them.

They soon learned that there was very little to be
gleaned from Teresa Lombardi's phone and Internet
records. She had no landline and almost never used her
Lombardi mobile phone, other than to make and receive
calls from her leadership group, and those were short,
mostly less than a minute. She had a high-speed fiberoptic
Internet connection that she used almost exclusively to read
up about art, news, watch movies online, and other benign
activities. Even her Internet search patterns were boring

and raised no suspicions. She had no social media accounts of any kind, and her emails were few and far between. As Teresa Lombardi, she was, from what they could see, living a cloistered life.

Looking at the Liana Verdi part of her life, at first glance, it was even less exciting. She used an encrypted satellite phone, though unbeknown to her, the Mossad had broken the encryption years ago. There were records of quite a few calls made from Rome to a satellite phone located in Naples, and although those calls were made quite often, the last call was made more than four years ago. The phone in Naples, according to the NSA, belonged to the late Ricardo Lombardi.

There were also regular calls to a satellite phone in Rome that belonged, according to the NSA, to Aziz Abdul-Salam Awad, the part time professor of Middle Eastern Studies at Università Cattolica del Sacro Cuore, Rome campus. Brandt and McArdle already knew he was Liana Verdi's business manager.

Even though Liana Verdi's electronic footprint was minimal, it was the records of calls to and from Moscow that got their attention. In early June 2014 she had made a call to a satellite phone owned by a person in Moscow. In February 2015, eight months after her first call, she had received a call from the Muscovite. Then there was a lapse of about seven months before she made another call to the Muscovite and received a return call a few weeks later.

Brandt and McArdle looked at each other and were about to ask the same question when the video call came through from CIA headquarters. It was Stacie.

"Hi boys, I guess you have a few questions for me?"

Brandt grinned. "We sure do."

"Okay, let's see if my extrasensory perception is still

functioning properly. That phone in Moscow belongs to Olesya Kharlamova. That's what you wanted to know, right?"

"Spot on and…," Brandt said.

Stacie held her hand up to stop him. "Still testing my ESP abilities. And we have in our databases just one person with that name who lives in Moscow. A few inquiries to our Russian desk provided us with a few photos, and the facial recognition system was so kind as to find us a match. Miss Kharlamova, sixty-six, joined the KGB directly out of Moscow University in 1976. Reached the rank of major by 1991 when she was made redundant and went into business for herself."

"What kind of business," McArdle asked.

"Organized crime. She's a *vor*, Russian Mafia, or *Bratva* as they call them. One of a very few women who ever made it in the Russian underworld."

"What type of work did she do in the KGB, and what's her fiefdom now?" Brandt asked.

"Part of her KGB training was a six-month stint at the Swallows Nest. She was a swallow aka a sparrow or honey-trap who, according to our records, excelled at sexpionage. And that's what her modern-day business is all about. Gathering and selling of information."

"At sixty-six is she not a bit old for that kind of excitement?" McArdle asked with a big grin.

"I wouldn't know, I am still a few years off that age. Maybe John will know better what women in their sixties are capable of." Stacie laughed and said, "Just pulling your legs, boys. No, she's the boss these days, she runs the brothel."

"That begs the question, what information would Lombardi want from her?" McArdle murmured.

"I'd guess Kharlamova might have contact with former KGB colleagues, such as that sleazeball, Frolov. If not, she has the ways and means to find the likes of him, others that are into illegal arms dealing," Brandt said.

"Exactly what Bryan and I thought," Stacie said.

"So, for now, we'll assume that Kharlamova made the introduction between Lombardi and Frolov," Brandt said.

"That seems to be the case. There are no records to show that Lombardi made a call to anyone other than Kharlamova in the lead up to that meeting with Frolov in Narva," Stacie said.

"I take it you've already started delving deeper into Kharlamova and put tabs on her?" Brandt said.

"Indeed. I'll keep you posted."

Chapter Forty-Six

JET SKIS AND A PICNIC ON THE BEACH

Port of Naples, Italy

Sunday, September 6, 2015

Rex and the team very carefully studied Donna Teresa's surveillance information, gathered by the CRC team over the past few days. By road, the house was a little over two miles from where the *TOMATS* was moored at the Marina Molo Luise. Greg's team included, apart from Catia, Rehka, and Marissa, the IT gurus at CRC headquarters back in Arizona with whom they had uninterrupted video contact. They soon got the complete floorplan and zoomed-in satellite images of Donna Teresa's property.

Naples, with its thriving drug trade, feuding Camorra clans, and lots of desperately poor and deprived people, was a breeding ground for all manner of illegal activities and violence. Therefore, those who could afford it, of which Donna Teresa was one, took great care and paid a lot of money to shield themselves from the criminal elements, and of course, she never spent a moment's thought that she was one of the criminals.

Lombardi's property, surrounded on three sides by eight-foot concrete walls topped with razor wire, powerful LED security lights, and built-in motion sensors, was also protected by three armed guards during the day and four at night. The security lights that pointed away from the property would turn night into day if even a dog strolled into the motion detectors' range.

On the water side of the property there was no fence—it would have spoiled the view. The perpendicular hundred and fifty-foot cliff was as good as or better than any man-made obstacle. In case an intruder had the guts and skill to scale the cliff, the guards had a view of the seaside edge of the property from their guardhouse which was rigged with motion sensors connected to security spotlights and an alarm. The lights were a few yards away from the edge of the cliff and pointed in that direction.

At the front gate was a camera atop the wall which gave the guard a full view of a visitor who would state his or her business via an intercom. If the guard decided to let the visitor in, the gate would open, the visitor would drive forward about ten yards, and stop in front of a double row of vicious metal spikes in the road. Behind the visitor the gates would close automatically, effectively locking the visitor in. The guard would then assure himself of the visitor's identity before pushing the button that would make the spikes recede allowing the visitor to drive up to the front of the house where the visitor would undergo a thorough search for any weapons by another guard before being escorted into the house.

On Sunday morning, while studying aerial photos of

the Posillipo area, Marissa came across an article about the history of the area. Her attention was drawn to a part of the article that talked about the private wharves which many of the seafront properties had since time immemorial. Many of those didn't exist anymore, but what was most fascinating was that some of them had tunnels, carved out of the rock by slaves, leading from the private jetties up to the owner's houses on the clifftop.

I wonder if Teresa Lombardi's place could have one of those? She called up the aerial map and zoomed in on the house. There was no jetty. *That doesn't mean there had never been one.*

She called Josh and Rex over to show them what she had found.

"Two ways to find out," Josh said. "One, delve into the historical archives and the city council's engineering department records to see if we can find more information about these piers and tunnels. Two, send a reconnaissance team out there to try and find it."

By now, Catia and Spencer had joined the conversation.

"We've got four jet skis and a number of SEALs who haven't been in the water for a long while," Spencer said. "The water might be a bit chilly, but the sun is shining, and we've got enough wetsuits and drysuits."

Rex was quiet for a while, and then he nodded. "Okay, here's the plan. We're going to have a picnic on this little beach right here." He pointed to a beach on the map almost right at the foot of the cliff bordering Lombardi's property. However, before we go; Greg, you and Rehka and the rest of your team try to get into those archives and find us some helpful information, if it exists.

"Declan, I'll need volunteers, three of the SEALS each with a female companion. Two per jet ski."

"What about the fourth jet ski?"

Rex looked at Catia and said, "It won't be the same as your Streetfighter on the open road, but that's the best I can offer you for now. You can drive. What do you say?"

A big smile lit up her face. "I'd love it."

"But… hang on we don't want her to be seen by anyone out there," Josh protested.

"No one would," Rex said. "We're all going to be wearing full-body drysuits."

"Okay, but I'd have very much liked it to take Marissa for a spin on the water," Josh said.

"Yeah, cold water or not, it would be great," Marissa added.

"Okay, Declan, make that two SEALS with female companions," Rex said.

Posillipo, Naples, Italy

Three hours later, shortly after 1:00 P.M., four jet skis with eight people, all of them covered from head to toe in wetsuits, were cruising slowly along the shore of the Posillipo area, enjoying the view of the spectacular houses on the clifftops. It took them just a few minutes to travel the one and a half nautical miles from the Marina Molo Luise to the spot below Teresa Lombardi's house.

Rex and company were happy to see they were not the only crazies out on the water. There were lots of them ignoring the cold water, skiing behind boats, kayaking, paddle boarding, and jet skiing, making the most of the sunny weather before winter would arrive.

Before they left the *TOMATS*, Greg and Rehka reported that their searches in the historical archives didn't produce anything useful. However, they did find some information in the records of the Naples City Council's engineering department. Although they weren't detailed architectural drawings, there were markings on the map of the area showing where the entries and exits of known tunnels were. From what they could see, there was a marking for an entry to a tunnel that seemed to be right on the border with the property next to Teresa Lombardi's. They couldn't find an exit for it on the map though.

The four jet skis were about thirty or so yards away from the shore as they rode slowly past the properties. Every now and then one or more of them would very excitedly point out another luxurious property to the others. After a while they pulled up to a small sandy beach area, about fifty yards wide, which bordered the left side of the Lombardi property.

They knew it was a private beach; there were signs telling them so in Italian, but there was no one around to tell them so verbally and shoo them away. If anyone turned up to order them away, they would apologize profusely, in any language other than Italian or English, and leave. In the meantime, they would enjoy the food and drinks they brought with them in watertight backpacks.

No one troubled them while they were picnicking, and two of the SEALs explored the area bordering the Lombardi property where the map showed a mark for a tunnel entry.

Rex couldn't help but miss Digger and think of how much he would have enjoyed getting off the boat and running around on the beach. And of course, Rex would not have been able to stop him from taking a dip in the sea —he loved to get into the water. Digger hadn't been happy when he saw Rex getting on the jet ski and realized he was not going with him, and he had made it known. But Simona and Rehka were there and managed to pacify him. They were more than happy to keep Digger entertained while Rex was away.

The two SEALs, Tanner Giles and Ronnie Hagen, were away for almost forty minutes before they returned with smiles on their faces. Fortunately, the owner of the private beach had not turned up.

They reported that they had found the entry. It was on the side of the big rock outcropping at the end of the beach. In the past, there'd been an iron gate at the entry, but now there were only a few rusty remains. Tanner had entered and found the tunnel to be safe.

About ten yards beyond the entry, the tunnel forked into two. It was abundantly clear that no human had set foot in there for a very long time. The tunnel forking to the left led up to the Lombardi property. Following the stairs up the tunnel in the light of his small penlight, keeping track of the number of steps and the angle of ascent, he'd ended up at a dilapidated rusty iron grate from which protruded the roots of the lawn and plants above. He had done a little digging with his bare hands and found the layer above the opening to be about six to nine inches thick.

"That iron grate would not withstand the attention of a small crowbar," Tanner said. Looking at the aerial map Rex had brought with him, the SEAL marked the spot where he estimated the exit would be. It was in the middle of the three terraces, about ten yards from the border of the property, and by the looks of it, among a large patch of lush teucrium shrubs. And most fortunate of all, outside the detection range of the security lights' motion sensors.

Chapter Forty-Seven

LIKE ROBBERS

Aboard the TOMATS, Marina Molo Luise, Naples, Italy

Sunday, September 6, 2015

Upon their return to the *TOMATS* they gathered in one of the meeting rooms to plan. Their challenge was to get into the house, plant the surveillance bugs, and get out without being noticed. That was the ideal.

Around the table with Rex, were Catia, Marissa, Josh, Spencer, Greg, and the two SEALs, Tanner Giles and Ronnie Hagen.

The discovery of the tunnel was a bonanza. They didn't have to worry about getting over the eight-foot walls, razor wire, and motion sensors. Through the tunnel they had a way into the Lombardi fortress with very little risk of being detected. Once on the property, before they could get to the house, they would have to neutralize the guards. Then they had to get into the house, which they strongly suspected was protected by a top of the range burglar alarm system.

The use of knockout gas was a consideration, but they didn't have any. The incapacitating gasses and sprays so prevalent in pulp fiction novels, movies, and television shows were just that, fiction. The only substances in existence that could knock their targets out were remifentanil and carfentanil, derivatives of the drug fentanyl, used by Russian Special Forces during the Moscow theater hostage crisis in 2002. However, they knew, as the Russians had proven, it would almost definitely cause fatalities.

After quite a few hours of brainstorming, Rex finally said, "It looks like our best option is to make it look like a well-planned and executed burglary.

"We'll have to move in and neutralize the guards all in one go, before they can raise an alarm. Then inject them with enough propofol to keep them down for an hour or two. While they're unconscious, we've got to get into the house, disarm the alarm, neutralize the woman, plant the bugs, mess up the place, and carry away enough valuable stuff to make it look like a robbery."

Catia smiled. "What you have described there *is* a robbery, Rex."

Rex grinned. "I suppose you're right." He looked around the table and asked, "Any other ideas?"

"I can think of a lot of things that can go wrong with your plan but less so than any of the other options we've discussed," Spencer said.

Everyone nodded their assent.

"Great. Now we need to map out the detail," Rex said. "Unless we find a reason not to, I'd like to go in early, say around two in the morning. That leaves us with a bit more than twenty-four hours to plan and prepare."

It was after midnight when everyone had agreed on the details and decided it was time to get a few hours' sleep.

Shortly before mid-day the next day, they got another windfall when Greg reported that the electronic surveillance team had intercepted messages from Li Voti about a meeting that night at Dina Martelli's estate, Vincola del Martelli. Donna Teresa was going to be at the meeting, which was scheduled for 9:00 p.m.

Although Teresa's absence at the house that night would make things much easier for them, it meant they had to move their timelines. It didn't take them long to agree it was too good an opportunity to pass and make the necessary adjustments to their plan. The weather also played along nicely when it became overcast and a light drizzle set in which, according to the weather forecast, was going to last for the next two days.

Posillipo, Naples, Italy

Monday, September 7, 2015

It was 8:45 P.M. when the two Inflatable dinghies with their small, near-noiseless, electric motors were lowered into the water from the stern of the *TOMATS*. Rex, Digger, and Tanner were in the first one; Josh, Ronnie, and another SEAL from the crew, Darrin Tipton, in the other.

Under their dark rain-ponchos, they were all dressed in

black, with black balaclavas rolled up on their heads. Each of them had a small, military assault pack in which they had night vision equipment, gloves, powerful pencil flashlights, taser guns, and Sig Sauer P226 pistols with silencers, which they hoped they would not have to use.

Digger had his harness on. His equipment, which included a mini microphone and earphones, video camera, and doggles, tactical night vision optics with infrared capability designed for dogs, were in Rex's pack.

The intemperate weather ensured that no one saw them when they left the marina, neither when they made their way across the water to a location about a hundred yards from the tunnel entry. The trip took them about ten minutes.

When they reached the landing spot, they quickly pulled the dinghies out of the water and hid them among the rocks. From there, staying in the shadows close to the cliff wall and among the rocks, they made their way quietly to the tunnel entry.

On the *TOMATS*, Spencer, Catia, Marissa, Rehka, and Greg were in the communications room watching the high-resolution surveillance imagery produced by the Global Hawk drone circling at 10,000 feet above. They had been tracking the six red dots all the way from the *TOMATS* across the water until they disappeared.

Inside the tunnel they took off their ponchos, folded and stashed them into their packs. Rex stood at the entrance where he could get radio reception, switched on his throat mic, and contacted Spencer to report their arrival and that the signal would be lost until they got out of the tunnel. He fitted Digger's equipment, tested it, and whispered to Tanner, "All set here, you can lead the way."

They moved up the stairs in single file, Rex and Digger bringing up the rear.

Reaching the top of the stairs, Tanner showed them the old rusty metal grate that covered the exit and went to work on it with the crowbar. And it was, as he told them the previous day, no match for it. Within minutes the grate was out of the way, and Tanner started cutting the roots away and removing the soil. In the meantime, the rest of the team took their pistols out and fitted the silencers.

When the opening was big enough for them to go through, Rex and Digger moved up the stairs past the rest of the team, stood on the second to last step, only Rex's head protruding above the ground, and contacted Spencer.

"Padre, Ruan here, can you hear me?"

Spencer's first name, Declan, was an Irish name meaning 'man of prayer' hence his callsign, Padre. They had agreed to keep their radio communications informal and deliberately not follow standard military radio protocols just in case someone was listening.

"Yep, I can hear you well."

"Okay, we're good to go, what do you say?"

"Mouse and one Golf left twenty minutes ago. Eagle says, only three Golfs left. All of them inside now."

They couldn't hope for much more to go their way. The only unknown was how long Teresa and the guard would be away. But the drone operator had been tracking her vehicle to Dina Martelli's estate and would let them know the moment it started moving from there.

"Thanks Padre, we'll stay in touch."

Rex went down on his stomach and crawled out of the tunnel to find a position among the shrubs. He called Digger to join him. Within seconds Digger was flat on his belly next to Rex, eagerly awaiting his orders. Rex scratched his ears, pushed his nose against Digger's wet nose, and said, "Clever boy. Okay, Digger," he said as he pointed to the right and ahead of them, "Scout and Hide."

As Digger disappeared like a ghost among the plants, Rex removed the patch of cloth on his left forearm covering the six-inch screen to track Digger's movements.

Through the micro earphones located inside Digger's ears and the images streaming back from the night vision camera on his back to the screen on Rex's arm, Rex directed him around the property even past the guardhouse. The rest of the team had also crawled out of the tunnel and took up positions on either side of Rex, waiting and listening to him directing Digger around the property. Ten minutes later, Digger emerged out of the dark next to Rex and pushed his wet nose into Rex's face.

He got another round of hugs and praise from Rex while the rest of the team smiled in wonderment. It had started raining softly again when Rex whispered into his throat mic to the team, "Okay let's go."

Two minutes later, the five men and Digger were outside the guardhouse. All the guards were in the TV room watching Terminator 1, dubbed into Italian, on full volume. Rex could only smile and shake his head at the irony when he heard Arnold Schwarzenegger's famous, "I'll be back," in Italian *'aspetto fuori'* which meant, 'I wait outside'.

Unfortunately, there was not enough time to give the guards a better translation.

The door was unlocked, Rex took his taser out of the holster, nodded at Tanner and Josh to do the same, and with hand signals told Digger, Ronnie, and Darrin to wait outside. He didn't want them to get in each other's way when they entered the TV room. It turned out Rex had nothing to worry about, all six of them could have marched in there, and the guards would not have noticed. The TV was so loud, and the guards so caught up in the movie, none of them saw the three men entering the room behind them. The taser darts hit them all at the same time, and they went down as in a choreographed scene in a play. Two minutes later, they were tied up and gagged and each had a dose of propofol coursing through their veins, off to dreamland.

They would wake up in about two to three hours feeling very giddy with no idea what had happened to them.

Rex and Josh studied the panels and switches in the control room and found the switches to disable the alarm system in the house as well as the security lights and cameras. They also found the keys to the front door. Sure that the guards were not going to give them any trouble, they walked over to the house where Josh unlocked the front door.

On the *TOMATS*, Spencer smiled when he saw the six dots appear from the guardhouse and make their way to the house. "Looks like the team did it."

A minute or so later, Rex's voice came over the speakers in the communications room. "Padre, nice place we've got here. We'll need a hand to move a few things. Can you help?"

"No problem, help is on the way."

Thirty seconds later, a white Mercedes Benz Vito van, waiting in the parking space ten yards from the gangplank to the *TOMATS* with two SEALs inside, drove off. The van was one of the three vehicles which the CRC surveillance team in Naples had hired and parked close to the *TOMATS* for use by the crew as required. The van would arrive at the front gate of Teresa Lombardi's house in about five minutes. On arrival the SEALs would let Rex know they were there, and he would open the gates for them and deactivate the metal spikes in the driveway so they could drive right up to the front door.

Working with surgical gloves to avoid leaving any fingerprints anywhere, it took them the best part of three-quarters of an hour to finish the job inside the house. Every room in the house and the entire guardhouse was now under video and audio surveillance from the best observation technology on the planet, totally undetectable by any counter surveillance equipment known to the CIA, FBI, or any other western intelligence agency. Every bug was tested and verified by Greg and his team to work.

Ten of the most expensive original paintings decorating the walls had been removed, wrapped in blankets, and stashed in the van. The wall-mounted 65-inch Samsung QLED TV, various ancient statues and artifacts, and a number of genuine Persian carpets also found space in the van. The contents of the safe found behind a bookshelf in the study, which Ronnie opened with a carefully shaped charge of Semtex, included a big bundle of cash, jewels, precious stones, a stack of gold coins, and other valuables. Those were placed in a leather attaché case and taken to the van.

None of them had any idea what the value of the loot was; they had no intention of selling it, but that didn't prevent them from guessing. Their guesses ranged from two to ten million Euros.

None of them had any compunction about relieving the crime boss of her ill-gotten possessions.

Like robbers would have done, they left the house ransacked, even raiding the fridge. The front door and the main gates they left open. The van with its precious contents took off to one of the storage facilities Catia had been renting for many years in the name of a shell company to use for the field agents she supported when on missions.

Rex and his team went back the way they came and left the opening of the tunnel uncovered.

By 10:30 P.M. everyone was back on the *TOMATS* waiting in the communications room for Donna Teresa and her bodyguard to return.

Chapter Forty-Eight

TO REPLACE THE IRREPLACEABLE

Posillipo, Naples, Italy

Monday, September 7, 2015

At 11:40 p.m. Teresa's red S-Class Mercedes Coupé pulled up in front of the open gate at her house. There was no guard in sight and no voice over the intercom. "Stop!" she shouted as the car rolled forward slowly. "Something is wrong. Back up. Park over on the other side of the road. I'll phone the police."

Within seconds she had Rinaldo Fara on the line, told him what she had found, and ordered him to come over immediately.

Fara had not yet reached his home after the leadership meeting. He made a U-turn and stepped on the gas. He arrived on the scene fifteen minutes later, parked behind Teresa's car, retrieved his service pistol—a 9-millimeter

Beretta 90-Two—from its holster under his left armpit, and approached Teresa's vehicle.

She was in the back seat behind the driver. She lowered her window when Fara approached and told him to get in on the other side. When he was inside, she told him that they had arrived at the open gate, there was no sign of the guards, she was convinced there had been a robbery, and the intruders might still be on the premises.

Fara told the driver to follow him and Teresa but to stay in the car and lock the doors. He and the guard who'd been with her at the meeting approached the guardhouse with guns drawn. They found the three hapless guards tied up and gagged, moaning and groaning on the floor. Fara pulled out his mobile phone and called for backup while the guard untied his ill-fated colleagues.

Within minutes, backup arrived in the form of a convoy of police cars with flashing lights and howling sirens which managed to wake up anyone in the neighborhood who was not already awake. Within half an hour there were more than twenty police officers and detectives on site. They swept the house and the property and found no intruders.

The quintessentially calm and collected Teresa Lombardi was beside herself. Her emotions were fluctuating between shock, lachrymosity, and trembling fury. It was the first time in his life that Li Voti, who had known her for more than twenty years, had seen her in such a state.

On the *TOMATS*, the team was watching and listening. Fara told Teresa that it would be best if they arranged alternative accommodation for her for a day or two while the detectives and forensic team gathered evidence and the property was secured.

Teresa told him, "I'm not leaving this house. I'll stay

here, they can do their work while I'm here. It's the job of the police to protect me. Make it happen."

Fara nodded in submission.

"Oh, and it is also the police's job to find out who did this. And it's your responsibility to make sure they don't drag their feet," Teresa said.

It was only the next day when the detectives made another inspection of the garden that they discovered the opening to the tunnel on the middle terrace among a dense patch of teucrium shrubs and figured out how the robbers gained access to the property without triggering any alarms.

Teresa, the guards, the gardener, even the maid were questioned, but none of them had prior knowledge of the existence of the tunnel.

Two days later, to a question from Teresa to Fara and the senior detective in charge of the investigation as to who could be responsible, they both raised their shoulders.

"We have no idea yet, Miss Lombardi," the detective said. "So far we haven't found any fingerprints or anything we can use to run a DNA test. The rain the past few days has wiped out all tracks except for in the tunnel.

"I'm sorry to say, but we have no leads at the moment. It is obvious that these people were professionals; they must have been studying this place for a while and were waiting for the right moment to make their move."

"It's blatantly obvious they were professionals, and by the looks of it, the police are not," Teresa retorted.

The detective made no reply. "I understand your frustration, Miss Lombardi. Although we have very little to go on now, eventually at least one of them will talk. Criminals like to boast about their accomplishments. Besides that, at some stage they'd want to sell what they've stolen, and that might lead us to them."

"Well," Teresa said, "you've given me no confidence you'll be able to find the perpetrators."

The detective made no reply and tried to change the subject. "I take it you had everything insured?"

"Yes, I had, but what you obviously don't understand is that those paintings and statues were one of a kind. How much money do you think it would take to replace the irreplaceable?"

The detective shook his head. He had no answer.

Chapter Forty-Nine

GET INTO WALID'S MEETINGS

CIA Headquarters, Langley, Virginia, USA

Monday, September 7, 2015

Among the original Badr five it was the presence of Hassan Walid aka Imam Karim Al-Sadiq that caused the CIA analysts the most concern. Therefore, he was the topic of the next brief to John Brandt and Chris McArdle at CRC.

"We know Walid's name among the Badr five is no coincidence," Stacie said. "With his background I'm sure he's not hanging around in Naples to preach to a few hundred Sunni Muslims to whose sect he doesn't even belong.

"We know he's in regular contact with the Beneduce-Longobardi clan through Valter Li Voti via telephone calls lasting less than a minute on average. Nothing of substance can be discussed during one-minute telephone calls. So, there must be in-person meetings, and we need to 'invite' ourselves to those ASAP."

Brandt smiled. Stacie certainly had a way of getting to the point, and he liked it.

Bryan Shafer added, "Another thing that we find disquieting is the fact that, apart from the odd benign email, the imam seems to never communicate with the rest of his pals in the Badr group. As far as we know, after months of surveillance, he almost never leaves the Muslim enclave. We know he is part of the group, and he plays a vital role in their operation. So, he *must* be communicating with them. We need to know how he is doing it."

Brandt nodded. "I'd guess he's got couriers working for him. And I'd venture another guess that our professor of Middle Eastern Studies in Rome, Aziz Abdul-Salam Awad, might be the intermediary."

"That might be so," Shafer said. "So, that's your brief. Get into Walid's meetings, uncover his networks, and put tabs on all of them."

Muslim Enclave, South of Naples, Italy

Friday, September 11, 2015

For observant Muslims, Friday is a sacred day of worship. In the Qur'an there is a chapter about *Al-Jumah*, the day of assembly, which is also the word for Friday in Arabic. It states, "O ye who believe! When the call is proclaimed to prayer on Friday (the Day of Assembly, *yawm al-jumu'ah*), hasten earnestly to the Remembrance of Allah, and leave off business. That is best for you if ye but knew! And when the Prayer is finished, then may ye disperse through the land, and seek of the Bounty of Allah: and celebrate the Praises of Allah: that ye may prosper."

Friday, September 11 was also the fourteenth remembrance of the September 11, 2001 attack on America.

The masjid was packed as every soul in the enclave attended the *Al-Jumah* service, but it didn't prevent the Imam from taking notice of two people he had not seen before. After the sermon, one of the congregation members introduced him to the newcomers who had, according to the man doing the introductions, arrived in the enclave late on the evening before. It was an old man, Yaman Hilal, who Al-Sadiq estimated to be about early to mid-seventies, and his granddaughter, Rasha Hilal, whose age Al-Sadiq could not guess because of the burka she was wearing, covering not only her whole body but also her face.

Their host told the Imam that his guests were from Aleppo, Syria, and that they spoke Arabic. Al-Sadiq greeted them and asked them to tell him how it came about that they were there.

The reedy old man spoke softly and slowly when he told the Imam of their trials and tribulations since their escape from the horrors of Aleppo. His wife had been killed eighteen months ago when government airplanes dropped a bomb on their house. The old man had miraculously escaped with only a broken arm and damaged eardrums all of which had healed completely.

About a year ago, he confided, Rasha had been a victim of a chemical attack by government forces which, by the mercy of Allah, she survived. But it had left her with damaged vocal cords which made it difficult for her to speak.

His tale of troubles continued three months ago, when, on the day they fled the city, his son and only child, the father of his granddaughter, was killed by gunfire from Syrian government troops. He and his daughter-in-law, the girl's mother, and the girl managed to escape the attack.

But then, just three days later, they ran into a platoon of government troops who shot at them and killed the girl's mother, leaving only the two of them. That was when they decided to leave Syria and go to Germany where the old man's brother had apparently been able to get residence and work and hopefully would be able to help them.

They had been traveling, hiding, begging, and starving for the last three months. One of the refugees whom they met along the way told them about the sanctuary they would find among Imam Al-Sadiq's people in Italy. The weight of the tale bowed the old man's body lower and lower, until he was almost bent at the waist.

Al-Sadiq almost had tears in his eyes when the old man stopped talking. He put his hand on the old man's shoulder and said, "You've come to the right place my brother. Stay with us, I'll see to it that you and your granddaughter are taken good care of. And when you've regained your strength and are ready to travel to Germany, I'll make arrangements for that."

The old man thanked the Imam and shook his hand. The Imam invited him and his granddaughter for lunch at his house the next day.

If Al-Sadiq had checked their story, he would have learned that Yaman Hilal and Rasha Hilal gave him their real names and that she was indeed the old man's granddaughter. He would have learned that they were, in fact, from Aleppo in Syria, and they did escape from the city during one of the government's attempts to conquer the city. He would also have learned that the old man's wife, son, and daughter-in-law were in fact dead, killed by government forces.

But that was where the lines between truth and untruth became blurred. Yaman Hilal's family were all killed in one attack three months before. Rasha was never a victim of a chemical attack, neither was there anything wrong with her vocal cords.

What really happened was, Yaman Hilal, who was actually sixty-one, and his family were supporters of President Bashar al-Assad's government who had the support of Hezbollah, Shia militias, and Russia. And he worked as an informant for *Shu'bat al-Mukhabarat al-'Askariyya*, (Military Intelligence Directorate) Syria's secret service. But when Yaman saw the carnage caused by Assad's forces in Aleppo, he and his family became totally disillusioned and turned to the Syrian Opposition. However, they soon learned the opposition forces were infested by extremist groups such as the Levant Front, al-Qaeda, ISIS, and others. They were just as bad if not much worse than Assad's regime.

Soon after joining the Syrian Opposition, Yaman was recruited by an undercover agent, whom he suspected had connections to the CIA or MI6, to spy on ISIS. The agent had given him some basic training in spycraft and surveillance techniques, the use of dead letter boxes and such.

For the year Yaman worked for this agent, the information he had passed on was used to cause substantial losses to the ISIS forces which had already conquered large parts of Syria and Iraq, committing the most outrageous atrocities against the populace in the areas under their control.

Then three months ago, his wife, son, and daughter-in-law were all killed in an airstrike by Asad's forces, leaving only him and his granddaughter. After this traumatic event, his handler told him it was time for him and his grandchild to get out of Syria and arranged for their exfiltration.

A few days later, he took them to within a few miles of the Turkish border where they were met by a team of five Special Forces operators, two of whom spoke Arabic, who took them across the border where a truck was waiting for them.

Yaman later learned that those men who helped them were a SEAL team from America.

From Turkey they were flown to the US Naval Support Activity base near Naples, Italy, sixty miles south of Gaeta. The base hosted more than fifty different commands and had more than 8,500 personnel.

At the base, their presence was kept as clandestine as possible while they were waiting for the slow-turning wheels of bureaucracy in Washington to finalize the paperwork that would grant them residence in America.

It was at this base where Rex Dalton and Declan Spencer had turned up a few days ago and recruited Yaman and Rasha Hilal for one more mission before they would depart for the land of the free and home of the brave.

The two of them were put through a few hours' training in the planting of electronic surveillance apparatus and briefed about their mission. Rex and Spencer assured them that they had the means to watch them very closely during the mission and would extract them the moment there were any signs of danger.

They were then fitted with old and worn out clothes, dirtied up, given a small tracking device to hide in their clothes, and at about 9:00 p.m. they were dropped off a few miles from the Muslim enclave and walked the rest of the way. While the overhead drone kept watch, Rex, Josh, Tanner, and Darrin followed them in a van about 300 yards behind until they were inside the enclave.

Chapter Fifty

AN ÉDITH PIAF PERFORMANCE

*CIA Headquarters, Langley, Virginia and CRC
Headquarters, Arizona, USA*

Saturday, September 12, 2015

Stacie knew they were onto something when one of her
analysts showed her the intercepted emails between OLTA
Travel, a Russian travel agent based in Moscow, and Olesya
Kharlamova.

Apparently, Miss Kharlamova was planning to take a
week-long trip to Paris, France. Whether the trip was for
business or pleasure or both was not clear from the emails.
But Miss Kharlamova's business was not the kind she would
want to reveal to anyone in any event. Whatever the
purpose of the trip, it was important to get a surveillance
team to Paris to 'welcome' her and make sure that she was
always kept under close watch in case she had a meeting
with anyone of interest.

A few minutes later, Stacie and Shafer were talking to John Brandt and Chris McArdle to request their help with the surveillance job in Paris.

Stacie found it a little strange that John Brandt was unusually quiet during the briefing, leaving most of the talking to Chris McArdle. To her it looked as if he were deep in thought.

Brandt accepted the assignment but said he needed an hour or so to check a few things and would get back to them.

When the video call ended, McArdle looked at Brandt and said, "I know that look, John. What's up?"

Brandt told him what he had in mind. McArdle was grinning when Brandt finished. "I like the plan, and of course it would give you the chance to kill two birds with one stone."

"What are you talking about?"

"Ah, well, I have it on good authority that there is a certain lady in Paris, ahh… what was her name again…? Proll, I think. Yes, that's it, Madame Proll. I believe she's a deputy director in the DGSE (General Directorate for External Security), in charge of clandestine operations. Maybe, she'd be willing to lend a helping hand?"

"McArdle, what exactly did Dalton tell you?"

"Not much. Just that she apparently knows you, worked with you on a few missions back in the Cold War days."

"Bullshit. Out with it."

McArdle laughed and put his hands up in surrender. "Honestly John, I don't know anything else. Oh, maybe one more little detail. According to Rex, in his opinion, this woman has the hots for you."

Brandt shook his head and said, "Dalton has to keep his

damn opinions to himself. Now, wipe that grin off your face and get Barrett and Shafer on the line."

Stacie and Shafer listened to Brandt's plan, and despite shaking their heads for the audacity of it, they agreed to it. However, they said the approval thereof was above their paygrade. Stacie left the meeting and managed to track the deputy director, Martin Richardson, down surprisingly quickly and led him to the video conference room.

Brandt explained his plan again, and Richardson said, "No. You can't do it. But, and please note I am not inviting you to do so, I can't stop you from ignoring my orders. And, if you decide to do so, and things go wrong, I don't know you."

"Hmm, sounds familiar," Brandt said. "Well, in that case, thanks for taking the time to listen to me. Please excuse me, I have a few travel arrangements to make to get to Paris in time to attend an Édith Piaf performance."

When the call ended, Shafer, frowning, said, "Édith Piaf? What the hell… I thought she was dead?"

Stacie laughed and said, "Yes, she died in 1963. But Piaf was known as 'The Little Sparrow'. Kharlamova, as you know, is an ex-KGB sparrow. Need more explanation?"

"It means he's going to do it?"

Stacie and Richardson were smiling as they nodded.

Chapter Fifty-One

LUNCH WITH THE IMAM

Naples, Italy

Saturday, September 12, 2015

On the Saturday after being introduced to the Imam, at mid-day, Yaman and Rasha turned up at Imam Al-Sadiq's house as invited.

Al-Sadiq was not married, but he had a woman who came in every day to do housekeeping and cooking for him. Rasha joined her in the kitchen while Yaman and Al-Sadiq retired to the family room.

Yaman was curious about the history of the enclave and the people who lived there, and Al-Sadiq was happy to tell him all about it. Of course, in his telling he made no mention of the connection with the Camorra, neither about his own background or objectives.

He was however happy to show Yaman his house, which the latter, after living for so long in the most horrible conditions imaginable, thought was an amazing place. Yaman asked Al-Sadiq if he would mind if Rasha joined them for the tour of the house, and of course, the Imam had no objection.

By the time the lunch with Imam Al-Sadiq was over, every room in the house had at least one electronic surveillance device in it, and the study and living room each had three. Unfortunately, they couldn't plant video bugs as those could not be planted as inconspicuously as the little audio bugs. Even so, the audio bugs would give them enough coverage to find out what was happening in the Imam's house.

A few days later, on Tuesday, September 15, Imam Al-Sadiq was kind enough to drive Yaman and Rasha to *Napoli Centrale*, the Naples Central Station, from where they would travel by train to Hamburg, Germany. The Imam paid for their tickets and gave them two hundred Euros in cash.

The two of them boarded the train, and soon after departure, they moved from their coach in the middle of the train to the back. A little while later, they moved to one right up front. It was a counter surveillance measure to see if there was anyone following them. They didn't detect any followers.

When they stopped at Formia station about an hour later, they detrained and were picked up by Tanner Giles and Darrin Tipton in a white Mercedes Benz Vito van and transported back to the US Naval Support Activity base.

Imam Al-Sadiq was now under close surveillance.

Chapter Fifty-Two

IN PARIS WITHOUT A SUIT

Paris, France

Monday, September 14, 2015

John Brandt was grateful that no one occupied the seat next to him in business class on the seven-hour flight from DC to Paris. He had never been one for small talk, and besides, he had a lot of rumination to do. He and Christelle Proll, the deputy director in charge of clandestine operations for the DGSE, *Direction générale de la sécurité extérieure*, (General Directorate for External Security) the French equivalent of the CIA or the UK's MI6, had known each other since their early thirties and had worked on a number of joint clandestine operations during the Cold War. Before meeting his wife, there was a time when the two of them were enamored by each other, but the nature of their work and the Atlantic Ocean between them proved to be relationship killers.

Christelle married a civil servant who turned out to be a total jackass that couldn't stand that she was making a success of her career while he was stuck on the bureaucratic treadmill. Unable to recognize that he was the cause of his own misery and that he should have thanked his lucky stars to have a woman like Christelle as his wife, he blamed her and everyone else for his misfortune. The marriage lasted ten years.

Brandt and Christelle stayed in touch but not regularly, unless contacting each other via email or text message once a year around birthdays qualified as regular. They had not seen each other for more than eighteen years. Brandt had called her a few weeks ago after he was discharged from the hospital to thank her for the help she'd given Rex and the team to rescue him. Before that, the last time they'd spoken on the phone was fifteen years before, when John's wife died, and Christelle had phoned to sympathize.

It was not as if they'd had a love affair that had been put on hold, just waiting to be kickstarted again. Even so, Brandt couldn't help but wonder if this visit might rekindle the spark between them. Christelle had less than two years to retirement, and Brandt, after his narrow escape from death at the hands of his tormentors, had been giving the idea of stepping down some serious thought.

From the moment he had the plan to intercept Olesya Kharlamova in Paris, he had been filled with excitement about the prospect of being directly involved in the mission. And even more exciting, he had to admit at least to himself, was the prospect of seeing Christelle again and maybe even working with her—just like the old days. However, now that the rush to catch the plane was over, with nothing else to keep his mind occupied but his thoughts, he was somewhat surprised that he felt a bit nervous. A bit of introspection soon had him confessing, to himself only because he would never confess it to anyone else, that the butterflies in his stomach had nothing to do with the mission; they had everything to do with the anticipation of seeing the charming Madame Proll again.

Of course, part of his unease was also the fact that his preferred plan hinged on Christelle's cooperation, and he wasn't sure if he still had enough influence with her to secure her collaboration. However, after giving it a lot of thought, he decided if he could not persuade her to help him, he would make an alternative plan, and it would still be wonderful to see her.

The Delta Air flight touched down at Charles de Gaulle Airport, Paris's main international airport, right on time at 10:45 A.M. on Saturday, November 7. He had only a carryon bag, and cleared customs without any problems. In the arrivals hall, his eye quickly caught the man dressed in a black suit holding a little white board with the name 'Mssr. Jake Baker' on it. He hadn't traveled on a fake passport; he just didn't want to have his name advertised to everyone in the hall. The Jake Baker moniker was Christelle's idea.

Two minutes later, the chauffeur opened the back door of the armored black Citroën C 4 Picasso with tinted windows for him.

His heart began to race when he laid eyes on Christelle Proll. On the plane, he had been thinking and trying to visualize what she would look like after all this time, but he was not prepared for what his eyes beheld in that moment. The blonde hair, the green eyes, the stunning smile—as far as he was concerned, the years had made little if any differ-ence—she was as sensational and alluring to him as ever.

There are more than 170,000 words in the Oxford English Dictionary, and in that moment, John Brandt could not recall a single one of them to say to Christelle. Eventually, more than just a few seconds later, he regained his composure, leaned over, and kissed her on both cheeks, French style, and said in a whisper, "Christelle, you are as beautiful as always. It is so good to see you again."

She smiled, took his face in her hands, kissed him on the mouth, and said, "Thank you, John. It's good to see you, too, and I'm so glad you haven't lost your ability to flatter a lady."

During the forty-minute drive to her apartment they kept the conversation light and cheerful. On arrival at Christelle's three-bedroom apartment, she showed him his room and suggested that he unpack his stuff, take a shower, and join her in the lounge where she had a spread of his favorite pastries and coffee waiting for him.

"You still remember what pastries I like?"

She smiled and nodded. "*Madeleines*, *Macarón*, and *Saint Honore*. Right?"

"The years have done nothing to your memory either. See you in fifteen minutes."

He was back in ten.

She handed him a plate with one each of the delicacies, asked him if he still took his coffee sans milk and sugar, poured them both a cup, and pointed to the chairs.

She waited for him to take a bite of the *Macarón* and have a sip of coffee before she started. "John, we can get to the point the long way or we can take a shortcut. Which is it going to be?"

John laughed. "The shortcut."

"Great. In that case, I'll do the listening and you the talking."

John took the rest of the *Macarón* and another sip of coffee and said, "Before I do that, I want to thank you again, in person this time, for the support you gave my agents to help find and rescue me in September. Were it not for your help, I wouldn't be here today."

Christelle waved her hand dismissively. "Don't mention it, John. I'm glad you're alive and that they were able to get to you in time. Besides, I'd like to think you'd have done the same for me if the roles were reversed."

"Without hesitation," John said.

"Thank you. Okay, now I'm all ears," she said.

John knew she already had some knowledge about Operation Badr, which she'd received from her counterpart at the CIA, Martin Richardson, when he had called on the NATO member countries to help with the operation.

John explained to her what progress had been made, Olesya Kharlamova's involvement, why he was in Paris, and how he thought she could be of help.

"John, what you're telling me, your presumptions about the potential significance of the use of the name Badr is disturbing. Beyond disturbing. The thought of terrorists getting access to weapons of mass destruction to use in some of the world's biggest cities, which could include Paris! It's downright terrifying.

"So, you're thinking this Kharlamova woman might be able to provide more information?"

"Yes, we think so. We suspect she introduced the Camorra woman, Teresa Lombardi, to Fedot Frolov. We'd like to know why him, specifically. Not only that, we'd also like to know if Kharlamova knows what was discussed at that meeting between Frolov and Lombardi in Narva in October."

Christelle was quiet for a long while, taking a few sips of her coffee before she said, "Kharlamova will be arriving on Friday, in six days?"

Brandt nodded. "She's booked under the name Irina Mikhailovna."

"Not much time. I'll need to discuss this with my director. It's an unconventional plan you have, and that's what I always liked about you—never afraid to be resourceful. I think I might be able to get the director's authorization for DGSE's cooperation. If he agrees, and if necessary, we might have to pull the DGSI in as well."

The DGSI (General Directorate for Internal Security) was the French version of the FBI or the UK's MI5.

Christelle told Brandt to help himself to more of the pastries and coffee while she called her director to set up an urgent meeting.

She was back in less than ten minutes. "Okay, Monsieur Brandt," she said with a big smile, "I hope you brought a suit and tie with you. The director was so kind as to cancel his appointment with the Minister of Interior to meet with us."

"Oh shit! Apologies. Hmm, we've got a problem. I didn't bring a suit. In fact, I don't even own a suit. When are we meeting him?" John was so caught up in his predicament, he didn't see the little sparkle in her eyes.

"What? You came to Paris with no suit? What were you thinking? You didn't even think you and I were going to go out for at least one nice dinner?"

Brandt started stuttering, and Christelle started laughing. "Relax, I'm not going to dress up either, you're good to go as you are. We must get going; he's waiting for us."

"Okay, that's a bit of a relief. But about the dinner thing. I… well I thought about that… a lot and…"

She put her hand around his waist, kissed him on the cheek, and said, "John, I'm just teasing you. There's no restaurant where I want to have dinner with you that will kick you out because you turned up without a suit and tie."

Brandt and the director had never met but knew of each other, and John was sure that Christelle would have told him about his visit to Paris. The director had canceled his appointment as promised and was waiting for them when his assistant led them into his office. He was a short stocky man with a balding head of thin gray hair, a firm handshake, and friendly demeanor. Brandt was relieved to see he was informally dressed in business casual fashion, gray slacks and a blue shirt with no tie or jacket.

He invited them to be seated and offered them a coffee. John eyed the decanter of cognac on the director's elegant credenza and thought if the director knew what was coming, he'd have offered them that and taken a healthy slug of it himself.

Just like Christelle, the director was aware of Operation Badr and the DGSE's involvement in it. He listened intently to Brandt's account, asked a few pointed questions, and then turned to Christelle and asked her, "What's your opinion about Monsieur Brandt's request?"

"Monsieur Director, I have no hesitation to recommend that we give him our full cooperation."

Brandt's impression of the director was of a pragmatic man who relied on the competence of his deputies. He was certain that would be especially true of Christelle Proll. In all the years she had been with the agency, she no doubt would never have served him with improper advice. Brandt waited for the director's verdict.

He said, "I'm convinced, from what you and Monsieur Brandt have told me, of the gravity of the situation, and I'm inclined to authorize your request. However, let's just take a moment to consider any political ramifications."

Brandt remained quiet while Christelle gave the director her opinion about it.

The director nodded, looked at Brandt, and said, "Monsieur Brandt, I know France and Russia have a different relationship than America and Russia, but I'd still like to hear your opinion."

Brandt grinned and said, "Monsieur Director, politics has never been my strong suit, but I can't see what political fallout there could be in this case. If a foreign person enters America or France or any country for that matter and commits a crime, the legal system of that country deals with it. It's not a political issue as far as I'm concerned."

The director smiled and said, "I agree." Then he turned to Christelle and said, "I leave it to you to manage from here and keep me up to date, preferably on a daily basis."

Christelle and Brandt thanked the director and left his house a little less than ninety minutes after their arrival.

The next order of business was for Christelle to set up a meeting with two of her senior operations managers to brief them. An hour after leaving the director's residence, she and Brandt were in a secured room with the two managers at the DGSE head office at 141 Boulevard Mortier, Paris XX.

The 20th arrondissement (*XXe or vingtième*) was the last of the consecutively numbered arrondissements of Paris, also known as *Ménilmontant*, located on the bank of the River Seine.

It was shortly after 6:00 P.M. when Brandt and Christelle left DGSE headquarters. The wheels were set in motion; there was nothing more they could do until the next morning when they would meet with the managers again to finalize their plans and preparations for the arrival of Olesya Kharlamova aka Irina (Ira) Mikhailovna.

Brandt then called Rex.

Christelle was more than a little amused as she listened to Brandt's side of the conversation.

"Dalton, I certainly hope I caught you at a bad time."

"I did?"

"Excellent. Now, give Catia a break, pack your stuff, and get you and your dog's asses ready to be in Paris by Wednesday morning no later than eight."

"Yes, Paris, France, geographical whiz kid."

"Yes, I'm in Paris."

"None of your business. Oh, and on that point, remind me to have a word with you about keeping your damn opinions to yourself."

"Text me your flight details when you have them."

"Yeah. Okay, see you Wednesday morning, and don't be late."

"No, I definitely don't want you here tomorrow. You're not welcome before Wednesday morning."

When the call ended, Christelle smiled and said, "You really love that boy, don't you?"

Brandt grinned and nodded. "Like he was my own son. But please don't tell him I said so."

She shook her head. "You certainly have a peculiar way of showing it, John. But allow me to let you in on a little secret. I got the impression, when I met him a few months ago, he feels the same about you. He is a fine young man."

Brandt nodded. "That he is. The best agent I ever had."

Christelle suggested that they return to her apartment so that Brandt could get some rest, but he replied, "We haven't seen each other in over eighteen years. I came to Paris to see you, and you want me to get some sleep? I'm not *that* old. So, unless you have made other arrangements, how about I take you out for dinner? You pick the place, I'll pay. We've got the rest of today and all of tomorrow for ourselves, let's make the most of it."

Christelle beamed. "John, if *you're* up to it, so am I. Guy Savoy it is."

The Guy Savoy was a Michelin-star restaurant owned by the chef who had trained the celebrity chef, Gordon Ramsay who starred in the popular American and British TV series, Hell's Kitchen. The restaurant offered a tasting menu which included among other delicacies, foie gras, lobster, and oysters. It was one of the most popular restaurants not only in Paris but in the world and all but impossible to get a booking in less than six months—unless, of course, your name was Christelle Proll, a personal friend of Monsieur Savoy.

Brandt and Christelle were among the first patrons to arrive when the restaurant opened for dinner and the last to leave when it closed at 10:30 p.m.

Chapter Fifty-Three

THINGS WERE ABOUT TO CHANGE

CIA Headquarters, Langley, Virginia, USA

Wednesday, September 23, 2015

At CIA Headquarters, Stacie Barrett and her team of analysts working on Operation Badr were getting impatient and frustrated with the lack of progress.

Since planting the bugs in Teresa Lombardi's and the Imam's houses, Greg and his surveillance team had been watching and listening to every word that was said. They meticulously recorded everything. Within a few days, they had gathered enough information to confirm what they already knew or suspected about Teresa Lombardi and her clan's involvement in drug trading, counterfeiting, racketeering, money laundering, and other proscribed activities.

It didn't surprise them to hear that Imam Al-Sadiq was deeply involved in human smuggling and the importing of drugs from the Middle East, which were sold to the Bene-duce-Longobardi clan.

But the wires remained quiet about anything related to Badr, terrorism, or an arms deal, neither had any meeting happened between the Imam and a courier of any sorts, nor was there any contact between Lombardi and Frolov or Al-Sadiq.

There was enough damning information about organized crime activities they could have handed to Italy's anti-mafia squad, which, if acted upon, could have led to several arrests and long jail sentences. The information would have implicated Teresa Lombardi, her entire leadership group, and Imam Al-Sadiq.

However, decision-makers above their pay grade determined it was not wise to do so at this stage. Though potentially being a step to prevent Lombardi and the Badr group from executing their plans, they argued that they could be dealing with the mythological Greek Lernaean hydra. The Hydra, according to legend, was a serpent-like leviathan with many heads that would grow two new heads in the place of every one that was cut off.

No. Until they knew about everyone that was involved in the Badr conspiracy and what their plans were, they had to patiently wait and listen, and prepare to act swiftly to remove all the heads in one fell swoop when the time came.

The surveillance teams following Frolov were also unable to produce any information of significance. All indications were that Frolov was an exceedingly wealthy man with more aliases than he himself could probably remember. He was always on the move, constantly traveling around Europe and Asia in chartered private jets, staying no longer than two to three days in the same place, every time under a different name, and under as many disguises. If ever there were a human chameleon, Frolov was it. There was no doubt that Frolov was up to no good, but the details remained a mystery.

It was frustrating to say the least.

He didn't have a wife or children. However, that didn't mean he had an aversion to women. On the contrary, he seemed to really like their company, which was probably why he kept at least one woman in every location he owned properties, such as the Bahamas, France, Pattaya in Thailand, and the Amalfi coast in Italy. He appeared to love luxury Italian sports cars and had a deluxe yacht anchored at the Isle of Capri, Italy, for the winter.

Two days after the meeting with Teresa Lombardi in Narva, he visited Belgrade, Serbia for half a day before flying to the Amalfi Coast where he spent two days on the yacht before flying to Pattaya in Thailand. And so it went, on and on, constantly on the move.

The missing scientist, Doctor Haroun Najm al Din Hadad refused to show himself. It irritated Stacie and Shafer to no end to know the scientist could be sitting somewhere busy building a very nasty chemical or biological weapon, and they didn't even have the slightest clue where to start looking for him.

The lack of information about the conspirators' plans and timelines remained a major worry not only for Shafer and Stacie but for everyone in the senior echelons of the CIA and every one of the team members involved in Operation Badr.

They would have been relieved to know things were about to change.

Chapter Fifty-Four

DO YOU HAVE ANYTHING TO DECLARE?

Paris, France

Friday, September 25, 2015

Looking back at everything a few days later, Olesya Kharlamova realized that the only thing that would have kept her from the nightmare awaiting her in Paris was if she'd never got on the plane that left Moscow on that fateful day, Friday, September 25.

As it were, without any premonition of what awaited her, she was on an Air France flight direct from Moscow to Paris, in first class. She adjusted her seat, leaned back, blew out a sigh of relief, and took a sip of her champagne. She told herself she deserved the break. She was tired, and she was going to relax for one full week. Sleep late, dine out, and enjoy Paris. No bodyguards, no followers, no male chauvinists to embitter her life—*just I, me, myself, Paris, and the cuisine and the sights and the shops.*

She had a limousine waiting to take her to the 5-star $2,200 per night *Hôtel Plaza Athénée,* in the heart of Paris's *Haute Couture*, with a view of the Eiffel Tower on the one side and *Avenue des Champs-Élysées* on the other. The *Avenue des Champs-Élysées* was one of the French capital's top attractions, visited by an average of 300,000 people per day. It was said to be the world's most beautiful avenue, by day or by night.

The customs officer that stamped her passport was very friendly, smiled, welcomed her to France, and wished her a good time. Her idyllic holiday was off to a good start, she thought when she thanked the officer and left.

Although she didn't know it at the time, the moment her holiday took a turn for the worse was when two uniformed agents, a man and a woman, of the DGDDI (*Direction générale des douanes et droits indirects*, Directorate-General of Customs and Indirect Taxes) commonly known as *les douanes*, appeared on either side of her just when she was about to enter the arrivals hall to meet her chauffeur. They asked her to accompany them. She was bit surprised, but in such high spirits that she was not alarmed.

The DGDDI was the French law enforcement agency responsible for customs services, immigration control, levying indirect taxes, preventing smuggling, surveilling borders, and investigating counterfeit money and more.

The two agents escorted her to a room with no windows, only a few uncomfortable, cheap, plastic chairs, a steel table, and video cameras mounted to the ceiling in each corner. In the room, her eyes first came to rest on a rather good-looking border security agent of about five foot eleven or so, with black hair, dark and penetrating eyes, and an athletic build. At the second look, she decided that while he was indisputably good-looking, his eyes transmitted intelligence… and danger. His name plate said he was Rowan Donnelly. Next to him was a big black dog.

The female border agent that accompanied her to the room stayed; the male left and closed the door behind him.

Donnelly greeted her in French, apologized for the inconvenience, explained it was just a routine random check, and said it would only take a minute. He also pointed to the security cameras and told her that everything was recorded. He asked if she had any objections to that.

She had none—she just wanted to start her holiday as quickly as possible, and this was just a nuisance.

Donnelly looked at his dog, tapped his own nose, and then pointed to Kharlamova's big suitcase and carryon, which were on the floor next to her.

The dog moved forward, sniffed at the two pieces for a few seconds, sat down, and looked at the man and then back at the luggage.

"Madame, did you pack your own luggage?" Donnelly asked.

"Yes, I did."

"Were you given any items by someone else to carry in your luggage?"

"No."

"Do you have anything to declare?"

"No."

"Did you lock your suitcases after you packed them and keep the keys with you at all times?"

"Yes, I did."

"And do you have the keys with you now?"

"Yes, I do."

"Thank you, madame. I'm going to put the suitcases on the table. I want you to unlock them, open them, and unpack everything inside please."

For a fleeting moment, Kharlamova was worried, but then she thought if they had problems with her fake passport, the customs agent who stamped it would have stopped her. And of course, there was nothing untoward in her suitcases. So, this must have been a random check as the agent told her.

She unlocked the suitcase and started unpacking. Halfway down she saw a small plastic Ziplock bag about four inches by four inches. She had never seen it before. Without thinking, she retrieved the bag, held it up, turned it around, unzipped it and took out the tinfoil packet inside. She turned that around a few times and ripped it open, saw the white powder, and felt the blood drain from her face. Her legs felt as if they couldn't support her weight anymore as she plonked down in the nearest chair, still clutching the plastic and tinfoil bags in her bare hands.

She began explaining that she had no idea what those items were, that she had never seen them, never touched them, and had no idea what was in them or how they happened to be in her suitcase.

Donnelly didn't interrupt, waiting instead for her to stop talking.

She didn't, not until she had switched from French to Russian and in a long rant, which included many colorful Russian profanities, proclaimed her innocence.

She probably believed none of the agents understood what she was saying. She was wrong; Donnelly was fluent in Russian but would not let her know he understood every word of what she was saying.

She gave a long sigh as she finally comprehended, she had been set up by someone, either in Paris or Moscow. One or more of her enemies could have done it—she had no shortage of those. Her despair grew in leaps and bounds as she realized that she had just put her finger-prints all over the plastic and tinfoil bags. And she knew, she didn't even have to think twice, hers were going to be the only fingerprints on those items. As for the white powder in the tinfoil bag, she had no doubts either—heroin.

She started another round of protesting and explaining, but then stopped mid-sentence, switched to French, and said, "I want to speak to someone from the Russian Embassy—right now."

The female agent stepped forward and said, "Madame, we'll get to that in due time. For now, we would appreciate it very much if you would just cooperate with us and do as we ask you.

"May I have your passport please?"

Kharlamova nodded and took her passport out of her handbag, handing it to the agent, who, with a latex-gloved hand, took it from her and placed it in a clear plastic bag. Next, the agent asked Kharlamova to hand her the Ziplock and tinfoil bags and placed them in a second plastic bag. She took two labels off the roll on the table, wrote something on each of them, and stuck them on the bags.

The agent stood, pointed to the security cameras in each corner, and told Kharlamova again that everything had been recorded from the moment she had entered the room. She told Kharlamova she was now going to hand the two bags to the forensics team at the airport and would report their findings within the next two to three hours. In the meantime, Kharlamova would have to stay in their custody.

Kharlamova only stared at the agent when she asked if she understood.

She asked Kharlamova if she required a Russian interpreter, but the latter shook her head and insisted again on calling the Russian Embassy.

The agent told her that she would get the opportunity to do so soon, that there were no charges against her yet, and that it would be wise to cooperate with them.

After a few more outbursts, in Russian, Kharlamova very reluctantly signed her false name on the piece of paper the agent had put in front of her containing the list of items she took from her. It was only after she handed the signed document back to the agent that it struck her; she had just provided them with another set of fingerprints to compare with those on the bags.

Two new agents arrived, a man and a woman. The woman relieved Kharlamova of her handbag and searched her before she and her companion escorted her to another room. This room could only be described as a jail cell.

Kharlamova walked in and heard the door lock click behind her. Though she could see no one, she knew someone watched. She sat down on the chair at the table, dropped her head on her arms, and waited. Although her mind was in turmoil, her KGB training kicked in as she made every effort to calm down, assess the situation, think about the possible scenarios, and plan for them—as best she could.

Two hours later, guards escorted her from her cell into yet another room. This room had a window, but she couldn't see through it. She knew it was a one-way window; this was an interrogation room, and someone was on the other side of that window, watching.

Her suitcase and carryon stood in the corner of the room.

A few minutes later, Donnelly and the big black dog and a tall, slim woman of athletic build with piercing green eyes and blond hair, dressed in a charcoal pantsuit, entered the room. The two of them sat down in the chairs on the opposite side of the table. The woman placed the two plastic bags containing the passport, the Ziplock bag, and tinfoil bags in front of her on the table.

The first impressions Kharlamova got of this woman were that she was intelligent and attentive. Not to be messed with. Donnelly's dark, penetrating eyes reminded her of staring down dual gun barrels. The dog sat down on the floor between Donnelly and the woman and stared intently at Kharlamova.

The whole scene was unnerving, but she made every effort not to show it.

Chapter Fifty-Five

TIME TO NEGOTIATE

Paris, France

Friday, September 25, 2015

The woman said, "I'm Madame Proll. I work for the DGSE. I've been told that you've already met Monsieur Donnelly."

Kharlamova frowned. "DGSE? What the… Never mind, my name is Irina Mikhailovna, but I guess you already know that. Now I'd…"

The dog growled softly.

"No, I don't," Madame Proll interjected.

"What?"

"Know that you are Irina Mikhailovna."

"What do you mean? There's my passport, have a look."

Madame Proll nodded slightly at Donnelly.

He said, "We had a look at your passport. It has a photo in it that seems to be of you, and it says the bearer of the passport is Irina Mikhailovna. The problem is that it's forged."

"No! It's not. Get the Russian Embassy on the line right now and check it. And, by the way, I'm not going to say another word until I've spoken to a representative of my country."

The dog growled again; a bit louder than before.

That damn dog is going to drive me crazy.

"You will get your chance to speak to your embassy," Madame Proll said. "But before you do that, I'd strongly advise that you listen to what we have to say first. That way you can give the embassy a full account of the problems you're facing."

Kharlamova said, "Go ahead, but I'll need a Russian interpreter."

Madame Proll smiled and said in fluent Russian, "Not necessary. Monsieur Donnelly and I are both fluent in Russian."

Kharlamova's eyes widened as she realized that Donnelly would have understood every word she'd ranted earlier when her luggage was searched. She tried to appear unfazed and said, "Good. So, now tell me what exactly is going on here."

Proll nodded at Rex to continue.

"What's going on is that you have entered France on a false passport, to start with. Secondly, you were in possession of fifty grams of heroin, an illegal substance in this country. Third…"

"Bullshit! My passport is legal, and the drugs were planted in my luggage."

The dog snarled at her.

Donnelly grinned. "You told me you packed your own luggage, locked it, and kept the keys with you. You also told

323

me you're not carrying any items for another person. You want to have a look at the video recording?"

Kharlamova shook her head.

"The only fingerprints on those bags containing the drugs were yours."

"What's the third joke you want to share with me?"

Donnelly looked at Madame Proll and nodded for her to take over.

"Miss Mikhailovna, or do you prefer I call you by your real name?"

"Mikhailovna *is* my real name."

"Interesting. You see, our records say you're Olesya Kharlamova, a former major in the KGB. And that's the reason the DGSE is involved. You are working for the *Sluzhba vneshney razvedki Rossiyskoy Federatsii*, SVR, the Russian Foreign Intelligence Service."

"That's a lie!"

The dog woofed softly.

"What's a lie? That your real name is Olesya Kharlamova, or that you're an SVR agent?"

She was in a corner, and the damn dog's growling was really working on her nerves. "Okay, I'll admit my name is Olesya Kharlamova, and I did work for the KGB. But I left the KGB in December 1991. I have my own business and have never worked for the SVR, and I will never work for them, ever."

Madame Proll had an impassive look on her face when she replied, "We know all about your 'business' Miss Kharlamova. You received six months of training at the Swallows Nest during your KGB days. And you're still in that line of business. Extracting information by means of sexpionage and selling it to the highest bidders, which includes the SVR."

Kharlamova's face had gone pallid. She made no reply.

The dog let out a sound as if he was yawning.

Kharlamova interpreted that as some kind of threat.

Donnelly took over again and said, "Miss Kharlamova, you are facing three very serious charges here. As far as the DGDDI is concerned, you are to be charged for entering the country with a false passport. It carries a five-year jail sentence. The possession of the illicit drugs carries a ten-year sentence. As for the espionage, I'm not sure, but it could be life."

Kharlamova's head dropped to her hands. She knew she was in a corner. Despite knowing that her only true transgression was the false passport, she had lived under the KGB and Communism long enough to remember how easy it was to make trumped up charges stick. And in her situation, every shred of evidence so far, whether it was false or not, pointed at her and no one else.

The time to deny and protest was over, it was obvious these people knew everything about her. It was clear that they had a lot more information they had not told her about yet—a very unenviable position to be in when you were sitting at the wrong end of the interrogation table. And it was also very clear that they wanted something from her. It was time to try different tactics.

"What do you want from me? Let's talk about that."

Unexpectedly, the dog had what looked a lot like a big smile on its face. *What the hell? Is the dog now laughing at me? Or is it about to attack me?*

It took all her willpower to hide her anxiety.

Donnelly looked at Madame Proll, his expression grave but professional as he motioned for her to go outside.

Madame Proll nodded ever so slightly, turned her gaze back to Kharlamova and said, "I don't know if there is much more we want to talk about. As far as I'm concerned, the next step is to arrest you for those crimes, read you your rights, and allow you to make the phone call to your embassy.

"After your arrest, you will be taken to a prison where you will be kept until your court appearance where the charges will be put to you. I'm not sure how long that would be, it could be a day or two before your first court appearance.

"However, I need to point out that you will not get bail. We'll strenuously oppose it. So, after the first court appearance, you will be kept in custody until your hearing, and that could be anything between six and eight months from now, could even be a year."

Kharlamova had only two words to describe her emotions at that point in time—utter despair.

"We're going to give you a bit of time to think about everything. If there is anything else you think we should know, it might count in your favor to tell us when we come back."

Paris, France

Friday, September 25, 2015

Christelle, Rex, and Digger went to join John Brandt in the observation room from where they could keep an eye on Kharlamova.

Brandt was grinning when the two of them entered the

room. "That was the quickest surrender by a KGB agent I've seen in my life."

"SVR agent." Rex chuckled. "I guess they aren't training them like they used to in the KGB days. But, on the other hand, it could have something to do with the fact that Madame Proll, Digger, and I make an unbeatable team."

At that, Brandt growled indignantly, to the delight of Christelle and Rex. It seemed Digger appreciated the joke as well, since he heard his name and smiled.

"Okay, before the two of you start awarding medals to yourself, the real work starts when you go back in there. Keep in mind, although you've maneuvered her into a very tight corner, she'll also be considering the potential comeback from her clients if she betrays them. If you push her too far, she might just opt for a French prison rather than showing her face in Russia again."

Madame Proll nodded. "Good point, John. We'll keep it in mind."

"Good. I'm ready when you are, Madame Proll," Rex said.

"Just one moment, Rex," Christelle said. "I'm not going to ask you again to call me Christelle. The next time you call me Madame Proll I'm going to order my agents to arrest you. There are three of them that would dearly love nothing more than to do exactly that."

Brandt looked at her with a frown, waiting for an explanation.

"Oh, I see Rex hasn't enlightened you on how he treated three of our agents in Vietnam a while ago. Well, when this is over, ask him to tell you."

Rex was shaking his head but smiling. "I just can't get rid of my past, can I? Thanks for reminding me, Christelle. And of course, no thanks for telling the Old Man about it."

Chapter Fifty-Six

AN OLD-FASHIONED DEFECTION

Paris, France

Friday, September 25, 2015

It was an hour later when Christelle, Rex, and Digger were back in the room with Kharlamova. Christelle started. "*Mademoiselle* Kharlamova, now that you've had time to think through everything, is there anything else you think we should know?"

Kharlamova shook her head. "There is nothing else. I am guilty of entering France on a false passport but not guilty of the possession of drugs or spying. However, having said that, I know the evidence is overwhelmingly against me. But, that's not what this is about, is it?"

It was immediately evident that the break had helped Kharlamova to boost her courage and regain equanimity.

"I know you want something from me," she said. "So, tell me what it is, and we can start the negotiations."

But Christelle hadn't fallen off a turnip truck. She was not going to put her cards on the table. She shook her head. "There is nothing to negotiate, *Mademoiselle* Kharlamova, you've got it all wrong. You committed serious crimes, and you're going to be charged for it. All I'm doing is giving you the opportunity to come clean with anything else you might have done. You're already in so much trouble you'll spend the rest of your days in jail. What I'm doing is offering you an opportunity to mitigate your sentence."

Kharlamova stared at her and Rex in turn for a long while then dropped her head slightly, avoided their eyes, and looked at the table. Her voice had dropped to a whisper when she said, "I have something that might be of interest to you."

"And that would be?" Rex asked.

"My business records."

Digger let out what sounded like a long sigh and dropped to his belly on the floor—he was going to take a nap.

Rex and Christelle both managed to look uninterested.

"Why would that be of interest to us? Or wait… are you saying your business records might show more crimes committed in our country or somehow prove your innocence?" Rex played stupid.

"Mister Donnelly, my business records might not be of interest to the DGDDI, but I'm absolutely sure they will be of immense interest to the DGSE."

Rex shrugged and looked at Christelle.

"Why would the DGSE be interested in your business records, *Mademoiselle* Kharlamova? And what makes you think what's in those records would safeguard you against the French justice system?" Christelle asked.

Kharlamova took a deep breath and started talking. She

was shrewd enough to withhold the specific details, yet gave them enough information to let them understand the magnitude and gravity of it.

Christelle, Rex, and Brandt, who was behind the one-way window, soon learned that this woman, over the past twenty-four years, had gathered the motherlode of extremely damaging secret information from across the globe.

What the three of them heard scared the living daylights out of them. Especially so when she pointed at highly regarded and powerful citizens of their own countries and those of many of their allies.

Kharlamova knew she had their attention when she noticed that they didn't interrupt her. It took the best part of an hour to provide a high-level view of what she was offering and answer some of their questions while skillfully keeping the specifics away from them.

At times, it was near impossible for one or another of them not to gasp in shock. The sex traps Kharlamova and her team of sparrows were able to set up and extract information from their targets, some voluntarily and some through blackmailing, sounded so corny it was difficult to believe it could happen in real life.

Although all three of them had been trained in espionage techniques and between them had many years of experience in the spy industry, they couldn't help but be astonished at what secrets powerful men and women were prepared to share with a stranger who was willing to share a bed with them.

It sounded like the stuff of spy novels, movies, diplomatic folklore, political scandals, disgrace, humiliations, special prosecutors, investigations, and congressional hearings.

When Kharlamova stopped, Christelle, although intensely interested, managed to feign indifference. She shook her head and said, "So, let me see if I've got it right; you want to give us all this information, and in exchange for that, we should forgive all your crimes and let you go back to Russia?"

Kharlamova shook her head. "Miss Proll, you know as well as I do that if I give you this information I can never go back to Russia. The moment I give it to you I've signed my own death warrant. I won't last twenty-four hours, not in Russia and not in many other parts of the world.

"No, Madame Proll, what I'm offering you is a good old-fashioned Cold War type defection. I'll give you the information in exchange for a new name and face and a new life—freedom and safety."

Christelle nodded slowly.

"And if you don't accept my offer," Kharlamova said, "I'll take my chances with the French legal system. I'd rather spend my days in a French prison than fall into the hands of my enemies, especially those in Russia."

Kharlamova sat back, folded her arms across her chest, and waited for a reply.

Chapter Fifty-Seven

TWO MORE CRATES IN PORT SUDAN

Port Sudan, Republic of Sudan

Friday, September 25, 2015

Port Sudan International Airport was located 12 miles south of the city. On the north side was a big warehouse. The building was secured with high, barbed-wire fences, security lights, three permanent guards, and two vicious Rottweilers that roamed the property at night with the guards. Surrounding the property, about five yards away from the fence, was a four-foot deep and wide trench, and in front of the trench there was at least a thirty-yard swath of no-man's-land; flat, bare, red African soil and no hiding place.

Everyone working at the airport knew the warehouse was off-limits, a no-go zone. All they knew, mostly through gossip, was that there were apparently two men who worked and lived inside on a top-secret project. The warning signs posted were very clear—anyone caught within 50 yards from the security perimeter would be shot on sight. Neither the airport security nor any of the staff had ever met or laid eyes on the two occupants inside.

At night the lights in the building were on, but the windows were covered day and night. The guards never entered the building and never left the premises.

At least every second day, a small, unmarked truck with no license plates visited the warehouse, ostensibly to deliver food and supplies to the guards and occupants. But no one at the airport knew who owned that truck, where it came from, or what it delivered. And with the threat of being shot when getting too close, no one had any interest in finding out.

In the early 1990's, Israel Aerospace Industries developed a UAV (Unmanned Aerial Vehicle), a type of drone known as the IAI Harpy. It was what was called a loitering munition, which was a weapon system that while circling in the air around the target area, searched for targets, and attacked once a target was located. Loitering munitions had the benefit that they made for faster reaction times against concealed or hidden targets that emerged for short periods.

The Harpy was built to fulfill the SEAD (Suppression of Enemy Air Defenses) role in battle; that is, attacking enemy radar systems. It was designed to evade enemy radar using stealth technology and carried a 70-pound high-explosive warhead.

The Israelis sold the Harpy to several foreign nations, including South Korea, Turkey, India, and China. It was the sale of $55 million worth of Harpys to China that earned them the ire of the American military community, worried that the Harpy would pose a threat to Taiwanese and American forces in the case of a war with China.

In 2004, China returned the Harpys to Israel to be

upgraded, and that was when the USA demanded that Israel keep the drones and nullify the contract.

Publicly, the Israelis refused, telling the US that the Harpy was a one hundred percent Israeli-designed weapon containing no US-produced sub-systems at all. For all practical purposes, they told the US to shove it. "We built it without your help, and we can sell it to whoever we want."

In private, however, the Israelis didn't want to alienate their biggest friend and ally. In a half-gesture of goodwill, they returned the Harpys to China without being upgraded.

The Chinese, masters at copying technology, built their own version of the drone and decommissioned the Israeli Harpys. The retired equipment ended up in a warehouse somewhere in China—as the old saying goes—out of sight, out of mind.

The Harpy was about nine feet in length with a wingspan of almost seven feet. It was powered by a 38 horsepower Wankel rotary engine, had a maximum speed of 115 miles per hour, and a range of about 311 miles. It was built to carry a 70-pound, high-explosive warhead.

It was on two of those original, Israeli-built Harpys, which had belonged to China, that Doctor Haroun Najm al Din Hadad and his assistant, Hassan Hussain, an aeronautical engineer, had been working since September 15. First assembling the two drones, then making certain alterations.

What the final payload was going to be, they didn't yet know, neither what the target was. They didn't need to know, not yet. They had very detailed instructions about the changes to make and they were following them to the letter. The payload, accompanied by the instructions for its deployment, was due to be delivered within the next day or two.

They were also under the strictest of orders not to make

any contact with the guards or the locals. In fact, they were forbidden to leave the premises for any reason whatsoever.

Furthermore, they were to maintain in absolute internet silence, which meant they had no Internet. Their only contact with the outside world was with the two men in an unmarked and unregistered white truck who visited them at night to deliver their food supplies and any materials they required. But they were not allowed to have personal contact with the visitors, they could only communicate with them in writing via the guards outside. It was all set up so that no one would be able to recognize anyone else after the project was completed.

They had just completed the assembly and configuration of the drones when two more crates arrived at the door of their workshop.

Chapter Fifty-Eight

THE SPARROW OF PARIS

Paris, France

Friday, September 25, 2015

The time in Paris was approaching 4:00 P.M. when Christelle said to Kharlamova, "I will present your offer to the director of the DGSE and get back to you." And just to make sure to keep the pressure on Kharlamova she added, "That doesn't mean I support your request. Until I have a meeting with the director, you'll remain here, in custody."

Kharlamova sighed but nodded her understanding. She was sure they would accept her offer. She had no doubt that she was the victim of a very cleverly designed and executed DGSE operation, and she had no way out of it. But she was sure what she had offered them was exactly what they were after from the outset.

Rex and Christelle, with Digger in tow, left Kharlamova in the interrogation room and closed the door behind them. In the hallway, Christelle gave the guards instructions to move Kharlamova back to the holding cell, to give her some food, and to keep a very close watch on her.

On entering the observation room, they both noted the look of concern on Brandt's face. They didn't have to ask him about it; they felt the same. They would probably get from Kharlamova what they wanted, but they hadn't seen the details contained in Kharlamova's 'business records', yet. Nevertheless, what she'd alluded to was going to have ramifications which they, at that moment, couldn't even begin to fathom.

"I'll get hold of the director right now. I've got no doubt that he'll want us to accept the offer, but I want to make sure he understands the can of worms about to be opened."

Brandt nodded. "Yep, from what I've heard, this is going to cause a shitstorm of epic dimensions, to put it mildly. Heads are going to roll, people are going to jail, fingers are going to be pointed, and asses are going to be kicked. And that'll only be the beginning.

"I'd say, if the Director accepts the offer, we need to talk to Kharlamova first, get the Frolov and Lombardi information out of her, and then hand her over to a team of analysts to extract everything else."

"Agreed," Christelle said as she started dialing the director's number.

Less than three-quarters of an hour later, Brandt and Christelle were in conclave with the director of the DGSE in a secured room at headquarters.

There was no hesitancy from the director to accept Kharlamova's offer, provided, of course, that the information could be verified. As for the inevitable political fallout, his opinion was that it was the prerogative of the governments affected to decide how to deal with it. Therefore, he agreed to Brandt's request to inform Christelle's counterpart, Martin Richardson, and ask him to send a team of analysts over to Paris immediately.

Within half an hour, Brandt had made a call to Richardson who immediately tasked his most experienced interrogator to get himself and two of his most senior analysts over to Paris post-haste.

DGSE safehouse, Paris, France

Saturday, September 26, 2015

Shortly after midnight, Kharlamova was moved from the holding cell at the airport to a DGSE safehouse on the outskirts of Paris. She was not going to get any sleep that night and very little in the days to come.

Christelle told her that her offer was accepted and spelled out the provisos in no uncertain terms.

Kharlamova was introduced to an American man, Jake Baker. She instantly sensed it was not his real name but kept her opinion to herself. He was a tall man with gray hair and hazel eyes. He had a stately comportment and was in excellent shape for his apparent age, which she guessed to be late sixties to early seventies, a handsome man despite his age. Her assessment of him was that he was a tough guy, a straight shooter who had been in the black ops and spy game for a long time. A man who had seen it all, been there and done it all. She quickly surmised that she had to tread carefully around him. He was not going to take any antics from her.

She could only sigh as she reflected that she was in the presence of three highly skilled professionals, four if she added the damn dog who could sense every lie she tried to dish up. About Donnelly she also had no doubts. He never worked for the DGDDI, she was willing to bet half of her entire fortune on it that Donnelly was a special agent, a black ops operator, and a highly skilled one at that. The dog rattled her, and that was without doubt the purpose of his presence. How that dog knew how to keep her off balance throughout the whole process she would never know, but one thing was sure, that he played a major part in ruining her holiday.

Kharlamova understood and accepted the terms and conditions. She didn't mention her assumption she had been the victim of a brilliant setup by the DGSE and probably the CIA. It was not going to improve her situation if she did make a scene of it.

She gave them the login credentials to her cloud-based storage account where she kept what she called her 'business records'. She also gave them the credentials to all her bank accounts, which the two IT specialists that worked for Christelle, immediately accessed, then transferred the money in them to a numbered Swiss bank account, one of many kept by the DGSE.

Within five minutes, Kharlamova was penniless. She knew the only way she would see that money again was to be honest with her captors.

Within minutes after gaining access to the cloud storage account, her captors would understand that Kharlamova's 'business records' were not the standard type of business records kept by legitimate businesses. What was inside that online vault was close to three terabytes of damning information about her clients and her clients' adversaries.

It would also be evident that Kharlamova had no scruples about working for unsavory characters. So long as they paid her, she didn't care who they were and what they did. It was also obvious in her line of business there were no ethics equivalent to the legal or medical professions' attorney-client or doctor-patient privileges—sometimes her clients in one case were her targets in another.

Kharlamova had been meticulous with her recordkeeping. Every client had their own folder, inside each folder were documents detailing, in chronological order, every case, the steps that were taken, when, where, how, and by whom. It included bank account details and financial transactions, complete with dates, amounts, and details of services rendered.

Accompanying the narrative of the cases in the text documents were related audio and video recordings as well as photos.

On the first readthrough, they didn't open any of the video files or the photos. The names of the files were, in most cases, descriptive enough to indicate what would be found inside—and many of them not were to be opened in the presence of a lady such as Madame Proll.

John Brandt and Christelle Proll, both of whom had been part of the Cold War, knew that even in the age where espionage had become more technology driven, the oldest trick in the KGB manual was still one of the most effective. The list of victims of Kharlamova's entrapment missions was long, illustrious, and remarkably varied. It included high-ranking officials, politicians, clergymen, businesspeople, mafia bosses, ordinary men and women, bachelors and married couples, young and old, homosexuals and heterosexuals, military attaches and journalists, security guards and ambassadors. No category of humans, it seemed, had been immune from the charms of Kharlamova's professional seductresses and their male counterparts.

After the first glance of what was in Kharlamova's online vault, Rex asked the IT guys to find all the information pertaining to Liana Verdi and Fedot Frolov and copy it onto a flash drive.

They did so and handed him the device, which he would later plug into a laptop not connected to the Internet.

Christelle then instructed the two IT specialists to copy every bit of information from the cloud server. They were to verify that what they were copying wasn't corrupted in the process. And when they were done, they were to wipe out everything on Kharlamova's account, so no one else could get hold of it.

It was obvious that Kharlamova had kept these records as a type of insurance policy. Not the kind of policy peddled by insurance salespeople that would pay out a large sum of money at the occurrence of death or another unfortunate event. Rather, it was the kind of policy that would be used to keep her alive and prevent her from meeting sudden misfortune. It was the kind of information people usually gave to their lawyers or a trustee for safekeeping—to be opened and published in the event of the untimely demise or disappearance of the owner.

Despite Kharlamova's assurances that she wasn't lying, Christelle, Brandt, and Rex understood that they had no way of knowing whether she had kept copies of the same information elsewhere. Even so, they held the trump card—they would know where to find her if she had lied to them.

The deal was that once she had given them all the information and everything had been checked and verified and she had been properly debriefed, which she understood could take months, she would be handed her money, provided with a new identity, and flown to a country of her choice, excluding, of course, France, the USA, or any of their allies.

Chapter Fifty-Nine

ON SUSPICION OF TREASON

DGSE safehouse, Paris, France

Saturday, September 26, 2015

Rex, John, Christelle, and Kharlamova were in the study of the safehouse at 4:00 A.M., Digger was asleep on the carpet. Everything said in that room would be recorded and captured on video, and Kharlamova was made aware of it.

Rex had the laptop open and connected to a big TV screen. He first browsed to the Teresa Lombardi folder dated June 2014.

The text document gave a chronological account of events, starting with the call received by Kharlamova from Lombardi, followed by the details of the dinner at the Grand Café Dr. Zhivago and audio recordings of the dinner meeting and subsequent telephone call from Kharlamova to Lombardi in February 2015 reporting her findings.

There were also financial records showing payments totaling $270,000 USD broken down by date and amount. $100,000 USD paid to Kharlamova's Austrian bank account in June 2014—the non-refundable deposit. Another $20,000 USD was paid for various travel and accommodation expenses into an account in the Bahamas, and a final amount of $150,000 USD paid in February 2015 into a Swiss bank account.

Kharlamova obviously didn't like to keep all her eggs in one basket—a sound business principle.

Rex asked her, "How did you and Lombardi come to know each other?"

"I did some work for her father, Ricardo Lombardi," Kharlamova said. "I never dealt with Don Lombardi directly, always through his advisor or consigliere, as they called him, Valter Li Voti. The work I did for her father is all captured in the files I gave you."

Rex continued scrolling slowly through the document while they read it and opened the audio files of the recordings for them to listen to. It was the recording and accompanying notes of the February 2015 telephone call from Kharlamova to Lombardi to report her findings of who was responsible for the 2011 explosion in the Port of Naples, which sent cold shivers down his spine and no doubt John Brandt's. They heard Kharlamova telling Lombardi she was able to find out it was a joint Mossad-CIA operation, and that the mission support was provided by a Mossad agent in Rome, a female *sayan*. It was a big relief to Rex, though, to hear that Kharlamova was unable to get Catia's name, address, and photo.

But it was even more chilling to hear how close Kharlamova came to identifying Rex when she told Lombardi that the person responsible for the explosion worked for a black ops private contractor, operating out of Arizona, called Crisis Response Consultancy, who were contracted by the CIA for that mission. And although she couldn't get his real name, she was able to find out that this man went by the pseudonyms *El Gato*, *Alshaytan*, and the Ghost.

It took a lot of willpower from both Rex and Brandt not to explode in a fit of rage in front of Kharlamova and Christelle, neither of whom knew that Rex was the person referred to in that conversation.

The next bombshell was not contained in those audio recordings of the telephone calls and dinner meeting. It was in the rest of Kharlamova's written notes and a series of video clips she hadn't shared with Lombardi. It contained the name of the person who leaked all the information, a senior official at the CIA, Morris Craik, the personal administrator of Martin Richardson. The written narrative was accompanied by some very embarrassing and utterly condemning audio recordings and video footage.

There could have been many reasons for Morris Craik's betrayal, but there was no time to speculate about it. Nevertheless, it was perplexing how a staunch family man with a wife and three children and a top-secret security clearance could get involved in a five-month extramarital affair with a woman who appeared to be half his age. Whatever Craik's reasons, his frequent cavorting at the apartment of Kharlamova's sparrow were duly filmed and recorded for the sole purpose of blackmailing him.

It was of paramount importance to get him removed from his position immediately—he could jeopardize the Badr Operation. John Brandt shivered slightly when he thought about the second call in less than twelve hours he'd be making to Martin Richardson.

It was Saturday, 5:30 A.M. Paris time and Friday 11:30 P.M. in Virginia when Brandt's call roused Richardson from a peaceful sleep and shattered his promise to his wife that they would sleep in the next morning and take a quiet getaway together that week.

When Richardson saw the caller ID on his encrypted phone, he knew it was bad news, and his getaway plans had blown out the window. He was not a man easily given to indignant outbursts, but the news given to him by Brandt had exactly that effect on him. Morris Craik had been working for the CIA for more than thirty-eight years. He was a loyal and diligent worker, and Richardson, who'd appointed him as his administrator, trusted him unreservedly.

As the first shockwave of the treachery subsided, Richardson's next reaction was, "I can't help but wonder how much more sensitive information that idiot has been divulging, to whom, and for how long. How many people's lives has he put in danger? Shit, how many people are dead because of him? And he knows about Operation Badr—not much, but enough to cause us damage."

"We can only hope this was a once off indiscretion, Martin," Brandt tried to pacify his friend. "The man is in his mid-fifties. He could've been going through a midlife crisis, male menopause or some shit like that," Brandt said. "But, like you, I shudder at the thought that a man in his position could've been doing this for a long time."

"By God, I hope you're right about that, John. Right now, I feel like organizing a firing squad."

"I understand, Martin. It's never pleasant to discover a traitor so close to home. I'll send everything we have discovered so far over to you as soon as we end the call. You should have it within fifteen minutes or so."

"Okay, thanks. I'll wait for that, and you can be assured that Craik will not see sunrise tomorrow morning from his own bed. In the meantime, keep going with that Kharlamova woman; we need to get to the bottom of this Badr thing. I have a very bad feeling about this one, John."

"You're not the only one, Martin. We're about to start on the Lombardi-Frolov transaction now. I'll keep you posted. Hopefully we won't uncover more moles in our camp."

"Let's hope so. But I got the impression from your call earlier that Kharlamova has a lot more devastating information and that we're in for a rough ride for many months and years to come."

"You can bet on that. We just had a quick gander through her vault before we started with the Badr related information, and I can tell you it's hair-raising. The information this woman has collected over the past twenty odd years is going to rattle a lot of cages. This vault of hers is going to be like Mount Everest—it will make its own weather, and it's going to be stormy weather. But for now, I'll leave that to Shafer's team to uncover and pass on to you."

"Can't say that I'm looking forward to that," Richardson sighed.

By 3:00 A.M. Virginia time on Saturday, September 26, an FBI SWAT team had arrived at Morris Craik's house and taken him into custody on suspicion of treason.

Craik didn't attempt to resist arrest; he didn't ask any questions, nor did he give any explanations. Not to the FBI and not to his sobbing wife. In the interrogation room, he said he was prepared to cooperate fully but requested to have his boss, Martin Richardson, present when he made his confession. Within two hours he was facing Richardson, and in the presence of the FBI's chief investigator he spilled the beans—all of it.

Richardson was disappointed, hurt, and outraged but also somewhat relieved when he left the interrogation room with the knowledge that Craik's betrayal was, as Brandt had hoped, a series of indiscretions with the same woman brought on by what Craik blamed on a loveless marriage.

Chapter Sixty

TERMS ACCEPTED

DGSE safehouse, Paris, France

Saturday, September 26, 2015

At the arrival of dawn, shortly before 6:00 A.M. in Paris, Brandt, Christelle, and Rex were still in the study of the safehouse with Kharlamova. They were busy reading through the next Teresa Lombardi file in Kharlamova's 'business records' which had started on August 19, less than seven weeks ago.

Brandt looked out the window and sighed in silence. Dawn was supposed to be the time when one could see the sky being illuminated while the sun was still below the horizon as the sun's rays were reflected from the atmosphere. But there was none of that. It was a typical late September day in Paris: miserable weather, overcast, rainy, and foretelling the cold to come shortly. And his gut feeling was that they were about to experience a lot more misery from Kharlamova's records.

Kharlamova's chronicles of her second encounter with Teresa Lombardi started with the text entry and recording of a telephone call from Lombardi on Tuesday, August 19. She requested another meeting with Kharlamova in Moscow for the next day, Wednesday, August 20. The call was less than two minutes, more than half of which was spent on niceties before requesting another meeting in Moscow.

The three of them noted the financial transactions, $150,000 USD paid to an account in the Cayman Islands on August 20, the same day as the meeting in Moscow. That was the non-refundable deposit required before Kharlamova would move a finger. Then there was another payment of $150,000 USD paid into an account in Monaco, on August 30, ten days after the first payment. There was a final payment of $250,000 on August 31, the day after the meeting between Lombardi and Frolov in Narva. The last tranche went into an account in Switzerland.

Rex mumbled, "I guess we will soon find out what each of those last two payments were for?"

Kharlamova nodded glumly.

"You and Frolov were in the KGB at the same time. Did you meet each other then?" Christelle asked.

"Yes. We did. He was my senior by a few years, but I worked with him to get some of his arms deals through."

Brandt growled, "In other words, you used your special bedroom skills to persuade or blackmail a few unwilling parties to sign underhanded arms deals. Right?"

Kharlamova nodded slowly. "But you won't find any of that information in my business records. I only started collecting and storing information when I started my own business."

"We'll want the details about your previous operations later. Let's return to the Frolov-Lombardi case," Christelle said.

"You know Frolov goes by the name of Egor Zubarev now?" Kharlamova asked.

"Yes, we do," said Brandt. "We also know about his many other aliases and his ability to rise from the dead." Brandt was not going to let her know for how long Frolov had been pulling the wool over the eyes of western security agencies or how recently they were able to find out about it.

Brandt nodded for Rex to continue. But Rex had a question first. "Did Frolov supply weapons to Ricardo Lombardi?"

"Yes."

"And you were the go-between?"

"Yes. You'll find the details about those transactions in my records."

"Frolov supplied the weapons for the deal that got Lombardi killed in 2011?"

"Yes."

Rex nodded and opened the audio recording of the meeting on Wednesday, August 20, which took place at the Pyatyy Okean restaurant in Moscow on the fourth floor of Terminal F at Russia's busiest airport, Alexander S. Pushkin International.

Rex knew the restaurant; he had been there a few times. It overlooked the airfield, was decorated with classical Russian paintings, and offered excellent Russian hot dishes and other food.

As she did with all her meetings, Kharlamova had made a secret audio recording of the entire event.

After greeting each other, Lombardi explained that she was in a hurry; she had two hours to finish the meeting and check in for the flight back to Rome. They ordered food and drinks, and Lombardi got right to the point. "I need someone who can supply me with some special equipment and materials."

"What exactly do you have in mind?"

"I want nuclear weapons—briefcase nukes."

None of Kharlamova's interrogators should have been too shocked when they heard Lombardi's request. After all, that was what they suspected and speculated would be what the Badr conspiracy was all about—to deal the West a crippling blow, which would create a modern-day Badr-like turning point in Islamic history.

Nuclear weapons would do it.

But they knew suitcase nukes did not really exist. A nuclear weapon that could fit into a suitcase has never been developed. The word 'suitcase' in that context had come to mean portable. The smallest nuclear bomb ever developed was known as the W54 warhead. It had a maximum yield of one kiloton, equivalent to 1,000 tons of TNT. It weighed 118 pounds. The notion of a nuclear weapon that fit into a briefcase was a fallacy—only to be found on the pages of fiction books and the screens of movie theaters.

"Teresa, are you serious?"

"Yes, I am dead serious."

"Do you have any idea how much scrutiny has been placed on any country with nuclear weapons, including those who are aspiring to get them, and any scientist that knows how to build them? You can forget about it. You won't get your hands on them. And besides that, it's an assignment I'll never accept—not at any price."

They could hear Lombardi's sigh before she said, "Well, it was worth a try."

"I trust that you've not discussed this with anyone else?"

"No, I haven't. You have my word on that."

Teresa Lombardi was lying through her teeth. She and Hassan Walid, known to her as Imam Kazim Al-Sadiq, were the masterminds of the Badr conspiracy. Lombardi was a consummate liar. She had lived a double life for almost all her adult life, and she had learned how to exploit her petite, girlish looks to the maximum.

She had been meeting with Al-Sadiq in secret for years, without any of her leadership group's knowledge, including Li Voti. They'd been planning the Badr attack for the past three years or more in utmost secrecy. Al-Sadiq knew exactly what Lombardi was doing at that very moment. He was waiting for her return to find out if they would get their weapons. The two of them had already selected their target, months ago. And if they were successful, it was going to be the modern-day Badr event they were longing for.

They knew they had to keep the group that knew about the Badr plan small. The only other person on the planet that also knew everything was Al-Sadiq's superior in Lebanon, Esam Abbas Bitar from Beirut, a well-known politician, member of Hezbollah's political wing, Loyalty to the Resistance Bloc, and member of the Lebanese parliament. The remaining three Badr co-conspirators didn't know the details—each of them had a specific role in the operation and were under strict orders to not even try to find out what the others were doing.

Although Kharlamova was trained in spycraft which included recognizing when someone was deceitful, she hadn't detected Lombardi's lie. "Good. And it's my advice to you to *never* discuss it with anyone. Stay away from it unless you'd like to spend the rest of your life in prison or worse."

Rex paused the tape and asked incredulously, "You believed her?"

"Yes, I did."

"Well then you're much more stupid than I thought," Brandt interjected before Rex could comment.

Kharlamova didn't reply, she just stared at the table.

"Roll the tape," Brandt said to Rex.

A long silence followed before Lombardi spoke again.

"The thing is, Olesya, I need weapons that can do widespread and serious damage, mass destruction is what I want. Accepting that I can't get a nuclear weapon, the next best thing would be enough good quality fissile material for a real dirty bomb. Failing that, chemical or biological weapons or both."

"Teresa, I'm sorry to keep asking the same question, but are you serious?"

"Yes, absolutely."

"You are determined to have your revenge irrespective of the dangerous territory you'll be steering into?"

"Unequivocally."

"You're playing with fire, Teresa; it's going to destroy you."

"The pot calling the kettle black," Brandt murmured.

"Olesya, revenge is all I have lived for," Lombardi said. "It has been my *raison d'être* for the past four years. There is nothing more important to me in this life than that revenge. I want it more than life itself. I desire to have it with my entirety. I deserve it, and I *will* have it. If taking that revenge is the last thing I do on this earth, I'll be happy. I've given up every pleasure in life, I have no man or woman or friends to love, because I have no love to give.

All I have to give is hate, and my enemies deserve to get it."

"Teresa, I just want to remind you of the old truism; if you desire revenge you should dig two graves."

There was no reply from Lombardi.

Christelle looked at Rex, motioned for him to pause the recording, and said, "That woman is certifiably insane; she needs to be in an asylum for the mentally ill."

"No doubt about that," Brandt said and then turned his gaze to Kharlamova in disgust. He had a hard time stopping himself from grabbing her and smashing her head against the wall for taking on a contract from such a sick person just for the money. It had already dawned on all three of them that the deal had been made. They didn't even have to listen to the rest of the recording, it was obvious. Frolov was going to supply the weapons of mass destruction, otherwise there would have been no meeting in Narva or further payments beyond the initial $150,000 deposit.

All that remained was to find out what type of weapons Frolov was going to supply, when, and where. "But Miss Russia here had no compunction to make a deal with her, irrespective of who is going to get killed or how sick in her head this woman was." He turned his gaze to Kharlamova, "In your world innocent lives don't matter; money trumps virtue—always. Right?"

Kharlamova made no reply.

Rex was quiet. He understood some of Teresa Lombardi's pain. His entire family—parents, brother, and sister—had been killed by terrorists in the 2004 Madrid train station bombings. That event had changed his life. Before the explosions he was heading for a career in the diplomatic service. But that tragedy had made him an embittered man.

Bent on revenge, he'd entered the shadow world of spying, black operations, and assassinations. For the most part of his life after the killing of his family, he'd been driven by an insatiable desire to avenge their deaths and those of the innocent people killed by terrorists anywhere in the world.

He could almost sympathize with Lombardi, were it not for one fundamental difference in the origins of their drive for vengeance—his family was innocent; hers was not. Lombardi's family was the enemy, collaborating with terrorists, the very people he had devoted much of his life to eradicate. Untold thousands of innocent people had died on the streets of the cities of Europe and the Middle East because of drugs and illicit weapons and explosives, which Lombardi's family had provided for one reason only—money.

Rex resumed the audio.

"Can you help me or not?" Lombardi asked.

A lengthy silence followed before Kharlamova said, "It's going to cost you a lot, not just for my services but for the goods, if my contact can even do it."

"Money is of no concern. What I want to know is if you can help me, or should I shop somewhere else?"

Another long quiet spell followed before Kharlamova said in a soft and measured voice, "Here's how it's going to work. One hundred and fifty thousand today. Non-refundable. I need two to three weeks.

"If I'm successful in establishing contact with the source, and he is agreeable, I'll let you know. Against payment of another one hundred and fifty thousand, I will provide you with a name, venue, and a time for a meeting.

"After the meeting, this person will let me know if you are able to make a deal. Upon his confirmation to me that he will be able to supply you with what you want, you'll pay me another two hundred and fifty thousand.

"And that's it, Teresa. You and I will be done—forever. I'll have nothing else to do with you from that point onward. Don't even try to contact me ever again. This is our last business transaction. Those are my terms, and they're non-negotiable."

"And if you're not successful to get this contact of yours to supply me with what I want, can we still do business in the future?"

"No. I'm putting myself in grave danger even trying to contact this person. So, if you insist on going ahead with this crazy idea, it is the last deal we'll ever make. I already told you, you're playing with fire. I intend to stay as far away as humanly possible from that fire."

Another long period of quiet followed. "Terms accepted. Give me your bank account details, I'll arrange for the transfer right now," Lombardi said in a firm tone.

Chapter Sixty-One

FAR, FAR TOO MUCH OF IT

Getting their hands on a nuclear weapon was an erotic dream of many a terrorist leader and the egomaniacal power hungry. But, fortunately for the world at large, so far, it remained just that—a carnal dream.

The activities of rogue states, those who threatened world peace, such as Iran, Syria, Iraq, and North Korea, who all had nuclear ambitions, kept the world on the edge of their seats and prevented terrorists from acquiring nuclear weapons.

Across the globe, security agencies spent obscene amounts of money to prevent nuclear proliferation—the spread of nuclear weapons, fissionable material, and weapons-applicable nuclear technology and information to nations not recognized as 'Nuclear Weapon States' by the Treaty on the Non-Proliferation of Nuclear Weapons (NPT), commonly known as the Non-Proliferation Treaty or NPT. Security agencies knew about every single nuclear physicist on earth and kept a watch on them. Many of them couldn't go to the toilet without the knowledge of one or more security agency.

The Islamic terror groups knew their chances of acquiring a nuke were virtually none. Therefore, to them, the ultimate prize, more valuable than gold, diamonds, and rubies, so desirable they would sacrifice themselves and their children, give their eyes and teeth, take insane risks, was fissionable material.

With that they could build a dirty bomb.

Even their scientists understood enough of physics to know that when enough fissionable material was packed with enough explosives, it would generate enough lethal radiation over enough land area to render any one of the largest cities of the world uninhabitable for at least two and a half decades.

Though the death toll would not be as instant and hefty as that of a nuclear explosion, it would not be trivial, either. Three quarters of a million or more people would die within a few years from cancer caused by the radiation.

A dirty bomb was not a weapon of mass destruction on the same level as a nuclear bomb, but it definitely was a weapon of mass disruption.

And despite the Non-Proliferation Treaty and the efforts of the security agencies of signatories to the treaty, fissionable material was available on the black market—far, far too much of it.

Chapter Sixty-Two

THE ISLE OF CAPRI MEETING

DGSE safehouse, Paris, France

Saturday, September 26, 2015

Rex opened the document titled Isle of Capri dated August 28, 2015, in the Lombardi-Frolov folder. It contained the notes of a meeting between Kharlamova and Frolov on the Isle of Capri, Italy; right on Teresa Lombardi's doorstep so to speak, less than 25 miles (44 kilometers) from Lombardi's residence in Naples.

They immediately saw that contrary to all Kharlamova's notes in the other files they'd read so far, the notes about this meeting were, to say the least, very sketchy, just a few bullet points. And there was no recording of the meeting.

Rex asked her to explain.

"Since leaving the KGB, I've had contact with Frolov only once before this meeting. Frolov has a reputation as a temperamental man, easily given to outbursts of fury and violence. People who know him fear him. I am one of them.

"The last time I saw him was in 2011 to ask him to fulfil a weapons order from Ricardo Lombardi, the Don of the Beneduce-Longobardi clan, the late father of Teresa Lombardi. My role was only to introduce Frolov to Li Voti. I had nothing else to do with the transaction."

"Say you," Rex said. "But you didn't do it for free. Right?"

"No, I didn't," Kharlamova mumbled.

"We're still waiting for your explanation as to why you didn't make proper notes or a recording of this meeting."

"You know how the previous deal turned out. The Don, his sons, and twenty-seven others were all killed. That made Frolov extremely nervous. It was not easy to get an audience with him this time. I had to go through a number of inter-mediaries before I could see him.

"Frolov is an exceedingly careful man. He is also an evil and ruthless man."

"And you're an angel?" Brandt growled.

Kharlamova paused for a breath, shook her head slightly, and continued. "He frightens me. He would've killed me without blinking an eye if I'd even tried to record that meeting. In any event, he would not let me near him until he had me strip-searched and clothed in garments he provided. With Frolov, I wouldn't take any chances."

"Okay, I get it. You were too scared to take the risk to try and record the meeting. What prevented you from making proper notes afterwards?" Rex asked.

Kharlamova shrugged and said, "I don't have an expla-nation other than that the man scares me witless. When he heard who my client was, he went into a fit of rage, called me a moronic bitch for even contemplating doing business with the Beneduce-Longobardi clan again."

"I'm starting to like this Frolov guy, he seems to be very perceptive," Brandt said.

"Okay, let's see how well your memory functions," Rex said. "Tell us in detail what happened at that meeting on his yacht at the Isle of Capri..."

"Miss Russia," Brandt interjected, "before you start, let me just give you a piece of good advice at this juncture. If you are going to tell us, don't lie, and don't leave anything out." He looked at Rex and nodded.

Rex thought the nod was for him to continue but then, to his surprise, Brandt pointed to Digger and said to Kharlamova, "You might manage to fool us, although that'd be just temporary, but you won't get past him. And he gets really, really upset when people lie to us."

Rex had a hard time suppressing his urge to laugh. Not about Digger's abilities to detect lies, at that the dog was exceptionally good, but about Brandt's change of attitude towards Digger lately. The words 'damn dog' had disappeared from his lexicon. It seemed as if Digger was now accepted as a friend and 'agent' in Brandt's CRC or at least as an assistant to an agent.

Josh and Marissa must've really had a long and interesting chat with the Old Man.

Rex called Digger, whispered in his ear, and pointed to Kharlamova. "You're up, clever boy. Make sure she doesn't lead us astray."

Digger got it immediately. He walked over and sat next to Kharlamova and stared at her, letting out one soft growl and baring his teeth in a snarl, as if to say, "Pay attention. If you lie, you'll regret it."

Christelle had never seen Digger in action before the

earlier interrogation at the airport and again now. Fortunately, Rex had told her how good a play actor Digger could be. She was also struggling to not smile at this scene.

Kharlamova was terrified. She didn't know who to look at, Rex and the rest or Digger next to her. Her head kept swiveling between them as she told them in detail about the meeting with Frolov.

Rex did the questioning, and Digger played along as always with deep yawns, soft growls, lolling tongue, and sometimes a smile, which if one didn't know, looked a lot like a threat. Whether Digger made his noises always at the appropriate time was debatable. Nonetheless, it had the desired effect on Kharlamova.

When she finished, they were all satisfied that she had been honest and had left nothing out, but it was not what they hoped to hear. In essence, her account came down to: she met Frolov, explained who Teresa Lombardi was, and miraculously survived his outburst. She then told him what Lombardi wanted, and Frolov's response was to convey the time, date, and place where he would meet Lombardi in Narva. That was the full extent of the meeting.

After that, Frolov contacted her, through an intermediary, the day after the supposed Narva meeting had taken place. The message contained a code phrase, agreed between them at the Isle of Capri meeting, which meant Kharlamova could go ahead and invoice Lombardi for her final fee. Kharlamova took that as a sign that an agreement had been reached. The details of which she had not the slightest idea.

Brandt said, "Kharlamova, we have made a deal with you, and we'll have to honor it, but let me tell you this; innocent people are going to die if we don't stop Frolov and Lombardi.

"You might want to think you can wash your hands of this deal. But you're the one who started it. And only to make a few bucks.

"The day when those bombs or chemical weapons or biological weapons are deployed, and women and children die, I want you to look around for me. I am going to look you up, not to kill you, because I must honor our agreement, but to remind you of what your role in it was. I hope that your conscience will prosecute you to your grave and beyond."

Kharlamova was a hard woman who made a living in the harsh and merciless underworld of organized crime, but Brandt's words had given her reason for pause. Although her conscience never bothered her much about the morality of what she did for a living, she was never so heartless that she would target children. She had to admit to herself she was blinded by the money she could make out of Lombardi and didn't consider the consequences. She should have walked away from this one. Her eyes were filled with tears because she knew he was right—she was the one who had set it all in motion.

Christelle saw Kharlamova's emotions getting the upper hand and used the moment to get a message across. "If there's anything you can think of, even an opinion or speculation as to what weapon, where, when, and how it's going to be delivered, you'd better tell us. I'm not entirely in agreement with Jake that we *have* to honor the agreement with you at all costs. What you did here was not your usual business where your targets always had a choice how they wanted to behave. What you did here was to conspire with terrorists, and I'm not convinced our agreement exculpates you from that."

A tear was streaking down Kharlamova's cheek as she

whispered, "Honest to God, I have left nothing out. I have no idea what Frolov and Teresa agreed. All I can say is what you already know; it's going to be a weapon or weapons with immense destructive capability. I believe it won't be a nuclear device, although I can't categorically exclude the possibility. However, I have no doubt it would be chemical, biological, or even a dirty bomb. Frolov is capable of getting access to any of those, that I'm confident of."

"How and where?" Rex asked.

"I don't know. I can only speculate. Frolov must have maintained contact with ex-KGB agents, SVR agents, and high-ranking former Soviet Bloc military staff. Apart from those, I wouldn't exclude contacts in China, North Korea, and Pakistan. I don't have details to give you. If I had the information, I'd certainly give it to you. There will be very few items he won't be able to get. Those are my opinions, purely speculation and gossip I've picked up over the years."

Rex, Brandt, and Christelle looked at each other. It didn't need saying; there was nothing more to be gained from Kharlamova about the Badr case for now. It was time to hand her over to the interrogation team to extract the other information from her while the three of them considered what to do next.

Chapter Sixty-Three

A HAND ON A HOT STOVE

CIA Headquarters, Langley, Virginia, USA

September 26-27, 2015

It started when Stacie was studying the satellite tracking reports of the ships of 7SSC, (Seven Seas Shipping Company) a big shipping business based in Riyadh, Saudi Arabia, owned by Saiyyad Rahal, one of the Badr Five. It was about the time when Rex et al started the second round of interrogation with Kharlamova in Paris.

The log of the Rahal III, one of 7SSC's ships, caught Stacie's attention when she made her first discovery. The ship which, according to the manifesto, was carrying a load of farming equipment, had plotted a route from Alexandropouli, Greece, through the Suez Canal for Mumbai, India.

When the Rahal III reached the Red Sea at a point opposite Port Sudan on its starboard side, it stopped.

According to the report, Rahal III had been at anchor about twenty nautical miles from Port Sudan for close to three hours.

Why?

Time was money in the shipping business. Across the world, cargo ships' speed and courses were tracked and logged in real time. Late delivery meant penalty payments for the shipping companies. And since the start of Operation Badr, 7SSC's ships had been singled out for closer scrutiny than any of the other companies.

Doing what? And why didn't the Saudis pick it up and report it? That's if they even spotted the anomaly.

The information was already seventy-two hours old.

Stacie reached for her phone and called for the surveillance footage of three days ago captured by the satellites and drones that kept a constant watch in those parts of the world. Within half an hour she had it all, and with the help of an experienced analyst, she studied the footage—hoping against all odds it would have captured something about the Rahal III.

It was her lucky day.

An old steel-hull fishing boat, with no name on it could be seen in the satellite footage. It had gone out from Port Sudan, met with the Rahal III, and moored to it. First, two wooden crates about the size of a three-drawer filing cabinet were lowered onto the boat with the ship's cranes. Then two men disembarked the ship and got onto the boat with the two crates.

"I guess we are looking at some kind of smuggling operation here," said the analyst.

"Yep. But what are they smuggling?"

Lady Luck stayed on Stacie's side as it turned out the drone had picked up both men's faces when they looked up into the sky. The facial recognition system made short work of identifying them.

Sudan was a terrorist paradise, where government forces and a plethora of terrorist groups were involved in genocidal wars on minority ethnic groups, massacring, raping, and pillaging. In the process, they had killed over 2.5 million Sudanese. There was a good reason the country had been on the United States' list of state sponsors of terrorism since August 1993. In other words, if a true definition of a shit-hole had to be created, Sudan could be used as an example.

The two men on that boat with the two crates were well-known jihadis of the Al-Qaeda ilk. Therefore, it was critical to find out what was in those crates and for whom they were destined.

Unfortunately, at that stage Lady Luck abandoned Stacie—the satellite and drones had collected no further helpful information.

Stacie 'M1' Abrams was chagrined with the Saudi's failure, whether deliberate, accidental, or by carelessness didn't matter. "How many more of these types of incidents went undetected or ignored?" she wondered out loud.

It took less than a minute to make up her mind, and she called for the attention of her team. "I want you to drop what you're doing for an hour or so. Go back to July, when we started this operation and placed the ships of 7SSC under closer surveillance. Check the satellite data. We're looking for a repeat of what we just found."

Within the hour they had checked every one of 7SSC's ships and found one more almost identical incident. On September 15, The Rahal IV had been carrying a load of consumer electronic goods from the Port of Shenzhen, China, destined for the Port of Naples, Italy when it stopped and anchored about 25 nautical miles from Port

Sudan. There it transferred two big crates, about six to seven times bigger than the ones unloaded three days before. The same old steel-hull fishing boat with no name on it had gone out from Port Sudan, met with the Rahal IV, and taken delivery of two crates. The same two men who were involved just three days before were there, disembarking the Rahal IV. They'd boarded the fishing boat and escorted the crates.

Again, Lady Luck abandoned Stacie—the satellite and drones had collected no further helpful information.

Five minutes later, Stacie and Shafer were explaining to Martin Richardson why it was crucial for him to immediately pick up his secured phone and talk to his counterpart in Saudi Arabia.

Richardson didn't need much convincing.

The Saudi director in charge of counterterrorism and clandestine operations told Richardson that he had assets in Sudan as well as in the Port Sudan area. He understood the urgency and undertook to brief two agents right away to locate the boat, the two men, and those crates. As a parting remark, he mumbled something in Arabic, of which Richardson understood very little, but he would have put money on it that it had something to do with kicking the asses of his analysts who had missed those incidents.

When the phones were back in their cradles, all Stacie could do was wait—not one of her strong points.

Richardson must have seen the frustration on Stacie's face. "Stacie, there's nothing more we can do now. We just have to wait for the Saudis to do their job and get back to us."

"I'd never have been a good field agent—I don't know how to wait."

"It's all relative. As Albert Einstein explained, 'Put your

hand on a hot stove for a minute, and it seems like an hour. Sit with a pretty girl for an hour, and it seems like a minute. That's Relativity'."

Stacie had her hand on what she experienced as a 'hot stove' for six hours while waiting for the Saudis to report back. She and everyone else who knew had little doubt those crates and those men meant trouble.

While she was enduring the relative effect of her hand on the 'hot stove', many thoughts crossed Stacie's mind. This could be the break they were looking for. But it was a gut feeling. No one would act on it. On her gut feeling, the President of the United States would not order an invasion of Sudan—as she would have—hours ago.

Then the Saudis finally got back to Richardson. They could not find the two deliverymen, but they found the boat and its captain. He didn't have a clue who the men were and what was in the crates. The crates were moved off his boat with a crane, and as far as he was concerned, that's where his curiosity and responsibility ended. He had no idea where they went. He was asked to do a job; he did it, got paid for it, and that was it.

The Saudi agents prodded the security guards at the harbor entrance, who looked at their handwritten logs and told them that the truck that had picked up the crates on both occasions belonged to a moving company based in the city of Port Sudan.

The moving company owner told the Saudi agents, masquerading as local police, where the crates were delivered—at the front gate of a warehouse in a secured area near the airport.

The Saudi agents didn't go into the area, the warning signs were enough of a deterrent for them not to take a chance unless they had specific orders and a lot more armed men.

The Saudis provided the GPS coordinates of the warehouse, and within minutes Stacie and Shafer and the Operation Badr team were studying the satellite images of the warehouse.

Within the hour, a satellite was tasked to monitor the place permanently, and a drone was circling thirty-thousand feet above. The warehouse would be under constant surveillance from that moment on until they knew what was going on there.

Finally, Stacie was able to take her hand off the 'hot stove', although she was not entirely satisfied to still be in the dark as to what was in those crates and who was in that warehouse.

The fact that the ships that had transported the crates on both occasions belonged to Saiyyad Rahal was enough to keep her and everyone else suspicious.

Chapter Sixty-Four

TIME TO GET HEAVY-HANDED

DGSE safehouse, Paris, France

Sunday, September 27, 2015

Christelle, Rex, and Brandt were in the family room, sitting in reclining chairs in a semicircle in front of the fireplace where a nice log fire was going. They each had a mug of French hot chocolate, made from whole milk, heavy cream, powdered sugar, and chopped bittersweet dark chocolate. The warmth of the fire and the delicious hot drink were more than welcome, an escape from the past twenty-four hours of no sleep, little to eat, and bad news.

Before he had left the *TOMATS* for Paris, Rex had instructed Greg and his IT team to check, double check, and recheck for any evidence of money that had passed from Lombardi's and any of the Beneduce-Longobardi clans' accounts to Frolov.

By the time the three of them started their deliberations

372

in front of the fireplace, Greg and his team had not found anything yet.

Brandt pointed out that didn't mean no money had changed hands. In the empires of the Beneduce-Longobardis, Teresa Lombardi, and Frolov, it was to be expected that vast financial transactions would be taking place, almost all of them for illegal purposes, and a big effort would have been made to obscure them.

Rex said, "Let's forget about tracking down the money for now. That's Greg's and his team's job. Frolov is going to deliver something to Lombardi, otherwise he would not have met with her, nor would he have given Kharlamova the green light to invoice Lombardi for the 'success' fee. In other words, the agreement was made; the goods will be delivered if they haven't been already."

Christelle said, "We still know absolutely nothing. We don't know what has been or will be delivered, where and when and who or what the target is, or when is D-day."

"Yep, that's about the size of it." Brandt said.

"And I know where to get all of that information." Rex chimed in.

Brandt and Christelle stared at Rex for a short while and then Brandt grinned. "Yeah, and I think I know what you have in mind. It would be a complex mission, it would be risky, it's doable, and you'll never get official permission for it."

"What are you two talking about?" Christelle asked.

"Rambo here wants to launch an international rendition operation. Frolov, Lombardi and Al-Sadiq. Right?"

Rex grinned. "No, that's not what I was thinking."

"Enlighten us then."

"I also want the clan leadership, all of the Badr group, and everyone else who has anything to do with this."

Christelle was on her feet. She was about to protest when Brandt's satellite phone rang. It was Chris McArdle. Brandt held his hand up for them to stop talking.

McArdle said he was in a conference call with Martin Richardson, Bryan Shafer, and Stacie Barrett, and they wanted Brandt to join.

Brandt told them that Madame Proll was with him and asked if they had any objections if she joined the conference. Richardson had no problem, in fact, he welcomed his French counterpart to the meeting. It was not often that the French and US intelligence agencies worked together like they were doing on Operation Badr. And that was largely due to Madame Proll's influence. He knew nothing about Brandt's and Proll's history. Brandt also mentioned that one of his agents was also in the room but did not mention Rex's name. It was part of the security protocol that no one in the CIA could know the names and faces of CRC's agents.

Rex remained off-screen and quiet for the entire meeting.

Brandt updated them with the information gathered from Kharlamova during the second round of interrogations, and they all agreed that although they now had confirmation of the deal between Lombardi and Frolov, they didn't learn much more.

Stacie then explained what had transpired in and around Port Sudan over the last three days and about three weeks ago.

Richardson told them that the US and Saudi intelligence agencies had put the place under tight surveillance with satellite and drone cover as well as feet on the ground. They were now waiting to see what they could garner from this observation.

Rex was shaking his head wordlessly. He was of the opinion they were wasting valuable time. The tactics of waiting for the Badr conspirators to show their hands was a risk—by the time they did, it could be too late to stop them. The critical information they needed was in the heads of Fedot Frolov, Teresa Lombardi, and probably others—all of whom they had tabs on, knew where they were, and could pick them up. It might not be an easy operation to execute, but with a team of highly trained operatives, the impossible could be possible. As far as he was concerned, they had only one strategy to follow now, and they should not wait to execute it.

Brandt saw the dissatisfaction on Rex's face and in his demeanor and must have guessed what was going through the younger man's mind. He got Rex's attention and signaled for him to remain quiet, indicating with a gesture that they would talk after the call ended.

He felt the same as Rex. It was time to get heavy-handed with the Badr group and their cohorts. But this meeting was not the place or the time to bring it up. He wanted to discuss it in detail with Rex and McArdle before even thinking of asking the CIA and DGSE to sanction the plan. Or rather, get sanction with the usual 'no, you can't do it, but we can't stop you from ignoring our orders. However, if you do ignore our orders and the mission fails, we don't know you'. In other words, approval with plausible deniability. Brandt would be happy with such an approval. It was how CRC had been operating on most of its CIA-ordered missions for years.

Chapter Sixty-Five

PUT THAT HAZMAT SUIT ON

Port Sudan, Sudan

Sunday, September 27, 2015

Their working and living areas inside the warehouse were well defined, separated by partitions of plywood. They were not allowed to enter the rest of the warehouse, thus had no idea what was stored there. There was no need for them to know. If they could have wandered about, they would have laid eyes on Fedot Frolov's stock-in-trade; thousands of assault rifles, rocket launchers, ammunition, surface to air and antitank missiles, explosives, landmines, antipersonnel mines, a few armored personnel carriers, and other instruments of death and destruction.

Inside their designated living area, they had a kitchenette, two single beds, a bathroom and toilet, a wall mounted TV, and two reclining chairs. The kitchen was stocked with dried and canned food to last for quite a few weeks. They got hot food at least twice a week when the supply truck visited. Their work area was well equipped with tools and workbenches to enable them to do their job.

But Doctor Haroun Najm al Din Hadad and his assistant, Hassan Hussain, a man with a Master's degree in aeronautical engineering from the University of Stuttgart, Germany were, to put it mildly, wholeheartedly fed up with everything; the food, the living conditions, the isolation, the degrading work, and no sunshine.

They were told they were working on a major project. They were told the final product was going to help change the history of Islam and the world. But after a few weeks of what was mind-numbing and humiliating work for two highly intelligent scientists, their initial excitement had made way for dreariness.

As scientists, they didn't care for, nor appreciate, all the secrecy and need-to-know and all the spy stuff. They felt as if they were being treated like freshmen high school students when they were not informed of what exactly they were working on and for what purpose. Scientists always worked with an objective in mind, knowing what they wanted to achieve, working toward an end goal. Now they just had to follow orders, like zombies. And the orders were coming to them piecemeal, just enough to do the next task.

Their first job was to assemble and overhaul the two former Chinese owned Harpys to make sure they were in tip-top flying condition. An impossible task without being able to take it outside for test flights. Once they were happy with the drones' flying condition—as happy as scientists could be without testing their work—they started making modifications to the drones to take the new payload. They were given the dimensions of the payload containers but were not informed about what was going into those containers.

While they waited for the arrival of the payload, they were tasked with a very menial job. It was this task that drove them to the verge of absconding. They had to paint and restore the outside of the craft to its original Israeli colors. All traces of Chinese ownership had to be removed. If that by itself was not enough of an insult for two devoted Muslims, having to paint the Star of David, the sign of the hated Jews, on the sides of the drones, made them feel defiled. They might as well have been ordered to cover the drones with pigskins.

If they hadn't both been religious zealots, which was the only factor that kept them motivated rather than the scientific challenge they thought they would be presented with when they were recruited, they would both have walked off the job many days ago.

Just when their boredom and irritation reached a new low, just before midnight, two wooden crates, each about the size of a three-drawer filing cabinet, were delivered to them. They took the crowbars to the crates with new-found enthusiasm. Inside, they hoped to find the payload for the drones and the instructions of how to install them.

Al Din Hadad ripped away the first pieces of wood when he spotted the bright yellow plastic-looking material. He pulled it out. *A hazmat suit* was his first thought. As a chemical engineer he knew what a hazmat suit looked like and had worn them many times. That's exactly what it was.

A chemical weapon? Was his second thought.

He looked over to where Hussain was ripping away the panels of the second crate, stopped, and retrieved the bright yellow hazmat suit from his crate and held it up.

"So, finally we have graduated to the next level. We are

allowed to know the payload is some kind of chemical weapon," he said.

"It seems to be. But what kind I can't say yet. Let me see if I can find the instructions; then we'll know for sure."

He removed more of the slats and found an A3-sized envelope with his name, Dr Haroun Najm al Din Hadad, typed in big fat black letters. He opened the envelope, took the documents out, walked over to his workbench, sat down on the chair, and began to read.

Al Din Hadad had never built a bomb. He understood that there was a science to it, but as a scientist he found the concept of using one's brains to build something so intricate with so much care and then destroy it at odds with what he believed science was all about.

At the elementary level, bombs were simple devices; explosives were set off to cause death and destruction. It was the composition of the explosives, the way it was packed and wrapped, the target to be destroyed, and the timing of the explosion that required the attention of skilled scientists.

The bombs he and Hussain were expected to build, in terms of the instructions he was reading, were, at the basic level, the simplest kind imaginable. It would have a core container which would be surrounded by explosives. Set off the explosives and it would disperse what was in the container over a wide area.

But that's where simplicity ended. The core container held radioactive material. They were to build a dirty bomb, also known as a radiological dispersal device or RDD.

Hussain was standing next to him waiting for an answer. Within a few minutes he could see that his partner's face had gone pallid, and sweat was starting to pearl on his forehead despite the air-conditioning. "What's wrong, Haroun?"

"We need to put on those hazmat suits—right now," Al Din Hadad whispered.

He and Hussain both knew that no suit would protect them against ionizing radiation hazards such as gamma rays, X-rays, radioactive particles, and such. But the hazmat suits would shield them from contamination. In other words, it would keep the radioactive isotopes away from their bodies.

They could only hope that the sender of the crates had packed the radioactive core containers in lead cases.

Chapter Sixty-Six

THE MOST TERRIFYING WORDS

DGSE Head Office at 141 Boulevard Mortier, Paris XX, France

Sunday, September 27, 2015

Christelle, Brandt, Rex, REX, and McArdle established a new secured video conference between the four of them as soon as they were done with the Langley call. Digger was fast asleep in front of the fireplace letting out the occasional grunt of satisfaction with his cozy environs.

Rex's mood had deteriorated gradually during the conference call with the CIA. By the end of it, his patience was all but gone. He had been away from Catia for almost a week and he missed her, which probably made him a bit more sensitive than usual. But the main reason for his vexation had to do with the fact that he had made his assessment of the situation, and it was a waste of precious time to keep conjecturing.

Therefore, Rex gave them a piece of his mind. "No one knows how much time we have left. And as Christelle said before, we actually don't know anything else. What we do know from Kharlamova's files are that Frolov sold Donna Teresa chemicals, or viruses and bacteria, or fissile material for a dirty bomb or, God forbid, a nuke. Any one of those can kill as many or more than nine-eleven.

"However, contrary to nine-eleven, and there is no getting away from it, this time we know something nasty is heading our way. We have some of the pieces of the puzzle, and those we don't we know where to get. So, if we don't go and get them and prevent the calamity these terrorists have in mind for us, what are we going to tell the people we're supposed to protect? Not to mention how we're going to live with our consciences when we know we could have stopped it but didn't.

"Besides," Rex concluded, "is it just me, or do any of you also get the feeling that Stacie might just have tripped over our missing scientist, Doctor Haroun Najm al Din Hadad?"

He was answered with three yeses.

From the fireplace, Digger let out a long and noisy yawn as if he was trying to tell them he was really bored by all this talk and stress about things he already knew.

Christelle, Brandt, and McArdle, without saying so, knew Rex's line of reasoning was impregnable—no necessity to debate it any further, and they said so.

Brandt said, "If those crates delivered to Port Sudan were indeed for Al Din Hadad, and those crates contained the materiel that pathologically insane Lombardi woman bought from Frolov, the end is near."

"Port Sudan is an odd place to build a bomb," Christelle said.

382

"Maybe not," said Brandt, "if your target is close by. Say in Israel, or Riyadh, or US military installations in the Middle East. We already know Lombardi has got her dagger out for Israel and the USA. In that area are a legion of targets."

"Okay, but if so, then the bomb or bombs have to be transported to their targets."

"Which is why they have Saiyyad Rahal, the owner of 7SSC, the Seven Seas Shipping Company, on the 'board of directors' of Badr," McArdle said.

"We're chasing our own tails here," Rex interjected. "Let's make a few safe assumptions. One, Frolov has delivered. Two, the bomb or bombs are in the final stage, but it's safer to assume they are ready. Three, they know what the targets are, but we don't. Four, that means we have no time."

It took them less than a minute to agree that what had to be done was to get Rex's rendition operation going without further delay; get hold of Lombardi and her clan leaders, the Badr five, and Frolov. Hold their feet to the fire until they talk. But they also understood that they were not entitled to make such a decision and execute it on their own. So, despite their unanimity they knew the first hurdle was political in nature.

The problem was their targets were citizens of other countries; Italy, Russia, Lebanon, Saudi Arabia— snatching them from their own countries was tantamount to a declaration of war, especially Frolov in Russia and Esam Abbas Bitar, the Lebanese politician. From the Russians, they supposed, they could expect no cooperation. From the Italian officials, they might get some cooperation, but they were so infiltrated by members of organized crime syndicates it would be a gamble. About

Lebanon's cooperation they had no doubt—there would be none.

Rex was getting worked up again. "Yep, that might be so, but is that enough reason to stop us doing anything about it? If so, why don't we just all take a nice holiday, far from the Middle East and Europe, and enjoy it while we wait for disaster to happen?"

Christelle, who understood the intricacies of politics much better than any of them smiled at Rex. "Hmm, we are really testy today, are we not? Rex, of course none of us wants to do nothing, but we will have to get the cooperation of our own and other governments to mount an operation like this."

"The most terrifying words in the English language," Rex groaned.

"What was that?" McArdle asked.

"Ronald Reagan. He said the most terrifying words in the English language are, *'I'm from the government and I'm here to help'.*"

They were all smiling.

"A very wise man," Brandt said.

A short discussion followed during which it was agreed that Brandt would talk to Martin Richardson. If he could get Richardson over the line then the two of them would approach the Director, Howard Lawrence, and from there up the food chain to the President. Christelle would approach the director of the DGSE who, if persuaded, would be talking to the French president.

Brandt and McArdle frowned in unison when Rex said he might be able to help get the French President to cooperate.

Christelle knew what Rex had in mind because she was kept informed by her Director during the saga almost two years ago when the Russians devised a plot to extort a signature from the French president on an agreement to build a gas pipeline from Russia to France. They would have succeeded, either to get President Aguillard's signature or topple him from power. But Rex and Digger were also involved, and now, two years later, Aguillard was still president of France and no Russian gas pipeline had been built.

Seeing the questioning frowns on Brandt's and McArdle's faces, she smiled and said, "It seems to me when this is over it might be a good idea if the three of you arrange a get-together, crack a few beers, and let Rex tell you about his adventures of the last few years."

"That's for damn sure," Brandt mumbled.

They agreed that while Brandt and Christelle were trying to get the political and bureaucratic wheels in motion, Rex and McArdle would start working on the plan.

Chapter Sixty-Seven

PRESENTS AND PRIME MINISTERS

Langley and D.C., USA

September 27-28, 2015

The message bearers, Brandt and Christelle, pulled no punches. They made sure there were no uncertainties about how serious the situation was and how critical it was that their requests received the highest priority, immediately.

Whether it was their presentation skills, or their skills of persuasion, or their audiences' ability to recognize danger when they saw it, or a combination of it all, they got the authorizations they required; it was as Brandt noted later on, "… as if all our stars lined up."

The CIA's Martin Richardson was on board with the plan before Brandt and Christelle got a quarter of the way through it. He stopped Brandt, phoned Director Howard Lawrence's secretary, and told her that he was on his way.

When he arrived, the secretary was all but pushing the visitors out of the director's office to let Richardson in.

Brandt and Christelle were waiting in Paris at the DGSE's headquarters and were immediately dialed in on a secured and encrypted video link arranged by Christelle. This time Brandt got halfway through explaining when the director stopped him, picked up the phone, and dialed the President.

The President, as had many of his predecessors over the decades since World War II, campaigned on ending America's military involvement in the Middle East. When he came into office, he worked hard to keep those promises. He wanted an end to war and strife in the Middle East and to normalize relations with the nations inhabiting the area. Nevertheless, despite being a peaceful man, he had a beef with terrorists that was non-negotiable and on which he was ready and willing to take action.

The President didn't want another 9/11 on his watch. This time there would be no Intelligence Community to blame—he had been warned. During their first terms, all presidents want another term. During their second terms, all presidents strive to leave behind a shining legacy. This President had less than one year to go in his final term.

Therefore, given the facts and the danger facing the world, he gave his stamp of approval and asked to be kept up to date. He also offered to use his influence with the heads of state of other countries if required.

Paris, France

Sunday, September 27, 2015

On the other side of the Atlantic, in Paris, the Director of DGSE was quick to agree with the idea. However, as was expected of him, he had to consider the political ramifications because he expected the President was going to ask. There were many, but the severity of the potential political fallout had to be weighed against the potential loss of life. When he was told that for the plan to go ahead it was not an absolute requirement that French security forces should be involved at the sharp end of the proposed mission, he booked an urgent meeting with President Aguillard.

The Director was a little surprised at how easily President Aguillard agreed to the mission. He thought part of it was that the President was probably still more than a little exasperated about the dirty trick the Russians had tried to play on him about two years ago.

The director was half-right. What he had no way of knowing was their meeting was preceded by a meeting the president had with his most trusted friend and advisor, the Prime Minister, Lucien Laurent. The director knew that the Prime Minister was Margot Lemaire's uncle. He was aware of the saga with the Russians two years ago. But he didn't know that Margot Lemaire was in the center of that brooding international political storm that threatened to create an enormous embarrassment for the president—that part was a closely-held secret. The President, were it not for the help of Rowan Donnelly, would have had to leave office in disgrace. The director also didn't know that the Prime Minister's meeting with the president was preceded by a secured tele-phone call Margot Lemaire had with her beloved uncle, the Prime Minister. Neither did he know that Lemaire's call with the Prime Minister had been preceded by a call to her from Rex Dalton, whom the director knew as Rowan Donnelly.

Whatever strings were pulled backstage, Brandt was jubilant to get the news from Christelle that President Aguil-lard was on board. And not only that, he had apparently brushed the director's warning about the potential political upshot aside and made any and all of France's security resources available for the operation. He also undertook to speak to the Italian Prime Minister personally to try and get his cooperation.

Secured Video Conference Between Paris, France and Rome, Italy

Monday, September 28, 2015

The French were known as masters in the art of diplomacy. Whoever said that, to prove the point, would have used the example of President Aguillard's exhibition of his skill and tact when he spoke to the Italian Prime Minister. With his Prime Minister, the Director of DGSE, and the striking Christelle Proll by his side in the video conclave, it took Aguillard less than twenty minutes to put enough fear into the Italian's heart to secure his cooperation.

The Italian Prime Minister only had to hear once that one of the possible targets of the Badr group could very well be the Vatican and that ten of the fourteen conspirators were on Italian soil, before he agreed to take action.

The fact that the Italian conspirators were all, if not directly then indirectly, involved with the Camorra crime syndicate, convinced him that this was a job for the DIA, (Direzione Investigativa Antimafia, the Anti-Mafia Investigation Directorate). They were headed by a director and were a multi-force investigation body under the Department of Public Security of the Ministry of the Interior.

Within forty-five minutes, the Minister of the Interior was brought into the meeting and had gotten his orders to instruct the director of the DIA to cooperate with the French and the Americans.

When it came to the discussions about political consequences, the Prime Minister had a very pragmatic stance. "I guess there is not much I stand to lose if things go wrong. I've already served in office longer than most of my predecessors. As you know, over on this side of the Alps, the position of Prime Minister carries no job security at all. In fact, it's probably one of the most insecure jobs in this country."

Aguillard laughed. He knew the Prime Minister was referring to the fact that since the end of World War II, Italy had seated 61 governments. In other words, over the course of 70 years they had a new government every 13.8 months. This Prime Minister was already in his thirtieth month in office—one of the longest serving Italian Prime Ministers since the war.

An hour later, Brandt and Christelle were in conference with the Director of the DIA, Antonio Castello. This guy was a livewire. He had a serious gripe with the organized crime bosses. They had been threatening him and his family and his subordinates for years, and he was more than fed-up with them. He and his family were living as if they were in a

prison, under 24/7 guard. So were many of his senior officers. He told Christelle and Brandt that they could expect
his and his entire force's full cooperation. He made it clear
that taking out the Beneduce-Longobardi clan's leadership
would be a crippling blow to the Camorra, and he would
like nothing better than to do exactly that.

"My family and I have been living in a prison for long
enough. It's time for the real criminals to go to real prisons,"
he concluded.

Chapter Sixty-Eight

FOUR ASSUMPTIONS

International Video Conference

September 27-28, 2015

While Brandt and Christelle were doing the political egg-dance, Rex, Josh, and McArdle established a three-way secured video connection and started the planning. It was a complex operation with many moving parts and lots that could go wrong.

Applying the principles of Occam's razor, which dictated that no more assumptions should be made than are necessary, they made only four assumptions. One, the bomb(s) were ready. Two, therefore D-day was imminent—as in the next few days. There was a possibility that it could be further away, but they would not take the risk. Three, each of their targets knew the full extent of the Badr conspiracy. Therefore, they had to be apprehended all at the same time to prevent them from alerting each other and activating the bomb(s).

Greg Wade was called into the video conference to provide them with the information gathered by the ELINT (electronic intelligence) team over the past few weeks. Rex and McArdle were particularly interested to know what their targets' plans were for the next forty-eight hours.

The seven Beneduce-Longobardi leaders, including Valter Li Voti, were all going to be at a meeting on Monday night, November 16, from 8:00 P.M. onward, at the Vinicola del Martelli estate, on the north side of Naples, owned by the very rich spinster, Dina Martelli, one of the leaders of the clan.

Usually the leadership held their fortnightly meetings at different venues around Naples, but every now and then they preferred Martelli's chef's cooking and the exquisite red wine produced by the vintner of Vinicola del Martelli estate.

Greg's team knew everything about the meeting. Exactly when it would start, in which room, who were the chef and his two assistants, and what was on the menu.

Capturing this group of people, they thought, should be handled by a taskforce consisting of DIA officers led by one or two of Navy SEALS from the *TOMATS* and Marissa. Rex and McArdle had little doubt that the SEALS would say yes to such an adventure as part of their paid-for holiday on a luxury yacht. However, to make sure their careers weren't jeopardized by their involvement in an unsanctioned operation, an urgent request went all the way up the line to the President, whose sanction was the fastest way to authorize it. He signed an executive order immediately, cutting through any red tape they might have encountered.

It was a bit of a disappointment to learn that Donna Teresa would not be attending the dinner meeting. She had to be in Rome for urgent business. That's what she'd told Li Voti according to the telephone intercept.

Her phone recordings revealed that she would be visiting her Liana Verdi Art Studio and had a meeting scheduled for 9:00 P.M. that same night, Monday, November 16, after the studio had closed. The meeting was scheduled to take place at the studio with her business manager, Aziz Abdul-Salam Awad.

Obviously, they didn't want to be seen together in public. And that made McArdle and Rex reach the same conclusion at almost the same time; *this could very well be the last meeting, to make final arrangements before the bomb(s) go off.*

However, the secret meeting in the isolation of the studio after hours would make it easier for a small team of skilled operators. Maybe Josh, one of the SEALS and a few DIA officers could move in, grab them, and get out without attracting attention.

Greg told them that from the Monday onward Fedot Frolov was going to be in Cannes on the Côte d'Azur, aka the French Riviera, on the Mediterranean coast of France. It included famously glamorous beach resorts such as Saint-Tropez and Cannes, and the independent microstate of Monaco. In the 18th century the area was a popular health retreat but later became the playground of aristocrats, artists, and jet setters.

The ELINT team knew that Frolov's yacht had sailed from the Isle of Capri the week before and was at that moment at anchor in the Cannes Le Vieux Port.

But the ELINT team had no information about how long Frolov intended to spend on the Riviera. That was because he never told anyone how long he was going to be in any place or where he was going next. He often changed plans and destinations on the spur of the moment.

Rex and McArdle hoped Frolov would stay a few days because he would only arrive there on the Monday morning from Austria. Nevertheless, the unpredictability of Frolov's 'cooperation' was one of the complicating factors.

To abduct him from the crowded environment of the Riviera unnoticed was going to take careful planning, a lot of skill, and more than just a dash of luck. This, they agreed, was a job for a French SWAT team accompanied by Rex and Digger.

Imam Karim Al-Sadiq, aka Hassan Walid, would not pose much of a problem— he was going be in the Muslim enclave at his home or among his flock. Since the ELINT team had started tracking him a few weeks ago, they had never seen him set foot outside the enclave. If they had been tracking him since his arrival in 2007, they still would have found that he seldom left the enclave.

Having no wife or children, from eight in the evenings he was usually on his own at home, watching TV, reading, or writing. Occasionally he would have guests for dinner or coffee in the evenings. The people in the enclave were his protection. For the team who had to abduct him, the challenge was going to be getting in and out of the enclave unnoticed.

Saiyyad Rahal, the owner of 7SSC, the shipping business based in Riyadh, Saudi Arabia was a man with a fixed and predictable routine, a trait of many successful businesspeople. He was a man who prayed five times a day, went to the mosque near his house twice a day for morning and afternoon prayers, and if he was not in the mosque, he was either at work or at home with his three wives and eight children.

Snatching him would be the responsibility of the GIP (General Intelligence Presidency) aka the GID (General Intelligence Directorate), the primary intelligence agency of the Kingdom of Saudi Arabia.

Esam Abbas Bitar, the politician from Beirut, had no travel plans for the next week. His rendition however, presented a bit of a challenge. Beirut was jihadi country, inhabited by fanatical extremist Islamic terrorists. Infidels such as Americans, Jews, and others were not welcome. They would be placed under close watch from the moment they set foot in the country.

The only clandestine organization in the world who could conceivably launch such an operation with any hope of success was Israel's Mossad. Their agents in the top-secret *Kidon* department, (*kidon* meaning 'bayonet' or 'tip of the spear') were an elite group of expert operators, some say the very best in the world, responsible to serve the Mossad's needs in operations against the enemies of the state of Israel, such as assassinations, kidnapping, and other activities. No doubt Israel would have assets in Lebanon and Beirut.

Last, they discussed Haroun Najm al Din Hadad, the potential bombmaker, who had vanished but could possibly be in a warehouse in Port Sudan, close to the international airport.

The data collected by the ELINT team from the drones and satellites watching the warehouse showed that there were four guards during the day, and at night two Rottweilers were brought to the premises to assist the guards. The guards never went inside the warehouse. They had no landline, but each of them had a mobile phone, which were by now hacked and sharing all data on them, including any conversations, with the ELINT team. The guards also had handheld two-way radios with a range of a mile or so to communicate with each other when required.

The report of the infrared thermal images taken from the drones circling the warehouse told Rex and McArdle that there were two people inside the warehouse, and they never came out. There were no electronic communications coming out of or going into that building, no mobile phones or landlines, and no internet traffic. Communications must have been in person or in writing.

What was going on inside that warehouse was anyone's guess. The thermal images indicated the two people could be working in a type of workshop on what could be vehicles of some type or devices with lots of electronic circuits. But it was not possible to tell what it was.

It could very well be the missing scientist Haroun Najm al Din Hadad. If so, he must have gotten a helper. And even if it turned out to not be Al Din Hadad, every bit of information so far pointed to some kind of illicit activity going on in there. In the absence of any solid information about Al Din Hadad, the fourth assumption had to be that it was him in the warehouse.

A way had to be found to get a look inside that warehouse. The Saudi secret service agents in the city had been told to stay away since the drones and satellites were deployed. Rex and McArdle agreed that there would be only one opportunity to find out what was going on. Inserting a team of clandestine operatives into Sudan and getting them out after their mission without getting into a shootout with the Sudanese Military was going to take a lot of thinking and preparation.

This was a task that McArdle, and he was sure John Brandt would agree, knew only one man in which he had the confidence to deliver a successful outcome, and he was looking at him—Rex Dalton.

McArdle started to tell Rex what he thought, but Rex stopped him and said, "Just in case you had different ideas, this one is my mission."

McArdle grinned and said, "Couldn't have said it better myself."

At that moment Digger awoke, yawned loudly, got up, stretched his legs, did a down-dog stretch, and walked over to Rex. He sat down next to Rex, looked at him, and let out a soft yelp which Rex interpreted to mean, "*What was that about some operation I've heard?*"

Rex said, "Nothing wrong with your hearing, buddy. You've got it. There *is* an operation in the making. And by the looks of it, you and I will be going to Africa. Apparently, there are some bad guys over there begging for our attention."

Digger woofed once and wagged his tail in anticipation. Maybe he was hungry and was asking to be fed, or maybe he really knew what was going on.

"Yeah, yeah, I know you're ready to go. But keep your pants on. I have a few more things to do, pack our stuff and arrange a ride for us."

Digger smiled.

McArdle shook his head. The relationship between Rex and Digger, from the little he had seen and from what Josh and others who saw them in action told him, was an enigma. If anyone forced him to answer truthfully, he would have put his hand on a Bible and sworn that the dog spoke English—a version that only Rex understood.

Chapter Sixty-Nine

WHAT'S THE TARGET?

Port Sudan, Sudan

Monday, September 28, 2015

The assembly instructions came with the crates carrying the fissile material. They were detailed, set out in a step-by-step fashion. They were easy to follow, but in some places a bit ambiguous, and nerve-racking to execute. Nervous people, irrespective of education and intelligence, were not always logical.

Load the fissile material in the inner tubes of the payload container and seal it. That took a little more than an hour—handling fissionable material required great care and presence of mind.

Now pack the explosives around the tubes to fill up the rest of the payload container and seal it. Another hour—one could never be careful enough around explosives.

Now fit the electronic detonators that will set off the explosion into their slots on the outside of the payload container.

Al Din Hadad and Hussain stopped.

"Did the idiot who wrote this mean this thing will explode when I insert the detonators?" Hussain asked.

Al Din Hadad grabbed his copy of the instructions and read that part. "I see what you mean. That's what you get when you let a goatherd write technical instructions."

"So, what now. Do we insert the detonators to find out if we've been on a suicide mission all along, or do we ask for clarification?" Hussain asked.

Al Din Hadad wiped the sweat from his eyebrows. "If it was meant to be a suicide mission, we won't get clarification. If this thing goes off, it will only kill the two of us; and I stand to be corrected, but is it not the purpose of suicide missions to kill some of the enemy in the process as well? If they wanted to kill only the two of us, and I can't imagine why they'd want to, they could've done so long ago with much less effort and cost."

"Even so, my brother, why don't you slip those detonators into their slots and clarify what that instruction means while I take a stroll outside—far from here?"

Al Din Hadad shook his head, picked the instructions up, and read them again. He started laughing.

"What's so damn funny?"

"Just read the next line."

Hussain read it and managed to fix an edgy smile on his face as he read it out loud. "Do not test the detonators after you have inserted them." The words were followed by a row of smiley-face emoticons.

Half an hour later, the detonators were in place, untested.

They sighed in unison and agreed it was time for a break and extra-strong Arabic coffee.

The entire job, which should have taken them no more than an hour, took the two jittery scientists a little more than half a day with sweat pouring out of them, not from exertion or the heat but from nervous tension.

Send your report when you have reached this stage. You're done for now. The drones are ready. All that remains is to activate the launch sequence at the set time. The instructions will arrive shortly.

"Does that mean the attack is going to happen on the day we get the activation instructions?" Hussain mumbled.

"Maybe. Maybe not. But most of all I'd like to know what the target is," Al Din Hadad said.

It still frustrated them to no end that they were being treated like children, but at least the end was in sight now. The payment they would get for their work was good, but that was not what excited them. It was the prospect that they would be part of a watershed moment for Islam. They were told when they were recruited that their names would be eternalized in the chronicles of Islamic history.

Chapter Seventy

THE RENDITIONS

DGSE Head Office at 141 Boulevard Mortier, Paris XX, France

Wednesday, September 30, 2015

Brandt and Christelle were coordinating the arrest and snatch operations from a joint operations center (JOC) at the DGSE Head Office, which Christelle had organized. From the JOC, they were in video contact with Stacie's team at CIA headquarters in Langley, Chris McArdle at CRC headquarters in Arizona, the team on the *TOMATS*, as well as the SWAT teams on the ground.

The operation started at 7:30 P.M., Paris time, when six teams in four different countries, Italy, France, Lebanon, and Saudi Arabia, signaled to Brandt that they were all geared up and ready to move out to the target locations.

Brandt and everyone else involved knew that plans seldom worked out once they met up with reality, therefore they had, in the lexicon of field agents, prepared for the worst but hoped for the best.

Brandt and Christelle listened and watched with bated breath as the six missions unfolded. Every team had been instructed to synchronize their watches to Paris time to make sure that they captured all the targets at the same time.

Riyadh, Saudi Arabia

Wednesday, September 30, 2015

It was 9:45 P.M. in Riyadh, 8:45 P.M. in Paris, when the Saudi GID agents quietly surrounded the luxurious three-story house of Saiyyad Rahal, owner of 7SSC, the Seven Seas Shipping Company, and a member of the Badr Five.

In the darkness, eight of them moved forward very quietly. But then one of them fell over a rubbish bin, causing a ruckus that forced the rest of the agents to throw caution to the wind and rush the rest of the way to the house. With battering rams, they took the front and back doors down simultaneously and stormed in, guns at the ready.

Inside the house chaos had erupted. Women and children were screaming and yelling everywhere.

In Paris, Brandt was swearing softly and Christelle had closed her eyes.

"Let's just hope they disabled his landline and deployed the cellphone signal suppression before they approached the house, as we told them to do. It will be a disaster if Rahal get his hands on a phone and makes a call before they get to him," Brandt said.

Christelle's eyes were still closed as if in silent prayer. She only nodded.

Fortunately, the leader of the GID team had deployed the anti-communications measures. He also kept his head on his shoulders and immediately ordered three of his men to round up the women and children, get them out of the way, and try to calm them down while he and the rest of the team stormed up the stairs to the top floor to Rahal's study where they'd seen the light burning when they approached the house.

Rahal was born and bred in the Kingdom of Saud. He knew how the legal system worked, and he knew how the law enforcement and security agencies operated in the Kingdom. Therefore, he knew, all too well, how traitors and conspirators were treated in the Kingdom.

The GID team leader reached the top of the stairs with four of his men behind him. He had taken three steps in the direction of the study when a single shot rang out from behind the closed door.

They found Rahal slumped back in his swivel chair behind his desk. Most of the top of his head was gone, and his brains were slowly dripping from the ceiling onto his desk. The study was a big, opulent room, lavishly appointed with Arab taste. Rahal's blood and brain matter were ruining an exquisite Kashan carpet.

The team leader spoke into his throat mic and reported to his commander.

In Paris, Brandt and Christelle were listening. Both understood enough Arabic to make out what had happened.

"Damn. This was the guy who could tell us all about their shipping arrangements," Brandt said.

"I'm sure Frolov and Lombardi and maybe even Al-Sadiq will also be able to tell us," Christelle said.

"I guess you're right. But they have not been captured yet. And I hope and pray the rest of the missions don't turn out like this one."

The Riyadh mission was over by 9:57 P.M. local. It was 8.57 P.M. in Paris.

The Muslim Enclave, Naples, Italy

Wednesday, September 30, 2015

As a highly trained Amn al-Muddad agent, paranoia was drilled into him. "A laissez-fair approach to personal security will cost you your life," he was told repeatedly during his training, and he'd adhered to the advice for many years.

But, living in the Muslim enclave in Naples under the protection of the most influential Camorra clan, surrounded by his 'own' people, over the years, Imam Karim Al-Sadiq had become complacent.

At 8:45 P.M. in Naples, on Monday, November 16, he realized his mistake when two men dressed in black balaclavas and DIA SWAT gear appeared in the doorway to his TV room where he was relaxing in a recliner and watching the news on Al Jazeera.

His stomach churning, he jumped out of the lounger and dove for cover behind the couch. He made it to the back of the couch, but his right leg was protruding from behind it, and before he could pull it in, he felt two sharp, pinprick sensations on his lower right leg. His body began to convulse immediately, and then he lost consciousness.

When he woke up, he had a headache, a dry mouth, and felt groggy. He looked around and saw he was in a small room with no window, a steel door, and a light protected by a steel grid in the ceiling more than ten feet above his head. In the far corner, up on the ceiling, he saw a lens that he immediately recognized as that of a video camera. He was on a hard mattress on a single bed bolted to the floor, and there was a steel toilet in the corner, also bolted to the floor.

I am in a jail cell.

He remained on his back for a few more minutes then rolled off onto the floor where he prostrated himself and prayed to Allah in a loud and earnest voice. He had no idea which direction Mecca was, Muslims were expected to say their prayers while facing toward Mecca—one direction, one people, one God. But Al-Sadiq felt maybe Allah wouldn't mind the geographical misalignment of the body of his faithful servant in circumstances like these.

It was all a show put on by the 'Imam' for the people who he knew were watching him. He had never been a religious man. He had been faking Imamship for close to eight years while he helped to smuggle Islamic terrorists into Europe and traded drugs grown in the Middle East for money and weapons to further the cause of radical Islamic jihad across Europe and the Middle East, especially against Israel.

But now, more than ever, he had to keep up the façade of the peace-loving Imam. The hour of reckoning was less than twenty-four hours away, depending on how long he had been unconscious. It could even be less than that. He had to resist and delay all attempts to pry from him information about the disaster the Badr group was about to visit upon the infidels, especially Israel and America.

It was 9:30 P.M. in Naples and Paris.

Liana Verdi Art Studio, Rome, Italy

Wednesday, September 30, 2015

In Rome, at the exact same time as the other five SWAT teams descended upon their targets, a SWAT team of three DIA officers, accompanied by Josh Farley and one US Navy SEAL, disarmed the alarm system of Liana Verdi Art Studio in Rome, then picked the lock of a side door and entered the building.

When Josh and one of the DIA officers approached the manager's office on the ground floor, they were not surprised to see the door was open and the lights on, though there was no one else in the building. They could hear the voices of a man and woman talking but couldn't make out what was said.

When Josh and the DIA officer stepped through the doorway, Aziz Abdul-Salam Awad, seated behind a desk facing the door, stopped talking mid-sentence, and his eyes shot wide.

Seconds later, Teresa Lombardi seated in front of the desk facing Awad and the window behind him, spun around in her chair, saw the two men with black balaclavas over their faces and DIA tactical gear covering their bodies, taser guns pointed at her and Awad, and screamed. It was high-pitched but would not reach the ears of anyone on the outside of the building. The next moment, it looked as if she was trying to get to her feet, but her body would not cooperate with her brain, and she slumped back in the chair.

In shocked silence, Lombardi and Awad each received and read their 'Letter of Rights'. It included information about the charges and the suspect's basic rights such as the right to be assisted by counsel, to be informed of the charges, to remain silent, etcetera. Italy, like all European Union countries, had enacted the principle of the right to information in criminal proceedings the year before, 2014. It was essentially the equivalent of the American Miranda rights.

Lombardi and Awad said nothing and made no attempt to resist. When requested to turn around to be handcuffed, they did so in silent subservience.

Their pallid faces and shaking bodies made it clear they were shocked out of their wits. Nonetheless, to Josh it was bizarre that they didn't utter a single word—the silence for such an extended period was abnormal. He checked them for any visible signs of drug use but found none.

They were placed in two separate SWAT vehicles and transported to the Carabinieri Station Roma Talents where they would each have their own private prison cell.

The entire operation from the moment the SWAT team entered the studio to the moment when the cell doors close behind Lombardi and Awad took fifty minutes.

It was 9:35 P.M. in Rome and Paris.

Beirut, Lebanon

Wednesday, September 30, 2015

It was 9:45 P.M. in Beirut, Lebanon, 8:45 P.M. in Paris. A team of three Mossad special agents led by a *kidon* were in place at the home of Esam Abbas Bitar.

Bitar lived alone. His wife had died two years ago, and his four children were all adults, living their own lives.

The team easily overpowered the two guards, one at the security gate and one roaming outside the house. They tied and gagged the guards and shoved them into the toilet of the guardhouse at the front gate. Two of the team donned the clothes of the guards and took their places.

For the *kidon* and remaining team member, gaining entry to the house was a walk in the park. They disarmed the archaic alarm system in less than ten seconds, and the lock of the front door surrendered in twenty-five.

There was no one home, which meant they had unfettered access to search the place and collect everything of interest. But it also meant they had to wait until Bitar returned from his meeting with, they suspected, leaders of the Jihad Council. They had a tracking device on Bitar's car, which had not moved in the past two hours. They had no idea when the meeting would finish, so they had to wait.

In Paris, Brandt and Christelle were listening, both a little nervous. This was one of the missions that could go wrong very badly. Pulling off a stunt like this in enemy territory was a big risk, always. The fact that they became aware of Bitar's unscheduled meeting at the eleventh-hour complicated matters further. But Brandt assured Christelle that if there was a secret service agency on the planet who could pull off something like this, it was the Mossad. When it came to the execution of clandestine missions in the Middle East, they had no rivals.

It was about an hour later when the Mossad team saw the signal that Bitar's car was moving. He was on his way home and should be coming through the front gate in about fifteen minutes. The two men inside the house shoved all documents, laptop, tablet PC, and a number of flash drives into their backpacks and left the house to take up their positions.

Bitar was in the back seat of the black Mercedes SUV behind the driver when they pulled up to the security gate. The driver rolled his window down and pushed the button on the wall to activate the intercom. He said his name and gazed into the camera. The gate opened and he pulled forward up to the boom blocking his way. The gate closed behind the car, effectively locking it in between the gate and the boom. A guard approached from the guardhouse. The driver looked at the guard and opened his mouth to say something when a man with a black balaclava over his face, clad in black from head to toe, appeared right next to him. It was as if the man had risen from the ground next to the car.

The next thing he became aware of was the gun barrel pushing against his ear. Then he heard the back door of the car opening behind him. He was too scared to turn his head to see what was happening and too busy trying to get control of his bladder, which was threatening to empty itself.

The driver didn't see the blow coming, neither did he expect it; he just felt a short, sharp pain in his neck before everything went dark.

What the driver haven't seen was Bitar in the back seat,

feebly trying to stop the second man who appeared out of nowhere next to him from opening the door. Bitar's hand had never reached the door handle. He was unconscious from the blow to his head a few seconds after the driver's. The propofol injection administered to Bitar immediately after the blow to the head was going to keep him unconscious for at least one more hour.

Given the short time frame in which they had to plan, prepare, and execute the mission, the Mossad had decided that it was too risky to try smuggling Bitar out of the country. He would be taken to a safehouse in Hazmiyeh, one of the better suburbs of Beirut, where he would be interrogated.

By 11:15 P.M. in Beirut and 10:15 P.M. in Paris, Bitar was in a basement room in the Mossad safehouse. They were ready to start questioning him the moment he woke up.

When Brandt got the message, he and Christelle both let out a long breath of relief.

Estate Vinicola del Martelli, Naples, Italy

Wednesday, September 30, 2015

At exactly 8:45 P.M., in Naples and Paris, the DIA SWAT team of eight accompanied by two Navy SEALS, Nathan Cook and Peter McGovern, with Marissa Bisset as observer, were in place. They were hidden from sight in the shadows outside the main house on Dina Martelli's estate, Vinicola del Martelli. The SWAT team leader looked at his watch and spoke into his lip mic to everyone. "Time to move in."

Marissa was grateful that the Director of the DIA had issued specific orders that this raid be done without the usual hullabaloo and press. It was a tactic which they often used when taking down crime bosses so that the public could see that something was being done by the government to stem the tide of lawlessness and that they were not afraid of the mobsters.

Tonight's operation was going to be executed in secret; quietly, quickly, and professionally. Once the captives had given up the information about their involvement in the Badr conspiracy, the press would be called in to have their day.

Valter Li Voti and the six clan leaders were having a good time. The food was delicious, and so was the wine which was flowing freely.

The villa was not guarded, and no doors were locked. Although the burglary at Donna Teresa's house a few weeks previously should have made her more careful, clearly, Martelli hadn't done anything to put security in place at her estate yet. She probably believed no one would be so stupid as to try to plunder the house of a senior Camorra member again.

At 8:47 P.M. the SWAT team entered the house silently through the front door, back door, and side door.

Three of them appeared in the kitchen, their taser guns pointed at the chef and his two helpers. They signaled for them to be very quiet and unmoving. The chef and his helpers froze in place, their hands up in surrender.

The diners were oblivious as to what was happening behind the kitchen door a few yards away from where they were seated at the large round oak table. They didn't even notice the silence that suddenly fell in the kitchen.

Seconds later, a deathly quiet fell on the seven when balaclava-clad men dressed in SWAT gear clearly marked with the insignia of the DIA materialized out of nowhere around the table.

Rinaldo Fara, the Naples police officer, was the first to find his voice. "Who the hell are you? What are you doing here?"

The team leader ignored Fara and said in a controlled voice, "You are all under arrest. It would be in your best interest to cooperate with us. It will avoid unpleasantries."

"Under arrest! For what? Do you have any idea who I am? Who *we* are?" Fara was red in the face.

"You're being arrested for your participation in various crimes. The details will be given to you soon. As for who you are, we know exactly who you are, Rinaldo Fara, police officer of the Naples police. We also know exactly who everyone else in this room is. You might even be very surprised to learn how *much* we know about all of you."

Fara opened his mouth, the team leader raised his taser gun, and Fara closed his mouth.

The team leader handed each of the seven a typed, personalized 'Letter of Rights'.

The seven were handcuffed and loaded into seven different vehicles and transported to the Carabinieri Comando Stazione Napoli Chiaia where each of them was honored with their own private prison cell.

From the time the SWAT team entered Martelli's house until the interrogations could start took ninety-one minutes. By 10:46 P.M. in Naples and Paris, the rendition of the Bendeduce-Longobardi leaders was complete.

Outside Cannes, France

Wednesday, September 30, 2015

Frolov's welcoming committee consisted of a SWAT team of eight DGSI agents with Rex and Digger embedded. Frolov being paranoid about his own security and never letting anyone know about his comings and goings had to be followed with drones and feet on the ground and the signal of the tracking device planted on his Ferrari.

It was only when he drove out from the marina in Cannes and took the road to a winery at 7:00 P.M. that they got an idea of what his plans were. While he was having dinner at the restaurant at the wine estate about ten miles outside Cannes with an unknown man, the SWAT team had enough time to pick their spot and get themselves ready for his arrival.

There was only one narrow and winding road leading to and from the estate to the main road.

The time was approaching 9:00 P.M. when, in the dark, the SWAT team heard the high-pitched noise of the Ferrari engine, which must have been doing close to top speed, a good fifteen seconds before they saw the light through the trees. According to the ELINT team he had two call girls on the yacht awaiting his return. No wonder he was in such a hurry. The night was still young.

The SWAT team had barricaded the narrow country road with two SUVs just around a sharp bend. The dense trees and bushes on the side of the road would make it impossible for Frolov to see the blockade until he came around the curve. However, he would have to slow down to get through the bend without running off the road. By the time he would see the barrier and stop, two SUV's would have blocked the way behind him, and he would be boxed in.

The Ferrari flashed past the two SUV's hidden among the trees off the road. Frolov was probably too occupied preparing to maneuver the powerful car around the bend to have noticed them. At that speed and with a bottle of wine in his system he had to concentrate; otherwise his beloved Ferrari was going to end up in an embrace with the stone wall on the side of the road. It was a scenario Rex was desperately hoping would not occur. He needed Frolov in a healthy and mindful condition to have a chat with him. But there was nothing Rex could do about it.

Just at the moment when Rex thought the bad scenario was going to unfold before his eyes, Frolov stepped on the brakes, the car's nose dipped, and the tires screamed on the road. Miraculously, the car stayed on the road and went around the curve with the outside tires missing the gravel by less than an inch.

The next moment, the brake lights came on again. The tires screamed as they slid along the tar, leaving black smoke in their wake. The car came to a dead stop. Two black DGSI SUVs pulled across the road a few yards behind the Ferrari.

The brake lights went out and the car moved forward slowly toward the SUVs blocking its way. Becoming clearly visible in the headlights of the Ferrari were a network of vicious-looking metal spikes covering the full width of the road.

The car came to a stop again. On the driver's side of the car, three men in black tactical gear, with faces hidden behind black balaclavas and armed with Heckler & Koch HK416 F assault rifles appeared.

"Nowhere to run and nowhere to hide, you son of a bitch," Rex mumbled.

The next moment the Ferrari's doors shot up in the air, Frolov jumped out on the passenger side and ran for the trees.

Not bad for a seventy-something-year-old bastard, Rex thought.

The SWAT team were raising their rifles. Rex saw and shouted, "No! Don't shoot! My dog will get him. Go Digger!"

Frolov had taken about ten to twelve steps before he went face down in the cold wet soil with Digger on his back. He was screaming obscenities in Russian.

Rex was a few yards behind and shouted to him in Russian, "Frolov, don't move! That dog will rip your throat out if you so much as twitch your eyes."

Twenty minutes later, the Dassault Falcon 8X private jet took off from the nearby airport heading for Paris. It was a one-and-a-half-hour flight.

Rex had a satisfied grin on his face, and Digger had curled himself up on the seat next to him and gone to sleep.

Rex looked at Frolov in his seat, to which he was tied opposite. Frolov was glowering at Rex, but he also noticed something more than just anger on the Russian's face—triumph.

What the hell is this sleazeball up to?

By 11:00 P.M. local time in Paris the entire rendition operation was complete. The interrogations had already started.

Chapter Seventy-One

THE INTERROGATION

DGSE Head Office at 141 Boulevard Mortier, Paris XX, France

Wednesday, September 30, 2015

In the JOC in Paris, Brandt and Christelle were now also linked in by video and audio to the interrogations happening in Rome, Naples, and Beirut. Brandt was going to question Frolov himself.

It was part of the agreement made between the US, France, and Italy that the Badr task force analysts and agents would get the first opportunity to interrogate the suspects before handing them over to any law enforcement or security agency who had jurisdiction.

Carabinieri Station Roma Talents, Rome, Italy

10:00 P.M. in Rome and Paris

With Josh in the interrogation room was the Navy SEAL that was on the SWAT team with him during the arrest of Teresa Lombardi and Aziz Abdul-Salam Awad earlier. The SEAL was a six-foot seven giant of a man, and his rough features always reminded Josh of the famous actor, Robert Kovaks. Even his smile was intimidating. His SEAL buddies ironically nicknamed him Tiny. Those who knew him knew that despite his looks he was really a very gentle creature, but only for as long as he didn't lose his patience and go on a rampage. Then he was worse than Arnold Schwarzenegger in any of his action movies. To the uninitiated, especially in an interrogation room, his mere presence would make anyone think twice about lying.

A SWAT team member escorted Teresa Lombardi into the room and guided her to the only empty chair, opposite Josh and Tiny.

Lombardi looked at the two of them in turn impassively. It was the first time she had seen their faces without the balaclavas.

Josh and Tiny said nothing, they just stared back at her wordlessly until she turned her eyes away.

Then Josh said, in English, "Miss Lombardi, you might not be aware of it, but the entire leadership group of your Beneduce-Longobardi clan was taken into custody a few hours ago. Rinaldo Fara, Valter Li Voti, Dina Martelli, and the rest."

Lombardi made no reply. She fixed her gaze on the wall

behind Josh. On her face there was no recognition, no sign of shock or denial, nothing, no emotions—detached.

"And they are saying a lot of really nasty things about you," Josh lied. The interrogation of the clan leaders had not even started.

"Italian. No speak English," she said.

Josh grinned and shook his head. He knew Teresa spoke Italian and English, he could speak English, Arabic, and Russian; and Tiny, an advocate for one universal language, the merits of which he could debate for hours, only spoke English. So English was the lingua franca. "Oh, I know for a fact you speak and understand English very well, Miss Lombardi. You want to know how I know?"

She said nothing.

He nodded at Tiny.

Tiny cleared his throat which sounded a lot like a big motorbike being started. Lombardi's head jerked to the side. Her eyes settled on Tiny. He flipped the switch on the portable audio player on the table in front of him. The voices coming out of the device were speaking English.

It took almost a minute before Lombardi's eyes flickered wide momentarily, as she must have recognized her own and Olesya Kharlamova's voices. It was the recording of the meeting between the two of them on Wednesday, August 20, at the Pyatyy Okean restaurant in Moscow on the fourth floor of Terminal F at the Alexander S. Pushkin International airport.

Josh nodded and said, "Yep, your good friend, Olesya Kharlamova. She stabbed you in the back. She is in our custody. Gave us this tape and many others and made a sweet deal for herself. Same as your other good friends, Li Voti, Fara, Martelli, and the others."

Lombardi was shaking her head.

"Oh, I almost forgot," Josh said. "I wanted to tell you we also have in custody other friends of yours, Egor Zubarev from Narva, Estonia, and Imam Karim Al-Sadiq."

For the first time Josh saw the microscopic signs of fear on Lombardi's face. But she didn't move, nor did she respond.

Josh pushed a bit more. "The interesting thing about those two friends of yours, apart from the fact that they also stabbed you in the back by telling us exactly what you've been up to, is that for some reason they're ashamed of their real names."

Lombardi was looking at him in silence.

"Did you know Zubarev is actually Fedot Frolov and Al-Sadiq is really Hassan Walid?"

Lombardi started to tremble slightly; she shook her head and mumbled something inaudible.

Josh grinned. Before stepping into the interrogation room, he had been thoroughly briefed by CRC's resident psychologist, Rick Longland. Therefore, Josh knew she was a pathological liar, and she was good at it. Longland also warned him that the woman had been living a life of deceit and unreality for so long that it might take a long time to get her into the realm of reality and get any useful information out of her.

Longland was watching and listening from the CRC headquarters in Arizona.

"Okay, now let's talk about Badr," Josh said.

"Noooooo!" It sounded like a wolf howl. Then she started mumbling incomprehensibly; her voice had dropped to a whisper. The next moment she exploded in a howl again. "Noooooo!" Only the white of her eyes were visible, her hands were clamped over her ears as if she didn't want another sound to enter.

Then she started shaking slightly and making a new kind of noise. At first it sounded like a soft giggle, then it grew louder and louder until Lombardi was laughing out of the pit of her stomach. Tears were streaming down her cheeks. Her whole body was shaking violently now. Slowly, the sounds of laughter coming out of her throat changed to something that was spine-chilling, haunted.

Then Josh saw her eyes—wild, empty, disconnected—*the eyes of insanity, or deceit?* he wondered.

Josh was a little startled but much more skeptical. Tiny was unmoving as if this was the most boring thing he'd ever witnessed, apart from a politician at a podium trying to explain to the audience what a nice place he would make the world if everyone would just vote him into office.

Longland's voice came over Josh's earpiece. "Josh, I think you'll have to stop there for now."

Josh got up and walked out of the room to talk in private with Longland. "Is she bullshitting us, Rick?"

"It's quite possible. She's been, as we already know, a supreme bullshitter her whole life. She might just be playing for time, the one commodity we don't have in abundance right now. I suggest you put her back in her cell and I'll observe. We should be able to get some indicators about her sanity within a few hours."

Brandt who had been following the conversation from the JOC in Paris said, "Okay Josh, get Awad in there and question him. Let's hope he's not going to try and pull the same tricks as his boss."

Carabinieri Station Roma Talents, Rome, Italy

11:00 P.M. in Rome and Paris

Ten minutes later, the shaking, ashen-faced professor of Middle Eastern studies was facing Josh and Tiny in the interrogation room.

Josh had made his assessment of the professor, and Longland had agreed with him. Although he was also a terrorist, he was not a battle-hardened jihadist. He was an academic. Josh and Longland agreed that Awad probably didn't have the mettle to withstand any measure of harsh interrogation even without physical harm.

Josh didn't waste any time on pleasantries. "Awad, I am not in a good mood. I don't like to shoot people, but that Lombardi bitch gave me no choice. I warned her more than once not to lie to me, but she ignored my advice, and now she's in the morgue downstairs. So, for the sake of *your* longevity and *my* emotions let's keep this short. That's unless you want to be brave and commit suicide by lying to me."

"What do you want to know?"

"Now that's more like it. If Teresa Lombardi had been as obliging as you are, she would still be alive.

"Tell me about Badr. Just remember, and I am giving you only one warning, I know everything about Badr, who you are, all of you. I know when you started plotting the Badr scheme. I know what weapon you're going to use, when, and where.

"I'm just making sure the others told me the truth. You are a truthful man, Awad, are you not?"

Awad nodded and began to speak. He kept talking for ten

minutes uninterrupted. He told them who the Badr Five were. It confirmed what they already knew. He explained the use of the name Badr and confirmed it was, as they had speculated, going to be a seminal moment for Islam. He further confirmed that he was the manager of Liana Verdi Art Studio and in that capacity, and with his background in Middle Eastern history and current affairs, he was the scout and go-between for Teresa Lombardi in buying and selling of illicit antiquities. He also told them that he was the messenger who carried messages from Imam Karim Al-Sadiq to Esam Abbas Bitar in Beirut and Saiyyad Rahal in Riyadh. His job as professor at the university was the perfect cover.

Then he stopped talking as abruptly as he started.

Josh frowned and Tiny let out a low groan of dissatisfaction.

"That's all I know," Awad said quickly.

"Awad, you want me to believe you were a messenger for your group but didn't know what the messages said?" Josh made a show of pulling his gun from its shoulder holster.

"I didn't need to know. Please put the gun away. There's no need for it. The messages were hand-written and encoded. I had a look at one of them and have no idea what it said."

He also had no idea where Haroun Najm al Din Hadad was or what the scientist was doing, neither did he have any idea what the weapon was, the target, or the date. Awad explained that the Badr group used the principle of compartmentalization of information. "We only know what we need to know when we need to know it to do our part. Nothing more."

Five minutes later, Longland's voice came through in

Josh's earphone. "I think he's done; you won't get much more out of him. I think he was honest."

Brandt's voice came next over Josh's earphones. "Okay Farley, get your ass on that plane. You can sleep on the way to Paris and Saudi Arabia. Hopefully Lombardi will regain sanity soon. If so, we'll get her transferred to Naples so that Marissa and Declan can question her."

In Paris, Brandt shook his head. Things were not going their way. He knew Lombardi definitely had the information they needed. From Awad, although disappointed that he didn't know a lot more, Brandt knew there was nothing to be gained from talking to him any longer. The Badr plot had been put together and controlled by professionals. The only other prisoners he expected might know the full story would be Frolov, Bitar, and Al-Sadiq. He didn't hold out any hope that the clan leaders, except maybe Li Voti, would know anything about Badr.

It was 11:30 P.M. in Rome and Paris.

Carabinieri Comando Stazione, Napoli Chiaia, Italy

10:15 P.M. in Naples and Paris

At CRC's Headquarters, Rick Longland was looking at the video footage of Al-Sadiq in his cell in Naples. Declan Spencer and Marissa were waiting on Longland to give them his assessment of the suspect.

It was 10:15 P.M. local time when Longland spoke to them, with Brandt and Christelle listening in Paris. "I have studied the information we have about this guy, and I looked at the observation tapes. Be aware, if you're not already, this one is intelligent and devious. He is going to try stringing you along as he takes you down the garden path."

"I don't want to waste time on him," Brandt said. "Declan, Marissa, give it a shot, but the moment you get the idea he's playing games, pull a bag over his head, tie him up, and put him back in his cell. No food, no water. Oh, and don't forget to put on the music for him."

A few minutes later, Al-Sadiq was led into the interrogation room and pushed down in a chair. His hands and feet were cuffed to the table, and the bag over his head removed.

He blinked his eyes against the bright light and then settled his gaze on Spencer, completely ignoring Marissa as if she didn't exist.

But Marissa had a plan to quickly get under his skin. "Let's start with your name. Your real name, not the fake one you're using."

Al-Sadiq didn't look at Marissa. He looked at Spencer and said, "If this woman is with you, you should teach her some manners. She has not been spoken to. Tell her to shut up until I speak to her."

Spencer had read Al-Sadiq's file. He despised the man, and the feeling was growing rapidly as he observed the terrorist's misplaced arrogance and air of superiority. But he was not going to let Al-Sadiq see that. He ignored the comment and kept a steady grin on his face while he met the man's gaze.

"I see you want to play hardball," Marissa said. "Well, I'll be more than happy to oblige... I..."

Al-Sadiq started to object again, but Spencer interjected. "Listen, you son-of-a-bitch. You're in civilization. We respect our women, and we respect each other. We don't interrupt each other when we're talking. The lady was talking, so you shut your pie hole until she's done."

"I won't be intimidated by you, and I won't defile myself by talking to this whore," Al-Sadiq shot back.

That's exactly what Spencer and Marissa wanted; to annoy him to the point that he would drop his guard. Marissa nodded and said, "Well, I've tried to stop it, but now I won't. The Saudis are desperate to have a word with you. Apparently, they've been looking for you for a while. It sounded to me as if you've caused them lots of trouble. I won't stand in their way any longer. At least you will not be asked questions by a woman while you're with them."

"Are you sure you want to do that? Hand him to the Saudis?" Spencer feigned incredulity.

Marissa nodded. "Yeah, he's left me no choice."

"Okay, Al-Sadiq," Spencer said, "that's it, she's my boss, I can't stop her. I feel sorry for you. All I can see in your future are heavy-duty truck batteries connected to your genitals and nipples with crocodile clamps and then… wait, ah… a big shiny scimitar right at the end of your life."

Al-Sadiq made no reply. He didn't show any emotions.

"Okay, you've made the choice," Marissa said. She made a big show of going to the door, calling two of the SWAT team members, and telling them loud enough so that Al-Sadiq could hear, "Our guest says he'd rather spend time with the Saudis than in our wonderful company. Can you please take him back to his cell, and make sure he is comfortable until they come to fetch him?"

The bag went back over Al-Sadiq's head, and in his cell, he was cuffed to the wall in a standing position spread-eagled. He began praying again loudly, but then he was interrupted by the most disconcerting and disjointed sounds he had ever heard. There were some notes from a violin, piano, a trumpet, a cello, all of it discordant, interspersed with blood-curdling sounds of people yelling and screaming and begging, glass breaking, mumbling, the sounds of cars braking, and fire alarms.

Al-Sadiq shouted, "Stop this noise! I am praying. Allah will punish you!"

But the divine didn't intervene; therefore, neither did the guards.

Brandt, Spencer, and the others had their confirmation —Al-Sadiq was not going to easily and quickly give up information. Eventually he would, but they didn't have time to wait until Al-Sadiq broke. It could take days, even a week or more.

Mossad safehouse, Hazmiyeh, Beirut, Lebanon

11:30 P.M. in Beirut, 10:30 P.M. in Paris

When the *kidon*, Yakov Jessel, team leader of the Mossad team, removed the bag from Esam Abbas Bitar's head, the captive had made a full recovery from his propofol induced sleep and was staring at him in defiance.

Jessel's men pulled Bitar up by his arm and pushed him down in a chair against the wall, where his feet and arms were tied to the chair.

"You have signed your own death warrant, Jew. My people will get you, and they are going to make you suffer, you pig. You will beg them to kill you before they are finished with you."

"Yeah, yeah, I am already shitting in my boots. Seeing

that, according to you, I don't have much time, you and I need to have a quick chat before your platoon of goatherders arrive to kill me."

"There is nothing I have to say to you, infidel."

"You sure you don't even want to hear my question?"

"Absolutely."

Jessel shrugged, pulled his Glock 19 pistol from the small of his back, screwed a silencer on, and shot Bitar in the left foot.

Bitar screamed and cussed in very graphic terms, not only about Jessel but also his sister, mother, grandmother and other members of his lineage.

When he stopped, Jessel said, "Oops, I actually aimed for your head. Those beers I had earlier must have interfered with my aim. Okay, let's try again." The next shot went through Bitar's right foot.

Another tidal wave of curses erupted from Bitar. This time it took a bit longer for him to stop screaming and moaning. "You're going to kill me. So why not make it quick, Jewish scumbag?"

"Believe me Bitar, I am trying. I've got no use for you since you don't want to even listen to me, but I'm really struggling to shoot straight. So just be patient, I'll eventually get to your head. I am just working my way up from your feet."

The next shot shattered Bitar's left knee.

Bitar's mouth opened in a scream, but the only sound that came out was a long sigh, and then his body went limp. He had passed out from the pain.

Brandt and Christelle were able to hear what was happening in Beirut but could not talk directly to the leader. Brandt had a link to the Mossad team's commander in Tel Aviv, Dannie Halevi. "Dannie, tell your *kidon* to not kill the bastard. The man is seriously obese; I'm worried his heart will give in before he starts talking."

"Don't worry, John. The guy handling things over there knows what he's doing. One of his team is a specialist medic, he's keeping an eye on Bitar. He's going to start talking within five minutes after he wakes up."

Halevi was right. Ten minutes later, the medic held a bottle of smelling salts under Bitar's nose and he stirred. A minute or so later he was fully aware and in excruciating pain. There are not many kinds of pain that can be inflicted on the human body as severe and intense as a shattered knee. Bitar started howling.

Jessel stood in front of him, gun in his left hand and a mug of coffee in his right. He took a sip and said, "Bitar, just hang in there, I only have one more knee, two hips, and two shoulders to go before I get to your head. It should be over soon." He raised the gun and aimed at Bitar's right knee.

"Stop! Don't shoot me again, please! What is it that you want to talk about?"

Jessel lowered the gun and said, "Okay, let's talk."

"Give me a painkiller first," Bitar demanded.

"Sorry, we don't have any. But if you talk quickly and answer honestly, I'll see if I can get a doctor to attend to you."

"What the hell do you want from me?"

"Badr. Tell me all about it. Don't lie. I already had word with your acolyte in Naples, Imam Al-Sadiq aka Hassan Walid. I don't know what you did to the guy, but he hates you. He said you're a piece of shit for getting him into this trouble. He said your wife was a whore and that you are not the father of your children. He told me in great confidence that your father slept with his camels and a lot of other unseemly things about you and your family.

"But I don't know if I should believe everything he told me. For instance, the story about the Badr plot you guys have been working on. I always say a man who can turn so easily on a friend can't be trusted. So, I want to hear your version."

"Badr. What is that?" Bitar said.

Jessel raised his gun and shot Bitar through the left calf muscle. "Not what Al-Sadiq told me. He said you know all about it. Teresa Lombardi said the same thing, and so did that Russian arms supplier... what was his name again, Igor... no wait, now I remember, Egor Zubarev from Narva, Estonia."

Bitar's eyes betrayed his shock.

Jessel saw it and said, "Yep we've got all of them, and they are all talking, and they're all blaming it all on you. Some loyal friends you've made there, Bitar."

Bitar broke down in tears, and the next moment, his body went limp again. He was unconscious.

It was 12:20 A.M. in Beirut and 11:20 P.M. in Paris.

Carabinieri Comando Stazione Napoli Chiaia, Italy

11:00 P.M. in Naples and Paris

From 11:00 P.M. Naples time, the Beneduce-Longobardi leaders were brought into the interrogation room one by one. It took Marissa and Spencer a little over an hour to confirm what was on the surveillance audio and video tapes;

the seven of them were professional criminals. They traded in drugs. They counterfeited and embezzled money and consumer goods. They ran racketeering schemes. They abducted people. They assaulted and bullied people, and from time to time, they killed people. They were scum, but they knew absolutely nothing about Badr.

They were definitely going to spend the rest of their lives in jail for criminal activities, but not for terrorism.

DGSE Head Office, Paris, France

11:30 P.M. Paris

Frolov still had that same smug, triumphant look on his face he'd had on the plane when he was brought into the interrogation room and shoved into the chair across the table from Brandt.

Brandt was about to start when Frolov said in English, "Do we do this in Russian or English?"

"I speak both. Let's start in English and see how it goes," Brandt said.

Frolov nodded and said, "We don't have to waste time on this. I see you're also past your best-by date. I'm seventy-four years old and had some good innings while it lasted. I don't feel old, there is still a lot of life left in me, but, sad as it might be, I know my hourglass has run out. Not only have you caught me, I just got the news that I have an inoperable malignant brain tumor."

Brandt didn't for a moment believe what the man was saying. However, he couldn't help but think if the story about the brain tumor was true, it would be poetic justice for a diabolical man such as Frolov. He showed no emotion and made no reply.

"So, you don't have to threaten me with violence or pain or truth serums or trick me into anything. I will tell you everything. What I'm going to tell you will be the truth and nothing but the truth. However, in exchange for that I have only one request for you. I'd like to know how you did it. I know there are many security agencies across the world looking for me. They've been looking for me for decades. For decades I've been able to stay out of their hands. How did you get to me?"

Brandt was on high alert. Frolov was not to be trusted, there was a good reason he had managed to stay out of sight of the world's security agencies for all his adult life.

We'll see where this goes.

"Only if I hear no lies."

Frolov began by telling Brandt in detail about his childhood in Narva, how he had joined the KGB, and with the collapse of the Soviet Union and communism, had gone into business for himself.

With pomp and fanfare, Frolov stepped Brandt through his curriculum vitae. He was not a man who discriminated when it came to his selection of clients, he explained.

Brandt listened, seemingly impassively, although he was getting more exasperated by the minute. He had to translate Frolov's dazzling words of self-aggrandization into what they truly meant in real life.

Frolov traded with dictators, and he traded with rebels. He sold his instruments of death and destruction to 'freedom fighters' irrespective of the legitimacy of their grievances, and he had no reservations to make deals with genocidal psychopaths and maniacs who slaughtered the innocent. Wherever, whoever needed weapons of any kind, Frolov was the go-to man.

He never picked sides in a conflict—he supplied them both—it prolonged the fight and increased his profits. Frolov, in his lifetime, had destroyed countries and people, and he had become obscenely wealthy while masterfully concealing his activities to the rest of the world.

Frolov fancied himself an astute businessman. And he was proud to tell Brandt that he had used his wealth to acquire luxurious homes in idyllic locations across the globe, a luxury yacht, the latest sports cars, and strings of beautiful women who were passionate about the world's primary aphrodisiac, money.

To Brandt's growing chagrin, which was reaching new levels as Frolov talked, it was obvious that he enjoyed talking about himself and his achievements with no thought spared for those his merchandise had killed. In fact, it seemed that Frolov hadn't even made a connection between the weapons he sold and the people they killed.

Brandt couldn't help but think of March 11, 2004. The day of the Madrid, Spain train station bombings that killed 193 innocent civilians including Rex's parents and siblings. Bombs that this lowlife might have supplied to the terrorists. He couldn't help but think of the millions of innocent people killed across the world as a direct result of the weapons supplied by this self-adoring maniac over the past forty-plus years.

In Arizona, Longland was not only watching Frolov on the screen in front of him, he also kept a close eye on John Brandt. He had known Brandt for many years, knew the Old Man had a very short fuse, knew him well enough to see the anger building up that was about to erupt like a volcano at any moment.

Longland spoke to Brandt in his earphones, while Frolov was yapping on. "John, the man wants recognition; his entire life he has been operating in the dark. No one, or very few, know what he's done. He's never gotten a 'well-done' pat on the back from anyone. Psychopaths love recognition and attention. He knows he has come to the end of the road. He wants someone to listen, he knows this is his swan song. Don't interrupt him, give him free rein. Keep your cool, John, it's going to be worthwhile to endure it."

Brandt grunted softly and nodded slightly.

It was Thursday, October 1, 12:45 A.M. in Paris, one and a quarter hours after his interrogation, or rather his soliloquy, started, when Frolov grinned and said, "That's my biography. I guess now you want to talk about the reason you've brought me here?"

Brandt made no reply. He took a sip of the dregs in his coffee mug; it was cold and tasted horrible, but it helped to stop him from killing Frolov. This was the most surreal interrogation he'd ever had. That was if it could even be called an interrogation. It was more like being taken by the hand, by Frolov no less, and led through the dark alleys of the evil soul of a delusional psychopath who had no idea how much death, pain, and suffering he had caused, nor would he have cared about it.

Oblivious to the danger he was in, 'Frolov the Great' continued. "Okay, you've captured me, so you must have captured the rest of them."

It was not a question. Brandt didn't respond.

"Well, it all started on August twenty-eighth of this year when a former KGB colleague of mine visited me on my yacht at the Isle of Capri."

"Olesya Kharlamova," Brandt said and saw the surprise

434

on Frolov's face. "Yep, we have her in custody. She told us about the meeting. Continue."

Frolov went quiet for a while, shrugged, and said, "It is what it is... Anyway, so she came and saw me. Asked me to help this woman, a client of hers, to avenge the death of her family who were killed in an explosion in the Port of Naples in 2011 in an arms-for-drugs deal. I supplied the weapons for that deal."

Brandt was about to jump over the table and strangle the man but remembered Longland's advice and controlled himself.

It was 1:00 A.M. in Paris.

Chapter Seventy-Two

EAT AND SLEEP WHEN YOU CAN

En route to Saudi Arabia

Thursday, October 1, 1:00 A.M. in Paris

With a top speed of 644 miles per hour, the Dassault Falcon 900 B was one of the fastest private jets in the world. It had space for 19 passengers and a range of 4,598 miles. The French Air Force as well as the DGSE had them in their fleets.

Rex, Digger, and Josh, accompanied by three SEALS, Tanner Giles, Ronnie Hagen, and Darrin Tipton were aboard a DGSE Dassault Falcon 900 B, organized by Madame Proll.

At 1:00 A.M. they took off from the French Air Force base Brétigny-sur-Orge about 17 miles south of Paris. The SEALS were supposed to have had six weeks of R&R on the *TOMATS* but got pulled into Operation Badr—they loved it. Where else would a SEAL get a free holiday on a luxury yacht in the Mediterranean and a bit of action to boot?

The three SEALS boarded the plane in Naples. From there they made the short trip to Rome, where Josh boarded after questioning Teresa Lombardi and Aziz Abdul-Salam Awad. They landed in Paris shortly after 12:30 A.M. to pick up Rex and Digger.

At cruising altitude, the pilots set course for King Faisal Naval Base at Jeddah Saudi Arabia, 53 miles from Mecca.

Their tactical gear and weapons were packed in the cargo section.

Rex and Josh had experienced the luxury of travel on private jets on some of their missions in the past. For the three SEALS, it was a first. They thoroughly enjoyed the reclining seats, espresso machine, and a spread of food to pick and choose from which, compliments of the DGSE and Madame Proll, was enough to last them for days.

Tanner Giles had a slight grin on his face when he said, "Rex, Josh, I know we're not supposed to ask who you work for and all that, but this outfit of yours, do they have any vacancies?"

Rex smiled. "We always have vacancies. But just remember we don't always travel in luxury like this to get our asses shot at."

"Well, none of us has *ever* traveled like this to get our asses shot at. I reckon I can get used to this very quickly." Ronnie Hagen chuckled as he got up from his seat to get another espresso and pastry from the kitchen.

The plan was that after landing at King Faisal Naval Base, a US Military helicopter would pick them up and drop them onto a US submarine in the Red Sea. The sub would get them close to the beach at Port Sudan from where they would infiltrate the city at night and make their way to the warehouse.

The team knew they could be on a wild goose chase. That warehouse and its occupants, though undoubtedly busy with something illicit, might have nothing to do with Badr. Nonetheless, they would be remiss if they didn't investigate what was going on, especially since Saiyyad Rahal's ships were involved.

In Port Sudan, the interim measures until Rex and the team arrived were to add one more drone over the warehouse to get a better view of the place. A five-man team of armed Saudi secret agents were tasked to find hideouts as close as possible to the warehouse and be ready to go into action on short notice in case it became necessary.

Brandt's face appeared on the TV screen. "Okay, boys, just a quick update with the information gained from the interrogations so far."

Everyone swiveled their seats so that they could see the big screen.

In typical John Brandt fashion, he kept the briefing short and to the point. "As you know, Saiyyad Rahal declined the invitation to our party and went off to meet his maker.

"Lombardi, as Josh already knows, seems to have lost her mind.

"Awad. Other than remembering his own name and occupation, and confessing to dealing in illicit antiquities with terrorists, knew nothing more than we already knew. The Badr masterminds obviously understand the need-to-know principle.

"Al-Sadiq decided to play hardball, so we've put him back in his cell for now. We'll chat with him again a bit later. Since we put him back in his cell, he's been calling upon

Allah to descend from the heavens and smite us all. But it seems he is not in good standing with the Almighty—all of us are still in good health."

Rex and Josh were smiling, and the SEALS were roaring with laughter at Brandt's choice of words.

"The clan leadership admitted to everything except the killing of JFK and the fake moon-landings and of course any involvement in the Badr plot. None of them had a clue about it.

"That left us with Frolov and Bitar. Bitar is in and out of consciousness—seems he's been having a real shitty time in the company of a *kidon* and a few of his mates. Bitar has been mumbling about Israel attacking someone and that *Yawm al-Qiyamah*, the Day of Judgement, is upon us. I spoke to my friend, Yaron Aderet, at the Mossad, but he says Bitar is hallucinating.

"POTUS also confirmed it with the Israeli Prime Minister—Israel is not about to attack anyone.

"Frolov. Now let me tell you, there's an enigma. I've never experienced anything like him. He is so keen to talk, I'm not getting a word in. The problem is I can't stop him, I'm under strict orders from Rick Longland to let the reprobate talk and not interrupt him. Rick gave me some psycho-analytical babble about psychopaths' craving to be heard and given recognition. Can you imagine, sitting there desperately wanting to kill the sonofabitch and instead having to pat him on the back in admiration and praise for being instrumental in the killing of millions of innocents? That's what I've had to endure for the past hour and a half.

"I'm about to go back in, and hopefully we'll get to Badr in the next hour or so."

When the call ended, Ronnie Hagen looked at Rex and Josh and asked, "Your boss?"

Rex and Josh just smiled and nodded.

"He certainly has a way of getting to the point." Ronnie chuckled.

Rex smiled. "Oh, I thought he was a bit longwinded today. I guess he got nervous when he saw you guys."

"He didn't strike me as the nervous type," Darrin Tipton said with a big grin on his face.

Soon after, the five men made themselves comfortable and tried to get some sleep. It was the SOP (standard operating procedure) of Special Forces operatives and field agents anywhere in the world; eat and sleep when you can because you don't know when you will get the next opportunity to do so.

Digger had gone to sleep on the seat next to Rex's soon after he had been fed, which was before the video conference with Brandt.

Their destination was 2,751 miles away, just shy of five hours at the plane's cruising speed of 590 miles per hour.

Chapter Seventy-Three

FINAL INSTRUCTIONS

Port Sudan, Sudan

Thursday, October 1, 3:32 A.M. Port Sudan, 2:32 A.M.
Paris, France

Al Din Hadad was roused out of a deep sleep by the
cacophonic noise of someone beating on the steel side door.
It sounded as if the person was trying to break the door
down.

"I'm coming! I'm coming!" Al Din Hadad shouted. He
got out of the bed mumbling, "Don't break the door down.
I'm on my way." He arrived at the door and shouted
through the door, "I'm here. What do you want?"

"I want nothing. There's a parcel for you."

Al Din Hadad quickly donned one of the balaclavas
they kept at the door to use whenever they interacted with
the guards and opened the door. The guard had already

left. He looked down and saw a bubble-wrapped parcel about the size of a shoebox on the ground in front of him.

When he got back to their sleeping quarters, he heard Hussain snoring. He went to the kitchenette, filled the kettle with water, and plugged it in. While he waited for the water to boil, he used one of the kitchen knives to remove the wrapping from the parcel and read the message that came with it.

"Hassan, my brother, wake up! We've got work to do."

Hussain moaned and groaned in protest but managed to open his eyes and glance at his watch. "At three-thirty in the morning?" he yawned.

"I agree. These people have no sense of time. But let's rejoice. These are the final instructions." He held the typed pages up for Hussain to see.

"Final instructions you say? Well, in that case let's do it, and let's get out of this hellhole and go home."

Inside the box were two satellite phones. They were to fit those on the inside of drone, next to the canisters containing the fissile material and explosives. They did that within a few minutes.

Now, you have to make a connection between each drone and its satellite phone. Follow the step-by-step instructions below to configure it correctly. When you see this message 'ADFXX MHTRQ' on the screen, it means it has been configured correctly.

It took them a little over fifteen minutes to get the success message.

Now, you have to disable the phones' flight mode so that it can connect to the satellite. Wait for the success message to appear on the

phone screens. Leave the phones on. Some software will download
and install itself on the phones and the drones' computer systems.
Wait until the process is completed before shutting everything down.

It took another 15 minutes before the software was
installed and they could shut down the satellite phones and
drones.

By 4:00 A.M. in Port Sudan, 3:00 A.M. in Paris, they
were done. Everything was connected and communicating
as expected.

"We're never going to know the coordinates of the
target or targets. Those would have been preprogrammed
into the phones or downloaded remotely directly to the
drones," Hussain said.

Al Din Hadad shrugged and said, "Yes, it seems to be
so. But, eventually, when these things have exploded, we will
find out."

Hussain nodded. "I can't wait for eight o' clock to come.
I just want to get out of here and as far away as quickly as
possible."

Their final instructions were to launch the drones at
8:00 A.M. Before launch they were to power up the satellite
phones and the drones' computers to make sure they were
connected, and then start the engines. And at exactly 8:00
A.M. they were to push the launch button.

From that point onward, the drones would operate on
their own.

The two of them had no way of knowing how the
mission was going to play out, not even where those drones
were headed. If they did, they would have known that the
drones were programmed to fly to the target coordinates,
and when they'd reached them, to ascend to one thousand

feet. Reaching that altitude, the explosives would detonate, which would not only destroy the drones but disperse the radioactive material over a wide area.

When the drones had launched, Al Din Hadad's and Hussain's mission would be over. They were to get out of Sudan, immediately.

Chapter Seventy-Four

CIA Headquarters, Langley, Virginia, USA

Wednesday, September 30, 10 P.M. Langley Virginia, USA. Thursday, October 1, 4 A.M. Paris, France

In the Badr ops room, CIA Headquarters, the analyst, Leigh-Anne's red head popped up from behind her screen as she told Stacie, "Action in Port Sudan!"

"What's happening there?"

"One of the drones and the satellite have picked up two satellite phones being activated within a few seconds of each other. The phones made connections to BulgariaSat, one of the comms satellites serving the Balkans, Europe, and the Middle East. From BulgariaSat a link was established to a computer in southeastern France. Checking the location now... Côte d'Azur, the French Riviera. According to the coordinates, the phone is located in the... Cannes Le Vieux Port marina."

"A yacht if I would have to venture a guess," Stacie said and paused for a moment. "Frolov's yacht! Is there a recording of the conversation?"

"No voice or video, only text data. It's just finished downloading a packet to the satellite phones in the warehouse. Looking at our copy of it now."

"Encrypted?" Stacie asked about twenty seconds later.

"Yep."

Stacie experienced what felt like a quart of acid being squirted into her stomach. "Get it to the cryptography team and tell them Stacie Barrett, M1 Abrams, the Battle Tank of the Analysis Directorate, wants that decrypted within the hour."

Leigh-Anne smiled and got busy. She didn't know Stacie was aware of her reputation and nickname.

Stacie went out in search of Bryan Shafer and Martin Richardson.

Mossad safehouse, Hazmiyeh, Beirut, Lebanon

3:50 A.M. in Beirut, Lebanon and 2:50 A.M. in Paris, France

In Beirut, Bitar was delirious from pain and shock, his heart was beating irregularly, and he was mumbling incoherently. "Today … bombing … *Yawm al-Qiyama* is today."

Yawm al-Qiyama… the Day of Judgement. "Who? Where?"

"Won't… tell… you… infidel."

"Put more smelling salts under his nose," Jessel told the medic.

446

Bitar recoiled when the bottle was held under his nose but breathed in enough of the powerful ammonium carbonate fumes to shock him back to full consciousness.

"Bitar," Jessel said, "my patience with you is at an end. I'm going to ask you once more. You answer me, or I finish what I started. And this time I won't stop until you're dead. You tell me now, and I stop now and call a doctor, or I kill you."

Bitar didn't respond immediately.

Jessel raised his gun and aimed it at Bitar's healthy knee.

"Mecca! They're going to bomb Mecca."

Jessel shook his head. *How much more pain is this man willing to endure before he stops lying? Mecca. He's hallucinating.*

"What kind of bomb? What time?"

Bitar opened his eyes and looked at Jessel, shook his head once, and said in a clear but soft voice, "A nuclear bomb. Today. I don't know the exact time. You can't stop it." He made an attempt to laugh, but it sounded more like a dog's snarl.

Jessel raised the gun again, but Bitar had passed out again.

DGSE Head Office, Paris, France

3:55 A.M. Paris

Frolov had just got his second wind. "This woman came to me as Liana Verdi, but I told her I know she's Teresa Lombardi. Kharlamova told me her real name.

"She had a brilliant plan. Her only problem was the

weapon. She said her first choice was a nuke; I couldn't help her. She then said if she can't get a nuke, she wanted a chemical or biological weapon or a dirty bomb.

"I could've supplied her with all three of those but had to explain to her that chemical and biological weapons required a lot more effort to prepare and deliver. 'A dirty bomb is so much smaller and easier,' I told her."

"Why did you make a deal with her? I'm sure you didn't have any interest in her plans for revenge."

"You're right, I am not a vengeful type of person."

How nice of you. But you're a mass murderer.

"I did it to build my reputation, my legacy so to speak. No one has ever set off a dirty bomb successfully. To this day it remains a theoretical device, yet to make it is very simple. Getting the fissile material is a bit of problem for most people, but not for me. Through my contacts throughout the former Soviet Bloc military, I have access to as much of it as I want. I've just been waiting for someone to ask me for a dirty bomb. You see, in business it's always about supply and demand."

"Obviously, you didn't bargain on being captured. So, there goes your legacy," Brandt said.

Frolov laughed.

"What's the target?"

"Mecca."

Brandt felt an ice-cold shiver running down his spine. *Surely, he's lying.* "Mecca. As in that city in Saudi Arabia?"

"Yep, that's the one."

Brandt had a hard time not showing that his jaw has gone slack as he realized that Frolov was not lying. "When?"

"What's the time?"

Brandt glanced at his watch. "Five past four."

"In a little less than three hours."

Seven o' clock in Paris, eight in Mecca. Brandt's mind was working at warp speed.

"How's it going to happen?"

"Two drones will deliver it."

"From where?"

"Port Sudan."

So, Stacie was right, that warehouse is part of the plan.

"You *will* stop it."

Frolov laughed again. "I can't. It's already in progress, it can't be stopped. Even if I could, why would I want to stop it? I kicked off an irreversible routine before I left my yacht last night. Not even I can stop it. You see, I'm still going to go down in history as the first one to build and successfully deploy a dirty bomb. If you hadn't caught me, can you imagine the publicity my business would've gotten out of such a feat?"

Brandt made a silent pledge to himself that he was going to kill Frolov when this was over. He would've done it there and then, were it not that he was rearing to get out of the room to start organizing a response.

But he had one more question, which he knew was important. "Why Mecca? The Badr Five are all Muslims. Mecca is the holiest place for Muslims of all stripes. How the hell did they agree to target Mecca?"

"Ah, that was easy. I acquired two Israel Aerospace Industries UAVs, known as IAI Harpys. Got them for a song from a Chinese friend. Their military had no use for them anymore. Over the last few weeks, the electronics and communications systems of the drones have been modified while on the outside the Harpys were restored to their original condition—complete with Israeli colors, markings and insignia, even the Star of David.

Brandt felt his whole body tensing and his fist clenching as he realized what a cataclysm the world was facing.

"So, as you can see. It's a brilliant plan. Israel will get the blame for turning the Muslims' holiest of holies to a wasteland for at least three decades. It doesn't matter what the Israelis say afterward, once the origins of those drones are linked to them, Muslims will unite and attack them. When that happens, America will get involved, and so will NATO and…"

Brandt's punch connected with the tip of Frolov's chin. The power of the blow lifted the Russian clean out of his chair and smashed him into the wall. His jaw was broken, something he didn't know yet, but he was going to become painfully aware of it when he regained consciousness.

Chapter Seventy-Five

DGSE Head Office, Paris, France. CIA Headquarters, Langley, Virginia, USA.

Thursday, October 1, 4:10 A.M. in Paris

Brandt rushed into the JOC and found Christelle standing in front of a map on one of the big screens. Her arms were folded across her chest, and she was trembling slightly as if she were cold. Her face was drained of all color.

"Oh my God, John. This is going to be Armageddon."

"Only if we allow it to happen. We've got less than three hours to stop it."

"How?"

"I've got some ideas. First, we need to divert that plane with Rex and his team to Port Sudan. They could be there in less than two hours. An hour before the drones take off."

"If the plane will be allowed to land," Christelle said.

"We'll need your president and ours and the King of

Saudi Arabia to put pressure on the President of Sudan. That plane *must* be allowed to land, and the Sudanese police and military *must* be ordered to keep their noses out of this scrap."

"Let's get onto it," Christelle said.

As Brandt turned to connect to the Operation Badr center in Langley, Stacie's face appeared on one of the big screens on the wall. She was in a conference room, and with her was Director Howard Lawrence, Deputy Director Martin Richardson, and Bryan Shafer.

Christelle took a seat next to Brandt.

"John, we've got independent confirmation that Frolov didn't lie when he told you that the target is Mecca, and it will be executed by drones to be launched from Port Sudan.

"We intercepted the communications between two satellite phones inside the warehouse, which went through the BulgariaSat satellite to connect them to a computer on what we believe is Frolov's yacht in the Cannes Le Vieux Port marina.

"Software was uploaded from the yacht's computer to the satellite phones. Our IT gurus deciphered the software code and found it's the launch and flight instructions for those drones, and the coordinates of the target is Mecca, as Frolov told you."

Brandt nodded slowly.

Director Lawrence took a sip of coffee, cleared his throat, and said, "We have, as far as I can see, a few options. One, we send armed Reaper UAVs from our Navy ships in the Red Sea to bomb the warehouse and everything inside it off the map. The Reaper MQ-9 drones are armed with a variety of weapons including Paveway II laser-guided bombs and Hellfire missiles. That should do the job.

"However, notwithstanding the fact that two Reaper

drones dumping their munitions on that warehouse would obliterate it, it will in all likelihood also trigger the dirty bombs and leave Port Sudan a nuclear wasteland. So that's our least favorable option."

Everyone nodded.

"Second option; in the same vein, but with less danger to human life, let the drones take to the air, wait until they're over the Red Sea and shoot them down there. The dirty bombs could still go off, but at least it will be far away from people."

"Three, we can try to pressure the Sudan government to send in their security forces and take care of the problem. But I'm not confident that they have the skills to disarm those bombs, and I'm not sure we would get their cooperation. Even if we could, we don't have enough time for them to organize it all.

"Four, we could ask the Saudis to send a taskforce from Jeddah over to Port Sudan to take care of business. But I don't know if they have a contingent of Special Forces operators stationed there. And we still have the time issue; the Saudis will probably not be able to make it in time.

"Five, we can send a taskforce from one of our Navy vessels to try and do it. But again, we have the time issue.

"I'd say our choices are between option one and two."

"Director, there's another option," Brandt said into the silence.

"Let's hear it," Lawrence said.

"We have dispatched, as a precautionary measure, a team of five special operators to Jeddah. They left Paris three hours ago on a DGSE Dassault Falcon. The plan was to infiltrate them into Sudan from one of our submarines, and to go have a look at that warehouse.

"We can divert them now. They could be landing at Port

Sudan within less than two hours, which, if Frolov didn't lie about the time, would give the team an hour to get to the warehouse and neutralize the drones."

Lawrence looked at each of the attendees in turn, waiting for more suggestions. There were none. "In that case, option one is now the special ops team. Failing that, we must decide whether we bomb the drones while they're still on the ground or wait for them to reach the Red Sea. All in agreement?"

Everyone agreed.

The Director looked at his watch and said, "Martin, while I get over to the White House, I need you and the rest of the people here to work out what has to be done to make this happen. I will contact you from the Situation Room in fifteen to twenty minutes. You have my authorization to divert that plane to Port Sudan, provided Madame Proll can get authorization from her Director."

Christelle was already on a secured line to her Director by the time Lawrence reached the door of the conference room. Fortunately, she had kept him up to date with the progress of the renditions and interrogations as they unfolded. Within minutes, she brought her director up to speed with the latest information and the request to authorize the diversion of the DGSE jet.

The Director approved it before she could finish her request and told her that he was on his way to Élysée Palace, the residence and offices of the President of France.

Christelle immediately established a link to the DGSE jet and told the pilots to change course and head for Port Sudan. They did so without question and confirmed their new bearings. They agreed to increase their speed and calculated that, barring any unforeseen issues, they would land at the new destination by 5:30 A.M. Paris time which would be 6:30 A.M. at Port Sudan.

"I take it by the time we get there we'll have clearance to land?" the main pilot asked.

"We're working on that. We'll let you know as soon as we have it," Christelle said. "Don't worry; we won't ask you to land without clearance."

Brandt activated the secured link to the cabin of the jet, turned the volume up, and said in a loud voice, "Dalton, wake up, the party is over."

Rex was not really asleep; he was in a state of restful awareness. It was a state which all Special Forces operators and field agents knew very well. He opened his eyes, looked at the screen, and said, "What's up, John?"

By now, everyone else in the cabin had swiveled their chairs to face the TV screen.

"We've got a tanker-load of sewage to deal with," Brandt started, and within minutes he and Christelle had explained the scenario.

Rex and the rest of the team were not stressed about the new destination and the prospect of going into battle immediately after landing. They were heading in that direction in any event. They would just get there much sooner now. Of course, they would have liked to have the opportunity to scout the place and plan their approach, but they had enough experience to know that the best laid plans, more often than not, changed during the execution. There was an adage among Special Forces operators; there are only three things in life that are certain—death, taxes, and changes.

They were however more than a little surprised about the terrorists' choice of target and weapons.

"Shit man, those idiots would start Armageddon," Rex said.

"Exactly what Christelle said earlier," Brandt said. "And I agree with that summation. The Middle East is the breeding ground of conspiracies, propaganda, and misdirection. This is a false flag operation that might just work out for them exactly as they've intended. No Muslim is going to believe that Israel had nothing to do with the bombing of Mecca. No one is going to convince the Muslims of the world that any Muslim of any sect would ever bomb Mecca.

"Once they find the pieces of those drones and identify them as Israeli in origin, the world's one point eight billion Muslims will forget their differences and unite against the state of Israel. The US and NATO would not stand by while Israel gets annihilated.

"If I've ever seen a detonator that could spark World War Three and a nuclear holocaust, this would be it."

The five men in the cabin were staring at Brandt and Christelle wordlessly, as the gravity of the situation settled in their minds.

"Boys, if you can't stop it, we'll drop bombs on the warehouse, or we can shoot them down over the Red Sea. Needless to say, we would prefer not to do that because of the inherent risk that our bombs might set off the dirty bombs," John said.

"Okay, John, if you could get Greg and Stacie Barrett to make sure we have the aerial maps, plans, and everything about that place and surrounding areas, we'll do everything we can to be ready to go into action the moment we hit the ground. We also need all information about those drones. We might have to disable them if we get there in time.

"Provided of course, that you have arranged clearance for us to land, and that the Sudanese police, military, militia, and any other adventurous types stay out of our way."

"That's being worked on as we speak. Both the DGSE and CIA directors are about to enter the offices of their presidents. We'll keep you posted," Christelle said.

It was 5:00 A.M. in Paris, 6:00 A.M. in Port Sudan. Two hours to H-hour. A little less than one hour flying time to Port Sudan.

The Supreme worked on as to shall Both the DOSE and IA decisions are agreed as better for other of other regulations. Two things required IA? Colombia side. It was 2004 M. in Fire, 600 MW 40 as Solution to John 24 were 8 articles that that plea from 8 8% the article.

Chapter Seventy-Six

THE REALM OF POSSIBILITIES

Paris | Washington D.C. | Tel Aviv | Riyadh | Khartoum

Thursday, October 1, 2015

Generally, when dealing with government officials and politicians, the wheels tend to turn gallingly slow. They were a breed of people who liked to consult widely and carefully consider all ramifications, including the risks or benefits to their careers, when making decisions. But every now and then they will be challenged by a situation like this. A situation where decisions have to be made in seconds, not days, weeks, or months. Actions had to be taken immediately, not somewhere in the future. Policies and procedures could not be followed, and the buck stopped with them. All of which required them to break out of the mold and surprise everyone, even themselves.

In an unprecedented demonstration of astonishing speed and efficiency, the staff at the White House had the

President of the USA, the President of France, and the Prime Minister of Israel on a video conference by the time Director Lawrence arrived at the White House. The French President and Israeli Prime Minister had already been briefed by the directors of their respective intelligence agencies when the call started.

The US President, with the Secretary of Defense and the Chairman of the Joint Chiefs of Staff next to him, got straight to the point and told his counterparts that they had one window of opportunity to stop the drones from leaving that warehouse in Port Sudan. But they had only ten minutes to decide if they were going to use the opportunity or not.

Within minutes it was agreed, Rex and his team would attempt to stop the drones from taking off. The US had a military presence in Saudi Arabia and the Red Sea, which would be called upon to support Rex's team.

The French had no military assets in the region but would provide support in any way they could.

Israel would stay out of it as they couldn't mount a military response in time. It was decided that the Israelis' time and effort would best be spent on preparing not only an international press release but also putting their security forces on high alert for the inevitable reprisals if all attempts to stop those drones from reaching Mecca failed.

Next, it was agreed that the King of Saudi Arabia had to be brought into the fold. He had to decide if he wanted to shut down and evacuate Mecca, and if he was willing to help the US and French presidents to convince the Sudanese president to help avert the crisis.

The king was the absolute monarch of Saudi Arabia. He served as head of state and head of government and head of the House of Saud, the Saudi royal family. Ex officio, he was also the Custodian of the Two Holy Mosques, a title not only signifying the king's jurisdiction over the mosques of Masjid al Haram in Mecca and Al-Masjid an-Nabawi in Medina, but also his responsibility to protect them. No wonder the king looked nauseated when he heard about the target and the weapons destined for it.

The king had no problems making decisions on his own. He decided, very quickly, that it was not wise to attempt to evacuate the one and a half million residents of Mecca, which in any case didn't include the hundreds of thousands of pilgrims in the city at any given time. "After all," he said, "we're not going to allow those drones to even reach Saudi airspace. Are we?"

"That's our intention, your Highness. But I want to be clear, there are no guarantees," the US President said.

"Understood," the king said.

It was a bit more of a challenge to get the Sudanese president on the line, another demonstration of Einstein's theory of relativity—the ten minutes it took before the President of Sudan was on the line felt like an hour.

While they were waiting for the President of Sudan to make his appearance, the Secretary of Defense in America issued his first orders to the Naval Commanders of the Fifth Fleet, responsible for the Persian Gulf, Arabian Sea, and the Red Sea. They had to ready themselves for a mission that had, in fact, already started.

The President of Sudan, of course, had no idea about Badr, and no idea that his country was being used as the launchpad for an attack on Mecca that could trigger the start of World War III. As could be expected, he was shaken by the news. And maybe he also felt just a little overshadowed by the three authoritative men who called him. He had never met the US and French presidents, had only seen them on TV. The King of Saud he had met on quite a few occasions.

Despite both being Muslim-majority countries, historically the relationship between Saudi Arabia and Sudan had its ups and downs, fluctuating between cooperation and conflict. Fortunately, at the time of this call, the two countries were experiencing an era of good relations, the result of Sudan's decision to expel Iranian diplomats from their country and send troops to support Saudi Arabia in the fight against the Houthis in Yemen.

Although the Sudanese president was also a Muslim, just like the Saudi King, and they were on good terms, it still took fifteen very precious minutes to inform him and get him to understand the consequences if he didn't act and agree to the requests from the three heads of state who called him.

Once the Sudanese President had a grasp of the gravity of the situation, even though he was still on the conference call, he began issuing orders for his staff to get hold of the top officials of the country's military and law enforcement agencies. His orders to them would be to shut down the airport at Port Sudan, divert all planes except the DGSE plane elsewhere. In addition, he'd have them set up a protective perimeter no less than two miles around the airport and the warehouse and make sure that no one entered or exited the area.

Twenty minutes before the DGSE jet was due to land, Christelle informed the pilots as well as Rex and his team that they had clearance for landing and could expect no resistance from the Sudanese military or law enforcement.

Two minutes later, the control tower at Port Sudan airport confirmed that they were cleared for landing.

Brandt and Christelle were experiencing the first tiny

461

jolts of optimism as they were kept abreast of the rapid, and to say the least, surprising, progress made by the various heads of state.

"John, maybe, just maybe, we can stop those drones on the ground," Christelle whispered.

"It's not beyond the realm of possibilities," Brandt replied.

Especially with Rex Dalton and that dog of his leading the charge, he thought but didn't tell her.

Chapter Seventy-Seven

AS PER THE PRESIDENT'S ORDERS

Port Sudan International Airport, Sudan

Thursday, October 1, 2015 6:45 A.M. Port Sudan,
Sudan, 5:45 A.M. Paris, France

Rex and the team retrieved their tactical gear and weapons out of the cargo hold and looked at the maps and aerial photos collected by the drones.

Once on the ground, the team would be in communication with each other through their headsets and lip microphones. Through one of the drones circling above the target they would also be patched through to the JOC in Paris, the CIA's operations center in Langley, and the communications room on the *TOMATS*.

Rex was a little apprehensive, and so were his teammates. They were rushing headlong into a situation without enough intelligence, without a plan, and without backup. As for the latter, Brandt told them that he had the assurance

from US Naval command that two MH-60S Sea Hawk helicopters as well as two fully armed AH-64A Apache attack
helicopters were on their way to Port Sudan. Two Reaper
drones with a full payload were heading in the same
direction.

They were also told that they could expect no interference from the Sudanese.

Brandt, who had been placed in charge of the coordina-
tion of the ground mission in Sudan, had also arranged
with the Saudis that their agents watching the warehouse
would pick the team up from the airport and take them to
the warehouse.

Rex hoped the Saudi agents would be able to give them
more information than what he could glean from the aerial
photos.

In Port Sudan, General Yohannes Eltayeb was in charge
of the operation to secure the area around the airport and
the warehouse.

Brandt found it utterly frustrating that both his
requests to be put in direct contact with General Eltayeb
were refused, and he was told that all communications had
to go through General Ahmed Burhan Hashim, the
commander of the Sudanese military. For a moment,
Brandt considered throwing his toys out of his crib and
asking the US President to get King Al Saud to interfere.
But he dropped the idea—there was no time for it, not
even to vent his irritation. The plane was ten minutes
away from touchdown.

General Eltayeb was a rising star in the Sudanese military.
At 43 years of age, he was young for a general, but he held

an English university education and spoke several languages.

What neither Brandt nor Rex and the team, and for that matter very few people, knew was that there was a time, long ago, when Eltayeb supported his president. But his views had changed. The president was 70; according to Eltayeb, he was too old to run a country like Sudan with all its challenges. On the president's watch, which started in 1989, way too long according to Eltayeb, the war in Darfur during which more than 400,000 were killed, took place, the Second Sudanese Civil War took place, and by the end of it, South Sudan's secession took place. Eltayeb had decided, long ago, that his president was a corrupt, useless politician, and a fraud. Sudan deserved better.

Eltayeb had ambitions, and he had mapped out his own career path years ago. The first step to achieving his end goal was to become the commander of the Sudanese military. In other words, his commander, General Ahmed Burhan Hashim's job. After that, his next position would be commander in chief. He couldn't stand the notion that this president was the commander in chief. Although the president had joined the Sudanese military in his youth, attended the Egyptian Military Academy, and eventually became a paratroop officer, Eltayeb was sure the man had forgotten which side of a gun the bullet came out of. But the president's most grievous and unpardonable sin was that he was a half breed—African-Arab from a Bedouin tribe in the middle of North Sudan. Eltayeb, on the contrary, was an Arab, pure bred. He loathed the Africans and even more so those who interbred with them.

Eltayeb was not only a bigot; he was also a hypocrite. His goal was to get the power, all of it. He wanted to be the supreme and sole ruler of Sudan. He wanted closer ties with Russia and China. He wanted the Americans and British out of his country. And to this end, he was slowly but surely building his base and his wealth for the day he would get his chance.

One of his many private enterprises was his share in the trade, which was conducted out of that enormous warehouse not far from the airport in Port Sudan. The stock levels of the merchandise inside varied according to the economic principle of supply and demand. At present, the stock consisted of ten million rounds of ammunition, two thousand RPG-7's with ten thousand rockets. The RPG-7 was one of the best weapons ever made. Simple to operate even by a teenager who, with a few minutes of training, could take out a tank, or an armored personnel carrier, even a Black Hawk attack helicopter—the great equalizer. There were hundreds of mortars and missiles for it. Thousands of AK-47s, the assault rifle that gave power to the powerless and voices to the voiceless masses of the world. There were handguns, sniper rifles, and grenades. Landmines, antipersonnel mines, explosives, and much more.

All in all, the current stock was worth about fifty million US dollars. Eltayeb's share was thirty percent, and for that all he had to do was protect the warehouse and make sure shipments were received and delivered on time to customers throughout Africa and the Middle East. His troops did the guard duty, and the government paid them. It was a sweet deal he had with a man who he had never laid eyes on, and whose name was Szabó. Whether that was the man's first or last name, he didn't know. Eltayeb didn't care, the money was good, and it was flowing in at a steady clip—the perpetual conflicts of Africa and the Middle East assured that.

Eltayeb had received the President's instructions second

hand through one of his lackeys, Sudan's commander of the armed forces, General Ahmed Burhan Hashim. To the general, he had given the assurance that his orders would be executed. What Eltayeb's understanding of those orders were, General Hashim never asked for.

The thing was, Hashim's interpretation of the president's orders, if executed, would put Eltayeb's private enterprise in jeopardy. From what he could gather, reading between the lines, an attack force of undetermined origins, was on its way to execute a mission against that warehouse and its occupants. Who the occupants were, he had no idea. What they were doing there, he also had no idea. All he knew was that he had to set up the working and living spaces for the two occupants and then had to withdraw without meeting them or finding out what they were doing there. His responsibility was to assure they were guarded, supplied with food, and to pass encrypted messages between them and someone on the other end of his secured satellite phone—who it was, he had no idea. He suspected it could have been his faceless business partner, Szabó.

It didn't matter to him who received the messages. As long as the money kept pouring into his pockets, he was happy.

By the time the DGSE jet touched down at the airport, General Eltayeb had set up his command post in the control tower from where he could direct his operation. The airport had been shut down as per the president's orders. His soldiers had set up a cordon around the airport and the warehouse as per the president's orders. The streets were cleared of civilians, and the airport staff were told to go home.

Chapter Seventy-Eight

GO GET THEM BOYS

Port Sudan International Airport, Sudan

Thursday, October 1, 2015, 6:45 A.M. Port Sudan,
Sudan, 5:45 A.M. Paris, France

Rex and the team were looking out the windows as the
plane approached the airport and touched down. Digger
was on his feet, fully geared up, excited and ready to go.
The team were in black tactical gear complete with body
armor, assault rifles, HK 416s, a German manufactured
Heckler and Koch carbine, and Sig Sauer P226 pistols. Two
of the drones above were brought down to 2,000 feet to
provide a detailed view of the target area and stream it to
the watchers in the operations centers in the US, CRC
headquarters in Arizona, Tel Aviv, Paris, Riyadh, the
TOMATS, and a few US Navy ships in the Red Sea.

The first thing that got Rex's hackles up when he and

the team reached the bottom of the stairs, was that there were no vehicles waiting as they were told there would be. He was just about to let Brandt know when he spotted a single white dilapidated Toyota panel van racing toward them across the tarmac.

The van skidded to a stop a few yards from them. The driver had a companion with him in the front passenger seat. Both of them were in bush-camouflage uniforms. The one in the passenger seat had an AK-47 protruding from the open window. The driver shouted at them and waved for them to get in. Rex told his men to hang back and cover him while he and Digger approached and checked out the van.

Rex kept his HK 416 across his chest, finger on the trigger, as he approached the van. The driver was yapping on in a language Rex didn't understand. He assumed it was Basa Sunda, a Malayo-Polynesian language spoken by the majority of Sudan. Rex ignored him and looked over his shoulder at the space in the back. The side windows in the back were covered with black paint, and the only way to get into that space was through the double doors at the back. The seats were two benches against the sides of the van facing each other. Satisfied there was no danger lurking in the back, the driver still babbling and gesturing nervously, Rex signaled for the team to approach while he spoke to the driver for the first time, in Arabic. He got only a blank stare from him. He got the same reaction from the passenger. Next, he tried in English, still no comprehensible response. He rapidly went through a simple greeting in all languages he spoke, but that seemed to just worsen the vacuous stares of the two men.

He walked around to the back, out of earshot of the

driver and his passenger, flipped the switch on the lip mic, and said, "John, I guess you're seeing and hearing what's happening over here. Our taxis haven't turned up. If this is our ride, it's okay, but the problem is these guys don't speak any language that anyone of us know. I take it there was a change of plan?"

"Not that I was informed of. But I'm not seeing any other vehicles approaching either. So, that *must* be your ride."

"Okay, we'll take it. But I'm not convinced everything is kosher here."

Rex turned to his men. "Guys, I don't like this. We were supposed, as you know, to be met by two vehicles driven by two Saudi intelligence agents whom I assumed would at least speak a few words of Arabic. These guys don't even know how to return a simple greeting in Arabic. Neither do they speak English, Russian, German, Italian, French, or Chinese. I would've expected at least basic Arabic from them. I'm not sure if they are our ride or not. Neither is John, but we don't have time to wait around to find out. John said there are no other vehicles approaching. So, let's get in but stay sharp; I don't trust these guys at all."

"Maybe we should mitigate the risk and hijack the van," Josh said.

"It crossed my mind," Rex said, "but I don't want to make too many enemies too quickly," Rex said and motioned with his head to the contingent of soldiers on the roofs of the airport buildings and a platoon of them on the tarmac in front of the buildings, about three hundred yards away.

Josh opened the back door of the van and climbed in, followed by the rest. Rex and Digger were last. When Digger was in the van, Rex said, "Digger, stay," and walked around to the passenger side. He opened the door and gestured for the man with the AK-47 to go sit in the back with the team. The man hesitated, shook his head, and started talking rapidly, clearly not willing to swap seats. Unceremoniously, Rex grabbed the man by the arm and pulled him out of the van. The man kept his protests up as Rex led him around to the back and pushed him inside.

"Digger, watch this guy," Rex said before he closed the door.

Digger growled once, and the man instantly went quiet.

Rex returned to the front, got into the passenger seat, and held his hand up to the driver to let him know he should not take off yet. He took his satellite phone out and pulled up the map of the airport and warehouse on the screen and showed it to the driver. The driver nodded. Rex tapped on the location of the warehouse and with a hand signal told the driver to get going.

The driver nodded, gave Rex a thumbs up, smiled broadly, showing off his broken and smoke-stained yellow teeth, and put the van into gear.

Everyone in the team had memorized the roads and buildings and possible routes from the airport to the warehouse.

When the van started moving, in the control tower, General Eltayeb lowered his binoculars, sighed in relief, and allowed a smile to break across his face.

The van sped across the tarmac heading for gates on the north side which was the opposite direction of where Rex expected them to go. The warehouse was on the south side of the airport.

By the time they approached the gate, the rattletrap was doing close to sixty miles an hour. The driver barely slowed down as he made a sharp right turn after they went through the gate. The wrong direction again. Rex was expecting him to go left, which would have brought them to a T-junction a few hundred yards away. From there, he would have had to turn left again to drive in the direction of the warehouse.

Rex shouted at the driver to stop. He didn't respond, didn't even look at him. Rex tapped him on the arm, but the driver only threw a quick glance at Rex and stepped on the gas. They were by now on a gravel road doing close to seventy miles an hour and accelerating. When they passed the eastern most corner of the security fence surrounding the airport, and the driver passed another road leading south, Rex spoke quietly into his lip mic to the team, "Guys, this asshole has no intention of taking us to that warehouse. Be ready for action on one. Three, two, one."

Rex grabbed the handbrake between the seats and pulled it up in one powerful jerk. The van's rear end fish-tailed; the driver struggled with both hands on the steering to keep control as the van skidded to a stop.

In the back, everyone was hanging onto the seats not to be thrown off. By the time the van came to a standstill in an enveloping big red cloud of African dust, Josh had the barrel of his Sig Sauer firmly in the ear of their guest in the back. Rex had the business end of his HK 416 pointing at the driver's head.

There was no need to understand each other's language anymore. A 9-millimeter Sig Sauer and HK 416 were enough to take care of any language barriers.

Twenty seconds later, all the watchers across the world saw the van emerge out of the dust cloud and go back the way it came, at high speed. As the dust drifted away, they saw two forlorn figures on their stomachs next to the road. Their arms and legs seemed to have been tied.

In the control tower at the airport, General Eltayeb lowered the binoculars and swore under his breath.

In Paris, Brandt grinned, Christelle looked worried, and on the *TOMATS*, Catia's fingernails were digging into the material of the armrest of her chair.

"Go get them, boys," Brandt whispered.

Chapter Seventy-Nine

SIT TIGHT BOYS

Port Sudan, Sudan

Thursday, October 1, 2015, 7:00 A.M. Port Sudan, Sudan, 6:00 A.M. Paris, France

The van, with Josh in the driver seat, was now speeding in the right direction. The warehouse was less than three miles away. Barring any holdups, they would get there in under three minutes.

They had an hour left.

Rex was just beginning to get optimistic when Brandt's voice came through in their earpieces and told them there was a technical speeding toward them on an intercept course. Seconds later, the technical burst into view about 200 yards ahead of them from a side street and came to a stop, blocking their way.

A technical, sometimes called a non-standard tactical vehicle (NSTV), or the poor man's Humvee, was an improvised fighting vehicle popular in Africa and South America. Typically, they were constructed from four-wheel drive, open-backed civilian pickup trucks. Toyota was the most popular make. On the back of the truck was mounted a rotary cannon or a recoilless anti-tank gun or other types of heavy weapons. This technical had a belt-fed 12-millimeter machine gun on the back.

"It's probably a bit too optimistic to hope that those guys are here to escort us to the warehouse?" Darrin Tipton could be heard mumbling.

For five men in a ramshackle panel-van, although armed and highly trained, the technical with its four AK-47-wielding soldiers and a fifth one manning the 12-millimeter machine gun on the back, posed a serious threat. For starters, they were outgunned.

Okay, what is this? Friend or foe? Rex wondered.

He got his answer in quick order when the four men with AK-47s dismounted and took up positions behind the vehicle with their guns pointed at the white panel van. The machine gunner was apparently struggling to load the gun.

Rex shouted to them in Arabic but got no reply. He tried in English and got the same response. "Does anyone in this country speak English or Arabic? Or are you all under orders not to understand it?" Rex said loud enough so that only his team could hear.

"That's if they even got orders not to interfere," Josh added.

Rex was silently working through the options; If they attacked the technical and its occupants now before that machine gun could be brought into play, they might have a chance. When the gun was ready, they would have no chance.

In Paris, Brandt was desperately trying to explain the situation to Sudan's commander of the armed forces, General Ahmed Burhan Hashim. The general quickly understood what Brandt was telling him, but instead of getting on the radio to General Eltayeb, Hashim wasted more than two minutes going off on a tangent about the insolence of General Eltayeb. By the time his ranting and raving was over, the machine gun was ready and brought to bear on the van.

Rex told Josh to reverse. Fifteen yards away there was a road to their right. As Josh did so, Rex saw a short spell of chaos around the technical before everyone jumped back onto the vehicle.

On the alternative route that would take them through a decrepit neighborhood to the warehouse, Brandt informed them that the technical had followed them, and soon afterward Rex and Josh, in their side mirrors, saw the vehicle about 250 yards behind them. But it didn't try to close the gap.

Not a mile further, Brandt told them that another technical was about to appear out of a side street and block their way. Thirty seconds later, they had come to a stop, boxed in between two technicals, two 12-millimeter machine guns and eight AK-47s now pointing at them.

The weird thing was that no one from the technicals approached them, no one was talking to them, and no one was shooting at them.

Then the reason for it became clear when Brandt told them that three police vehicles were heading their way.

"So much for no interference from the locals," Rex said to Brandt. "It seems to me they are under orders not to shoot but to delay, hence calling in the police. Someone wants us delayed long enough so that those drones can take off."

"And I think I know who," Brandt said. "Sit tight, I'm going to raise some hell right now."

A minute later, Brandt was in a verbal battle with the US Secretary of Defense who was in the Situation Room with the president, chairman of the joint chiefs of staff, and other high-ranking officials. "Mister Secretary, I don't care about causing an international incident by firing the first shots. You are playing into their hands. It must be clear, even to you, that our task force can't be delayed. Not one minute longer."

"Mister Brandt, I won't be dictated by you."

"Mister Secretary, shut up. You're wasting time. Order one of those drones to shoot those damn technicals out of the way or I order my men to start shooting their way out of this. Any deaths on our side are on your head."

"Mister Brandt..."

"Enough!" The president roared. "Divert one of those Reapers and take out those vehicles now, immediately."

Brandt leaned back and grinned.

Christelle was shaking her head ever so slightly.

Brandt said to the team, "Sit tight, boys, the cavalry will be there momentarily. Stay in the van and keep your heads low."

The soldiers manning the technicals never knew what hit them. Two hellfire missiles hitting their vehicles at virtually the same moment left only two smoldering heaps of metal and tiny parts of their bodies dispersed into an area more than a hundred yards around ground zero.

In the control tower at the airport, General Eltayeb saw the contrail from the two missiles streaking down from the sky, heard the explosions which sounded almost like one, and swore loudly.

Seconds later, the van was racing toward the warehouse again.

It was 7:35 A.M. in Port Sudan, 6:35 A.M. in Paris.

Chapter Eighty

IT'LL BE OVER IN MINUTES

Port Sudan, Sudan

Thursday, October 1, 2015, 7:38 A.M. Port Sudan, Sudan, 6:38 A.M. Paris, France

About 800 yards or so away from the warehouse, as the van skidded around a corner, a barricade of three technicals and about twenty armed soldiers came into view.

This time they fired the moment they saw the van. Bullets were hitting the engine and body of the van. The front window cracked into thousands of pieces as at least three bullets hit it. Rex used the butt of his HK 416 to clear out the glass while Josh threw the van into reverse to get back around the corner.

"How much more of this kind of non-interference do we have to take?" Rex muttered.

When they were out of the firing line, Rex quickly took

stock. Josh had taken a bullet in the left upper arm. It looked as if it went through without hitting bone.

"I'm good," he said to Rex.

A bullet had grazed Darrin's right hip. He was also good to go, he told Rex.

The van was in worse condition. Steam was blowing out from under the bonnet and the engine was dead. Then they all smelled the smoke before they saw it.

They didn't have to be told to get out, spread out, get cover, and prepare to fight off the soldiers they expected to come rushing around the corner very soon.

"Okay, John, I take it you saw that our friendly neighborhood Sudanese army has just helped us get on our feet."

Brandt replied, "Yeah, I did. But not to worry, take a deep breath, sit back, relax, and enjoy the show."

Rex was about to ask for clarification when he heard what in that moment, he thought was the most beautiful sound he had ever heard, even more beautiful than Catia's voice. The unmistakable thumping sounds made by the blades of two AH-64A Apache attack helicopters.

Very few people on the receiving end of an Apache attack helicopter had lived to tell how much devastation and mayhem those pale horses of the biblical apocalypse could cause.

Rex and the team heard but couldn't see what exactly happened. Nonetheless, when the smoke and dust cleared, there was no barricade and no soldiers, only their remains.

It was 7:45 A.M. in Port Sudan when the team moved out toward the warehouse again.

When they rounded another corner, and the warehouse came into view about 100 yards away, the first thing they noted was the two Harpy drones sitting on launch ramps. But there was no one near them.

Probably took shelter when the Apaches took out the blockade, Rex thought.

Brandt came back in their earphones and said, "There's nothing like a warm welcome by a lot of fans to make one feel right at home. Is there?" He told them the spy drones above showed there were another 50 or so soldiers in the trenches surrounding the warehouse just on the outside of the chain-link fence waiting for them. They had six RPG-7s, three 12-mm machine guns and the rest were armed with AK-47s.

From studying the maps on the plane, Rex knew in order to get to the warehouse they would have to cross 30 yards of flat ground with no cover. It was suicide to try and do it in broad daylight with 50 soldiers hiding in the trenches on the other side.

"Patch me through to the Apache pilots," Rex demanded.

Brandt did so in less than a minute.

"Guys, we need a little more of your help over here to clear out those trenches around the perimeter," Rex said to the pilots when they were connected.

"No problem. We're on our way," the pilots replied in unison.

"Thanks. But be careful. Make sure you don't hit those two drones on their launch pads in front of the warehouse."

"Got it," one of the pilots said. "You watch out for the RPGs; we'll take care of the rest."

Rex took Darrin with him and moved to the north side of the building. Josh, Ronnie, and Tanner were covering the south side. "Our job is to neutralize those RPGs when those Apaches come back."

Less than a minute later, the Apaches came in for the first pass with their machine guns blazing. Rex and the team took out two of the RPG operators, the Apaches took out two more. There were two left and an unknown number of soldiers.

When the Apaches came roaring in for a second sortie, the two remaining RPG operators tried a different tactic and jumped up when the Apaches were still far away on approach. They never got their weapons shouldered as they were showered with bullets from the Heckler Koch assault rifles carried by Rex and his team.

It was 7:58 A.M. A deathly silence had descended.

The team started traversing the open space one by one while giving each other cover as they did so. There was no one shooting at them.

In Paris, Brandt placed his hand on Christelle's shoulder and said, "We're almost there. It'll be over in minutes."

Christelle nodded as she kept her eyes glued to the screen displaying the images streaming from the spy drones.

The Warehouse, Port Sudan, Sudan

Thursday, October 1, 2015, 8:00 A.M. Port Sudan, Sudan, 7:00 A.M. Paris, France

As they arrived on the edge of the trenches, they checked to make sure no one in there was still alive who could shoot them in the back when they entered the premises. Rex, Digger, and Darrin, after they had established there were no survivors in the trench on the north side, crossed the dugout and cut a hole in the fence.

Josh told him they were doing the same on the south side.

Darrin stayed back to cover them, while Rex and Digger rushed to the front of the warehouse. But before Rex could get there, gunfire erupted on the south side followed by Tanner's voice over the earphones shouting, "Damn, I've been hit."

Josh said, "Stay down, Tanner. I'll come and get you. Ronnie sort out that bastard that's still alive, and make sure there're no more of them."

Rex and Digger were up against the north wall moving forward quickly, assault rifle ready, when he heard the sound of two engines coming alive. "They've started the drones' engines. I'm moving in," he said into his lip mic as he broke into a full sprint.

They came flying around the corner to the front of the warehouse just in time to see two men running back inside through the double doors. When Rex saw the men next, they were standing side by side at a workbench about ten yards away. One of them, he recognized from his photos, was Dr. Haroun Najm al Din Hadad; he had what looked to Rex like a remote control in his hands and was looking at the buttons on it. The other man, a stocky guy with an unkempt black beard and hair, Rex didn't know.

Shit. They're going to launch those drones.

The one without the remote looked up, saw Rex and Digger, shouted something in Arabic which Rex didn't catch, turned, and ran farther into the warehouse.

"Get him, Digger. Attack!" Rex shouted as he pointed to the fleeing man and dropped to his knee.

Before Digger could reach his target, two rounds, one in each eye, from Rex's HK 146 made a complete mess of al Din Hadad's head. The device dropped from his hand, and by the time his body hit the ground, Digger was flying through the air toward the back of his charge.

Rex ran up to al Din Hadad and pumped three more rounds into him just to make sure. He picked the remote up from the floor, looked at the small screen, and let out a long sigh—it was not switched on.

Maybe the device malfunctioned, maybe the batteries were dead, maybe the man didn't get a chance to switch it on.

Then Rex became aware of the runaway's screams.

Digger was on the bawling man's back, with his teeth sunk into the back of the man's neck. Rex approached and said, "Listen asshole, you better stop screaming and wiggling, or my dog will kill you."

The man stopped immediately.

"Digger, would you mind keeping him down there for a few minutes? I have to go and shut those engines down."

Digger's muffled growl, Rex understood to mean, "No worries, mate, I've got him. Take your time."

When Rex turned around, he found Josh, Darrin, Tanner, and Ronnie standing a few yards away. Tanner was holding his left shoulder; blood had stained his tactical vest. Josh's left arm was soaked in blood, but he still seemed fighting fit and in good spirits.

Josh grinned and said, "Rex, thanks, it was great being here to watch you take care of it. But do you think next time you and Digger might be able to give us a chance to be part of the action?"

"I'll have to discuss that with him," Rex motioned with his head over his shoulder in Digger's direction. "I'll let you know what he thinks of the idea."

Tanner sat down on the floor with his back against the wall. Josh and Ronnie moved toward Digger and his captive to retrieve the man and tie him up. Darrin accompanied

Rex outside to the idling drones where they quickly found the switches and turned the engines off.

"Okay, John," Rex said into his lip mic when the engines died, "the drones won't leave the ground. You can send in the experts to disarm the bombs."

"They're on their way. Good job, guys." Brandt said, and then his voice trailed off but not enough for them not to hear him saying, "I'm too old for this shit. Time to think about retirement."

Christelle who was in contact with the pilots of the DGSE jet, told them to take off immediately and head back to Paris.

On the *TOMATS*, a roaring applause erupted. Catia and Marissa were hugging each other and crying with joy. Since the first day the two of them met, they knew there was a bond between them because of the work that their men did, and they had quickly become good friends.

In Paris, Christelle Proll had taken John Brandt in a breath-squeezing embrace and whispered into his ear, "Do you think there might be room for me in your retirement plans?"

"That's why I want to retire," Brandt murmured, "to be with you."

In Langley, Stacie Barrett, Bryan Shafer, Martin Richardson, and the Badr Operation team high-fived each other.

In the White House Situation Room, the President and all present in the room as well as those who were on the video conference from Paris, Riyadh, and Tel Aviv cheered and clapped their hands. And although they all knew the post-mission reviews would soon start, one by one they started smiling.

Among the attendees there were only a few, and the

President was not one of them, who knew about the Khar-lamova 'business records' and had an inkling of the brouhaha about to erupt in the days, weeks, and months to come.

Two navy Navy MH-60S Sea Hawk helicopters arrived at the warehouse soon after Rex spoke to Brandt. One of them carried the two bomb disposal experts in protective gear and hazmat suits. The other carried two medics.

The Apaches stayed around, but General Yohannes Eltayeb's forces had apparently had enough—they were nowhere to be seen.

General Eltayeb himself had left his command post at the airport, and the last time he was seen was in an armored vehicle heading out of the city. Where he went, no one knew. He was never seen or heard of again.

In Africa, jungle justice was often measured out quickly and without publicity.

An hour later, Rex and his team were in the back of a Navy MH-60S Sea Hawk helicopter en route to a US Navy ship in the Red Sea. The bombs had been disarmed, the drones taken apart, and all of it loaded into the back of the second Sea Hawk.

Epilogue

Within two days, the four remaining Badr conspirators arrived in Saudi Arabia as per King Al Saud's request. As Custodian of the Two Holy Mosques, of Masjid al Haram in Mecca and Al-Masjid an-Nabawi in Medina, it was his obligation to protect it and prosecute offenders.

There would be a trial for the four of them. It would happen within a week or two. It would not be a public trial. And no one expected that the suspects would be found not guilty. The Mabahith, Saudi Arabia's secret police, tasked with domestic security and counterintelligence, had a reputation to be swift and thorough in their investigations and never brought people to trial who were innocent.

The Mabahith—a law unto itself—ran its own prisons, its agents operated with impunity. Enhanced interrogation techniques, including waterboarding, denailing, flagellation, beatings, sleep deprivation, starvation, and the old favorite, electrocution, were standard operating procedures.

All judicial proceedings in the Kingdom were conducted in secret. Witnesses, lawyers, juries, and evidence was a waste of time in a legal system dependent almost exclusively upon signed confessions obtained by the police.

Whenever an accused appeared before a judge and repudiated the signed confession, the judge would refer the matter back to the police for further investigation. Rumor had it no one had ever gone before a judge for a second time to revoke their declaration of guilt—a testimony to the efficiency of the Mabahith.

The Badr four were soon going to find out about the power of persuasion wielded by a heavy-duty truck battery fitted with a few lengths of electric wire, ending in alligator clamps clipped onto the genitals and nipples.

There was no speculation about the sentences the four would get—in the Kingdom, for treason, there was only one sentence—public beheading.

Fedot Frolov, although King Al Saud wanted him handed over as well, was spared the one-way trip to the Kingdom for now. There were a number of intelligence agencies across the globe who first wanted to have a chat with him. With the cancerous brain tumor killing him slowly with every passing moment, he probably didn't have enough time left to oblige all his fans with an audience. Besides, for the next six or so weeks, it was going to be difficult to understand him with his jaws wired shut—a serious constraint on a man who liked to blow his own trumpet.

Donna Teresa, Valter Li Voti, Rinaldo Fara, Dina Martelli and the remaining four Beneduce-Longobardi leaders were in the hands of the Italian anti-mafia squad. The veil was finally raised for the media, and they made sure that the world knew about the crippling blow dealt to the Camorra. Many more arrests were expected over the weeks and months to come.

Across Italy, most people were happy to hear the news,

but in the Campania region there were many who were worried about what would become of them now that their main benefactors were behind bars, and by the sounds of it would stay there for the rest of their lives.

Olesya Kharlamova's capture and interrogation was kept a secret. Her 'business records' were getting the attention of an international team of intelligence analysts. It was going to take weeks to work through all of it and drain all the information out of her before she would be sent on her way to set up her new life under a false name in an undisclosed country. Then the political fallout would start. Some of the information would be revealed and actions would be taken. Some of it would be used for leverage; some would be used for outright blackmail, and some of it would just be swept under the carpet.

Next in the Rex Dalton K9 Thrillers Series

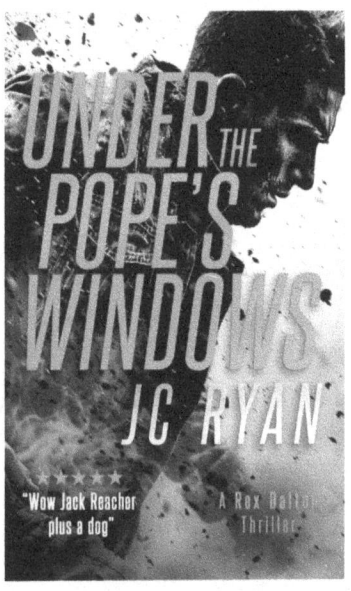

www.vinci-books.com/popes-window

Stolen libraries, hidden agendas, and a race against time to uncover the truth.

Rex Dalton, his wife Catia and their loyal military dog Digger embark on a perilous mission to recover ancient Jewish libraries stolen by the Nazis in 1943. As they navigate a treacherous landscape of neo-Nazis, anti-Semitism and a shadowy cabal of elites, the stakes grow higher with each twist and turn.

Turn the page for a free preview…

Under the Pope's Windows: Prologue

Jewish ghetto, Rome, Italy

October 14, 1943

The Nazis had an insatiable lust for books, especially esoteric books such as the books of the *Biblioteca della Comunità Israelitica*, the library of the Jewish community of Rome, and the *Biblioteca del Collegio Rabbinico Italiano*, the Italian Rabbinical College Library; books and papers including incunabula and scrolls covering more than two thousand years of the history of the Jews of Rome.

On 30 September 1943, two uniformed Nazi officers turned up at the Jewish Ghetto and demanded to see the libraries. They visited again on 1 October to inspect the libraries again, and on the second they visited the chief rabbi's home, where they examined and confiscated all the books and papers they found there.

On 11 October, the two officers were back, this time in

the company of a man purporting to be a German scholar with expertise in book publishing. An eyewitness of the events wrote of this man: ...*He too is escorted by SS troops and appears to be just another German officer, but with an extra dose of arrogance that comes from having a privileged and, regrettably, well-known 'specialty.'*

This elusive, dread-inducing character makes his way into the synagogue building. While his men commence ransacking the libraries of the Rabbinical college and the Jewish community, the officer, with hands as cautious and sensitive as those of the finest needlewoman, skims, touches, caresses papyri and incunabula, leafs through manuscripts and rare editions, peruses parchments and palimpsests. The varying degrees of caution in his touch, the heedfulness of his gestures, are quickly adapted to the importance of each work. In those aristocratic hands, the books, as though subjected to the cruel and bloodless torture of an exquisite sadism, revealed everything. Later, it became known that the SS officer was a distinguished scholar of paleography and Semitic philology.

On 14 October the Nazis were back, it was the day when the Community Library and a portion of the Rabbinical Library were removed as the president, secretary, and sexton of the Jewish community looked on, helpless.

The rabbi ripped his shirt, threw himself to the ground, and poured dust on his head. When the sexton urged him to rise, he moaned, "How can a people live when the knowledge of their past is taken from them?"

"Some will perish, but our people *will* survive. It is written; 'I will bring back all the people unto thee.'"

The rabbi scooped up another handful of dust and poured it on his head. "It is also written; 'My people are destroyed for want of knowledge! Today the knowledge has been taken from them.'" He scooped up another handful of dust and poured it on his head.

"It was not you who stole the books, rabbi."

The rabbi remained inconsolable. "It is written; 'Where there is no vision, the people perish.' My people will perish because we lost the books... 'Ye shall perish among the heathen'."

Helplessly, the sexton repeated, "All is not lost. The Torah remains."

Oświęcim, Poland - Auschwitz extermination camp

October 21, 1943

The rabbi got the first bitter almond whiff of the Zyklon-B gas, hydrogen cyanide. In the airtight room many of the condemned vomited and retched and convulsed and banged their heads against the walls. He merely leaned against the wall, murmuring, "My people. The books! The books! The boo . . k . . .s . . . .s . . . . .s."

Under the Pope's Windows:
Chapter One

A SINGULAR EVENT

Rome, Italy

Saturday, May 7, 2016

"What's that?" She asked a few seconds after entering the room. She was pointing at the dress on the bed.

He struggled to hide his nervousness. This was the situation they could not plan for—it was the potential single point of failure of this entire mission. Nevertheless, he managed to keep a poker face. "If I'd have to venture a guess, I'd say it's a wedding dress."

"For whom?"

"I'd have to make another guess. I'd say it's for you."

She approached the dress slowly, picked it up, held it against her body, looked in the mirror, and whispered, "When?"

"Today."

"But... what about... I mean... you... the guests... a

rabbi… what…" Then she turned and smiled. He could see her eyes had turned aquamarine—the color they changed when she was very happy. Then she was in his arms and they were whispering to each other.

"Let's do it. I've been fretting too much about it for far too long," she said.

He made no reply; instead, he kissed her.

"How much time do I have?" she asked.

"As much as you need."

"What time is it now?"

"Six oh five."

"What time is sunset?"

"Eight fifteen."

"We'll start at eight twenty. Five minutes after the Sabbath is over."

He left and entered the next room with a grin on his face that said it all and told his accomplices they were on.

As he walked away, he quoted the famous words of the actor George Peppard, the cigar-chomping leader of the A Team in the popular TV series of the '80s, Colonel John 'Hannibal' Smith; "I love it when a plan comes together."

It had been a very special occasion, unique in many ways—weddings usually are. This was a small one—private, essentially a secret affair—attended only by a few close friends and no family. The couple had no family, no father to walk the stunning bride down the aisle.

Despite the absence of family, it was a joyous occasion which could easily not have taken place at all. The idea of a surprise wedding had been around for a while. It was a straightforward concept—the couple invites their guests to an event under the pretense of a party, dinner, or brunch, and then surprises them by announcing a matrimonial celebration.

In this case, however, due to the groom's misinterpretation of what a surprise wedding entailed, it was not the guests who got the surprise but the bride. That the groom had purposefully misconstrued would be proven beyond a reasonable doubt in the aftermath of the event.

Traditionally couples go to great lengths to make their big day a memorable one. Every now and then a pioneering couple will come up with an idea so outlandish it will get media attention—scuba diver fanatics getting married underwater, skydivers during a freefall from ten thousand feet, in an airplane a few miles up in the sky, in a hot air balloon a few thousand feet up—people seemed to never run out of avant-garde ideas.

If the media had been allowed at this wedding, which they were most definitely not, the choice of venue would have gotten some mention. It was on a luxury yacht, the TOMATS, at anchor in Roma Marina Yachting. That was the first marina to be built in Rome's historic, 2,000-year-old Port of Civitavecchia, also known as the Port of Rome, about fifty-five miles from the city center. The name TOMATS was derived from the first letters of Ernest Hemingway's classic short novel, *The Old Man and the Sea*.

The hybrid Christian-Jewish ceremony, co-officiated over by a rabbi and a Roman Catholic priest, was not unusual. It was the security clearances of both clergymen that would have been extraordinary to the media.

Some of the guests would have gotten a lot of media attention too. After all, it was quite possible that history was made by the French Prime Minister, Lucien Laurent, accompanied by his niece, deputy minister Margot Lemaire, and her little daughter, Rowena, attending a wedding within Italy's territorial waters.

Other notables among the guests were the deputy director of the DGSE, the French equivalent of the American CIA; the captain of the TOMATS, a former Navy SEAL; and the head of the Collections department of Mossad, Israel's intelligence agency.

Christelle Proll, the dazzling deputy director of the DGSE, was in the company of John Brandt, the CEO of a top-secret black ops American private military contractor known as CRC, Crisis Response Consultancy.

Declan Spencer, the captain of the TOMATS, former Navy SEAL Commander and life-long friend of John Brandt, was accompanied by Simona Bellucci, another one of the beautiful women who graced the yacht that day. Simona was formerly known as Sophia Maiorani from Naples.

The Mossad's deputy director, Yaron Aderet, had no companion, but he was the man whose arm the bride was holding when she walked into the room where the ceremony took place.

The bride, as usual, stole the day. At 5' 9" she was tall for a woman, only two inches shorter than the groom. In the high heels she was wearing, she looked the groom straight in the eyes. There was no dissension; she was the fairest of them all. Her shoulder-length waves of stunning auburn hair, flawless creamy skin, scattering of light freckles across her nose attesting to the natural red in her hair, and a near-constant dazzling smile that lit up her face made her breathtakingly beautiful. The groom would have told anyone who wanted to listen that her eyes were the color of the Mediterranean, blue at times and aquamarine at others, as they changed with her mood and what she wore.

The groom, at 5'11", with penetrating dark eyes, black hair, tan skin, the physique of a gymnast, and a stern-looking face, was not movie star attractive but certainly a very handsome specimen.

Everyone found the big black Dutch shepherd dog, who brought in the wedding rings on a dainty white satin cushion balanced on his nose, adorable.

That Rex Dalton, the groom, an American citizen, was a former black ops field agent and assassin in the employ of CRC, and his bride, Catia Romano, an Italian Jew, a former Mossad agent, now Ph.D. student at Sapienza (aka the University of Rome), would certainly have been newsworthy to journalists of any stripe.

Grab your copy...
www.vinci-books.com/popes-window

About the Author

JC Ryan is a bestselling author renowned for his intricate espionage, archaeological thrillers, and conspiracy mysteries. With over 30 acclaimed novels, including the popular Rex Dalton K9 Thrillers, Rossler Foundation Mysteries, and Carter Devereux Mystery Thrillers, Ryan has captivated readers around the globe.

Drawing from his diverse professional background—as a military officer, lawyer, and IT manager—Ryan creates compelling narratives that skillfully blend historical accuracy with thrilling adventure. He is celebrated as a master storyteller, known for crafting riveting plots, meticulous historical details, and engaging, multidimensional characters. Ryan's meticulous research lends authenticity and depth to each story, immersing readers in richly constructed worlds filled with intrigue, suspense, and adventure.

Fans of David Baldacci, Lee Child's Jack Reacher, Tom Clancy's Jack Ryan, Nelson DeMille's John Corey, Vince Flynn's Mitch Rapp, Mark Greaney's Gray Man, Gregg Hurwitz's Orphan X, Robert Ludlum's Jason Bourne, Daniel Silva's Gabriel Allon, Brad Taylor's Pike Logan, Brad Thor's Scot Harvath, James Rollins' Sigma Force, Steve Berry's Cotton Malone, and Dan Brown's Robert Langdon will find JC Ryan's novels equally compelling and unforgettable.

When not writing, Ryan enjoys spending time with his college sweetheart, whom he married in 1978. They are proud parents of two daughters, have two sons-in-law, and are grandparents to two grandchildren.